IMPEACH
IMPEACH
IMPEACH

NO
BL♦♦D
FO♦

NEW YORK

th Day
April

DOXOLOGY

NELL ZINK

DOXOLOGY

4th ESTATE • London

4th Estate
An imprint of HarperCollins*Publishers*
1 London Bridge Street
London SE1 9GF

www.4thEstate.co.uk

First published in Great Britain in 2019 by 4th Estate
First published in the United States by Ecco,
an imprint of HarperCollins in 2019

1

A catalogue record for this book is
available from the British Library

ISBN 978-0-00-832348-6 (hardback)
ISBN 978-0-00-832349-3 (trade paperback)

Designed by Renata De Oliveira

Printed and bound in Great Britain by
CPI Group (UK) Ltd, Croydon

MIX
Paper from
responsible sources
FSC
www.fsc.org
FSC™ C007454

FOR *Justin Taylor's cat, Emma*

ACKNOWLEDGMENTS

I wish to thank the Dutch Foundation for Literature for its provision of a six-week fellowship in Amsterdam and the Borris House Festival of Writing & Ideas (Ireland) and LitLink Festival (Croatia) for especially memorable outings. Thanks always to my wonderful agent, Susan Golomb, and excellent editor, Megan Lynch.

DOXOLOGY

I.

Unknown to all, and for as long as he lived, Joe Harris was a case of high-functioning Williams syndrome. He displayed the typical broad mouth, stellate irises, spatial ineptitude, gregarious extroversion, storytelling habit, heart defect, and musical gift. To the day he died, he had no more wrinkles on him than an action figure. He was never tested, because he lacked the general intellectual disability that was the syndrome's defining feature. However, his capacity to irritate others was near infinite. He spoke his mind, trusting everyone he saw.

For example, once when he was walking through Washington Square with his friend Pam, an elderly man of the kind who might be forty approached them and asked them to hold his asthma inhaler for just one second. Pam rolled her eyes and walked on, but Joe held out his hand, into which the inhaler was promptly placed in a forceful way that made it fall to the ground in two pieces. The man declared that replacing the broken inhaler would cost Joe fifteen dollars.

Joe replied, "I don't have fifteen bucks on me. But you could come with me to work! Most days I make more than that. Yesterday I made a lot more. You know what else I made? About a million paper napkins folded in half! After my shift I can give you all the money you need. My work is about a mile away. I can give you free pie, if we have pie that's stale. I'm going there now." He touched the man's arm. Shouting that bowl-headed faggots should leave him alone, the man ran away. Joe picked up the inhaler and yelled, "You forgot your thing!"

HIS FATHER WAS A PROFESSOR OF AMERICAN HISTORY AT COLUMBIA. HIS MOTHER HAD been a forever-young party girl in permanent overdrive who could drink all night, sing any song and fake the piano accompaniment, and talk to anybody about anything. In 1976 she died, running uphill and laughing, in the middle of a departmental picnic at Wave Hill. The students mimed heartbreak while her husband mimed CPR. Joe held her hand and said, "Bye-bye, Mommy!" He was only eight.

At her funeral in the Cathedral of Saint John the Divine, he clapped his hands through the syncopated bits of the doxology and lifted his voice meaningfully on "Father, Son, and Holy Ghost." Professor Harris immediately understood that the Holy Family had been redefined to resemble his own. The child schmoozed his way through the reception, telling stories about the funnest times with Mom. Adults patted his head and made meaningful eye contact among themselves. Joe, in their view, was not precocious. They had firm ideas on what to do with him, most of them involving boarding school on another continent. They were concerned about his dad's capacity to attract another wife.

Professor Harris changed nothing, on the theory that Joe, whom he loved, would be hurt less if nothing changed.

JOE WAS WAVED THROUGH PUBLIC SCHOOL AS THE SON OF A PROFESSOR. EVEN BEFORE graduation, he took up waiting tables at the Abyssinian Coffee Shop on Fourteenth Street. It was a small, old-fashioned diner with a cashier up front and a short-order cook in the back. He didn't have to memorize anything except codes like "S" for scrambled eggs and "P" for pancakes. The specials were eternally fixed combinations, and he never handled money except to put tips in his pockets. Most customers gave him a dollar for lunch or breakfast, a quarter for coffee, and two dollars for dinner. They were gracious because he looked fourteen. They thought he was saving money for college. The manager liked him because he was good for business, always rhapsodizing about fries and soda in a way that made them sound exponentially more wonderful than chips and tap water, plus he never stole.

With tips in his pockets, he felt rich. It was his good fortune to be a sucker in a time when the Village was not rich in expensive things. Dealers and hookers caromed off his chatty ways. He was afraid of loud noises and fast-moving objects. He never took the subway or crossed a street against the light. His instinct for self-preservation didn't extend to people, but he respected vehicles—and the dangerous subset of people who were loud and fast-moving—so much that on the whole he was safer walking around New York than a normal person would have been.

He started playing ukulele soon after his mother died. As a teenager he switched to electric bass because it also had four strings and was good enough for Paul McCartney. For his sixteenth birthday, his father took him to Forty-Eighth Street, where he picked out a lemon-yellow Music Man StingRay. At home he played unamplified, accompanying records and the radio. On days when he didn't hear a new song he liked, he wrote one. He wasn't egotistical about it. He didn't care who wrote the songs as long as they were there. He sang his favorites in public, with hand motions, louder than he could really sing, his voice ringing and rasping, the sound effortful, conveying obstacles overcome, the drama of stardom, the artist as agonist, in part as a side effect of singing outdoors against ambient racket and traffic.

When he turned twenty-one, he got access to his trust fund. That is, his father was able to tap it for his expenses and moved him from their rent-controlled duplex in the West Village to a two-bedroom in a nondescript building on Nineteenth between Fifth and Sixth. They shared a cleaning lady who doubled as a spy, assuring Professor Harris that Joe regularly ate real food and changed his clothes. With his own place, he could finally invest in a bass amp. Pam helped him parse the classifieds and bulletin board flyers. She located an appropriate Ampeg combo a short walk away in Hell's Kitchen. He fiddled with the tone knob on the Music Man, looked up at the seller, and yelled over the noise, "Fuck me sideways! I never knew this knob did anything!"

PAMELA BAILEY WAS BORN THE YEAR AFTER JOE, IN 1969. SHE GREW UP AN ONLY CHILD in northwestern Washington, D.C., between the National Zoo and the National Cathedral.

Her mother, Ginger, was a homemaker, active in their church—that is, the cathedral—and the friends of the local branch library. She had practiced what she called "Irish birth control" by marrying after she finished college and not before. She didn't approve of the Irish generally, but acknowledged a preference for lace-curtain Irish over shanty Irish such as the Kennedys. Pam's father, Edgar, was a career civil servant at the Defense Logistics Agency in Anacostia. Adolescent Pam suspected him of having committed atrocities in Vietnam. He had been partially responsible for supplying American forces there with cinder blocks. To her credit, he had materially enabled the invasion of Grenada by coordinating the movement of spare tires.

Ginger and Edgar were white Anglo-Saxon Protestants of the post-Calvinist variety. They didn't believe in predestination, but they behaved as if it were revealed truth. Every deviation from the straight and narrow was presumed a fatal wrong turn on the one road to salvation. An oft-cited maxim was "Spare the rod, spoil the child," albeit with a certain irony, since as belt spankers they never used an actual rod. With similar irony, they would say, "Children should be seen and not heard." Of course they expected Pam to be able to hold up her end of a dinner-table conversation. Maybe they should have had an extra child to practice on.

She went to public school and never had much homework. She liked to play with boys. At age nine she discovered Dungeons and Dragons. At twelve, she made up an outer-space-themed role-playing game that earned her $2,000 when her father licensed it to Atari in her name. But puberty was unkind to her. Her reddish hair made pimples and freckles stand out. Her friends went from talking swords and sorcery to planning careers in the U.S. Army Rangers, where they would acquire aluminum crossbows that kill silently. Her awakening critical faculties showed her a world of strictures where she had expected freedoms. The 1970s had suggested that in maturity she would enjoy communal solidarity and LSD. The 1980s coalesced from a haze of competition and AIDS. Between her childhood and her adolescence lay a generation gap.

She resolved to become a retro hippie earth mother. She began with a feminine school-sponsored extracurricular activity, modern dance. The teacher who ran it spent her time correcting papers. Her pupils stood outside the crash-bar doors of the gym, sharing cigarettes. Nothing was taught. At the year-end performance, Pam wore a black bodysuit and tights and crawled onstage to the sound of Leo Kottke playing "Eight Miles High" on a twelve-string. She was supposed to stare at the floor, but she peeked up to see whether her parents were moved. They were reading paperbacks.

At age thirteen she discovered a higher-stakes role-playing game. Her character: drunken punk in a crumbling, segregated, crack-saturated city.

She embarked on adventures at bars downtown. Bouncers let her into hardcore punk shows for free. She had a faceless West Virginia driver's license that said she was nineteen, so their asses were covered in case of a raid, and that's all they cared about. Grown men with jobs and money bought her drinks until the harsh light of last call or the restroom revealed that she was too young even for cocaine. To kill time until the Metro started running, she left clubs in the company of boys who said they had drugs. She would smoke crystal meth or crack with them and deploy the energy boost in walking home.

Mostly she was meeting boys she couldn't stand, seeing bands she didn't like. She was so tired all the time that if she didn't like the band that was onstage, she could put her head down on a table and sleep.

The band she loved was called Minor Threat. They laid claim to the "straight edge," foreswearing all substances and casual sex. Before going out to trade petting for a rush, she would draw Xs on the backs of her hands with black marker to signify her belonging to the straight-edge movement. She was well-read enough to know that a foolish consistency is the hobgoblin of little minds. She had seen what the striving for integrity had done to her father and mother. Dependence on a job supplying the troops had turned them into warmongering fascists, and hearing them say "I love you" made her sick. In contrast, Minor Threat's integrity thrilled her, and she would have given anything to hear their singer, Ian MacKaye, say "I love you." But she stood face-to-face with him only once, and she offered him sex. For self-evident reasons, she thought it was the most valuable thing she possessed. When he ignored her, she realized her mistake. Sex is not scarce. Girls with sex are like the stars of the sky.

By teaching her to value originality, the punk movement led her to the realm of art. How she longed to try hard and eventually to be known for making something the likes of which had never existed!

The summer before tenth grade she founded a band of her own, the Slinkies. Since practicing in a garage would have required asking someone's parents to move the car, they used their bedrooms. Rehearsal was a quiet affair, if not in the opinion of their families.

At the Slinkies' first and final gig, on a Sunday afternoon at the Jewish Community Center in Bethesda, they plugged into the previous band's equipment. None of them knew what a monitor was for. Pam couldn't hear her guitar after the drums came in, so she turned up its volume knob. It still didn't play audibly, so she cranked her amplifier. She sang as loud as she could and couldn't hear that either. The bassist crouched by her amp, trying to hear herself, and it must have been feeding back like a motherfucker, but nobody onstage could make out what she was playing, not even her. Into the clattering tornado of sound, Pam chanted her doggerel about sabotage in the voice of a tone-deaf auctioneer. The room emptied fast, except for two boys in black dusters who stayed through all three songs and said the Slinkies were a dead ringer for late-period Germs. That was not what she wanted to hear. The Germs' singer, Darby Crash, had killed himself in 1980, so by implication their sound was not avant-garde.

GINGER AND EDGAR WERE DIGNIFIED PEOPLE, NOT EASILY INDUCED TO YELL. BUT WHEN she would stumble in at five thirty in the morning on a weekday, having misplaced her skirt, her father couldn't help but intuit that she would be skipping school, and it made him crazy. Her mother yelled at her, starting when her father went to work and ending when she left for school. At times when no one else was yelling, she missed it, so she yelled instead. For two years, there were no conversations in the household that didn't involve yelling.

Her father developed an unfortunate habit of threatening to throw her out. Her mother would remonstrate, and he would relent. To make the mixed message complete, she would imply that her defense of her daughter betrayed excess motherly love, because in truth she deserved to be thrown out. The threat didn't seem harsh to either parent. Neither of them meant it seriously, though they expected her to move out when she reached eighteen. WASP culture had arisen in the poverty of desolate feudal places. Intergenerational solidarity had been impracticable in Anglo-Saxony, where brides required dowries and younger sons wandered off to settle distant territories like so many beavers. Pam's grandparents, who were alive when she was little, lived in Florida and Arizona. The Florida ones gave her ten dollars every Christmas to spend as she chose. The Arizona ones had an Airstream travel trailer with a bumper sticker that read, WE'RE SPENDING OUR CHILDREN'S INHERITANCE.

She didn't apply to colleges. Instead she told her parents, in her junior year of high school, that she was going to New York to train as an artist.

She didn't say what medium, just "artist." She asked for her Atari money from when she was twelve. It had been earning stagflation-style interest and was, she calculated, sufficient to establish her in an apartment in Manhattan. The money was held in her name as Series EE Savings Bonds. Her parents, being no stupider than their daughter, kept the bonds in a safe-deposit box and wouldn't say which bank. They said the money was earmarked for her education. There was disagreement as to the true nature of education. The yelling in the house attained exceptional duration and pitch.

The upshot was that in September 1986, as her senior year was officially starting, Pam marched down to the Greyhound station—on foot, because she had only the seventy dollars she'd earned by selling her father's audio receiver and VCR to a pawn shop—and boarded a bus to Port Authority.

From her seat on the smelly bus, the sight of the towers of Manhattan from the cloverleaf above the entrance to the Lincoln Tunnel was the most exciting event of her life, definitely including all her experiences of sex, music, nature, and drugs combined.

She emerged to the sidewalk at Forty-First Street and Eighth

Avenue. Street wisdom acquired in downtown D.C. told her it was not a place she needed to be spending time. She saw whores with recently hit faces. She walked east. To a mind unschooled in construction techniques, the city seemed carved from the living rock. Sheer cliff faces surrounded her on every side. Cave dwellings teemed with fairies, rogues, and barbarians, as on a D&D adventure. She quickened her pace. At Times Square she turned southward down Broadway. The whoredom transitioned to hustlers and dealers. She reached Fourth Street with a thrill. She saw some men playing handball. She had never seen handball being played.

She stopped to watch them. No one stopped to watch her. She was a leggy stranger in black jeans and a men's V-neck undershirt, with a backpack and sleepover bag, seventeen years old, lost, female, and invisible. She was exactly where she wanted to be.

NOT LONG AFTER HER ARRIVAL, SHE STARTED WORKING FOR A COMPUTER CONSULTING firm called RIACD. Everything about it was mismanaged, from the wordplay in the name, which was not an acronym and was properly pronounced as "react" only by foreigners, to the one-man marketing division. The address, far downtown on John Street in the financial district, lent the company pecuniary cachet along with crooked drop ceilings and gurgling toilets.

A possible exception to the general mismanagement was its thirty-year lease, signed in 1985. RIACD's founder, Yuval Perez, was a draft evader who had turned eighteen just before Israel's 1982 invasion of Lebanon. Owing landlords money didn't scare him. He didn't take contracts seriously as threats.

Only mismanagement could make a consultancy hire a dropout with radiation head to learn C from a Usenet tutorial, so Pam didn't fault it. (Radiation head was the world's easiest, and also worst, punk hairdo. Using scissors, the wearer cut his or her own hair really short, and the patchiness made him or her look like a cancer patient.) They met in a bar, where Yuval gave her an aptitude test and hired her to start the next day. The test involved imagining a set of ninety-nine pegs numbered left to right, one to ninety-nine, in a hundred holes also numbered left to right, with the right-hand hole empty. You were supposed to say how you'd move the sequence one slot to the right, reversing the order. A typical programmer's first move was to posit additional holes.

Pam had been raised on short rations. She never assumed additional anything. Thrift was a cardinal virtue in the business in those days. Computers were slow, with definite limits. Programs had no graphics or menus. Stinginess was called "elegance." In aesthetic terms it resembled the elegance of cutting your hair instead of washing it and wearing the same boots every day with no socks. Ultimate elegance was realized when all the programs in a mainframe lived naked and barefoot, sharing a single overcoat.

Her first project after the C tutorial was an auto-execute system for the American Stock Exchange. She wrote it in a day, and it compiled the first time. It ran on SCO Xenix on a 286 in a pipe room in their basement. The traders liked it enough to call her back to install anonymity—not security; the Morris worm hadn't happened yet. They wanted fantasy usernames, so as to lend deniability to stupid auto-execute positions.

Immediately, and for all time, she got cocky. Routinely, she neglected input validation, memorably writing an interface that crashed if a user entered an accented character. On one too many occasions, she left a client's system without turning off the debugging fire hose. Yet Yuval considered her a key asset. More conscientious consultants with better social skills regularly put them to use over long lunches, during which they argued that Merrill Lynch or Prudential might economize by employing them directly. Because of Pam's outbursts, meltdowns, and mistakes—universally regarded as aspects of her femininity—there was never a danger that a client would hire her away.

She was one of two women at RIACD. New colleagues often had trouble making eye contact with her in the one-on-one encounters they liked to bring about by blocking her way to the ladies' room, while others exposed her to the crass insults that passed for flirtation in Queens. Yet their respect for the RIACD receptionist, an angel-faced Yemenite in oversized tops and long skirts, no older than Pam, was deep and unfeigned. Pam deduced that in the fantasy universe of a Mediterranean American man's virgin/whore complex, it was best to come down on the side of the virgins. She told new colleagues she was gay. Sexists in those days were familiar with the work of Howard Stern. His sadomasochistic radio talk show invested the unapproachable lesbian with powerful taboos.

It didn't cost her any dates, because she never met a suit she wanted to date. Sex was part of the leisure-time world where she made art. In her mind art was ideally commercial, feeding and housing its creator. She loved coding's austere beauty, but she didn't regard it as an art. It was too restrained. It made the suits too happy. It was how she made money. An artist needed money in great abundance. Without it, she would bounce off Manhattan like a bird off a plate-glass window.

IN 1989, WHEN SHE MET JOE, HER ART PROJECT WAS A BAND CALLED THE DIAPHRAGMS. Even the name embarrassed her. She thought it sounded early eighties. Simon, the singer and bass player, claimed that his masculinity made it ironic. He was a grad student from Yorkshire on a fellowship to study opera practice at NYU. He possessed a bulky, sticky gray keyboard that incorporated an analog drum machine. She played a Gibson SG guitar. The band was supposed to be a No Wave power duo. Everybody except Simon knew it was shitty Casio-core.

Of course the Diaphragms had played CBGB. Anybody could play there once. All it took was signing up for audition night. Their gig was at seven o'clock on a Wednesday. Their twenty dearest friends ordered beer by the pitcher, but the manager still said their set needed work. When Pam asked him what aspects in particular, he shrugged and said, "Your set. The songs. How you play them. The arrangements. You know. Everything."

They rehearsed every weekend in a space in Hell's Kitchen. It charged a reduced rate of ten dollars per hour between eight A.M. and noon on Sundays. They arrived at eight, because rehearsing their set took forever. The songs were hard to memorize or tell apart. She had slept with Simon eight times and heard him refer to her in public as his "ex" on at least ten occasions. To compound her embarrassment, he was still her roommate. They lived in an overpriced doorman building on Bleecker near the folk clubs and Italian bakeries, in the eastern part of the West Village known to gentrifiers farther east as "Little Jersey." A flimsy drywall partition divided what had once been a one-bedroom apartment into a one-and-a-half. Simon had the half bedroom. It was too cheap. He would never, ever move out voluntarily. She was out of town a lot for work, and every time she got back, she could tell he'd been sleeping in her bed. They were not friends. She hated him. They were both on the lease.

JOE ADDRESSED HER HAIR ISSUES FIRST THING WHEN THEY MET. "YOU'RE GREAT-looking, except for your hair!" he said. "I love your body. It's so elongated. You have an incredible-looking mouth. Your eyebrows are moody, like you have a romantic soul. You should wear liquid eyeliner and have long hair all the way down to your butt!"

This was after he'd known her for not even ten seconds, or five. He'd tapped her on the shoulder while she was standing in line for fifty-cent coffee from a cart.

"That would take forever," Pam said. "Hair grows, like, an inch every three months."

"I don't do math," Joe said.

"Me neither, but if we call it a foot every three years, and it's three feet from my head to my butt, we're looking at nine years."

"Nine years!" He patted his own hair thoughtfully. It was mousy brown and wavy, cut in an inverted bowl shape. "How old do you think my hair is?"

"You are quite the mutant," she said, making so as to leave. She had ordered but neither paid for nor gotten her coffee. Before she could abandon him, Joe took hold of her arm.

She was in a mood to put up with it. She was at a cart on lower Broadway, buying weak coffee at four P.M., because she had been escorted out of Merrill Lynch for calling this one dickhead "fuckwad" in the presence of his subordinates. He had responded that he'd have her fired from RIACD. Immediately she had called Yuval, who observed that the term "fuckwad" is considered denigrating by members of certain ethnic groups, as in all of them everywhere, and she had yelled into Merrill Lynch's house phone that if he ever invested a dime in marketing RIACD's platform-independent programming language (her side project for slow days in the office), none of them would have to deal with dickheads like this fuckwad ever again. Then she had felt a strong hand gripping her arm. That had been half an hour ago.

Joe's touch was a pleasant contrast. He was beaming as though he'd been looking for her all his life and finally found her, but in a somewhat disinterested manner, as though she were not the woman of his dreams but something less essential, like the perfect grapefruit. He appeared to be contemplating her.

"You shouldn't be touching me," she said. "You dig?"

He let go of her arm and took a step backward. To her dismay, he started chanting. "Yo! Mutant MC, keep off the lady, hot like coffee, she got the beauty—"

"Don't be a goober," she said, giving the coffee man a quick fifty cents and moving away from the cart with the hot liquid that would arm her against Joe. "Stop the rapping. Never rap. Or, should you feel compelled to rap against your own better judgment, don't try to sound black."

"But that's what rap sounds like." Saddened, he looked down at the sidewalk.

She almost felt guilty. She said, "I didn't mean it that way. Rap if you want. Just not where anybody can hear you."

"I'm actually a singer," Joe said. "You want to hear a song? I write one almost every day."

"Sure," she said.

They walked north together, and he sang his tune du jour, loudly, with hand motions.

BEING AROUND JOE WAS RELAXING FOR PAM. THEY COULD TALK AND TALK, AND NOTHING she said ever offended him. Nobody picked on her once they saw him, and nobody could pick on him for long. If she got nervous walking without him, she would stop off and buy a cup of coffee. Hot coffee in a guy's face will stop him deader than a bullet, long enough for a skinny girl in jump boots to get away.

II.

Daniel Svoboda lived in a state of persistent ecstasy. He had no lease. His rent was a hundred a week in cash.

He was an eighties hipster. But that can be forgiven, because he was the child of born-again Christian dairy-farm workers from Racine, Wisconsin.

The eighties hipster bore no resemblance to the bearded and effeminate cottage industrialist who came to prominence as the "hipster" in the new century. He wasn't a fifties hipster either. He knew nothing of heroin or the willful appropriation of black culture. He was a by-product of the brief, shining moment in American history when the working class went to liberal arts college for free. Having spent four years at the foot of the ivory tower, picking up crumbs of obsolete theory, he descended to face once again the world of open-wheel motorsports and Jell-O salads from whence he sprang. Eyes schooled on Raphael and Mapplethorpe zoomed in on Holly Hobbie–themed needlepoint projects and xeroxed Polaroids of do-it-yourself gender reassignment surgery. Reflexively they sought the sublime beauty and violence they had learned from Foucault and Bataille to see as their birthright, and they were not disappointed.

An eighties hipster couldn't gentrify a neighborhood. He wasn't gentry. His presence drove rents down. His apartments were over-populated and dirty. Landlords were lucky if he paid rent. He wasn't about to seize vacant lots for community gardens or demand better public schools. All he wanted was to avoid retiring from the same plant as his dad.

The eighties hipster was post-sensitive. Having risen from poverty to intimate acquaintanceship with political rectitude (for collegiate women, it was the era of lesbian feminism), he knew what sensitivity was. He internalized it. He put a fine point on it. His speech acts reflected his awareness that its possession made him part of a vanishingly small minority. He drew attention to everyday prejudice and injustice through overemphasis. Witness his habitual attention to the crimes of Hitler and Stalin or the ill-fated band name "Rapeman," borrowed from a hero of Japanese comic books.

The eighties hipster practiced outward conformity in his dress and bearing. The mod, the glam rocker, the rockabilly, the punk, even the prep risked and defied the wrath of the homophobe, but the eighties hipster could get served a beer in the Ozarks.

The eighties hipster was the short-lived cap of spume on the dirty wave of working-class higher education, and it is right to mourn him, even if he did devote too much time to the search for authentic snuff videos and photos of nude Khoisan women.

ON A NOVEMBER SATURDAY IN 1990, PAM WENT OVER TO JOE'S PLACE TO LISTEN TO records. It was raining in sheets that whipped around the corners of buildings and blowing so hard that women in heels were taking men's arms to cross the street. Cars were plowing bow waves through puddles of scum.

Joe had a visitor. As he was letting her in the apartment door, a man emerged from the bedroom with a square sheet of black plastic in his hand and said, "Hey, man, you have the *Sassy* Sonic Youth flexi!"

"I subscribed to that magazine the second I heard of it," Joe said.

"It's not long for this world," Pam said, hanging up her coat. "What's the demographic supposed to be—thirteen-year-old girls who fuck? Advertisers really go for that."

"Nice to meet you," the stranger said, stepping forward and holding out his hand. "Daniel Svoboda."

"Pam Diaphragm," she said. "*Sassy* is the dying gasp of straight mainstream pedophilia."

"I read it for the political coverage," Daniel said, satirizing the readers of *Playboy*.

"I first heard of it from a bald guy who does in-flight programming at Eastern," Pam said. "So can we listen to this flexi?"

"I'm a Sonic Youth completist," Joe said, taking the single from Daniel and arranging it on the turntable. "The only record I don't have is the *Forced Exposure* subscribers-only single 'I Killed Christgau with My Big Fucking Dick.'"

"That's not a real record," Daniel said. "Byron Coley made that up."

Byron Coley was the editor of *Forced Exposure* and Robert Christgau was the chief music critic of the *Village Voice,* as Daniel did not feel called upon to explain to Pam. Nor did he find it necessary to tell her, one condescending beat later, that the record existed after all.

She found herself attracted to him. He had not asked her real name. His sophistication and knowledge seemed to resemble her own. She commenced phrasing a friendly remark. She put the brakes on. They say that you truly know a man only after you've seen him with his male friends, but this friend was Joe, who might not count. Furthermore, it had been demonstrated in empirical trials that a woman gravitates to the sexiest man in the room. Here, again, Joe was setting the bar low. She said instead, "It's Christgau who's a big fucking dick."

"I wouldn't go that far," Daniel replied. "But you can't grade music on a bell curve. Mediocrity is not the norm. Most records either rock or they suck."

"I'm kind of over grades myself. Did you just get out of college?"

"Yeah. You should see my awesome transcript and GREs. That's how I qualified to work as a proofreader."

"I'm a programmer, but I never finished high school."

"Silence, lovebirds," Joe said, dropping the needle. "Prepare to rock."

DANIEL LIVED IN AN ILLEGAL APARTMENT WHOSE EXISTENCE HE HAD DEDUCED THROUGH spatial reasoning. It was located above a shop on the edge of Chinatown, on Chrystie Street near Hester, facing a fenced-in, filthy park. Betwixt a dripping air conditioner and a sidewalk black with grime, Video Hit sold hot coffee, durian fruit, fermented tofu, one-hundred-film subscriptions to the latest Hong Kong action movies on VHS, lemon-scented animal crackers pressed from microscopic dust, fortune cat figurines, and introductions to local women whose photos blanketed the wall above the cash register.

It was his first inviolable space. Growing up, he had shared an upstairs room with two brothers. The three were close in age. One was a wrestler who wanted to be a doctor. The other was an adopted Somali epileptic with one leg. He couldn't stand up to the wrestler, and with the Somali, he wasn't allowed to try.

Technically it was a loft: high-ceilinged, unfinished storage above a retail space. It was accessible only through the store, which closed for five hours nightly via the lowering of an impenetrable steel gate to which he had no key. If he stayed out past one o'clock, he was sentenced to stay out past six. He was young. He dealt with it. The floor above his was connected to a jewelry factory next door through a hole in the intervening firewall. He heard footsteps in the factory at all hours of the day and night. Victor and Margie, his landlords, had tried putting inventory in the loft, but the floor sagged, and they didn't want to clutter up their shop with a pillar. For storage they used the basement, accessible through a trapdoor in the sidewalk.

They were immigrants from Hong Kong. When he suggested they let him move in, they saw the offer as money for nothing. They didn't want to rent to Chinese who would overpopulate the place. Daniel's meek demeanor suggested to them that he wouldn't cause trouble.

He'd been to rent parties in Soho, where a "loft" was a white-lacquered, vast-windowed domain of cleanliness and prosperity in a historic building framed in cast iron. His building was salmon brick, with wooden beams black from dry rot. You could drive a butter knife into his doorframe and turn it around. He guessed the structure was 150 years old.

His stairway was steep, and the door to it was narrow enough to be mistaken for a closet. On one occasion, soon after he moved in, a workman set down a new cooler and trapped him upstairs. It took serious yelling and pounding before Victor shifted it enough for him to go to work. He bought himself a fire safety ladder with hooks for the windowsill. When he was at home, he padlocked his door from the inside.

He assumed—romanticizing things a bit—that his trap-like secret lair had been set up for illicit activities and abandoned after a raid. From his first glimpse, he had taken away vague impressions of battered furniture and dusty slips of paper, which he looked forward to examining closely. By the time he moved in, the place had been swept and every portable object was gone, including the linoleum.

He installed a sink and a hot plate. He showered with a handheld, standing in a galvanized tub. He dumped the wash water down the toilet, which could always use a good hard drenching. On the street side, he observed blackout rules, with shades drawn during the day and opaque curtains at night. His rear windows opened on a small and sometimes sunny courtyard, miraculously free of garbage, cool and fresh, with no poisonous dry cleaners, no restaurants blowing rancid exhaust, and no living creatures but rats and pigeons. They squeaked and made coo-cooing sounds, but didn't otherwise interfere with his life.

HE WORKED NIGHTS, PROOFREADING DOCUMENTS FOR A BIG LAW OFFICE IN MIDTOWN. The job required an eye for detail. He had trained his visual perspicuity for four years at taxpayer expense while acquiring a B.A. in art history from the University of Wisconsin at Madison. He knew there was such a thing as a job in his major, but unless he counted the college faculty, he'd never met anybody who had one. His superfluous college career could be traced to—or blamed on—a sexy substitute teacher who rambled on about art and revolution for two days in eleventh grade when their regular world history teacher had the flu. He never forgot her. At any moment, he could have improvised a touching essay about how he was first inspired by Mrs. Ellis to believe in a power higher than Jesus Christ.

But eleventh grade was too late to adopt the praxis of art and create a portfolio adequate to gain admission to some kind of secular humanist academy. He could play an instrument—the clarinet—but stiltedly, due to a lack of instruction and role models, and it had never seemed potentially useful to him for purposes of art music, which he naively understood to include progressive rock. He gave it up when he got to college, because he loathed spending his free time at parades and football games. Also he feared it was giving him buckteeth. He wasn't vain, but—here, again, inspired by Mrs. Ellis—he sensed that he should hang on to what little beauty he had.

His good physical features were, in order of scarcity in the general population: broad shoulders and narrow hips; an attractive mouth (full lips, straight teeth, odorless); thick curly hair (dark brown). Not-so-good features: moderate acne scarring; incipient jowls; hairy feet; hairy back; hairy face (he had to shave all the way up to his eyes). Ambiguous feature: five feet eleven inches tall, a towering and uncomfortable giant among Asian immigrants and their furnishings, inconspicuous by the standards of Midtown or the financial district.

He never got his dream job at his favorite record store in Madison, but he regularly met musicians through his shifts at a Subway sandwich shop. By neglecting his studies, he was able to soldier his way upward through the hierarchy of the university radio station until he had a two-hour show on Monday mornings, shocking people awake with the Residents and Halo of Flies.

He had come to New York with $800 in savings expressly dedicated to the release of the seven-inch single that would put Daniel Svoboda on the map. Not as a musician. He wanted to found a record label.

By dint of his radio experience and strategic mail-ordering from ads in *Forced Exposure* and *Maximum Rocknroll,* he knew his single didn't have to be so great musically. What it needed was reverb on the vocals, chorus on the guitar, and compression on everything else. The sound would be "warm" and "punchy." The au courant midwestern sound was grunge with vocals lowered by an octave. The band posters showed nitrogen funny cars shooting flames. What he had in mind was something different: breathy female vocals over propulsive guitar drones, like My Bloody Valentine, only faster. The key element was the breathless woman-girl-child singer—a delicate, tight-throated slip of a thing, aspirating her lines like Jane Birkin on "*Je t'aime . . . moi non plus*" but buried under a mass of guitar noise. In terms of artistic lineage, she was somewhere between Goethe's Mignon and

André Breton's Nadia. He was eager to know whether Pam could sing.

AT HIS SUGGESTION, PAM AND JOE MET HIM AT NOON ON A SATURDAY IN FRONT OF THE Music Palace, a large cinema on Bowery. It was getting close to Christmas. The streets were full of shoppers looking for bargains on the latest Chinese-manufactured goods, such as dish towels and those little plastic rakes and buckets kids take to the beach in summer. They bought a six of Michelob at the grocery store next door and hid it in Pam's backpack. The theater was almost empty. A few men were sleeping toward the back and milling around the bathrooms behind the screen, recent Asian arrivals with nowhere else to go.

The double feature paired an action movie set in Mexico with a kung fu fantasy about medieval China. It ran all day and night. The action movie had already started, so they didn't get to talking until the intermission. Pam, hoping to arouse Daniel's curiosity, said how much she was dreading practice.

He said, "What kind of practice?"

Joe said, "She's in this hard-sucking power duo that has no songs."

"Like I always say, if you gotta suck, suck loud," Pam said. "The Diaphragms have rehearsal space, a drum machine, and no pride. I'd make a speech tomorrow at practice and say it's all over, but the bass player happens to be my roommate."

"Ooh," Daniel said.

"It's hellish. And the worst part is we really do suck. I use so much distortion that all I have to do is look at the guitar and it feeds back. I loop it through a delay and play along with myself. Does it sound dumb yet?"

"Potentially. Can you play bar chords?"

"Are you asking can I play guitar? Yeah, sure. I can even sing. But there's something about this band. I don't want it to be good. I want it to suck, so Simon's band will suck. It's the most self-destructive thing I've ever done, and that's saying a lot. I need to quit."

Daniel hesitated. "I don't want to be in a band," he ventured, not sure he would be believed. "I truly don't. You could say I'm more the camp-follower type. I like a certain kind of music, and I want to get people listening to it. I had a radio show in college. I want to start a label."

"What kind of stuff?"

Joe interrupted them, saying, "Let's have a band! We'll call it Marmalade Sky. It's me on bass, Pam on guitar, and you on keyboards. We all sing. We have three-part harmonies. We practice at your house. I write the songs. Prepare to rock!"

Daniel said, "You're barking up the wrong tree, man. I can't play keyboards. Maybe I could fake drums."

"There's too much drums in songs all the time," Joe said. "You play keyboards."

"I'm in," Pam said. "Next stop Marmalade Sky."

"So what's my label called?" Daniel asked Joe.

"Lion's Den, because of Daniel in the lion's den."

"That sounds like reggae, when 'Marmalade Sky' sounds like bad British psychedelia."

"Together they fit how we're going to sound, which is free dub-rock fusion."

"He could be right," Pam said. "He did without an amp for so long, he's the Charlie Haden of punk rock. I mean, relatively speaking."

"Pam's the worst lead guitar player in the universe," Joe said. "Her fingers move like it's freezing out and she lost her mittens. But in Marmalade Sky, she plays massive power chords she knows how to play, and I play the tunes."

"I play like I'm wearing the mittens," she corrected him. "It's the evil influence of Simon. He wants everything to sound like it's been dragged through candied heroin."

"He's your roommate and in your band?" Daniel asked. "You must be close friends."

"We're extremely intimate." She rolled her eyes.

"It sounds to me like you should cut him off and never look back. I mean, as a disinterested third party."

"I didn't mean to imply that he's on drugs. There are more things at the bottom of the barrel than drugs."

"Can you please play keyboards?" Joe asked Daniel.

"You truly don't want to hear me try."

"You have to," he insisted. "We can't have a band unless we're all in it!"

"I want to put out the band on my label, not play in it."

"It will be absolutely no fun being rock stars and getting laid and everything like that if you aren't in the band. You have to play something!"

"It's better money," Pam pointed out. "A manager gets twenty percent, but as a band member you'd get a third."

"Twenty off the top plus a third puts me at forty-seven percent," Daniel said.

"And we make it all back from record sales and touring!" Joe said.

"I have a day job already," Pam said.

"Me too," Joe said. "I mean touring in the city."

"What I have is more like a night job," Daniel said. "But fine, let's talk about how I'm going to hang it up because I'm raking it in with art for art's sake."

"We're going to be rolling in it," Joe said, as though reminding him of an established fact, "because I'm writing the songs."

Daniel and Pam exchanged a look that said the band would fail no matter what, if only because Joe was writing the songs.

There was a shared bemused affection for him in the look already. "You're going to be the next Neil Diamond," Daniel said.

"Hasil Adkins," Pam said.

"Roy Orbison!" Joe said.

WHEN THE KUNG FU MOVIE WAS OVER, THEY GOT TAKE-OUT PIZZAS AND WALKED TO Daniel's place to eat and listen to records. The first track he put on was "Suspect Device" by Stiff Little Fingers. Joe danced, throwing his arms up to jerk his body from side to side. Daniel put on Hüsker Dü's "Real World," Gang of Four's "Love Like Anthrax," and Mission of Burma's "Forget," until Joe said he was tired of dancing. He volunteered to sing a song he had written earlier in the day. Daniel and Pam exchanged the look again. Joe took a deep breath, clapped his hands to indicate a rumba, and sang, with so many North-African-style adornments that every syllable was stretched into three or four:

> This world is small
> I see you all
> Killing my head
> With how you bled
> And now you're dead
> Dead, dead, dead

He stretched the final "dead" into about ten syllables.

Pam said, "Joe, man! Are you emotionally troubled? Is there something I don't know?"

"Seriously, I think the melody's okay," Daniel said. He went to the rear corner of the room, under one of the windows to the courtyard, and returned with a warped flea-market classical guitar, wrongly strung with steel instead of nylon. It wasn't tuned. He gave it to Pam and said, "Here, play it on guitar."

Twenty minutes later, they had an intro, verse, and guitar riff. Daniel drummed gently with spoons on a book. Pam sang the song, and Joe sang the bass line. Finally he said, "That was the A part of the song. Now comes the B part."

The lyrics to the B part were about skateboarders. Daniel said, "Wait. Is this the chorus or the bridge? Does this have something to do with the A part?"

Joe said firmly, "It's about skateboarders. They're dead. There was gravel at the corner of Fifth and Fifteenth, and they were hanging on to the bumper of a cab, and *poof*!"

THE NEXT MORNING, PAM TOLD SIMON THAT SHE WAS GOING TO THE PRACTICE SPACE without him because she could afford it on her own. Ten dollars an hour isn't much for a programmer. She said she was done with the Diaphragms. The band had never worked. She had a new project that might work. To forestall any hopes on his side, she said he wasn't welcome in the new project.

The whole routine made her nervous. She stood by the door, guitar on her back and effects bag in her hand, making this insulting speech as if expecting immediate capitulation, knowing better than to expect it.

Simon said, "That's my practice space, not yours. I already advertised for a new guitar player."

"So why aren't you going there now?"

"I don't have one yet. But I will."

She set her things down and said, "Simon, I know our love was beautiful, but we need to break up."

"I'm not moving out. I can't even afford to practice by myself. You're the one who just said ten dollars isn't a lot of money. You move out. You can afford a place of your own. Just go." He turned sulkily toward the cereal box on the table and sprinkled a few more squares of Chex into his slowly warming milk.

DANIEL DIDN'T WANT TO REHEARSE ON SUNDAY MORNINGS. HE DIDN'T SEE ANY REASON to get up early, cross town, and pay money to do something they could do in his home if they didn't get carried away with the volume. Over miso soup on Saint Mark's Place—his first date with Pam—he said, "Why spend money when we can just turn down?"

"Tube amps don't work like that," she said. "They need to warm up to sound right, and they need to sound right to warm up. There's no headphone jack."

"Why don't you get a transistor amp, so you can practice at home?"

"No way," she said. "I've been down that road. We rehearse under realistic conditions." She sketched her experience with the Slinkies, saying it was time to move forward, at least into the eighties, now that it was 1990. There was nothing embarrassing about being behind. The sixties had hit pop culture around 1972, just as punk was taking off. "You ever see *Birth of the Beatles*?" she added. "We need to work like busy bees to get to the tippy top."

"Darby Crash died the day before John Lennon."

"Todd is God," she said. "But yeah, maybe Darby's what put Chapman over the edge."

Daniel suppressed a smile. He had nothing against John Lennon, and no sympathy for the man who shot him, but knowing that Todd Rundgren had composed "Rock and Roll Pussy" about Lennon, that Lennon had responded with an open letter to "Sodd Runtlestuntle" in *Melody Maker,* and that Mark David Chapman had cared enough to take the affair to its logical conclusion while wearing a promotional T-shirt for Todd's latest album—it was a kind of knowledge he didn't expect a woman to have, much less care enough to say something post-sensitive about. He was starting to get a serious crush on her. He personally had first heard of John Lennon the day he died. His family was more into Up with People.

LATE WEDNESDAY NIGHT, PAM WAS AMONG THE FIRST TO BUY THE *VILLAGE VOICE* AND turn to the real estate classifieds. She strode to a streetlamp to read. What she saw made her guts clench. Since her last move, her budgeted residential zone had shifted far away from Manhattan, past Brooklyn Heights. The studios she could afford were in places like Greenpoint and Astoria. Even Park Slope had apparently turned into a bourgeois hell of first-time homebuyers bent on pretending their stucco townhomes were brownstones on the Upper East Side.

She regarded Brooklyn as a cultural wasteland. A summertime stroll up Flatbush with the devoted Brooklyn fan Joe hadn't changed her mind. In a shop window she'd seen a dead branch spray-painted gold in a silver-painted vase for eighty dollars. She had attended an art opening in Williamsburg once, down near the water, and it still stuck with her as though it might recur as a final image of vacuity before she died. She had narrowly missed the era when Alphabet City was controlled by Latino crime syndicates and inhabited by the living dead—honest-to-goodness cannibals—but Williamsburg was creepier, because there was nobody around. No buildings standing open with dim-eyed figures guarding holes leading to cellars; just walls and chain-link on all sides, and she and Joe the only pedestrians for miles. Cannibals could have eaten them right there on the street, without taking the trouble to drag them inside a building. When they got to the opening, it turned out to be site-specific installations made of found objects. None of the so-called artists could afford supplies or a studio. It was literal *arte povera*. Then she sliced open the top of her right ear on a splinter of broken mirror some wannabe had hung from the ceiling with twine.

She read the ads for lower Manhattan again. Her hands and feet turned cold from the adrenaline, as if she'd been caught in a trap. To all appearances she was not leaving her lease on Bleecker Street. If Simon wasn't either, she would have to put up with him.

III.

Operation Desert Shield marched inexorably toward war. The USA was ranging its armaments against Saddam Hussein and preparing to lay waste to his country. Pam often wished aloud that the Selective Service System would draft Simon into the battle for Kuwait.

Daniel had talked about the draft so much that she didn't realize there was no draft. He was in touch with the American Friends Service Committee, on Joe's behalf as well as his own, preparing for them to become conscientious objectors. He even took Joe to a Quaker meeting, but only once.

There was officially a recession on. Corporate executives were moaning that double-digit annual profit growth was a thing of the past. Even RIACD's Wall Street clients were strapped for cash. They had installed networked PCs before firing the staff the PCs would make redundant. Two years earlier, when Pam parachuted into an office, she could be sure of seeing secretaries in motion, walking briskly in and out of their supervisors' offices, running files from room to room, controlling the speed of Dictaphone tapes with foot pedals, typing letters on IBM Selectrics. Now those same secretaries sat at bare desks half asleep, while their bosses answered correspondence privately on Lotus cc:mail. Occasionally one would stand up to take a print job off the printer in the printer room. At a big reinsurer, Pam saw a woman typing a chapter from the Book of Ezekiel. She learned that the company's desktop publishing pool had resolved, as a devotional exercise, to enter God's Word into WordPerfect documents. Not because anybody needed a printout; they all had the book at home. It was a means of communion with the Divine. It could not end well.

The winter settled in like a poisonous fog around the redundant American people. The war ramped up. Yellow ribbons appeared. The streets were dark at four o'clock. The wind whistled and rattled the signage. Pam and her coworkers sat idle in the conference room, watching a lot of TV.

In mid-January 1991, things got interesting. A CNN correspondent was trapped in Baghdad. He described his fear in great detail, conveying a sense that war was ultra-scary. The battlefields looked like barbecue grills—not arrangements of discrete wrecks and craters, but greasy charcoal melted to the pavement. America the Beautiful was taking no prisoners.

Pam went to visit Daniel after work and found him downstairs in the store, huddled up in his coat, watching CBS with Victor. He pointed at the TV and said, "They're landing Scuds on Tel Aviv. It's Armageddon."

Daniel was not remotely Jewish, and he didn't know any Israelis, but he had been raised in the kind of Christian household that promotes respect for the defense capabilities of Israel and belief in the apocalyptic consequences of putting its back against the wall. Not that Israel couldn't defend itself. Plucky little Israel had fended off repeated Arab invasions, and not through the power of prayer. It had fought valiantly and developed—with French assistance, though Daniel couldn't imagine why that was—a nuclear deterrent. Those who aided the enemies of Israel died. That's what they did.

For example, the British engineer who decided to help Saddam build a cannon big enough to put two tons into orbit. He just up and died of gunshot wounds in Brussels.

The respect was possibly overgenerous and the eschatological expectations overblown, but it was hard for Daniel to imagine Tel Aviv taking a Scud missile lying down. To make sure Pam knew what he meant, he added, "This is World War Three!"

"Are they with nerve gas?"

"They don't know yet. Nobody wants to be first to take off the gas mask and find out. But it can't be nerve gas, right? Israel would so totally nuke Baghdad. They want to draw Israel into the war, but they don't want to die. If Israel sends even one plane into Iraqi airspace, it could draw the whole Arab world into the war."

"What do you think, Victor?" she asked.

"Americans supply Israel with many things. Israel won't interfere in our war."

"I think Israel goes its own way," Daniel said. "They play off all sides against each other. They get less American support than you think."

"Israel and Iraq are nothing," Victor said. "If they nuke each other, it's not World War Three. It's jackals fighting over a desert."

"Whoa," Pam said, unused to hearing anything that could possibly have been construed as anti-Semitic.

"Any war that goes nuclear is World War Three," Daniel said. "And nuclear war involving Israel is Armageddon, any way you cut it up. So this is potential nuclear Armageddon. Babylon the great is fallen—is fallen . . . for all the nations have drunk of the wine of the wrath of her fornication!" He shouted the last bit because it was part of a Tragic Mulatto song.

"Let's wait first and see whether they use nerve gas," Pam said.

Victor offered to open a bottle of vodka to celebrate the coming

American win. Daniel's response was to proclaim, "Let us eat and drink, for tomorrow we die." Victor reached under the counter, and Pam expressed admiration at his stocking bootleg vodka, which counted as agreement to help them drink.

They watched TV until eleven o'clock. Pam said she was too drunk to go straight home on foot. She went upstairs with Daniel to have some herbal tea.

There they had sex for the first time. His doubts, hesitations, and regrets were as nothing in the face of the coming apocalypse. She felt none of the above. She wished she'd had the idea of sleeping with him long before.

SEX CAME AND WENT IN PAM'S LIFE. SHE HAD PICKED UP ENOUGH OF THE TAIL END OF seventies culture to call it "love." She never had sex unless she was "in love." She could fall in love in the space of fifteen minutes. She had offered many appealing strangers tender kisses, some of which became hand jobs in short order, while others quickly progressed to "making love."

As a result, all her boyfriends had been approximately as charming as Simon. She fell in love as a prelude to sex. Then she had ethical qualms about unloading people in the morning, because she was in love. Her ideal of sex was intimate and gentle, and she kept having it with strangers.

She knew all about bad sex. Not rough sex; she would have called that "assault." She knew that gay men pick up rough trade at the risk of being beaten to death, that submissive men role-play excuses for penetration, and that straight women take both behaviors to extremes. She understood herself to be a hedonist. She never sought out unpleasant consequences. They just kept happening.

Sex for Daniel was the opposite—consistently too much fun. His earliest sexual experiences had involved fondling the genitals of Christian schoolgirls he never once kissed. He'd even gotten a blow job from one of them once, and he wouldn't have kissed her for a million dollars after that. Her feelings were hurt, but what could he do? How were his sexual preferences his fault?

In college he'd gotten a crush on an eccentric and lonely black women's-studies major who slept around but never had intercourse with anyone. She never said why not, and she never touched him, so he never felt he had standing to find out. At times he thought they were two virgins, born to be together, and at other times he thought she was recovering from a rape trauma and subsequent promiscuous phase; he never asked. In her senior year she came out as lesbian, and he felt he'd missed his one chance. He had two years of college left to go, and nobody he knew of liked him that way.

At an art opening the fall of junior year, he met a Thai woman on an exchange program to the veterinary school. They corresponded for months. That was sexually rewarding (not). He'd never known Buddhists were so strict about premarital sex.

His senior year, he hooked up with a scraggly-haired anthropologist. She had sour armpits and annoying mannerisms such as picking her nose and relating everything to cybernetics, but she said she liked to get fucked. Once, early in their liaison, she diverted his member into her anus with her hand, and he didn't immediately notice. When he did, she explained that she had vaginal discomfort from a yeast infection. He suspected that she felt no sexual pleasure, of any kind, ever, and that it was a matter of indifference to her how he did what.

On one occasion, he was unfaithful to her with a pretty townie he met at a heavy metal show. When they were done, the townie said, "Did you know I'm fifteen?" He was terrified. She promised to keep quiet for a hundred dollars. But his friends at Subway knew that she was nineteen and an amateur, so it was okay.

In short, his previous experiences of sex had less than nothing to do with love. Pam opened a new chapter in his life. Where the other consummated affairs seemed to have emerged from the sewers of his mind like roaches swarming out of a toilet, Pam descended from above, bringing all he held most dear: beauty, art, music, cyberpunk, the Lower East Side. Kissing her was the most important thing.

Band practice was interesting after that. Joe sang his songs while playing counterpoint melodies on the bass. Pam looked straight down at her left hand, and Daniel focused on the brushes with which he played warped floor tom and broken snare. Every so often, the couple raised their eyes and nodded almost imperceptibly in greeting.

IN HIS FUNCTION AS MANAGER AND LABEL EXECUTIVE, DANIEL BOUGHT THE SELF-HELP manual *Book Your Own Fucking Life*. It was a punk rock venue guide to the USA and Canada, produced by an anarchist collective in Minneapolis. He observed that meaningful implementation of the book was predicated on possession of a vehicle. He was financially committed to Marmalade Sky to the tune of the $800 the first single was going to cost him. There was nothing in his plans about thousands of dollars for transportation. The thought of trying to store a van in lower Manhattan made his insides droop. Whether or not the street sweeping machines came, you had to move your car every day. Official car theft rates were kept low by the inconvenience of reporting crimes, but a car parked on the street still had annual insurance premiums roughly equal to its value. A worthless car could be relied on to stay put if you removed some vital part such as the alternator every night and took it upstairs.

He broached the necessity of renting a van some weekend to play Trenton or Philly, traditional springboards for ambitious and creative bands that had trouble cracking the mercantile culture of NYC rock.

Pam said, "What's next, Passaic? This city not big enough for you?"

Joe elucidated his view that New York City was the industry's one and only mecca. Bands from other places dreamed all their lives of playing there, paying serious money—like fifty bucks—for the privilege of presenting short sets in exploitative clubs such as Downtown Beirut. Marmalade Sky, an endemic growth, could play New York any time it wanted, by setting up out on the sidewalk or next to the fountain in Washington Square. He had seen a rig with a Peavey and a car battery. They could play wearing fun costumes. He had seen a girl dressed as broccoli.

"No, no, no," Daniel said. "I'm not busking for quarters! I have a job!"

He noted inwardly that Marmalade Sky's need for a label and a manager was not urgent, and possibly not even real. The band itself might not be real. He felt it might be helpful to know relevant people who could confirm the band's reality. If, say, he were on speaking terms with someone who booked clubs or a music journalist—he didn't know how or where to start, but he did have the idea. He resolved to acquire a kick drum and hi-hat cymbals.

He wasn't thinking straight. Pam worked days, and he worked nights. On weekdays they saw each other in the evenings, when she got home from RIACD and he hadn't left yet—generally from about seven to ten—which was enough time to cook or get takeout, fool around, get cleaned up, and go home to sleep and uptown to work, respectively. On weekends they went to shows. He was losing sleep.

When he finally asked her, Pam proffered her habitual disinterested analysis. Of all the factors in their success, she said, there was only one under his control: the debut single, which he should urgently bring to fruition. After it came out, other bands would hound him with demo tapes. For the sake of buttering up a label owner, they would offer Marmalade Sky choice opening gigs.

He replied, "I have the money to put out a single, but no band to put on it. Maybe you can tell me when Marmalade Sky is going to start being non-heinous."

"Put up a flyer at Kim's," she said. "Or an ad in the *Voice*. Find some band that has a decent cassette and offer them a seven-inch. Or record Joe as a solo project and let him sell it to his three hundred best friends."

A STRANGE PHENOMENON HAD TAKEN HOLD OF PAM'S CHECKING ACCOUNT SINCE SHE had met Daniel. It was growing. While single, she had not skimped on cover charges, restaurant meals, instruments, electronics, or liquor by the drink, and whenever she couldn't find her wallet—a regular occurrence—she had bought a new one to fill with new cash. Since meeting him, she had been spending money rather than hemorrhaging it, and she was saving hundreds of dollars a month.

But she didn't offer to contribute money to Lion's Den. It was his label, not hers. She had enough business experience to know that it wasn't a business. It was an art project. Investing in it would contravene the project goal, which was to be Daniel's art. He wanted autonomy more than he wanted success. He wanted to design record covers, compose press releases, and gain a reputation— among the handful of people who mattered to him—as a man of wit and taste. It had nothing to do with turning $800 into $2,000 in the fullness of time and paying her back.

She didn't try to explain herself. It was hard to explain. As an art form, rock's medium was commercial success. The tippy top was its guiding light. Having a band was about being a rock star, a fantasy of ultimate autonomy in which you got paid megabucks to be your worst self.

Meanwhile she was slogging away as a programmer, and he was sitting up all night setting Latin abbreviations in italics. Marmalade Sky might be art for art's sake, but if it didn't offer them at least a chance of rock stardom, it wasn't worth doing.

DANIEL TURNED HER SUGGESTION OVER AND OVER IN HIS MIND. JOE COULD PLAY MORE instruments, and play them better, than all three of them put together. He had no shortage of material. The missing element was the multitrack studio to produce the master tape.

He thought briefly of buying microphones and a four-track and learning to use them—or, more realistically, letting Pam figure them out—but the equipment would cost almost as much as pressing the single, and he'd still have to rent a soundproofed room, free of garbage trucks, car stereos, car alarms, and honking, to record it in, and hire a real producer to oversee the recording and mix it down. Inadvertent technical errors might commit to vinyl the excruciating sound of tape hiss or sixty-cycle hum, making the single too lame to distribute.

He said to himself, "Fuck it," as people often do when deciding to spend money they don't have. Joe instantly agreed to record a seven-inch with two three-minute songs in a single afternoon. Daniel booked a studio with an engineer in Hoboken, about three months into the future, and paid a deposit of $200.

PAM'S PERIOD WAS LATE. SHE DIDN'T WANT TO TELL ANYONE JUST HOW LATE. SHE AND Daniel had had unsafe sex more than once. It didn't feel like it counted, because it was such a small fraction of the total sex they'd had. Okay, she admitted to herself: five weeks late. If her period skipped another week, it would be an open-and-shut case. She would need an abortion.

She knew that if she told Daniel, he'd offer to pay, and there would go Lion's Den records. She had plenty of money. The only way to get an abortion and keep the single was to tell Daniel nothing. He was already in over his head, buying studio time for a friend when he could have pressed a clean master provided for free by strangers. In any case it might already be too late for a black-market poison-pill-style abortion with smuggled RU-486. It would make her sick all weekend, cramping and bleeding until she swore off sex for life, but at least she wouldn't have to make time for a clinic. She needed to hurry. She'd have to explain being sick to Daniel. Food poisoning, maybe? She would have to come up with what she ate and where. She didn't feel like rushing into being sick. Besides, the pregnancy might resolve itself unobtrusively. If she skipped the poison pill and stuck to old-fashioned abortion clinics, she had months left until the third trimester.

All she needed was to keep the information away from Daniel until she got organized and found out where they do second-trimester abortions.

She was a programmer and a punk, versed in the mortification of the flesh, accustomed to treating her body as a sink and a tool. She was young and inexperienced, not in tune with her own biology and nature. She was not thinking straight. She was not thinking at all to speak of. In the corner of D.C. where she grew up, abortions came from Mom. You told your mom you'd been stupid, and she made the relevant appointments. You handed off the thinking to someone else, like a user, not a programmer. Pam didn't make the appointments.

Right around week ten, she grabbed herself by the scruff of the neck, set herself on her feet, and confronted Daniel. She said, "Daniel, I do not feel good."

"Is something wrong?"

"I'm pregnant."

"From me? Hey, I don't know what you get up to after I go to work! Maybe you turn tricks under the viaduct."

"It has your eyes."

"When did you find out?"

"I haven't found out yet. I keep putting it off. I need to get on the stick and do something about it."

"Do you not want a baby?" Seeing her shake her head, he asked, "Is it because of the Art Strike?"

"A baby is not creative work!"

"Are you sure you don't want a baby ever in your life? Most people want one sooner or later. Like me. I always assumed I'd have kids someday."

"What are you saying?"

"I know we never talked about it, but right now I'm thinking, 'If not now, when?' You'd be a total bottom-shelf mother." ("Bottom-shelf" was positive, since in midwestern refrigerators the top shelf was where you put the cheap beer for guests to notice when they were making themselves at home.)

"And 'If not me, then whom?'" Pam said.

"Random unwed parenting is standard practice back where I come from! We Christians welcome every new Christian soul."

"It's standard everywhere," she said, "but not for me. And the reason we never talked about it is that we've been dating for maybe four months."

"Obviously," he said firmly, "abortion makes sense on paper. But I don't live my life on paper. I would have been happy to know you were pregnant with my child the first time I saw you."

"You're just weird," she said.

"If we have a kid now, we can be out of the woods at forty. I implore you!" He clasped his hands together pleadingly. "Besides, scheduling an abortion is work, but if you just let it ride, you don't have to do anything. Which I guess is what you've been doing. How far along are you?"

"That's so not true! There's prenatal care. I have to get sonograms and do Lamaze and La Leche League and turn into my mom. You're going to love that. Not to mention giving birth and the next eighteen years."

"It'll be easy. We're young and healthy."

"I should get a pregnancy test," she said. "Maybe it's just ovarian cancer."

THE DISTANCE SHE HAD PUT BETWEEN HERSELF AND HER PARENTS KEPT HER FROM indulging the notion that her child would inherit her traits. It would be its own person, transporting nothing of her into the future. It would be raised differently from the way she had been raised, in a different world. Yet already it seemed to embody personal weaknesses she thought she had learned to repress.

Nausea and latent disquiet, for instance. While still the size of a pushpin, Flora reopened Pam's eyes to the horror of existence. The Cold War had ended. The peace dividend was pouring in. All the thermonuclear warheads were still there. All, what, ten thousand of them? Twenty thousand? In any case, enough to cook every animal on Earth and leave the survivors licking their eyeballs off their maggoty faces.

Nuclear deterrence was a variant of predestination. Whatever happened to you was your fault, if you hadn't deterred it. It was life as an endless stud poker game in which folding equaled death. Any day now, life could become *The Day of the Triffids*, if the Triffids had been defense policy wonks and not evil plants from space. The Triffids in turn reminded her of *The Genocides*, a novella by Tom Disch in which alien farmers sow the unfortunate Earth with giant sugarcane. Millennia might pass before that happened, but by having a baby, she would be involving herself directly in the tragedy. It was no consolation to recall the survivors' stubborn capacity for joy or their relief at the conclusion of the harvest. As a willingly pregnant woman, she would at once be placing a long-shot bet that life on Earth would be idyllic forever and condemning a stranger to have its heart broken by her death.

She even worried about the coming Asian century, which she imagined as resembling Karel Čapek's *War with the Newts*. Western imperialism was still going strong. It would take fifty years to decline—and there stood the baby, all grown up, undernourished, lopsided from twelve-hour days in the sweatshop, enslaved by happy-go-lucky taskmasters who decorated its dormitory in red and gold. The red tide of slave labor was all around her in China-town. She just had to open her eyes to let it engulf her.

She was not getting any work done. She called Video Hit from her office and made Margie wake Daniel so she could say, "There's no way I'm having this baby. I'm sorry. It's over."

"All right. That's a shame." After a moment of dead air, he added, "Now I'm sad."

It crossed her mind that killing Daniel's baby might not be the most efficient method of removing heartbreak from the world. She said, "In fact, I haven't made up my mind yet."

"I wish you were here," he said. "I'm going crazy. I've been thinking about names. What do you think of 'Irene'? It means 'peace.'"

"Too nasal for New York. Plus I might not even be pregnant."

WHEN THEY WERE DONE TALKING, SHE WENT DOWNSTAIRS TO A DRUGSTORE ON JOHN Street. She had put off buying a pregnancy test. After all that time without her period, she wouldn't have believed a negative result, and a positive result wouldn't have told her anything she didn't know, so the parsimonious solution was to skip the test. It was positive.

She didn't call Daniel. Instead she walked into Yuval's of-fice, closed the door, and told him that effective immediately she would be disappointing her clients at the insurance companies in Omaha. Flying pregnant was out of the question, due to cosmic gamma rays. When the baby came, she would go on vacation for at least two weeks.

Yuval said, *"Mazal tov!"* It was not the Ashkenazi one-word *MA-zel-tov* that means "Congratulations," but the Sephardic two-word *ma-ZAL TOV* that means "Good luck with that."

THAT NIGHT SHE WAITED UNTIL DANIEL WAS JUST ABOUT TO LEAVE FOR WORK TO TELL him. Lying back on his bed, in the shade of the narrow section of wall between his two bright rear windows, she said, "We're going to have a baby."

He said, "I feel this is a good time to confess that I love you."

IN THE MORNING, HE CALLED JOE TO SAY HE COULDN'T AFFORD TO RECORD ANY SONGS, because he would be needing every cent he had to finance his baby. He would lose the $200 deposit on the recording studio, but that was better than paying the balance.

Joe said, "I guess she didn't tell her parents yet."

"How do you know?"

"Because you're worried about money!"

"What do you mean?"

"They're so rich, they live in a house with a yard and trees!"

As a native of Wisconsin, Daniel didn't consider a yard and trees proof of affluence. But that night in bed, resting up before work, he did go so far as to ask Pam to explain Joe's insinuation. He had always assumed she came from a working-class background similar to his own, if only because she hadn't finished high school. The news about her pregnancy had prompted him to subordinate his artistic ego to the expense of raising a child. Now he wasn't so sure. Was it conceivable that fatherhood might improve his finances instead of bankrupting him?

She said her dad was a career civil servant with a desk job who planned to retire at sixty. At that point he would commence a second career as a "double dipper," exploiting his contacts as a defense consultant while drawing half of his former salary. He wasn't rich, far from it. He made a little under a hundred thousand. In Washington that meant he could have a decent house in a safe part of town, with a wife who didn't work, living like it was the sixties. He also had—she said this was the problematic part, for her—a clean conscience, though she knew, or could guess, what he'd been involved in during the Vietnam War. She hadn't talked to him since she left home and had hardly talked to him before that; he was a distant, authoritarian father.

"I know you can do math," Daniel said. "Do you have any idea what a normal person would have to save to retire on fifty thousand dollars a year for life?"

"They're not rich. They're, like, slow-drip rich. They're middle class."

"You parents have zero worries!"

"Oh, no. I gave them plenty of wrinkles and gray hair." It sounded like a boast, so she added, "Or maybe it was napalming old people and kids that gave Dad wrinkles and gray hair. I don't know and I don't care."

"What's your mom like?"

"I don't know. The last time I saw her, she was a stingy, controlling bitch."

"When was that?"

"Nineteen eighty-six."

"So call her and find out."

"Call yours first."

"There's no danger mine will offer us money. More like second-hand baby clothes from the church basement. Mom will start crocheting a layette set and be done by the time it's ten months old."

"Racine's a safe distance. You can tell them. Though I guess they might want us to be married."

"I'll lie. If there's one thing evangelical Christianity teaches you how to do, it's lie."

"You can lie? I can't say I noticed."

"It's not a skill I get much use out of anymore. Christians unearth the innate lying talent of little kids and hone it like a razor. Like when they ask you to raise your hand in youth group if you've ever touched yourself, and then raise your hand if you've ever touched a girl."

"So does everybody pick door number two?"

"Hell, no! You'd be getting some girl in trouble. The point is to make you feel guilty and trapped. That's all. It makes you bond with the other Christians, because you're all telling the same lies together all the time and everybody knows it. It's like your platoon did a war crime, so now you're blood brothers."

"Did you raise your hand?"

"One time I did raise my hand and say I touched myself, and they acted like I'd come out of the closet. I guess it's the same thing. My hand touched dick."

"Can't have that," Pam said, touching his dick.

THE INITIAL PLAN WAS FOR HER SOMEHOW TO GET RID OF SIMON, SO THAT SHE AND Daniel and the baby could share the one-and-a-half-bedroom apartment in the doorman building. The size was perfect. They might never have to move again. Daniel's share would be double his current rent, but that would still leave it in manageable territory.

It was such an elegant solution that Pam presumed Simon would instantly see their side of the question and vanish from her life, if he had any utilitarian model of ethics whatsoever. He refused to budge. He liked his half-bedroom, which allowed him to live in a fancy apartment in an enviable location without paying Manhattan-style rent. Little Jersey wasn't chichi; it wasn't Soho or Tribeca; he couldn't brag that he lived there. It was more of a drinking theme park with shoe stores. But at least it wasn't a bridge-and-tunnel neighborhood where finding an affordable apartment required reading knowledge of Greek or Polish.

He said he'd be happy to look for a new roommate. With that location, so close to the bars, he could basically run auditions and keep interviewing until he found somebody who'd fuck him. The new roommate was guaranteed, he assured Pam, to be a better fuck than her, because she had never been anything special—too cerebral. He advised her to grow some hair, because it's sensual for men when women have some hair to grab on to.

He got what he was aiming for. She left in high distress. She couldn't imagine spending another night under one roof with him. In effect, she evicted herself.

THEY RENTED A U-HAUL TO DO THE MOVE A FEW DAYS LATER. SIMON HELPED CARRY HER dresser and platform bed from the elevator to the truck. He was unwilling to laze around like a pasha in front of Daniel. Daniel in turn noticed Simon's discomfiture when he packed up Pam's microwave. "You're going to miss this," he prophesied.

"I'll make sure the new roommate has one," Simon said.

"Never share an apartment with one person," she told Daniel as he drove. "Always live in a group situation where the total is an odd number, so you can have majority rule."

"That's a discouraging thing to say to somebody you're about to move in with," he said. She reminded him that she was two people.

They got married. Of course they got married. The possibility lay there, inducing vertigo, until they did it to get it over with— Daniel for reasons that were primarily romantic, and Pam because marriage made her an ex-Bailey. So they got married, a minor bureaucratic procedure in city hall, downtown, with no special outfits and no party.

Joe waited for them outside the building with a bouquet of wilting rosebuds he had bought at a newsstand and warm champagne that got all over his pants when he opened it. He sang a new song to their happiness, sucked the foam from the bottle, and passed it to Pam. Daniel said, "The bride never drinks at a shotgun wedding," and drank most of it himself.

IV.

K ill, kill, kill," Pam breathed. Daniel thought she was referring
in her delirium to *Faster, Pussycat! Kill! Kill!*, but she was at-
tempting a Unix shutdown of the birthing process. Sometimes
you have to send the "kill" command a good number of times.

It didn't work. She kept giving birth.

He didn't leave the room right away. But he had his limits, and
one of them was how much pain he could watch her suffer. He
tried to stay and even took part in the conversation about attaching a suction cup to the baby's head. Then he felt dizzy and left
to sit down in the lobby. A nurse came out to tell him it was over.

He called his parents collect. They congratulated him sincerely.
But as much as they treasured the birth of a new soul predestined
for heaven or hell, they couldn't see it as a special occasion. It was
routine, in the circles in which they moved, to welcome babies.
They'd been wondering where his babies were since around the
time he turned twenty. Flora was their ninth grandchild. They
promised to send a check for fifty dollars. They invited him to
come home sometime and bring his wife and daughter.

PAM DIDN'T CALL HER PARENTS. SHE DIDN'T WANT TO HEAR HER MOTHER'S OPINION ON anything—not on Daniel, not on her decision-making skills, not on her choice of hospital.

She'd picked one with a low rate of cesarean sections, and she was regretting it. She'd gotten a touch of fever right toward the end, and her ob-gyn suggested she let them induce labor. She ended up with one giant cramp that went on for seven hours until they hauled the baby out with the VE. It looked as though its birth had involved being thrown from a passing truck, the same figurative truck that had run over her pelvis. Its head was blue from the ears up, crowned with a puffy skin yarmulke for which the technical term was "chignon."

Looking at the baby filled her soul with the fear of death. Within a week she believed that without Daniel, it would not have lived. Without him, she'd be lying facedown drunk on the bed, headphones blasting Black Sabbath. He kept it warm, dry, and loved and brought it to her to feed.

After two weeks, to her astonishment, she bounced back. The trauma faded. She regained her appetite. She saw that the baby was cuter than she'd remembered. It looked to her less like a scrap of meat torn from her insides and more like a warm, dry, fluffy little human.

She asked Daniel to take a look at her vagina and see whether it too was recognizable as human. She was afraid to use a hand mirror, because it felt like it was in shreds. He said, "Babe, it's literally identical. Nothing's changed."

She looked at it herself and found that he was right. She cherished the hope that she might one day be herself again.

SHE STAYED HOME FROM RIACD TO RECOVER. BABY FLORA KEPT GETTING CUTER AND cuter. Joe came over to inspect her and declared her the cutest baby who ever lived, explicitly praising her purple-and-green head.

She was in fact a cute baby, after the swelling went down. She had Daniel's tan skin, quite striking with Pam's blue eyes.

He didn't get time off from the law firm for having fathered a child. He didn't even get a cigar or a pat on the back, since he had nothing to gain by telling them about it. Pam had better health insurance, and he felt that he looked to outsiders like an irresponsible character and nothing more: nine months from slum-dwelling loser to slum-dwelling loser dad.

She cared for the baby at the odd times when it wanted to be cared for, slept during the strange hours it saw fit to sleep, sat patiently through the eerie work routine of the rented breast pump, and let him pick up the slack. He was happy when holding Flora and a bottle, happiest when carrying her around the neighborhood hidden in a sling tied to his chest, and seriously indispensable when it came to cleaning, laundry, and shopping.

The medium-term plan was for her to work days while he went on working nights, so that someone was always with Flora. Six weeks after giving birth, she pumped three bottles full of milk and stumbled off to RIACD. Promptly the baby-maintenance scheme collapsed, and not because Daniel wasn't up to the task. Without napping during the day, Pam couldn't sleep enough to work. Maybe there are jobs you can do in your sleep, but fixing manual garbage collection in an undocumented big ball of mud isn't one of them. She went back to work on a Wednesday, and by the following Wednesday it was clear that something had to change. She didn't want to be the consultant who passes for a profit center because he has so many billable hours, at least until his clients bail.

Thursday morning she called in sick, pumped extra, put in earplugs, and asked Daniel not to wake her until she woke up on her own.

That happened around noon. When the vision came, she

opened her eyes and determined that he was next to her in bed, with Flora sprawled naked on his bare chest. She nudged him out of a doze and said, "Daniel. I found a solution."

"Pray tell."

"You get a day job, and we hire a babysitter."

He sat upright, clutching Flora close, and said, "No, no, no."

"Why not?"

"I am not letting some migrant worker take it out on my daughter how much she misses her kids. We don't have anyplace to put a Dutch au pair, as much as I'd enjoy hosting one, and we can't afford a qualified babysitter. We'd have to put her in day care, and there's no way on God's earth. Forget it."

"I meant Joe."

"Joe," Daniel said. "Isn't he, I don't know, not the most literate—"

"I know she's your daughter and everything, but she's also a newborn. She can communicate on his level until she's at least six."

"What makes you think he'd do it?"

"He has some okay shifts, but he averages, like, five dollars an hour. We offer him seven, and bingo."

"No way," Daniel said. "He trusts everybody. If somebody came up to him on the street and asked if they could hold her, he'd just hand her over."

"People will think he's the dad. If I were going to fence a baby, or even liberate it for my own use, would I go after the dad? Anyway, you just invented that crime, because I've never heard of it—playground-based baby trafficking. Come on. People around here keep an eye out for each other. You know what they say. It takes a village to raise a child."

"It takes a parent to raise a child. It takes a village to raise a stray cat. Joe is too trusting to be responsible for anybody."

"Look who's talking, the man who wants to hire a stranger! At least he's a known quantity. And he'll say yes, because he worships her."

In the evening they went to see him, bearing Chinese takeout. He didn't hesitate. Chief among the people he trusted was himself. If someone had offered him a job running the trading desk at Goldman Sachs, he would have taken that too.

He got so excited about his new opportunity that they had to remind him of the existence of the coffee shop. He said he was sure no one there would mind if he missed some shifts, and whenever he was done babysitting, he could pick up where he left off. For all they knew, he was right.

He did have a short attention span, but as Pam said, that might be an advantage. Babies have ways of getting themselves noticed. Joe's attention span might equip him with unusual patience, by keeping him from noticing that it was the same shriek over and over.

SHE CALLED IN SICK AGAIN ON FRIDAY, AND HE CAME OVER FOR A TRIAL RUN, ARRIVING at nine in the morning. She grabbed a bottle of breast milk from the fridge and warmed it up in the microwave. After she had arranged him feeding Flora, she lay down on the couch for a nap. She didn't want to disturb Daniel, who was asleep on the bed, having gotten home from work at seven.

Four hours later, she woke up. Joe was holding Flora and a fresh bottle, still sitting at the kitchen table. He said, "I changed her diaper."

"I'm sorry. I forgot to show you how."

"No problem. It's easy, compared to regular underpants. There's no front and back!"

Nodding affirmatively, she rushed to the bathroom, because she was having this phase where the desire to pee and peeing were sort of the same thing. Through the door, she could hear him singing a blues song to Flora:

Drink another bottle, it's almost two o'clock
I said drink another bottle, baby, it's almost two o'clock
You been drinking all this morning and I'll never let you stop

On the kitchen table, squirming on her back
I said baby's on the kitchen table, squirming on her back
I'm going to take her little pants off and show her where it's at

Daniel turned over in bed and said, "Your song is deeply disturbing."

"The last line needs work," Joe said. "In blues songs 'back' always rhymes with 'heart attack.' Maybe 'wipe her dirty crack.'"

"I think with regard to our professional relationship there should be an ironclad rule," Daniel said. "No songs about my daughter."

THEIR ONE CONCESSION TO JOE'S ECCENTRICITIES WAS THE PURCHASE OF A BABY carrier. Pam called strollers "traffic testers," because of the way caregivers in New York shoved them into the street to stop the cars. They had been transporting Flora in a ten-foot-long carrying cloth that circled the torso multiple times, with an X in back and another X in front, finishing with a knot you had to tie behind your own back. Joe's attempt to put it on might have worked as a vaudeville routine. For him they invested in a BabyBjörn. They didn't say it aloud, but they were both ever so slightly concerned that he might forget Flora somewhere if she weren't firmly attached to his body.

Daniel quit his night job, transitioned to Pam's health insurance, and signed on with a temp agency in the financial district. The hours would be unpredictable, but the pay was higher than for full-time work—eighteen dollars an hour. Within a week, he had an assignment that would last a year, sitting in for an administrative assistant on maternity leave at an employee benefits consulting firm way downtown, in windy maritime Manhattan, close to Battery Park.

His new colleagues expected almost nothing from him. They seemed thrilled that he knew how to alphabetize. They came to him for help printing spreadsheets.

After work he usually took the handoff, since Pam worked later. In the morning, he headed downtown while she waited for Joe.

The familial stress level declined to near zero. Flora continued to set new benchmarks for infant cuteness. By the time she was six months old, Pam, Daniel, and Joe were in agreement that for her to get any cuter would violate natural law. Her hair had come in wavy and almost black. Her eyes were dark blue. Her face was chubby as a peach.

LIKE DANIEL, JOE TOOK HER ON LONG WALKS STRAPPED TO HIS CHEST. HE HIT ALL THE record stores at least once a week. His former coworkers at the coffee shop fawned like grandparents.

One afternoon he came home and put her on the changing table just as his beeper went off in the pocket of his coat. He left her to go to the coatrack. He was feeling around for the pager's hard surface in a tangle of candy wrappers when he heard a *thump*. She was lying on the floor on her side, making a high-pitched groaning noise.

He ran downstairs to call Pam, who had called his beeper. He said, "While I was getting the beeper, Flora fell on the floor! I think she hurt herself!"

"Where are you?"

"Downstairs."

"Go back up and get her. Hail a cab to the emergency room at New York Downtown right away. I'll meet you there. Okay?"

"Her arm looked weird."

"Push her sideways into a box so you don't have to change her position. Pad it with blankets. I'll see you at Downtown Hospital. Okay?"

She didn't call Daniel because she had a bad feeling about what he might say. He confirmed her fears that evening when he arrived home to see Flora's elbow wrapped in blue bandaging. It was sprained. Joe had thought it was broken because he didn't really do shapes. Daniel said they couldn't go on letting a retard care for their child. He stopped himself and added, "He's not retarded. Of course not. I just mean—"

"What did he do differently from anybody else?" Pam demanded to know. "Do you really think there's any babysitter in the world that wouldn't have happened to? She rolled over. There's a first time for everything. And he was flawless. He charmed his way into pediatric orthopedic surgery before I could even get down there. She was fixed before I even caught up with them. She's fine!"

"She has a monster bandage," Daniel said. "What if she'd been bleeding?"

"What do we have to do, hire a registered nurse? I know Joe couldn't splint a broken arm to save his life, and the box he put her in was way too big. But he knew something was wrong, and he got her to the hospital. That's one of the reasons to live in Manhattan. It's never far to the best medical care in the world."

"He put her in a box?"

"I told him to. I don't know. When an animal's hurt, the most important thing is to get them to the vet without moving their spine, so you slide them onto something stiff like cardboard."

"Oh, my God," Daniel said. "She could have had a spinal injury, and you told him to pick her up and put her in a box!"

"Well, he couldn't just leave her there and call an ambulance. That would take forever."

"She might have been—I can't even say it—"

"What?" Pam protested. She knew what he was getting at.

Her throat seized up. "I didn't think of that," she said. "I can't even think about it if I try." It was true. No amount of effort could make her imagine Flora with a broken neck or back. It seemed like a sin, and tempting a lifetime's bad luck, to think about it, much less say it.

"We're getting rid of that table," Daniel said. "We don't need her airborne. There are no changing tables in nature." She whimpered in her crib, and he picked her up. "Baby Flora, the floor baby. Born to be in contact with the earth."

HE RESERVED THE HOBOKEN STUDIO AGAIN, THIS TIME FOR A FULL DAY, INCLUDING grudging supervision from a grouchy engineer, and recorded two Joe Harris tracks: an original entitled "Hold the Key" and a cover of "American Woman" by the Guess Who.

"Hold the Key" was taken straight from life. "Hold the key, kill the light, lock the door, lock it twice, and go down . . ." It had originated as a mnemonic device for leaving his own apartment, but in Daniel's opinion it could become a stoner anthem. He imagined crowds at festivals singing it, swaying, holding hands.

Joe said "American Woman" was easy to play and fun to sing, and he wasn't wrong. No one, hearing that recording, could have denied that he could warble like Mariah Carey and wail like Bono. Only the oddness of his ambitions marked him as an indie eccentric rather than a mainstream poseur.

Daniel didn't waste money on a printed sleeve for the seven-inch, knowing it was the glued-on label that mattered. He used xeroxed clip art and a free vector graphics program (CorelDraw) to make the Lion's Den logo. It showed a stylized lioness holding a large flower, something like a zinnia, in its crossed forelegs, with "Lion's Den" in sixties-style art nouveau script. He put the pre-ponderance of his investment into sound quality, paying double for heavy vinyl mastered at forty-five revolutions per minute to be shipped from England. He ordered one thousand of the singles, an insanely optimistic number, but Joe had committed to playing as many shows as it took to unload them, even if it took him the rest of his life. Daniel estimated twenty years.

JOE WAS IN THE LOFT ON CHRYSTIE STREET WITH FLORA WHEN THE UPS MAN ARRIVED with the fourteen stunningly heavy boxes. Victor helped him carry them up the stairs. Joe put one on the stereo, cranked it, and danced. It was immediately clear to him what he needed to do. He fed and changed Flora, strapped her to his chest, tucked twenty-five singles into his messenger bag, and marched off to the Abyssinian Coffee Shop.

He bestowed singles on all those who currently had shifts and stacked five more by the register for the remaining employees to pick up. With one exception, a pothead prep cook whose shift was ending, the staff added their gifts to the stack, from which two customers removed six singles before a homeless hoarder absconded with the rest.

His next stop was Tower Records. He asked to speak to a manager and explained that he was Joe Harris, seeking distribution for his new single, out now on Lion's Den. He introduced Flora, turning and lifting a corner of her blanket to show the manager her sleeping face. He talked too much and too loudly. He continued talking after the manager turned away. He was allowed to leave two singles. He left the store against traffic, through the entrance, turning around to wave goodbye.

He headed westward toward NYU's radio station. Failing to get past the security guard, he was told to try the U.S. Mail. At select bars and nightclubs, he pressed the single on whoever answered the door—in one case, a custodian holding a mop.

SHORTLY AFTER HE LEFT TOWER RECORDS, A JUNIOR EMPLOYEE WHO HAD WITNESSED the proceedings asked the manager if she could please, please have the singles before he threw them away. He said of course not; he would never throw them away, much less give them to her. They were the property of Tower Records, to be listened to in due time by the staff member responsible for selecting indie records for distribution.

She knew how many supplicants he had—dozens every day. She said, "At least let me listen to it. You have to!" She clasped her hands and bounced to indicate pleading.

"Fine," he said, holding out both seven-inches. "Take them."

"I don't want to keep them," she said. "I want us to distribute it, if it's any good. I want to hear it!"

"Why?"

"Because that guy was so cute, like an angel. Did you see his eyes? They were like stars!"

"Take them," the manager said, disgusted.

She put one in her messenger bag and brought one to the frat boy working the customer service desk.

Forty-five minutes later, after his ironic Anita Baker compilation tape was done playing, the store filled with a fresh and compelling sound. Joe had recorded all the A side's instrumental tracks on bass. Open strings played the part of Neil Young and Crazy Horse bass. High fretting was Phil Lesh meets the Congos bass. Fuzzy bass, courtesy of Pam's distortion pedal, stepped in after the bridge to play a solo. All the tracks were doubled, because he liked playing them so much. The sound was low fidelity, but the tune rocked like a cradle rocking, like someone casually pitching a melody from hand to hand, and he sang in a tormented voice about something it was hard not to take for loneliness. The chorus was a three-part harmonic cadence on the repeated word "down," careful and precise as a madrigal.

Annoyed by the challenge to his preconceptions, the customer service frat boy flipped it to hear the B side. Massive riffage blasted from the store's speakers while the same voice cried out, "American woman!" The vocals were lower in the mix than on "Hold the Key" and conveyed a note of pain definitely lacking in the original. It sounded as if the American woman really had the singer cornered this time. It was less a succession of throwaway insults than a cry for help. The bass recalled live Yes or King Crimson, with the kind of distortion that peels paint off distant walls.

"I'm in love," the stock girl said. "Do you think that was his baby?"

"It definitely wasn't his single," the frat boy replied. "That guy was a retard. That's who the breeders are. Not smart people. That's why we're devolving."

DANIEL BOUGHT *FACTSHEET FIVE*, THE FANZINE THAT CATALOGED FANZINES, AND PAGED through it, noting down the names and addresses of likely sounding targets. First he sent promo singles to riot grrrly magazines such as *Bust* and *Chickfactor*. (Post-punk women had exchanged duct tape on their nipples for heels and cocktail dresses without compromising their ironic focus on objectification by the male gaze and the appropriation of epithets intended to belittle and demean them.) Likewise he mailed promos to painfully masculine publications such as *Thicker* and the *Probe*. He tried for attention from mass-market monthlies with nationwide distribution (*Spin*, *Alternative Press*) and tabloid weeklies (*Village Voice*, *City Paper*), which got five singles each, instead of one, on account of their big staffs.

He truly didn't expect any competent reviewers to approve the single by this means, but it was all he had. Music being a matter of taste, and the urge to help a struggling artist rare, he counted on wasting hundreds of dollars in postage alone in return, if he got lucky, for three or four inattentive reviews.

After about two months, he had his first responses: amiable

paragraphs in modest publications—five-by-eight xeroxed, stapled, folded fanzines with circulations in the hundreds—all of which said that the single was "gorgeous." That was the adjective du jour. In the age of grunge, anything that didn't sound like a riding lawnmower was gorgeous. Several of the reviews arrived with demo cassettes from the reviewers' bands. The one he liked best sounded like lawnmowers ridden by nymphets playing banjos, but he didn't have the money to put out another single. Every time a review arrived, he cut it out with scissors and pasted it to the letter-sized sheet of paper he called the "press kit."

JOE LACKED THE ROCK STAR'S STANDARD NEUROSES. HE FELT NO BASELESS CONVICTION that he was a genius. He had never needed illusions to feel good about himself, and his illusions had never been exposed. Unencumbered by the guilty suspicion that he was secretly a no-talent impostor, he had zero inhibitions about telling the world. Soon hundreds of people with no interest in music and less inclination to buy seven-inch singles were quite pointlessly aware that he had one out. The mail carriers knew it, as did the transvestite from Essex Street with the Yorkies, the girl who made the egg creams on First Avenue, the schizophrenic who sat on the discarded end table next to the BMT entrance on Houston, et cetera.

He liked magazines and he liked helping Daniel, so whenever he came near it, he stopped into See Hear, a large alternative newsstand in the East Village that specialized in music fanzines. He leafed through every magazine—dozens of new issues each week—checking each one under *H* and *J* to make sure they didn't miss a review of his work. So it was he who found the notice in *Forced Exposure*.

Joe Harris. "Hold the Key" b/w "American Woman" 7"
(Lion's Den). Ruins meets Badfinger in a jar of Gerber's.

Mark my words: You don't need to hear this, and
whoever mic'd the drums on it should die facedown in
a pile of dog shit with an AIDS-infected needle up
his ass.

It was the first time he had seen a review before Daniel did.
He wasn't sure what to think. It was troubling enough that he
didn't even point to it and say, "Look! *Forced Exposure* reviewed
my record!" to the cashier when he paid for it. He paid and left,
walking with studied briskness toward Chrystie Street, repeating
key phrases such as "facedown in a pile of dog shit" to himself
with his first-ever inklings of self-doubt.

Daniel didn't mind being awakened from a Saturday afternoon nap (Pam was out clothes shopping) to read it. A review in
Forced Exposure was exciting to him.

"Admittedly hard to parse," he said, "but definitely positive.
Ruins is good." Ruins was a Japanese improvising bass and percussion duo widely regarded in avant-garde circles as ultimate rock
gods. "Badfinger means British invasion without the invasion.
They're saying it's not bluesy."

"And Gerber's?" Joe protested. "That's baby food!"

"They're saying you can't play guitar."

"But I don't play guitar, or drums either!"

"They're making a funny about the drums." Daniel turned to
the front of the magazine and glanced through the features. "Oh,
look. Here's a sex scene between you and Thurston Moore."

"A what?"

Daniel was too busy laughing to answer right away. "It's a fake
Sonic Youth tour diary. He loses his virginity to you in the ladies'
room at Wetlands. Definitely do not read this. They're not trying
to pluck you from obscurity, like they do with crappy Swedish
speed metal. It's like they think you're already famous."

Joe perused the tour diary entry. "'The probing, darting fist of it-boy Joe Harris,'" he read aloud. "I'm the 'it-boy'!"

"You're the it-boy," Daniel said. "High five."

He clipped the one-paragraph review and added it to the press kit, unobtrusively, at the bottom, with his official media relations glue stick.

V.

Daniel had assumed that Joe's first gigs would be open-mic nights at anti-folk clubs on Ludlow, squaring off against stoned women in fringed vests. But given the excellent publicity, he felt emboldened to try booking him into a rock club. It could happen. Most new artists had cassette demos and no press. Joe had a seven-inch forty-five and something approaching sanctification from *Forced Exposure*.

The first step was audition night at CBGB, as much as Pam dreaded the idea of ever seeing the place again. Her first reaction was an uncharacteristically whiny "Do I have to go?" She offered to stay home with Flora. When Daniel said he would buy her sunglasses and a floppy hat, she realized that she was being needlessly vain. No one would connect a backbencher holding a baby in Joe's entourage with the pitiful diva of the Diaphragms.

Since CBGB bought a weekly ad in the *Village Voice* to list the auditioning bands, Joe's name appeared in the paper. Dozens of people in New York City were regular readers of both the *Voice* and *Forced Exposure*.

"Dozens" doesn't sound like a lot, but the farther you got from New York, the more attention was paid to media, which, after all, serve to "mediate" between the individual and lived experience. Indie rock fans who couldn't afford basic cable were more likely to have heard of Slint than Nirvana.

As a result, the show wasn't entirely empty. The girl who had made off with Joe's singles from Tower Records—ensuring that Tower would never become his distributor—was there, accompanied by the friend on whom she'd pressed her spare single. They wore vintage flower-print housecoats over turtlenecks and thick wool tights and were drinking beer. When Joe took the stage, they yelled, "Hold the key! Hold the key!" Flora lay in Pam's arms, earplugs deep in her ears, swaying with the beat. Joe played through two amps—his own new bass rig and Pam's Marshall—with a Whirlwind splitter to divide the signal. The effects loop on the bass amp ran through her MXR distortion. The guitar amp, with the reverb turned way up and the treble way down, was fed through her Foxx fuzz-wah. Joe's voice and the grinding of his valiant Hartke cabinet's indestructible aluminum speaker cones cut through the haze of feedback echoing from the tortured Marshall, and he sang all his finest nonsense as though his soul were on fire. Instead of "American Woman," he closed with "Roll with the Changes" by REO Speedwagon.

When he was done, the manager's comment to Daniel was "Bookable. Get him a band."

Meanwhile, the girl from Tower approached Pam and said, "Your baby is so cute, I can't stand it!"

"Thanks," Pam said.

"Do you know Joe Harris? It looked to us like maybe you know him."

"We're friends."

"He's so talented. Does he—does he—" Her friend elbowed her, and she rephrased her question. "Are you his wife?"

"I don't think he's ever had a girlfriend in his life," Pam said. Seeing their disappointment, she added, "He's not gay. Just shy." She smiled at the absurdity of what she'd just said. Girls were shy of Joe, shying away soon after he opened his mouth to speak. Elevation onto the stage of CBGB, with well-rehearsed lyrics to sing at high volume, must have enhanced his sex appeal.

His new number one fan took the smile as reassurance. She giggled, not even trying to hide her relief, while her friend squealed at her, "I told you that wasn't his baby!"

"I should introduce you," Pam said. "He's coming over now."

The girls drew away to regroup. Joe hugged Pam, spoke with her briefly, and turned to stare at them both. They ran out of the club.

TO DANIEL'S SURPRISE, MAXWELL'S BOOKED JOE. HE WOULD HAVE BEEN LESS SURprised if he had seen the single up on the wall at Pier Platters, priced at twelve dollars, classed as a limited-edition rarity because he still hadn't found a distributor.

Maxwell's was a club at the far end of Hoboken, a full nautical mile away from the PATH train to Manhattan, specializing in new and obscure acts. Some were obscure without being new— Daniel had seen Sun Ra there not long before his death—but most were both. The club invited Joe to open for a band that was opening for a band that was opening for a band that was opening for the Honeymoon Killers.

Joe asked Pam to sit in on guitar. Drums could stay optional if he made the bass loud enough, but someone had to fill the chinks in his crushing wall of sound, or so he said. The debate went back and forth until her final stern refusal. She wasn't feeling very rock and roll—she weighed six pounds more than before she got pregnant—but her main reason was Joe's sound. On the single it was refreshingly open and airy, more like an arbor than a wall. A million indie rock bands (or what seemed like a million to her, meaning several, all from the Pacific Northwest) featured guitars screaming high over bellowing male voices. Only Joe saved that Fender Jaguar role for himself. His vocals soared over the percussive rumbling like Grace Slick's on "White Rabbit." If it took some electronics to make it work live, so be it.

That was her view, and Daniel more or less agreed, though he would have liked to see her onstage with Joe. She was female and women were trendy. But he wasn't about to force it. As she said, guitar didn't fit with what Joe was doing. The sound of the single seemed to them an accident of fate, but it was an accident they liked. In the silence of his brain, Daniel called it "bliss-core." He didn't plan to put that in a press release, though. A new set of accidents could change it at any moment.

THE SOUND CHECK AT MAXWELL'S WENT FINE, WITH THE USUAL EXCEPTIONS FOR strangers being irritated by Joe. He was delighted and excited by everyone and everything. He forgot to plug in his bass and sang half a song a cappella, proving once and for all that he didn't think the instrumentation much mattered. When Daniel yelled, "Plug in!" he found the end of the cable, shoved it into his bass, and finished the song in a storm of arpeggios. He looked ebullient about being so much louder than before. The soundman said he was meshuga, but he didn't seem to mean it in a bad way.

The hall wasn't full for his set, but there were people in attendance. Pam and Daniel could see that many were the proper kind—indie rock fans, as indicated by their pocket tees in dark colors, unbuttoned plaid flannel shirts worn as jackets, and vintage PF Flyers or comparable footwear. Also present were two men of a dubious sort. "Major label scouts," Pam hissed. They were dressed in sport coats and talked to each other in loud voices throughout Joe's opening number. She heard one of them call his music "rad," as if "rad" were current slang.

Carrying Flora, she went to stand in front of them. Every time they moved, she moved. When they eyed the rear of the club, plainly considering sitting down on the big PA speakers stored there, she went to those same speakers to change Flora's diaper. Seeing the diaper from the inside, the scouts decamped to the bar.

A less streetwise musician might not have chased major label scouts away from Joe. But indie rock had arisen from desperate necessity, to offer artists an alternative to exploitation. The recording industry had once paid musicians flat fees. The contemporary way to stiff them while cultivating an appearance of generosity was to charge publicity against their royalties. Every video, tour bus, and hotel room came straight out of the artist's pocket. Long before peer-to-peer file sharing and online streaming, a star could have big hits and be broke.

As Joe was starting his last song, Pam saw the cute girl from CBGB. She was alone, rushed and hectic, still wearing her coat. She had arrived when his set was nearly done. Pam could see the disappointment in her face. She strolled over. The girl noticed her with relief. She mimed looking at her watch and turned up her hands helplessly. She knew she was late. When the song was over, and she was done clapping and whooping and yelling "Encore!" and "Hold the key!" she turned to Pam and said, "I had to find someone to cover the shift after mine. That's why I'm late."

"What's your name?"

"Eloise."

"No way."

The girl closed her eyes in deep embarrassment and clenched her fists, and Pam realized belatedly that she was shy. Eloise fled toward the stage, where Joe was launching into his encore, "Splash 1" by the 13th Floor Elevators. He saw her and stared at her. He sang the entire song looking into her eyes.

The rock repertoire includes several songs an informed person might call romantic, such as "God Only Knows" by the Beach Boys, but few can compete with "Splash," the work of a mystic at the height of his powers. Soon after its composition, those powers defeated Roky Erickson, and he turned his genius to the service of the devil and the Martian voice in his head, but in "Splash" he was as yet untainted.

It was too much for Eloise. When Joe had finished emoting, she had to be alone. She ceased from clapping and hid in the bathroom to fix her face. The ladies' room at Maxwell's was a single. Because the mirror occupied the same space as the toilet bowl, a person could miss an entire set waiting in line. There she stood at the mirror and found herself wanting. She looked in vain for the neon splashing from her eyes.

Pam gave up looking for her and joined the queue. When Eloise finally came out, wincing at the sight of her, Pam hesitated briefly. She wanted to introduce her to Joe. She thought it might be of significant positive import for Joe's future. But she had to pee, so she stayed in line. By the time she emerged, Eloise was gone.

IN THE TAXI GOING HOME, SHE SAID TO JOE, "THAT CUTE GIRL INTRODUCED HERSELF TO me. Her name is Eloise. I think she likes you."

"I'm the original bitch magnet," Joe said.

"What cute girl?" Daniel asked.

"The Joe Harris fan club. She came in for the last two songs and stared at him in a trance, like she's from that tract *Hippies, Hindus and Rock & Roll*. Short brown hair, flowered dress?"

"Earth to Pam," Daniel said. "'Cute' means sexy, not frumpy."

"Frumpy and dumpy," Joe said. "When a guy says 'cute,' he means a model. Like you."

"I am not a model!"

"You're skinny and you have clothes like a model."

"Joe, I swear to you, man, she's Trixie and you're Speed Racer. She's your one true love."

"I wouldn't fuck her for practice!"

"Who taught you to talk like that?"

"He's quoting me," Daniel said. "I was being ironic."

"What the fuck, Daniel! Why pick on Eloise?"

"She's the scenester babe I always thought I would end up with. She's my bête noire, man."

"I want to be your bête noire man," Joe sang, to the tune of "Whole Lotta Love."

THE FAMILY WENT TO RACINE FOR CHRISTMAS. PAM GAINED WEIGHT AND UNDERSTOOD why Daniel was so tall. They stayed at a motel because there wasn't room in the house for five families of giants, but they ate with his parents. Every meal was like the miracle of the loaves and the fishes. Pie pans were in constant rotation. Meat from the deep freeze in the basement was thawing continuously on every countertop.

At first there was no conflict or even especial curiosity about her. No one had time to listen to anything she said. They sized her up and decided that she required a succession of big, bland meals. They lauded the chubbiness of Flora. Daniel talked with his relatives about people and places she had never heard of. It was hard to keep track, even after he explained. Only one topic addressed her directly. At the midday meal on Christmas Eve, Daniel's much older sister Debra advanced the theory that Princess Stéphanie of Monaco had a haircut similar to hers.

That evening, she begged to be excused from going to church.

"Are you sick?" Daniel's mother asked.

Stupidly, she didn't say yes. She said instead that she wasn't a Christian, and technically neither was Flora, because she hadn't been christened, so if nobody minded they would just go on back to the motel and rest up.

A doctrinal dispute erupted that shocked even Daniel. He had managed to put out of his mind how seriously his family took religion. They thought Pam's notion of infant baptism was sacrilege and that her ungrateful soul was bound for hell. Soon nine adults were tag-teaming her to yell about Jesus, drunk on Baileys and a blueberry dessert wine they pretended was festive rather than alcoholic. Flora was crying and they didn't care, because all the children were crying.

No non-Christian person had ever been invited to their home before. Even Daniel had originally appeared uninvited, so to speak. Nobody ever asked him what he believed, and he usually knew better than to talk about it. On this occasion, the role model provided by Pam herself—a person whose openness with her parents had produced a rupture she clearly felt was preferable to living a lie, or at least preferable to going to church—prompted him to come to her defense with solidarity. He said, "I don't believe in God or Jesus either, but it doesn't matter!"

FOR PRESENTS, HE HAD BOUGHT EVERYONE IN HIS FAMILY SOME INDIVIDUALIZED ITEM of exotic Asian strangeness from Chinatown, a figurine or odd snack. He and Pam were due to receive many socks and fruit-cakes, and Flora was getting hand-knit baby booties.

On Christmas morning, he took the Asian presents to his parents' front porch and tried to negotiate. It became clear that alone, without Pam and Flora—without evidence that he had his disobedient wife well in hand—he would not be welcomed, and that they would credit no personal profession of his faith. He would have to attend church with them and set an example by coming forward to be saved.

His heart sank because he knew he would never do it. Seeing that he was expected to be a patriarch, to rule over Pam, alienated him as nothing ever had before.

Flora didn't care about missing Christmas. She wasn't even two yet, nor entirely clear on which of those strangers had been Grandma and Grandpa.

Their return flight was postponed by thirty hours due to typical Wisconsin winter weather. The likelihood that they would return for a second holiday season in Racine diminished to a vanishing smallness.

JOE'S NEXT SHOW WAS BY INVITATION OF SIMON, WHO HAD STUMBLED INTO ENVIABLE gigs reviewing classic rock LPs for the new website Amazon and heavy metal for the magazine *Thrasher*. Dumb luck and connections had lent him the aura of success, and some indie rock band was trying to siphon it off by getting him to book opening acts for their CD release party at a storefront on Stanton Street called House of Candles.

The band members had their own label, the way Joe had Lion's Den, so they had no label-mates to pack the bill with. They were from Albany, so they had no fan base in tow except their girlfriends. They were paying rent for the venue, so they wanted bands with social circles, but not party bands that would steal the show.

Being something of an asshole, Simon invited bands that would help cement his professional position as a critic. He added Joe as an afterthought, to make sure Pam knew he could have booked Marmalade Sky and didn't. He told the indie rock band that Joe was an outsider singer-songwriter with a loyal following, which was true.

She stayed home with Flora. Joe was promised no share of the door but granted permission to sell merchandise. Simon encouraged him to skip the sound check, because he couldn't have cared less how he sounded. Thus Joe and Daniel didn't head over until eight o'clock, as the first band was starting. Daniel carried twenty-eight singles in a box labeled "$3."

Daniel set it down on a table in the back and looked around for Eloise. But she never showed that night, because there had been no publicity for anyone but the headliners. He stayed near the merchandise to make sure no one stole it.

Joe sat in the front row, bass on his lap, playing along quietly with the opening act, billed as Broad Spectrum. It consisted of a woman singer, a scared-looking boy playing tenor recorder, a sequencer that wasn't working right, and a keyboard player holding a tambourine. The keyboardist was responsible for the sequencer. She kept jabbing at it, shaking the tambourine at random, and alternating between two chords on the keyboard with her left hand. You could hear that she was right-handed. The woodwind looked frustrated, trying for low notes and getting overtones. The singer's dance moves kept taking her away from the microphone. Her voice could be heard when she stood still for the chorus, but it remained incomprehensible, because she cupped the mic with both hands, looking very earnest and sexy while it was practically inside her mouth and kept feeding back. The group performed as though they not only hadn't rehearsed, but had won the gig in a raffle, earlier in the day, before they founded the band.

After their first number subsided, the singer nudged the keyboardist aside and fiddled with the sequencer. The setup began to play "Sussudio" by Phil Collins. She returned to the mic, glared at Joe for singing along, and said, "It's a borrowed keyboard. Give us a minute." Three minutes later, the band continued its set with four-finger organ, tambourine duties devolving on the singer. The woodwind took a rest. The singer's yawping teetered on the edge of feedback until Simon, the soundman, rendered the mic inaudible. The whole thing was pathetic, and when it was done, everybody clapped for a long time.

Daniel thought, The name kind of fits, assuming they meant "broad" as in "woman" and the autism "spectrum." Also, in his opinion, their conceptual project didn't stand a chance against the art of music. Joe had craft, not a concept. He could hear himself play—he could really listen—and when he wasn't sounding good, he took steps to fix it.

He played three numbers, rocking out to his own conception of beauty, alone and weird. The applause was cursory, because there was no one in the audience but members and friends of Broad Spectrum. He sat back down in his seat in the front. An older but not repulsive man in standard-issue indie rock garb (Black Watch plaid shirt, Cubs cap) sat down next to him, introduced himself as Eric, handed over a business card, and said, "Call me if you're interested." Joe scampered to the rear, breathlessly waving the card, to tell Daniel he'd been scouted by Matador.

Matador was an important indie record label, Joe's favorite in all of New York next to 4AD. It turned out that Broad Spectrum was made up of people who had office jobs there.

Daniel had come to feel gloomy about distributing the single. If Joe got a contract with Matador, his work was done. The remaining singles would sell themselves. He said, "That's awesome!"

He knew that Matador was doing some kind of dance with Atlantic—an unequal partnership or a not quite acquisition—the idea being that collaboration would offer artists all the advantages of a major label with none of the degradation. What the reality was, he didn't know, but the company itself was respectable: it possessed bourgeois realness; it had offices in Manhattan and fine and noble founders, and it distributed its wares to the farthest corners of the earth. As for signing with Matador, there was little Joe could have possibly done that was more likely to get him fair treatment and decent money.

Daniel sold two singles that evening and gave away five to people who said they were reviewers for magazines whose existence he doubted, strengthening his resolve to nudge Joe from the indie rock gift economy into the big time. He offered to call Eric for him the next day.

WITHIN A WEEK JOE AND SOME GUY NAMED RANDY HAD SIGNED A MEMORANDUM OF understanding drawn up in ballpoint pen on a steno pad at a beer bar on Sixth Avenue. Joe signed it in the presence of Daniel—not in an official capacity; his role as Joe's label executive and manager was a combination hobby and joke—who saw nothing to criticize. Somebody somewhere had skipped Joe right over Matador and signed him to Atlantic, with an advance of $80,000 for a single LP. He might take home only $10,000 after taxes, recording, and publicity, yet spending even $10,000 was likely to be fun for him. On some level it was money for nothing, since he would be making music anyway. With a major label contract, he could make it in a fancy studio with professional engineers.

When the finalized contract arrived in the mail—eighteen pages of legalese—Daniel belatedly suggested getting a lawyer. Joe said no, because he trusted Eric and Randy. Daniel suggested involving Professor Harris. Again, Joe said no.

He wasn't anybody's ward. He was impulsive and vulnerable. His own weaknesses told him, directly, that he didn't need protection.

It wasn't paradoxical. It was tautological, like all the most daunting and bewildering things in life. Things are the way they are: unthinkable. Trying to understand can feel like a struggle, but the conflict is internal to each of us, ending in surrender each night when we close our eyes.

Looking through the countersigned contract months later and seeing points he maybe should have argued over, Daniel couldn't say for sure whether Joe had gotten a raw deal. Maybe other fledgling artists were being treated better; he didn't know. In absolute terms, it was a gift. Joe had gone straight from babysitter to rock star, while there was nothing in the contract that would oblige him to give up babysitting.

RANDY WANTED TO MAKE AN ANTI-FOLK RECORD WITH ROCK DRUMMING À LA BECK OR major-label Butthole Surfers. He claimed that Joe's vision of bubblegum dub was an audience-free joint that wouldn't even fly in Brazil. That's how he phrased it, thinking Joe would get bewildered and surrender. Joe did not. It seldom impressed him that things are the way they are.

"The bass on *Doggystyle* makes my vision go blurry!" he insisted to an elevator full of random label employees after his third chaotic five-minute meeting with Randy. "That's what I want! Deep music for deaf people!" He told Daniel, who was waiting for him in the lobby with Flora to go to lunch, that Atlantic was going to turn his lovely demos into crashy-bangy alternative rock.

"It worked for Suzanne Vega," Daniel pointed out. "They add kick drum and hi-hat to some folkie vocal thing, and there you are. That's how CBS made a number one hit out of 'Sound of Silence.'"

"That's the main substance of my lament!" Joe said. "With too many drums, you can't hear the music. I don't need drums. I have my rhythm in the music where it belongs!"

"That's good. Try that on Randy. Say what you just said to me."

"You do it! He doesn't listen to me."

DANIEL, IN HIS FUNCTION AS PRETEND MANAGER, CALLED RANDY THE NEXT DAY. IT wasn't a productive conversation. Joe had presented an irresolvable impasse as mere friction. Randy informed him that Joe was all set to make a record that the label would never release. Subsequently he would be free to go on making records for them at his own expense forever, until he happened to make one they liked.

Daniel replied, "That's a no-good deal, and you're a piece of shit."

"Am I now," Randy said.

"If you pile roadblocks on the creativity of Joe Harris, that's exactly what you are. An ignorant, self-defeating piece of shit."

"I didn't say he can't record any album he wants," Randy pointed out. "I just said we won't release it."

"Fuck you, ass-wipe," Daniel said, marveling at his own inarticulacy.

Randy referred him to a senior executive producer, a blond surfer-snowboarder of fifty who called himself Daktari.

DANIEL WENT WITH JOE AND FLORA THE FOLLOWING WEEK TO SEE DAKTARI, WHO TOLD them he'd be adding a rhythm track whether they liked it or not, and that from what he'd heard people saying around the office, *Music for Deaf People* would be an excellent working title.

Daktari was handsome and regularly spent time in France. Many years before, someone in Paris had told him it was a mark of breeding to insult people to their faces without breaking eye contact.

His skills were wasted on Joe, who replied in gratitude that he had resolved to call his opening track "Daktari." He started writing it right there. Tapping his foot, he sang, "Daktaree-ee-ee, is Randy's boss so maybe he can te-ell me, if we need drums on this so give the bass to me, I'll show you drums are not the sole reason to be."

"A percussion jam is a big crowd-pleaser," Daktari interrupted. "Don't you want to be bigger than Jesus?"

Switching back to normal conversation, Joe said, "Lots of Aretha Franklin songs don't have drums!"

"Afraid of the neighbors? We can find you rehearsal space."

"It's not the noise," Daniel interposed. "He has this inability."

"You mean disability?" Daktari looked closely at Joe's body. A flicker of horror crossed his beauteous mien at the idea that the label might have signed a disabled person.

"Inability," Daniel said. "He can't really listen to loud noises that sound like explosions all the time."

"Because of what, war trauma?"

"He's unable. It's like when you say you're unable to come to the phone or unable to forgive somebody. On the one hand, it's an admission of weakness, because you're saying you're at the mercy of forces beyond your control, but to other people it sounds arrogant, since those forces might be *you*." Flora was pushing a six-inch beanbag hippopotamus up his pants leg, and he leaned down to pet her head, the way he always did when speaking an eternal truth he hoped would accompany her on her way.

"In other words, it resembles my inability to put out a hit record with no percussion," Daktari countered.

"I didn't say 'no percussion,'" Joe said. "I love congas and bongos. Can we get a studio with congas and bongos?"

"Our studios have pro arrangers and session musicians and every goddamned instrument in the book," Daktari said. "Bring me hit tunes, and I'll record them any way you want."

RIDING HOME ON THE BUS, DANIEL LOUDLY MOURNED THEIR FAILURE TO SIGN WITH AN independent label. He was tortured by the illogic of their discussion with Daktari, who had bested him in negotiations without negotiating or even paying him any attention. Instead of gaining the label's assent to songs without drums, he had committed Joe to earning congas and bongos with all-new material.

They stood for a long time talking about it at the playground. Daniel set Flora down on the ground. Indoors she was a floor baby, but outdoors she was a baby rooting for acorns in mud. Sandboxes were rare in New York, considered dangerous because of pet feces. There was never an evening when she didn't need a bath.

"I screwed up," Daniel said, turning over a succession of fallen leaves with his foot. He saw a shard of broken glass and picked it up so he could throw it in the trash. "We should have signed with Matador."

"That guy likes hit songs," Joe said. "So I'll write hit songs. He's going to love my new songs. Everything's completely fine, so stop worrying."

"My feeling was that he hated us. I mean all of us, even Flora."
He looked down. She had placed a cigarette filter in a bottle cap
so that her hippo could eat it off a dish. When the hippo failed
to react, she mimed eating the filter herself. "That's a no-no!" he
said. "Don't eat litter!" She put it back. With her help, the hippo
extended its prolapsed pink mouth like an amoeba over the bottle
cap and its contents. "Hippos hate cigarette butts," he said, picking it up so he could throw it away. "Even though they're rich in
minerals and fiber. They prefer grass. Why don't you offer him
some grass from your open hand?"

"Where's any grass?" she said. "I don't see grass."

"I see dandelions," Joe said. "That's hippos' favorite food. They
call it hippo-pot."

"I see hippo-pot!" she said. She stood and approached a solitary
dandelion that was standing by a fence. With the hippo clamped
under one arm, she did her best to rip it out of the ground.

"That was pedagogically questionable," Daniel commented.

"You're so nugatory all the time!"

"I hope you mean 'negative all the time.'"

"Even about Daktari. He hates indie rock music because he
works for a major label. It makes total sense."

"So why the fuck did he sign an indie rock artist like you?"

"Because he's a prescient guy. He can tell I'm going to bring
him big hits!"

VI.

Joe's first girlfriend was the former singer of the defunct band
Broad Spectrum, a slim, dark-haired classical archaeology
major named Bethany. She was interning at Matador that
summer because it was too hot in Asia Minor to go on digs. She
wore hundred-dollar Laura Ashley dresses with Doc Martens,
the look Eloise's housecoats and Hush Puppies were supposed to
suggest. Her features were delicate. Her teeth looked like Chic-
lets. She shared a two-bedroom summer sublet in the West Village with an absentee figure-skating instructor. She styled herself a
"geek girl" because she wore glasses. In her spare time, she followed
New Dance. She had read somewhere that attending dance per-
formances can qualify a person to be a dance critic. Her father, a
banking executive, occasionally met her for lunch at Delmonico's,
where he assured her that dance was another arrow in her quiver.

She volunteered to sing harmonies on Joe's record. It surprised
her when he said no. She thought his trusting ways would make
him a pushover. Instead they made him assume she wouldn't mind
rejection. She didn't let on how mad she was, because she didn't

want to lose him. She believed that his surreal sense of humor made him a hard person to know.

Her relationship specialty was evenings out. She liked plays and recitals. He didn't care who paid. She led him to art museums and to restaurants with arty food. For several weeks that fall, they were regulars at American Ballet Theatre. She tapped his new American Express card for culture and comfort. In her own mind, she was educating him, so it seemed to her like a fair exchange.

Joe worked diligently on his songwriting, as usual. He mastered his demos on sixty-minute cassettes. Every time a tape filled up, he delivered it to Daktari's secretary. There was general consensus around the office that he was going to end up owing the label a lot of money. No one there believed in him but Bethany, who did it on principle because they were dating.

PAM HATED HER WITH GREAT BITTERNESS. SHE SAW HER AS A MOOCH AND A LEECH WHO was using Joe as an auxiliary dad, one of those upper-class women who aspire to be children all their lives. As an excuse for poor eyesight, the "geek girl" tagline bugged her big time. But what bothered her most was how Bethany's girlfriendly blandishments stained Joe's pure soul with egotism. All his innocent self-regard and faith in his innate value metamorphosed into campy self-adoration in the light of her approval. She heightened his pleasure in life when he was already living a joyful dream. She reinforced playful impulses that didn't need any encouragement. His behavior in her presence careened right past joie de vivre into something resembling hysteria. He called her "the orgasm factory" to her face, and she followed him around like a duckling. She constantly displayed to onlookers that she was with Joe—of all people—and this, Pam simply did not understand. How could some hot-looking, jet-setting, dance-theater-watching rich bitch be possessive about Joe? Had she reencountered him after the House of Candles show feeding hot dogs to squirrels, instead of walking the halls of Atlantic with a contract in his hand, would she have gone near him? (Hot dogs that spent too many hours in the slimy waters of the Abyssinian Coffee Shop burst and became unsalable, and then they were Joe's.) Any child of six could have told you she was a deluded social climber who'd boarded the wrong train. Why couldn't he see through it?

Stupid question, she knew. He trusted everyone, even bitches. His former life hadn't been long on the bitches. For a poignant half second, she wished she had kissed him, or even gone to bed with him, so that no star-fucker bitch could have been his first.

WHEN FLORA WAS THREE, DANIEL TOOK HER TO THE TRIENNIAL SVOBODA FAMILY reunion. She came back raving about tricycles and wagons, wearing a tiny gold-plated cross on a chain around her neck. He was no longer an accredited family member, but the Svobodas seemed to feel there was hope for her. He let her wear the cross until they got home. Then he said it was too valuable to wear every day, took it off her, and threw it in the trash. A week later, she asked for the cross again. When she couldn't have it, she cried.

A week after that, her hippo ate dog shit and had to be put out of its misery. She saw a crucifix in the window of a Santeria store and asked Joe to buy it. It was as though she couldn't get Jesus out of her mind and wanted him for her new stuffed animal.

Fortunately it was a cash-only store. The crucifix had been blessed by a voodoo priest and was very expensive. Joe couldn't help her out on the spot, but he told Daniel about her wish.

"If she needs a shirtless guy with a beard, we can get her a G.I. Joe," he replied.

"We'll make our own cross, and she can put him on it with rubber bands."

"If it's a cross she wants, we can—no. There's no way I'm

making her a toy cross! What's next? A toy cat-o'-nine-tails, so she can self-flagellate?"

"Jesus is weird," Joe remarked.

"You can say that again!"

"Why is he on the cross?"

Daniel raised his eyes to heaven. "Oh, man, Joe. Well, historically, he wasn't always on the cross. I think for something like twelve centuries, he was the risen Christ, fully dressed. Then there was Gothic art and, like, the black plague or something, so they switched to showing him on the cross. You know he died on the cross, right?"

"Why?"

"The weight of his own body, I guess. Makes it hard to breathe when you're hanging by your arms."

"But he's so skinny!"

"Not in real life! He was always eating out with rich tax collectors, and he could make food appear by magic and turn water into wine, so he was a total land whale. That's why he died so fast, like hours before the skinny dudes they crucified at the same time. The Romans didn't even have to break his legs."

"That is so gross," Joe said.

"And he's scared shitless up there, screaming out, 'My God, my God, why have you forsaken me?' But you know who God was, who could have helped him the whole time? His dad!"

"My dad would not do that."

"My dad would."

THE REVERBERATING CHRISTIANITY DEBACLE AGGRAVATED PAM'S SENSE THAT HER daughter was growing up without her. Every moment she spent at the office was a moment when some stranger and/or family member of ill will and worse intentions could plant a fateful wrong idea in Flora's head.

Joe tried to console her by recording selected playtime. It didn't help. The cassettes merely made audible how he kept Flora in stitches. He was giving her a solid grounding in verbal wit, pre-school style. Her parents' role was to drop by nightly and impose dour worries about nutrition and rest.

After the fourth and final taping session, Pam's path forward became clear. One dialogue passage was as follows:

JOE: Never rub your nub where people can see.
FLORA: But I want to!
JOE: [singing] Got to rub my nub in the club, rub my nub in the club, got to rub my nub in the club—now dub—see my nub nub nub nub nub nub nub nub in the club club club club club club club, it's like a sub sub sub sub sub sub sub—
FLORA: Don't make fun of me!
JOE: Then stop rubbing your nub and do the dance! [singing] Rub my nub in the club, chugalug in the pub, rub-a-dub in the tub . . . [etc.]
FLORA: [clapping along] Rub my nub I rub my nub I rub my nub I rub my nub I rub my nub [etc.]

Flora's improvisation of a contrapuntal rhythmic chant made her seem extraordinarily musically accomplished for her age. At the same time, Pam experienced a heretofore unsuspected and overpowering need to raise her child herself. Flora was getting old for a babysitter. She wasn't a baby anymore. Her psyche needed to be molded in Pam's image, or Daniel's at least. Otherwise, what was the point?

"I need to cut down on my hours," Pam said to Yuval the next morning as they stood drinking coffee in the office kitchenette. "My kid doesn't even know my name. She calls me 'Mom.'"

"So you want to spend time with Flora."

"Yes. The problem is maternity leave is unpaid, and it's a little late."

He sneered, wrinkling his nose. "Who told you that? Your union rep?"

"Very funny!"

"You're the funny one here, talking about part-time work when I bill for you by the day. Clients are always telling me how many hours you work most days, or should I say minutes?"

"Express yourself clearly, Yuval."

"That maybe it's almost better if you limit time offsite? Like, dress up like you're in marketing, run intense interviews about client needs, drip your famous honey sweetness on them, estimate billable days with some generosity to me, and deliver on time? Stay home. Work as you need. Flextime."

"I'd do that."

"But only two years. Maternity leave. In two years is performance review. I'll be counting your billable days."

She called Daniel at his temp job with the good news. He said, "Your boss has a Messiah complex."

DANIEL THOUGHT THE SONG WAS GREAT AND LACKED ONLY ONE LINE TO BE PERFECT: "IF my right hand should offend you, cut it off."

With Pam at the controls of a four-track and the vocal stylings of Flora and Daniel, Joe recorded a bass-and-foot-tapping demo of "Rub My Nub." The interplay between the four/four repetitions of "rub my nub I" and the syncopation of "cut it off, cut it off" was strikingly infectious. When Daktari heard it over the phone the next day, he said, *"Ç'est ça, mon ami!"*

Joe's reasonable response was "Sad monogamy?"

He was summoned to a studio in Chelsea to rerecord vocals and two bass parts. It took two days. Without consulting him, Daktari then laid the recording over a big-beat synth percussion track. He hired a contrabassist to shadow the bass and singers to imitate Flora, ran the results through a compressor with multiple bowls of reverb (reverb was measured in units of the kind bud), and cranked up the presence until the song could work as a ringtone on a Nokia.

The album *Sad Monogamy* (that was the working title; in the end it was released as *Coronation*) came together quickly, because Joe wrote a song almost every day. Daktari didn't care too much about the other tracks. He didn't even ask for changes in "Rub My Nub," except for the title, which became "Chugalug."

THE STILLS AND RUSHES FROM THE FIRST DAY OF FILMING THE "CHUGALUG" VIDEO astounded Daniel. Watching the shoot on monitors was even more disturbing.

He was a show business novice. His experience of comparing images with reality had been acquired firsthand. For example, he saw himself as an okay-looking guy who was not photogenic. In pictures he looked like a small-eyed, hairy potato. Smiling widened his strong jaw into something photographs invariably depicted as a moon face, right on the edge of pug. By contrast, he thought of Joe as not an okay-looking guy. He wondered how major-label-style publicity was supposed to work with a star like that. He imagined they would pose him far away, with contour makeup under dramatic lighting, or maybe on a beach, facing out to sea. Joe was short, five feet seven and a half at the outside with shoes on. He had a cute enough butt and square little shoulders, and if you issued him a smallish guitar—well, Dylan and Springsteen were little guys, right? Those were Daniel's not uncharitable thoughts on the subject of Joe's image. He was trying to be realistic.

On screen, Joe became a rock god. His Muppet mouth became a twenty-tooth smile. His small head became enormous eyes; his girlish chin, an asset at last. His mousy bowl cut required only one sweep of the oiled brush to darken to a mass of chestnut waves under the lights. His short stature and neck made him fit neatly in the frame. His size made cheap props, such as the foam-and-cardboard wingback chairs the director had bought from IKEA (to be returned for credit the next day), look vast and luxurious. The effect of the camera on his skin was strangest of it all. Joe in real life had a yellowish cast. He was anemic-looking, sallow, not olive; not a beautiful look. On screen he looked vibrant, yet blotless—smooth as the piece of paper the cameraman held up to get a white balance score. Reduced to two dimensions, with a script to follow, he became someone else who was also himself. The transformation wasn't instantaneous, because the two Joes were incommensurate and incompatible. It was like some strange proof of the existence of a parallel universe looming behind our own. Daniel could look up at the soundstage and see the frowns on the dancers straining to evoke eroticism in the presence of the goofiest man alive (they'd met him; he'd introduced himself and talked to them all before the shoot), lower his gaze to the monitors where similar women were writhing in a miasma of lust they felt for a handsome singer who was coolly delivering obscenities, look up again to see Joe gesticulating while the resentful troupers sweated their workout, look back down, look up again, see stars, see human beings, until his brain abandoned the effort of trying to reconcile them. The video was like a centrifuge, separating the world into a visual component that drained into the monitors propped on the floor and a bodily component that became more unsightly with every turn of the machinery.

The women did the dance, not Joe. The director said it was great to be able to surround a singer with built fly girls who could move instead of models. He told Daniel to be happy, because Joe was going to get film offers.

THE VIDEO WENT INTO ROTATION ON MTV AND VH1. STRANGERS NOW RECOGNIZED JOE in record stores, if the staff clued them in. They called him "Joe

Harris" rather than "mongo collector scum." He had been more notorious than popular.

Maybe he would have stayed notorious, never becoming popular, if he'd been easier to recognize. But his social skills and conversational arts couldn't discredit him in the eyes of the world. The disconnect between image and reality was total. Occasionally he was taken for someone who resembled Joe Harris, but only when something startled him into silence.

There was one recurring situation where he would be recognized and draw a crowd: if the song was played in his hearing. He would sing along and do the dance, no matter where he was—at home listening to the radio, walking past a bar where it was on the jukebox, shopping in a grocery store where an easy-listening version was streaming over the paging system. It made him oh-so-happy to hear it.

His mainstream career took off with an appearance on a morning talk show. Atlantic's publicist had negotiated a one-minute promotional segment. Prior radio interviews had established that a minute could be a long time. Thus there was debate as to how to handle him, until a production intern's boyfriend provided a timely eyewitness account of a performance in the dairy section of C-Town. The host of the show shook hands, said hi, and let the track roll. Seemingly a man of few words, Joe sang and did the dance. The camera zoomed to his face as the vision mixer cut to the shocked reactions of the host and other guests.

After that, many talk shows invited him on, but not to talk. The song gave rise to a vulgar and widely satirized dance craze. No wedding was complete without it. It was the go-to anthem of drunken groomsmen. The album sold and sold and sold, and the single reached number four on the *Billboard* Hot 100. Joe in his lewdness was compared with Elvis Presley.

As with Elvis, it was a lewdness only the unmediated had seen. The buzz around his first concert tour was accordingly significant.

Daniel began to wish he'd asked for a songwriting credit for his coda.

CURRENTLY BETWEEN JOBS, ELOISE STROLLED THE LOWER EAST SIDE IN SEARCH OF JOE. She looked out for Pam, Daniel, and Flora as well. But all of them were busier than they'd ever been. She didn't know where they lived. Joe was walking and shopping less, swamped with work and free promo CDs. He never again played a small club, having gotten signed before he could even occupy a feature slot at CBGB. The label was rationing his presence in preparation for a big-budget tour.

She watched cable in case his video came on. She bought magazines like *People* and *Vogue* so she could read short Q&As and capsule reviews. The scourge of commerce had driven the wedge of fame between them. She thought it was only natural, because he was a rock star and she was a speck.

VII.

Pam went to a party at Daktari's apartment with Joe and Bethany, while Daniel stayed home with Flora. The party was full of industry bigwigs, TV journalists, and stars. Daktari introduced Joe as the next big thing. Joe flitted from new acquaintance to new acquaintance, lingering over the females like Pepé Le Pew. It was painful for Pam to watch. He was no longer profiting from the most basic social corrective—the boycott, when women walk away. By the end of the night, he was single. She wished it could have been because he saw some flaw in Bethany. But he couldn't see flaws in women who were much, much worse.

Around two in the morning, he kissed Bethany goodbye and told Pam to say hi to Daniel and Flora so he could go on fondling a creature in a white puffy coat with the hood up. She looked to Pam like a sofa standing upright, upholstered in shiny nylon over down batting. Why did she need a warm coat indoors? Was she a junkie? Pam's thoughts were dire. She developed a sudden new appreciation of Bethany. Anything was better than this. Sofa Girl had a pinched face and horrible orange lipstick. Under the coat, she was tiny. Maybe she didn't have enough body fat to maintain 98.6 without a coat? Even as Joe was feeling her up, she was screeching and waving a cigarette around. She reminded Pam of Edie Sedgwick, the famous vapid cocotte from Warhol's Factory.

Pam fled the party downhearted, but not alone. At the corner of Thompson and Spring, Bethany touched her arm and said, "Hey, Pam. Let's share a cab."

"I'm walking," she said. "I need air." She crossed the street, but Bethany followed her.

"Did you see that girl?" Bethany asked.

"The anorexic dressed as a grub?"

"She's this bogus model who's been fired from, like, everywhere. She's on every drug in the book. She's horrible, awful, like, God! Why her?"

"Shut up, shut up. Just shut up," Pam muttered, as though to herself. She had a bad feeling. Bethany was more keyed up than she'd ever seen her.

"She's going to fuck him right at the party," Bethany went on. "How does Daktari even *know* her? She's not a music person. She's fashion!"

"You're an archaeologist," Pam pointed out.

"But I'm into music and dance. And she—you know what she's known for?"

"Bestiality shows in Tijuana?" Pam increased her pace, trying to walk too fast for Bethany to keep up.

Bethany didn't break into a run, but her heels pounded the sidewalk with a hastening, hollow pinging sound. From twenty feet behind Pam she called out, "Fucking backstage at fashion week!"

Pam turned to face her and said, "If you think it's all her fault, why don't you get back up in there and defend him?"

"*Defend* him? He's the one making out with a tramp. I have to *leave* him."

"Well, defend *her*!"

Bethany's irate sadness gave way to incomprehension.

"He's an aggressor," Pam said. "You are duty bound as a feminist to go back in there and stop her ass from getting nailed by a stud she can't handle."

She snorted and scoffed. "Stud."

"I'm going back," Pam said.

She stalked past Bethany, angling across Thompson toward Daktari's door. There she tried the doorbell.

She tried it several times over the space of four or five minutes. She finally slipped inside when a pizza deliveryman slipped out. Up in the apartment, Joe was nowhere to be found. Nowhere—everybody told her so—absolutely nowhere—meaning in this case a walk-in closet in the master suite, where he was clutching at a strange woman's hair with his pants down. He was yelping, but Pam couldn't hear him because of all the noise. She assumed they must have left while Bethany was distracting her with their altercation.

She emerged alone to the street. The jilted sponge was gone, but she could see five other women on the same block, on her side of the street alone, who were guaranteed to be better life-partner prospects for Joe than Sofa Girl. She walked home in a snit of foreboding, her thoughts mother-dark.

DANIEL WENT TO JOE'S PLACE TO PICK HIM UP THE NEXT AFTERNOON FOR A LUNCH DATE, and Sofa Girl was there. She answered the door in her sofa coat and an iridescent yellow bra. She was obviously drunk. Joe was in the shower, singing "Good Morning Starshine."

Daniel yelled, "Hey, Joe! I can come back!"

"You want a beer?" Sofa Girl asked. "Wait, we're fresh out. You want to get us some beer?"

"I'll come back later."

Joe yelled, "Stay! I need food!"

"And I need beer!" Sofa Girl yelled.

"We can go somewhere that has beer," Daniel said. "It's not hard."

Joe came out of the bathroom naked, holding his wallet over his genitals. Daniel wondered why he had taken his wallet with him into the bathroom, but only until he remembered Sofa Girl. It was hard, but not impossible, to piece together a chain of events that would make even Joe protective of his wallet—say, if a person were to take every single bill out of it, in his presence, to spend on something he didn't want.

Joe said, "Hey, Daniel. Could you possibly run downstairs and grab us some beer?"

"You don't need beer," Daniel said. "You need food."

"Right," Joe said.

"Beer and food!" Sofa Girl called out, waving her cigarette.

"This is Gwendolyn Charanoglu," Joe said. "Gwen, meet my manager, Daniel Svoboda." He put his wallet on the kitchen counter and returned to the bathroom.

"Oh, my God, I am so honored to meet you!" she squealed. "I've heard so much about you! He talks about you all the time!" She offered him her hand to shake.

The hand was sticky. The smell from under her coat was fetid. Daniel had a troubling vision of Joe's providing a lyrical description of him while Gwen sucked him off. He dismissed it and said, "You can go ahead and get dressed, so we can go out. It's warm outside. He'll be fast."

She looked down and said, "Oh, yeah. Oh, my God. I'm naked. I'm wearing nothing!" She wandered around the room, looking at the floor, until she found her tunic, clutch, and sandals. She put on the tunic and dropped the coat on the floor in its place. She took Joe's wallet from the counter and stuffed it into her clutch—it almost fit inside—and picked up her shoes. "I put on my clothes!" she called out.

"That's a crying shame!" Joe shouted.

He returned in his bathrobe and asked her for a cigarette. With difficulty, she narrowly squeaked one out of her bag. Joe's wallet almost blocked its egress.

"Come on, Joe," Daniel said. "You don't smoke, and I'm hungry."

"There's a time for everything," Joe said. He lit up.

"Seeing you with that cigarette makes me horny," Gwen said.

"I'm going now," Daniel said.

"No, stay!" she said.

"Yeah, stay," Joe said.

Daniel didn't know what to make of Joe's condition. He seemed energetic enough, but vocally subdued. He wasn't narrating. By his normal standards, he was a zombie. "No way, man," he said. "I'll call you later. We'll get dinner."

He didn't answer the phone. Daniel thought, If that girl ever sobers up, she'll notice she's with Joe, and we'll be rid of her.

As it turned out, that was a big "if."

SINCE PAM WAS "WORKING" FROM HOME A LOT, JOE CUT DOWN ON HIS BABYSITTING. HE and Gwen dated two or three times a week, mostly in the afternoon. Her evenings were busy. On weekends, she claimed to be visiting her father in Great Neck. She made it sound like a nice place, but she said that although their relationship was serious, she wasn't ready for him to meet her family. He introduced her to Professor Harris, who took it philosophically. Of course he preferred Bethany, but he had never been able to imagine her sticking with Joe for long. He saw the attraction of a squalid, angular airhead for a fun-loving young man.

Joe proudly titled her "my girlfriend." Pam and Daniel were in agreement that he was not her boyfriend, as much as he might like to presume otherwise. There had to be someone else in her life. Drugs were surely involved. Her manner toward them alternated between petulant statue and raging ermine.

With concern and sympathy for Joe alone, they analyzed the situation as follows: His life was a social life. He had never been alone. He was always in the company of people or recordings of them. It wouldn't have taken any time for solitary confinement to drive him insane. The shift to conversing with inanimate objects and gauging their responses would have been instantaneous. Arguably it had taken place long before, when he first took up singing alone on the streets of New York. And unlike his other friends, Gwen was there for him. They had work and kindergarten, and she had nothing. She was as forbearing and tolerant as Joe. Her reasons happened to be different—she was high all the time—but wasn't he high too, in his own way? She laughed at his jokes. She laughed at accidents. She laughed at the news. Her mood was consistently as good as his. To everyone but him, she was grating and repetitive, and that was the secret of their bond.

GWEN'S ANALYSIS DIFFERED. AS SHE SAW IT, HER ALOOF AND INCONSISTENT ATTENTION to Joe was only natural, because, you see, this guy Blake, an actor in the process of failing to make it, was her old boyfriend. He had gotten a part in a TV pilot that never got made into a series and then transitioned, embarrassingly, to theater. Recently he had played the role of a bug, with no costume or makeup. Most of his lines were a high inhuman whine that the audience wasn't supposed to understand, because he was a bug. It got a great write-up in the *Voice* but did not gain a mention in any of the dailies. So basically Blake was over, and Joe was her new boyfriend. His career was in ascendancy. Spending time with him was an investment that could pay off big. But obviously there was going to be some overlap, because an old boyfriend doesn't dissolve into thin air when you tell him it's over. Plus, a new boyfriend isn't always prepared to assume all of an old boyfriend's duties. Blake, for example, was a terrific, if not 100 percent reliable, source of speedballs. Some weekends they just binged straight through, at an apartment on the Upper West Side that this theater director friend was lending him while he got back on his feet after his acting fiasco. Joe had no drugs, no sources of drugs, and no interest in drugs. Supplying her with drugs was a boyfriend duty he couldn't and wouldn't ever properly fulfill. So the transition from Blake to Joe was going to take some time, obviously.

She was proud of having chosen Joe before he became famous, when he was merely the next big thing. Not entirely coincidentally, he was on the cover of *Spin* that month, and his album was featured in *Rolling Stone*. His tour of venues with room for a thousand people, such as gutted 1930s ballrooms in large midwestern cities, would involve not buses and hardship but airplanes and room service. She couldn't accompany him without losing Blake—that is, without leaving Blake alone for so long that he would find someone else and leave her—that is, for two to three weeknights in a row. She estimated the time Blake could spend alone on a weekend with his pockets full of drugs before meeting someone new at around twenty minutes. The length of time she could spend without drugs on a weekend in the presence of a man who had drugs without at least blowing him was likewise around twenty minutes. But it seemed to her that Joe's specialness made a resolution effortless: he didn't have drugs, and he wasn't jealous. She and Blake would meet new people.

Gwen wasn't a victim of childhood trauma. She had tried drugs because she was an uninhibited, fun-loving person, and she was addicted because that's what drugs will do. She submitted to lesser traumata of all kinds to get them, because she feared the greater trauma of doing without. She was a trauma avoider, not a

trauma reenactor, as trauma victims are. There was no masochism in her rejection of effort and no egotism in her devotion to
Joe. Selflessly she put the needs of drugs and men before her
own, subordinating herself, as though they had picked her up
after the modeling agency dropped her. And she was a lost soul,
because she was having a great time. No one felt inspired to intervene. No one felt her destiny had ever been that of a productive member of society, not even her parents, sadly. Her mother
had moved to L.A. when she was seventeen, and they partied
together. Her father never remarried, and he also threw great parties. Her one talent was walking. She wasn't creative, curious, or
beautiful. If anything, that last was her trauma—the lack of a
bankable face for print ad campaigns. She was skinny, though.
That was good enough for drug dealers, and they did their part to
keep her that way.

She never came willingly to Chrystie Street. She couldn't
stand Pam and Daniel, long walks, or Flora. The adults were
judgmental, the walks didn't match her shoes, and she opposed on
principle all special treatment for people who happened by luck to
be ultra-petite and cute. She knew better than to say so. She had
matured a lot since driving her modeling career into a ditch. She
knew herself and what she wanted out of life—which was definitely not to be the kind of beauty has-been who marries a rich old
man—and what kind of situations she could handle. She ignored
the Svobodas. No one encouraged her not to. Joe was happy to
have their undivided attention.

DANIEL TRACED OUT THE TOUR ROUTE IN AN ATLAS. THE DISTANCES TO BE COVERED
astonished Joe. He knew his way around the city, but he hadn't
known it was so tiny compared with the rest of the country.

Not that there was anything unusual in that. Most of his
inabilities were so common that the music industry had institu-

tionalized ways to manage them. Disorganization was universal, so assistants told him where to go and when. Dowdiness was endemic, so stylists told him how to dress. Lateness and inarticulacy likewise, so publicists escorted him to interviews and told him what to say. No one had to tell him to put on his solemn Adonis face at photo shoots. After an hour of posing, it came on its own. Photo editors waited for it. They accepted nothing less. In this, they were typical. Most people who met him were in the business of selling him. They accentuated the positive.

Given his aversion to vehicles, there was initially some concern about transportation, but his first chopper trip to Daktari's place in the Hamptons from East Thirty-Fourth Street had made it apparent that he wasn't afraid of flying. He had no issues with distant panoramas, whooshing, or steady roars.

Only for one inability did an exception have to be made: drums. Daktari tried putting him in front of a trap set, but he flinched as if the kick drum were bombs and the snare were gunfire. He kept turning around to stare at it, even with earplugs in. It was agreed that there would be no drummer on his tour. Canned beats from a synthesizer would be mixed for the ears of the audience at the soundboard. The only percussion in the monitors would be the soft click of a metronome.

A touring band was hired. This was accomplished via classified ads that included the time-honored condition "No big hair." Appropriately collegiate-looking men were auditioned and inspected. Joe liked them all, so the decision was left to Daktari, with nonbinding input from Daniel. Since Daniel wanted to protect Joe, and Daktari wanted to protect his investment, their taste in companions for him turned out to be similar. They hired three placid, mature, competent men with forelocks—Sebastian the Chilean American rhythm guitarist, Kevin the Irish American rhythm bassist (Joe played lead bass), and John the Pakistani

American keyboardist, all in their midthirties, darker than Joe, with boyish looks persuasive at a distance.

A few weeks before the tour began, Joe called Daniel to say he wanted a rider on his contract. To wit, he could no longer play a live show without four unopened quart bottles in the dressing room: gin, rum, bourbon, and tequila.

"Did the guys ask for this?" Daniel asked, disappointed.

"No," Joe said. "Gwen told me I can put anything I want in the rider, and they have to give it to me."

"Huh? Since when do you want a gallon of schnapps?"

"Her friends can't afford drinks at bars. She said if I put it in the rider, it's free."

"Tell her no. Musicians get free drinks when they're playing. Tell her to drink your drinks."

"But if I'm in love with her, I give her what she wants."

"No, you don't," Daniel said. "When you love a woman, you give her what she needs. That's plenty enough to keep you busy."

"She gives me what I need, because she loves me," Joe said, dangerously close to logic.

"But you don't need her," Daniel said. "I bet any girl could give you what you get from her. Just saying."

THAT AFTERNOON, JOE GOT INTO A TUSSLE WITH A STRANGER AFTER TOUCHING HER waist at a crosswalk. His woeful attempt to explain saved him from disfiguration by passersby.

He came over in the evening, and he and Daniel walked out on the Manhattan Bridge. Daniel administered an urgent talking-to that was the opposite of the birds and the bees. It addressed a mandate to confine sexuality to the imagination. Beyond the principle of the thing, he felt that Joe should be prepared for civil liability. Any girl he offended would surely sue, he said, the second she found out he was rich.

Joe objected that rich guys get girls.

"Sure they do," Daniel said. "But then the girl hands them the check and says, 'That'll be ten thousand dollars, please.'"

"Like prostitutes."

"You got it. Never pay for sex. With girls it's not 'You break it, you bought it.' It's the golden rule. Repeat after me. *Never pay for sex.*"

"Never pay for sex. But what if the girl needs money?"

"Girls need sex, or they need money, but never both at the same time. It's not sex unless it's free. It's not sex unless the girl's so into it, she's paying you!" Daniel could hardly believe the asinine things he was saying, but he felt the situation demanded more than honesty.

"Gwen never needs money," Joe asserted.

"And that's the one good thing about her—no, let's be real."

He meant to correct himself and label her Joe's doxy. But something clicked in his mind first. Joe was right; she never needed money. She bartered sex for other things. What kept her from pursuing an arrangement in which Joe paid her rent was that her father paid it. She didn't accept checks from anybody but her dad, and that made her a nice girl, in theory.

He said, "Gwen's a barnacle. You're a ship on the ocean of life, and she's along for the ride."

"Stuck to my underside," Joe said approvingly.

JOE PLAYED A SHORT ACOUSTIC SET AT A LOFT IN SOHO, A PRIVATE BENEFIT FOR A FILM-maker with cancer whose wife knew Daktari. There he premiered a song about his discovery that there are no limits on fantasy. Daniel stayed home with Flora, but Pam heard it live, to her dismay. The tune was excessively catchy. Joe sang:

This song is a letter
From my pants to your sweater
You make me feel better, and better, and better

You blow me for an hour
I wash off in the shower
Still feeling the power, the power, the power
[etc.]

Pam felt that any self-respecting woman now would leave the room. Instead of leaving, she looked around to see who else was leaving. Gwen, for better or worse, was beaming beatifically, hands clasped to her chest, swaying on a stool to Joe's left. She didn't seem to know she was onstage. When the song ended, she teetered over to him and gave him a big, smacking kiss.

"You looked great up there," Pam said to her afterward, both of them standing by the table with the free white wine.

"Avoid!" Gwen said modestly. "When I was ugly, nobody cared, but I have glowing skin now. You—you should get it." She hiccuped.

"'Glowing skin'?"

"Duh, Pam! My skin?" She turned her head from side to side. "Are you looking?"

"It's incredible," Pam said. "I can't believe it. Can you excuse me a second?" She turned her back and walked away to try to meet a well-known sculptor.

Meanwhile Joe stood out on the sidewalk below the venue, smoking a cigarette and holding forth on his recent discovery of Beethoven's Fifth Symphony. He was singing the closing movement as "laa-laa-laa, la-la-la-la-la-laa," and so on. No one interrupted him. A half-circle of young people eyed one another cautiously as they listened, struggling to make out whether he was high or being ironic.

"I'd be into getting dinner," a woman ventured, wondering whether he'd offer to take them out.

Instantly he stopped singing and smiled at her. "Me too! Let's go get crackers!"

"This guy's a trip," someone said. The crowd of nine began to move, surrounding him and leading him. He didn't know which direction it was to the nearest grocery store, but the purposeful movement of informed participants swept them all away at the proper angle.

Joe said at the entrance, "I like crackers because they're crisp." He charged down the center aisle and looked around in bewilderment, saying, "Do you see crackers?" He didn't see crackers. It was an unfamiliar store.

The others brought him products to review and reject while he stood his ground, waiting for crackers. A mood of hilarity took hold as they competed to find out which product would elicit the most troubling poetry. It turned out to be a bag of apples. "Don't curdle my blood with tree fruits," he said. "They're replete with earwigs."

Nobody brought him any crackers. Eventually he paid for two sixes of beer and returned to the gallery alone. Years later, the others were still telling the story about the time Joe Harris bought them beer on acid. They said you had to be there.

THE TOUR WAS A SOLD-OUT TRIUMPH, WITH EPIC AFTER-PARTIES. GWEN HAD FLEETING sex, of a kind, with Sebastian, Kevin, and John, but only before it came to her attention that she would have no access to drugs unless groupies were to bring them. Her new dealer, Kenneth, had a network, but it didn't extend past Tenafly. For drugs to happen, she had to hang back, even from Joe.

Possessiveness would have been beneath her dignity as common-law wife. That's how she saw herself, though he never stopped calling her "my girlfriend."

He still used the term "rock star" loosely to mean anyone in a band. A "groupie" was any woman or girl in his hotel room. "My girlfriend" played the part of groupie wrangler, ensuring that access to his room was limited to those with dissolute good looks and the appearance of money. Once a party established itself in a hotel room, it was only a matter of time before one of the groupies called a local supplier and ordered in. Most of them were old enough to have legal sex but too young to buy legal alcohol, so they knew where to find drugs.

The press said he was spiraling out of control. But his wishes corresponded to the innocent desires of a fun-loving adult. He was used to having fun, and he saw no reason to cut back just because his being a rock star raised the number of people who cared.

Most stars, however dim their astral radiance, are at first surprised, soon perturbed, and ultimately warped as social beings by the ease and pleasure habitually bestowed on success. No sycophancy is necessary for corruption. Anyone accustomed to normal life—particularly in New York—can succumb to delusions of grandeur when faced with mild helpfulness and a willingness to ignore slights. Even without a retinue of paid handlers, much less true fame of the inconveniencing kind, Joe lived as he always had, trusting everyone, assuming the benefit of the doubt, surrounded by friends—if anything growing more frolicsome as decisions were taken out of his hands. The transition to life among toadies barely registered.

Life among groupies, however, got his attention majorly. He liked everything about them, even the way condoms slowed them down.

He liked to drink, but he rejected competing modes of self-medication. Downers reminded him that he appreciated himself the way he was. LSD made him hide under a blanket. He tried cocaine and ecstasy and didn't notice any effects. He could learn from experiences with pills and powders because he didn't automatically trust them. They weren't other selves, the way people were. They were more like speeding cars.

His life as a libertine sybarite amused Pam and Daniel. They felt that anything was better than exclusive commitment to Gwen. His wedding to her was a worst-case nightmare scenario they made jokes about. When Flora was around, they kept quiet about his adventures, and so did he. He knew which of his stories were rated PG-13 and which were R and X.

VIII.

Pam, Daniel, and Joe bought bricklike cell phones so that they could coordinate picking Flora up from kindergarten.

One pretty spring afternoon—it was Daniel's day to pick her up—she emerged wanting to know whether she was gay.

"Why do you ask?" he said as they walked, holding hands. "It's your choice. Do you feel gay?"

"Haejin asked me if Joe is my dad. I said no, but he takes care of me. And she goes, 'You have two dads, so you're gay.'"

"Tell her he's your friend. Isn't he your friend?"

"That's what I said! And she said I don't have any grandma to take care of me and that's why I'm adopted and gay."

"Whoa," Daniel said. "That's normative in so many ways, it makes my head hurt! Does it make your head hurt?"

She touched her head cautiously. "No. My head's okay."

"Being gay is nice," he said by way of general information. "But only for gay people. It has to do with sex, so it's very grown up—except on Halloween, when we go to the gay parade."

"Are rainbows gay?"

"No," Daniel said. "The rainbow stands for ultimate evil."

"It does not!"

"Do you know about Noah's ark?"

"Kind of. There's animals."

"In the Bible, it says that a long time ago, God killed almost everybody in the whole world, and almost all the animals, using a big flood to drown them. When it was over, the only survivors were on a boat, Noah's ark, and God said to them, 'You know what? I'm going to put this rainbow up every time it rains now, to remind myself not to drown you guys ever again, because you're perfectly good at killing each other without my help.'"

"That is not in the Bible!"

"Check it and see. Genesis, chapter eight, verse twenty-one. And the Lord said in his heart, the imagination of man's heart is evil from his youth, and the fear of you and the dread of you shall be upon every beast of the earth, and upon every fowl of the air, upon all that moveth upon the earth, and upon all the fishes of the sea, and surely your blood of your lives I will require. It's the curse of the evil rainbow!"

"It is not!"

"God drowned every single unicorn, and you know why?"

"They aren't evil!"

"You don't even want to know. What do you think they do with that horn?"

"I don't know—kill stuff? Like, put it on their horn?"

"You got it! You stay away from those bad boys!"

THAT NIGHT IN BED HE SAID TO PAM, "FLORA'S GETTING TEASED BECAUSE SHE HAS NO grandparents. Are you sure you couldn't take the plunge?"

"It would be weird, after all these years."

"It can only get weirder," Daniel said. "You just have to take a deep breath and jump. I bet your mom will be happy no matter what. Flora's her only grandchild. The first one always gets their attention."

"I don't know. I don't think so."

"Not to get Christian on you or anything, but did you ever think about how your mother feels? I mean, not whether she has a right to feel that way, but just how it must feel to her having an only child and not even knowing whether she's alive? I mean, I'm not close to my parents, but at least they know where I am."

"She can look me up. I'm sure she already has. She's not stupid."

"How would she find you, even if she knew you were in New York? You had your number on Bleecker disconnected, and you married me and changed your name to Svoboda before RIACD got a website. Be real. Call her. Tell her she has a five-year-old granddaughter and see how fast she turns around."

PAM DIDN'T CALL HOME RIGHT AWAY. THE POSSIBILITY OF MAKING SUCH A MOMENTOUS change with so little effort induced vertigo. The call would take her all of thirty seconds, and it would bring her parents back into her life. She waffled. She didn't want to hear her mother's reaction, but more important, she didn't want anyone to hear her cry.

At heart, she was sorry. She pitied her parents. Now that she had a daughter, she didn't want to know how it must have felt to have one out alone in 1980s downtown Washington nightlife. When she thought about it, it didn't surprise her that her parents had yelled at her. It was more surprising that they hadn't locked her up in a psychiatric ward in the interest of saving her life.

She sent a postcard with the return address of RIACD's post office box.

Dear Mom and Dad, long time no see. I hope you're well. I'm well and happy and still in New York. My husband, Daniel, and I have a daughter, Flora. She's five now. She

asked about you. You were always saying I shouldn't burn my
bridges. Well, write back! And please forgive me.

Love, Pam

Two days later, at five thirty in the afternoon, she got a call
from the receptionist, saying her parents were at the office.

"Pass my dad the phone," Pam said. "Hey, Dad."

"Pam," he said. "It's good to hear your voice. Where do you
live?"

She gave him the address on Chrystie Street. Then she summoned Daniel and Flora to the kitchen table for an announcement.

SHE WENT DOWNSTAIRS TO THE STREET TO WAIT. MEETING HER MOTHER IN PUBLIC
would surely lead to some kind of awkward public display, but it
wouldn't be as embarrassing as having her parents hunt around for
a doorbell until Victor or Margie showed them the narrow ply-
wood door equipped with a hasp and padlock behind the beverage
coolers.

A blue Chrysler LeBaron pulled up, and Ginger sprang from
the passenger seat into Pam's arms. "I'm going to find parking!"
Edgar called out, easing the car away.

"Oh, Mom, I can't believe it," Pam said.

She was, in fact, straining to believe what she saw. Her strait-
laced mother had turned from a prematurely middle-aged conservative prep with gold door-knocker earrings and a perm into
a hippie earth mother with wavy gray locks. Instead of a white
turtleneck, she was wearing an Indian print top. Her face hadn't
changed, at least not the important parts. Her eyes were the single
most familiar and persuasive thing Pam had ever known. They
were the original definition of trustworthiness, and her smile was
the paradigm of all affection. She hadn't seen anything like them
since she was twelve.

Her mother held her tight while Pam whimpered. She said, "Boy, am I glad Daniel and Flora can't see this. They'd be so freaked."

"You probably told them we're monsters," Ginger said, retreating to see her reaction.

She wiped her eyes. "I never mentioned you to my daughter. I know it's crazy. But at least you're starting off with a clean slate. She didn't figure out something was missing until somebody told her about grandparents in kindergarten the other day."

"What's she like?"

"Cute. Pretty. You're going to go nuts. I'm never going to get you out of here."

"Is she smart?"

"More like quirky?"

"I can't wait. What's keeping your father?"

"I should have told him there's a garage on Essex."

"He'll find something."

"So"—Pam hesitated—"are you guys healthy? Are things okay?"

"Except for that untraceable daughter bit that broke my heart into little pieces, it's been a fairly smooth journey. Ed's almost to retirement. That's another thing I can't wait for."

"You look so different."

"Did you really expect losing a daughter not to change me?" She bit her lip. "I went through some serious down time there. I was at an ashram in New Mexico off and on for two years. I was in the hospital for depression, twice."

"I'm so sorry."

"I found out a lot of things about myself. Parts of myself that I'd wanted you to become, because I wasn't becoming them myself. You know? I got to know my boundaries a little better and acknowledged that it was all me. You were my vicarious vessel. So I changed."

"I kind of know what you mean," Pam said. "Maybe."

"The world you came into didn't inspire you to be what I wanted for myself. I was inspired differently when I was young. It was a different time. I hope you've been able to live in tune with your inspirations."

Pam said, "I'm doing okay." Her mother's affirmation of creativity and self-realization as valid life goals embarrassed her deeply. An unpleasant suspicion arose in her mind. Punk rock and New Age esotericism had both arisen in the seventies. Could they be more similar than she liked to think?

"Here comes Ed," Ginger said, indicating her husband, who was approaching them with long, lively strides, one hand in his pocket, holding his wallet to deter pickpockets.

"My baby," he said, bear-hugging Pam with closed fists.

"Is the car legal?" she asked.

"I found valet parking at a restaurant. At least I think I did. Maybe it was just some guy in a vest stealing my car."

They proceeded into the store, greeted Margie in a casual way, and went with minor jostling up the stairs.

When Pam opened the apartment door, Daniel was facing it with his hand protectively on Flora's shoulder, and for a moment, she felt she was making a terrible mistake.

Flora dealt with the tension by yelling, "Grandma!" and flinging herself into Ginger's arms, as if she'd been systematically prepared by a course of pro-family brainwashing to think grandmothers were Earth's most beneficent beings. She snuggled and let herself be petted, instinctively opening her mouth like a baby bird.

It wasn't Daniel's doing; all he'd done was feed her a piece of toast and say that Pam's parents were coming to take them out to dinner. She had picked it up at kindergarten. Most of the kids spent their nights being disciplined by harried New Yorkers and their days being spoiled by sweet old Chinese and southern ladies.

"That's Grandpa," Ginger said, pointing.

Edgar genuflected so that Flora could throw herself against his chest, humming with glee as if she were eating a giant cookie. "So nice to meet you," he said, smoothing her hair.

Disengaging, she solemnly asked him, "How do you feel about dim sum?"

"That's a New York thing," Edgar said. "I don't even know what that is."

"I can eat eight," Flora said.

"That's impossible," Ginger said.

"Les jeux sont faits," Daniel said. "I guess we're going out for dim sum. Nice to meet you." He put out his hand to Edgar. "I'm Daniel Svoboda, and this is Flora."

"You're my favorite man in the world right now," Ginger said, hugging Daniel on tiptoes while he shook Edgar's hand. "I never thought I'd be this happy again." She was crying soft tears that she called "tears of joy."

GINGER HAD BEEN FEELING VERY MUCH IN CONTROL. BUT THE STRANGELY TRUSTING AND even disrespectful way Flora greeted her and Edgar—it was like coming home to a lonely dog—had unexpectedly reminded her that when Pam was that size, she had still been spanking her with hairbrushes and coat hangers. For major infractions, Edgar whipped her bare bottom with a belt. It always made her roar and squeal snotty tears like a baby, even though the belt barely grazed her and never left a mark. The hard part was holding her down to get a clear shot.

Ginger at the time had regarded Pam as a worthy adversary and her sorrow as suitable penance for the messes she made. Seeing Flora so puny and gullible made her aware of her past depravity. She sensed for the first time the depths of her subjection to a culture of violence. Prior to their meeting, she had been able to luxuriate to some extent on the moral high ground where Pam's cruel defection stranded her. Flora's self-evident vulnerability made her realize she'd been a fascist mom after all.

She felt an urgent need to be Flora's fairy godmother. It was too late to grant her a childhood of the gentlest enchantment enveloped in flowers and birdsong, but with Pam's approval, she bought her new bedclothes in blue flannel with a pattern of white sheep. Her current sheets and pillowcases had stiff yellowish stains that wouldn't wash out. Pam and Daniel had carried on long, bemused conversations about what they could possibly be. (They were Duco Cement from a tube Flora found on the street and liked to sniff. Fortunately she left the cap off, and it dried out.)

The one act of truly petit-bourgeois despoliation they allowed Ginger was to escort Flora to FAO Schwarz to buy a doll. The two spent almost all day in Midtown, with detours to Rockefeller Center and the Russian Tea Room. They returned with a plush stuffed horse in chestnut brown, a foot tall, with yellow eyes and a white star on its forehead. Edgar named it "Secretariat." Flora said the word over and over, as if it were a present comparable to the toy.

When Ginger got back to D.C., she went back into therapy.

SHE CAME UP ON THE TRAIN ONCE A MONTH OR SO, SOMETIMES WITH EDGAR, SOME-times without, continuing to stay in hotels. She always brought clover, picked in their backyard and packed in a sandwich bag. It had taken adamantine insistence to persuade her that her daughter's family was not needy and that gifts of money would have been useless to them, whereas it made everyone happy to serve clover on a plate and summon Secretariat from his cardboard stall to share in a meal of flowers. Daniel had done Boy Scouts under a survivalist scoutmaster, so he knew that clover petals were nature's candy.

The Svobodas didn't go to Washington. Pam saw no reason to leave New York except on work assignments. Her youthful declaration of internecine war had never been superseded by a peace treaty. She had run away for reasons she still found valid. She accepted her parents' apologies because she'd had her revenge, eleven years of it. She willingly granted them Flora. Flora was a different person, new to them—obviously—and impressionable, even by the standards of little kids. Maintaining superficial harmony for her sake was so unselfish, it felt like love.

Ginger and Edgar, for their part, were terrified of Pam. The truce was too recent. The stakes were too high. One false move might lead to rejection and loss. They tiptoed around Pam, careful not to cross her. They performed tasks they found surreal: breakfasting on Krispy Kremes behind blackout curtains and a padlock, surrendering Flora to her louche mooncalf babysitter for walks that left her too tired to eat. No matter how the child's upbringing shocked them, they voiced no criticism, as though Pam had become the patriarch that Edgar no longer was.

FLORA WOKE UP MOLTO EXCITED ABOUT THE FIRST DAY OF FIRST GRADE AT P.S. THIRTY-Two. Daniel, Pam, and Joe brought her to the towering steel gate. She tore herself loose and raced off to a group of her friends from kindergarten who were standing in a circle on the asphalt, comparing backpacks.

When Pam picked her up at the end of the day, she didn't look quite so happy. Flora held Pam's hand as they walked home and sat dolefully in front of her plate of cookies, obviously troubled.

There were a number of kids in the class whom she had not encountered before. Pam bit back the impulse to suggest she make new friends. Flora knew all that; she had acquired two new best friends within a week of starting kindergarten. She said hesitantly, "I don't think Vanu even went to kindergarten."

"Why's that?"

"He doesn't know stuff. He doesn't know the alphabet. He hits everybody."

"Did he hit you?"

"No. Just Julie."

The next morning, after leaving Flora with her friends in the schoolyard, Pam continued inside to chat with the teacher, Ms. Shahrokhshahi. She sat at her desk, with a French manicure and long dark hair in a ponytail, looking at a math teacher's manual with much the same expression that Flora had used on the cookies. Pam introduced herself as Flora's mom.

"You can call me Ms. S.," the teacher said. "I adore your daughter."

"Me too. I wanted to ask you about some kid named Vanu she says hits everybody."

Ms. S. rolled her eyes. "If he's been in school before, I'm a monkey's uncle. He can't sit still unless I'm literally touching him, standing by his desk, touching his shoulder. I've got to get him out of my classroom."

"Does he belong in special ed?"

"He belongs in kindergarten. I think he's five and big for his age. He comes up to my shoulders."

PAM SAW MS. S. AGAIN AT PARENT-TEACHER NIGHT. THERE WERE ONLY TWO OTHER moms and a dad from Flora's class, so they had time to talk. "I adore Flora," Ms. S. said again.

"She's tops," Pam said. "How's little Vanu?"

"He calls me Ms. Ass and pats me on it. But I'm not allowed to get more than five feet from him, or he heads for the window. It's first grade. I'm in loco parentis. I'm going crazy."

"Isn't there anything you can do?"

"Like what?"

"Is he hyperactive? They have Ritalin for that."

"I take that back; I'm not in loco parentis. I'm at the mercy of his parents. Des Hernandez—he teaches fifth grade—said the older sister pretended to be a cat until she was fourteen. Their mother has a strong cat preference."

"So the family has mental health issues."

"If you see drugs as a mental health issue. Des says she hurt her knee working for the Ice Capades, like, twenty years ago. She's on disability and addicted to some kind of pain medication."

"So get Vanu some Medicaid-sponsored Ritalin."

"She'd sell it to buy cat food."

"Maybe he's hungry."

"Have you seen him? Phew."

"It's not really my business."

"I wish I knew whether it was my business." Ms. S. sighed. "I'm supposed to be teaching, and all I do is micromanage his moods."

"Special ed," Pam said.

"What century are you from? If he had Tourette's, they'd still put him in my class. It would be a learning experience for the kids. *Big dick cocksucker cock! Fuck Ms. Ass!*"

"You sound kind of traumatized."

"You could be right."

TWO WEEKS LATER THERE WAS A SCHOOL-WIDE BROUHAHA ABOUT MS. SHAHROKHSHAHI. Flora's version was that Vanu had wanted to get up out of his seat and go to the window. Ms. S., who was standing by him as usual, had tightened her grip on his shoulder and asked him to stay in his seat. They argued, as usual. Then Vanu—this was the unusual part—stood up and kicked her in the shin. Her hand on his shoulder made him lose his balance, and he fell down backward, bumping his head on a desk.

Vanu told a different story. There were no witnesses, just a bunch of six-year-olds; it was he said, she said, like any assault that takes place in a closed room. The physical evidence pointed to the grave culpability of Ms. S. There was a bump on Vanu's head. The examination by a school-appointed physician turned up all sorts of interesting scars and bruises on Vanu, some of them recent enough to be pinned on Ms. S., who was placed on suspension, barred from the school grounds, and fired a week later. It being her first job after student teaching, she didn't have the seniority to be assigned a spot on a couch somewhere in an administrative building.

Pam tried to get her phone number from the school—she had liked her—so she could drop by, or call and console her, but the appealing Ms. S. was gone from her life forever.

THE NEW TEACHER WAS NAMED MR. MILEWSKI. HE FELT HE WAS UNDER NO OBLIGATION to teach the kids anything, since he was a substitute, marking time until a replacement for Ms. S. could be found. He carried on long debates with Vanu, paying no attention to any other child.

Flora began taking books to school. As a city kid, she knew how to tune out noise. It wasn't a skill; it was automatic. She'd never been on a camping trip to the woods outside town or anywhere that didn't have a roaring sound in the background—not even the planetarium. To enjoy herself in class, all she had to do was ignore Mr. Milewski and Vanu the way she ignored most things, most of the time.

That was the key difference between her and Vanu: he cared about what went on around him. In the world's most exciting city, he was drawn to the window. Flora was an introvert. In a more just world, he would have been allowed to move and play. She was far better suited to a Romanian-orphanage-style environment of superficially ordered neglect.

To Pam, she seemed happier. She had the best of both worlds, socializing at lunch and recess while enjoying the benefits of homeschooling. Her curriculum, chosen from the shelves of the public library, consisted of cheap nonfiction chapter books with minimal illustration. Many were paperbacks from the seventies with plastic-coated library bindings. The information wasn't up-to-date, but then again, it was first grade. The exact lineage of the human species was less important than knowing it had evolved.

They saved math for after school. Cookies were good for adding, subtracting, multiplying, and dividing.

Week by week, Flora seemed to mature, becoming more focused and able to concentrate for longer periods. It was a little disturbing to Pam that the school was doing such a good job all of a sudden.

She went to see Mr. Milewski on parent-teacher night. He praised "the shy, retiring bookworm" Flora and emitted hail-fellow-well-met chuckles about his "problem child" Vanu, who was "too big for his britches" and deserved "fifty lashes with a wet noodle." He obviously preferred boys to girls. By being larger and more aggressive than the other kids, Vanu had a leg up in terms of masculinity. Mr. Milewski was not nearly old enough to be talking like Howdy Doody, in Pam's opinion. He was one of those men who start balding at twenty, raised in an era when young people were maximizing hair, and had been taken for his own father all his life. There was a creepiness to his affection for Vanu, but on the other hand, it reassured her that his neglect of Flora was a good thing.

IN SECOND GRADE, FLORA WAS CONSIDERED OLD ENOUGH FOR AFTER-SCHOOL ACTIVITIES. She chose basketball on Tuesdays and Thursdays. Music lacked the glamour of unfamiliarity. Art, drama, and dance were distant rumors. Tutus on Halloween were all she knew of ballet. But she had been watching cool strangers play basketball since the day she was born. She hoped to impress people in the park. Her parents were fine with it, since watching her try to sink layups was frankly hilarious.

She was old enough to shoot hoops by herself, within view of whoever was minding the store. It might be her parents, if she was shooting hoops; they knew how to work the register, and when Flora was in the park they sometimes volunteered, to give Victor and Margie a little time off. The landlords had no children of their own. They invested a lot of hours in Flora without paying her much direct attention. They conspired to give her Tootsie Rolls and sugared sodas and tell her parents she had eaten an apple and drunk white milk, but not every day. They knew that on afternoons when she was a latchkey kid, if Joe (or occasionally Ginger and/or Edgar) didn't come to pick her up, her strict parents would be home by five thirty, right around the time the big boys took over the basketball courts.

JOE TOOK HER OUT WALKING, WHEN HE HAD TIME. BEING A ROCK STAR WAS NOT A DAY job, and even if it had been, he wouldn't have given up his walks. He still made new friends every day. Unless they were stationary, like clerks and homeless people, or refused to be shaken loose, like Pam and Daniel, they were soon neglected, but never forgotten entirely. Flora stood by while he queried psychotics about their sores and frozen dessert vendors about their flavors in the same tone of disinterested fascination, oblivious to class boundaries, adding no boundaries of his own.

He was hopeless at cash registers and one-on-one, but he ordered a video segment of her team bouncing basketballs in time to his song "Nitchpakroyd." Where they weren't in rhythm, they could be corrected in postproduction.

His follow-up record came out with three videos, a lot of press, and a plan for a major tour. It was entitled *Viscosity*. The success of *Coronation* had given him a measure of artistic control, and as he told Daktari, he liked to say "viscosity." If he was going to be saying a word over and over in interviews, he might as well pick one he liked. That was also how he came up with the singles: "Foursome," "Noodle Bleach"—both fun to say, while the latter could be understood as a play on "nude beach," at least by twelve-year-olds—and "Nitchpakroyd," to which the lyrics were mostly "Nitchpakroyd like an android!" It could be taken (in the context of the video) to imply precocious excellence in basketball or something to do with race, pedophilia, emotional detachment, or drugs. Nobody knew, too many people cared, and Joe never gave it any thought. The sound of *Viscosity* was melodic and a tad heroic, with overdubbed odd noises. The multiple bass tracks remained. He saw them as his trademark, and everyone indulged him, because the sound did well live.

In due time, he set off again on a three-month tour with Gwen. It wasn't an around-the-world tour, though the press materials called it that. Going west, he only skimmed East Asia before returning to California, and he never got as far as eastern Europe heading east. But it was still a lot of dates. None of them were in football stadiums, but several were in basketball arenas.

Daktari had coached and encouraged him to be a more dynamic performer. He strode around the stage in three different costumes in the course of two hours, sometimes handing off his bass to a roadie so he could concentrate on singing. The instruments and mics were wireless, so there was no danger he would trip.

He had two female backup singers. After ten shows, they were hoarse and their voices had to be put on playback as a precaution. He gave them the night off in Nagoya and asked the male instrumentalists to lip-synch their parts. That went over so well that Daktari gave him the green light to do it during a song called "Wet Pot" for the rest of the tour.

DANIEL STUDIED THE TOUR ITINERARY CLOSELY. HE WOULD HAVE LOVED TO GO IN Gwen's place, or as Joe's manager, or a member of his entourage, or even a fly on the wall. The hotel names reawakened youthful fantasies of decadence without debasement. In two cities Joe would be conveyed to them by helicopter. Daniel's inability to share in the spoils of rock stardom made him think dark thoughts about fatherhood. But it wasn't an outcome anyone could have predicted—that his babysitter would make the big time, rendering it impossible for him to leave his child alone—and he accepted it as his fate.

SLOWLY THE TWENTIETH CENTURY GROUND TO A HALT. THE MAW OF THE WORLD WAS choked with too many things. The tech community saw salvation in the abandonment of things, which would be replaced by information. Information was imagined as helpful knowledge, the kind librarians provide at the reference desk. The internet was conceived of as a gigantic library. The world's naïveté was grotesque.

The final significant event of the 1990s, at least on Chrystie Street, was that Victor and Margie bought a thousand shares of Amazon stock. When the bubble burst in March 2000, they took an $80,000 loss of their own free will as if they could punish the company by divesting. They raised Daniel's rent to $800, an increase of 100 percent. It would bring them an extra $80,000 over seventeen years. He didn't fight it.

The city had lost all its cheapness. The finest burgers no longer cost five dollars but twelve. All the dollar-egg-and-cheese-on-a-roll snack bars had been turned into Au Bon Pains. Lunch at Aureole had broken the twenty-dollar mark. The rich were richer, and poverty had become impracticable. All over Manhattan the middle-aged middle class was standing in the wreckage of its defined-contribution retirement plan, waiting to lose its position in middle management. The economy kept on tightening, and with every turn of the capstan, more people dropped out, like undersized fish in a net. Daniel's temp assignments no longer served the exclusive purpose of saving executives the stigma of vacant desks outside their offices. He was performing identifiable tasks as outsourced labor. He didn't like it.

He turned toward Pam one Saturday morning in bed and said, "I know this is a personal question, but how much money do you have, anyway? Did you lose anything in the crash?"

Yuval didn't offer himself or his employees 401(k) retirement accounts, because he was not the kind to defer gratification. But even without tax-exempt matching grants, Pam had been saving upward of a thousand dollars a month since moving in with Daniel. In the crash, she had lost precisely nothing. She replied, "That's so cute. You've never read one of my bank statements?"

"I don't read other people's mail!"

"I have maybe a hundred K. I'm not sure."

"Thousand? It's high time we got a bathtub in here, like one of those freestanding ones with claw-and-ball feet."

She said she didn't think the floor would take the weight and that it was her retirement money. She provided a synopsis of the Katharine Hepburn movie *Holiday*. "I'm not putting off quitting until I'm a little old lady in tennis shoes," she summed up.

"I prefer the 1930 version with Mary Astor," he replied, "where Edward Everett Horton gets more screen time."

"The problem is this town," she said. "Who knows what rents are going to be like when we're fifty? But if I put my money into a down payment to buy something, what do we live on?"

"You're forgetting two things. One, that you're married to an economic powerhouse, and two, that anybody can make a fortune in real estate with no money down."

"Nope. If you don't have money to play with, don't invest it. It's like going to the racetrack. You only take as much as you can afford to lose. How much do you have saved?"

"Six hundred, maybe? I mean dollars, not thousands. Maybe I should be putting in for an allowance from you. Almost everything I make goes to rent, groceries, and paying Joe."

"You still pay Joe?!"

"He takes care of my kid. Why would I not pay him?"

THEY DIDN'T INVEST IN REAL ESTATE. THEY CLOSED DANIEL'S BANK ACCOUNT AND MADE him joint owner of Pam's money.

She had never found a reason not to trust him. The marriage

might end sometime—it was only realistic to think that—but it wouldn't be because her husband lied, cheated, stole, dissembled, or misled. He was as transparent and honest as a machine. His output was as good as his input. With regular maintenance, he might last forever.

Sharing, however, had chopped her savings in half, and she considered getting depressed. She kept sleeping through boom-and-bust cycles, making nothing beyond her salary. RIACD was Yuval's sole proprietorship. It turned a profit, but not in the new postmodern way, with extra zeroes behind every number. It still billed by the day. It churned steadily through the bowels of finance, tinkering with system-critical infrastructure, independent of happenings on the surface. As a regret minimization framework for a boom, it was deficient.

Over the years, many employees had left to join startups, where some were paid in worthless shares, some in worthless options, and some in nothing at all. It was hard for Pam to get excited about startup odds while working on sure bets like life insurance. Still, the office was regularly abuzz with tales of IPOs cashing out on fantasy products—sucker VCs funding AI image recognition software that couldn't tell a cat from a washing machine, that sort of thing—and although the tales made everybody sad, no one could crack the code of how other people made money for nothing.

A client at a university library where she maintained RFID antitheft software invited her to a party at a startup in Williamsburg. The client said she wasn't sure what the guys did (she'd been dating one of them for two months), but they were definitely making excellent money, even after the dot-com crash.

Pam went to the party and took Yuval along. It was immediately obvious that they weren't making excellent money. Seven developers were sharing a two-up, two-down row house. Bunk beds were involved. There was nothing to drink but beer. They were creating software that would enable the anonymous transfer of large sums of money across international borders. Their backers were in Manhattan, in the financial industry. If the project succeeded, it would be illegal. Federal law required that sums over $10,000 change hands under surveillance.

When Yuval pointed this out to one of them—that they were taking their investors for a ride and exposing prospective customers to criminal liability—he denied it. He said it was like when an armaments startup develops a new gun. The product could be used in the commission of a crime or as a paperweight. The patent and SEC filings would say it was a paperweight. Besides, until they scaled it up, it was a paperweight, so it didn't matter.

Yuval said that his consultancy had a deep bench for issues of scalability and database recalcitrance. There was no answer. Pam remarked that Windows NT, clearly identifiable by its screensavers, was an odd choice of development environment for banking software. The developer said he had meant scaling up from the PowerPoint presentation to a video with music. They would start making the fund-raising video as soon as they were done designing the graphic interface.

A deliveryman arrived with pizza. The party guests held out bouquets of one-dollar bills to defray costs. "Let's scale up," Yuval said. They decamped to Peter Luger for steaks and bourbon. That was Pam's sum total firsthand experience of startups.

IX.

In the presidential race that crowned the millennium with ignominy, Daniel supported Ralph Nader of the Green Party USA. He had known the name since childhood. Nader's organization, Common Cause, had coined his favorite slogan, "Unsafe at Any Speed." It served him as a kind of tacit personal motto, complementing Pam's motto, "Fast, Cheap & Out of Control," which she had taken from the title of a movie, coincidentally also having to do with cars. As a basis of affection for a political candidate, it was eccentric, but not unusual.

He fatigued his friends with his defense of third parties and his newfound interest in parliamentary democracy. Pam assured him he was wasting his time, because New York always goes Democratic. It was the Empire State's machinelike reliability that gave her the right to be apolitical, and she felt he was doing her a disservice by working to disrupt it. But even Joe could tell there was something wrong about supporting a third party in a two-party system.

The only friend Daniel had who was innocent enough to

support Nader was Flora. He took her along canvassing on two successive Saturdays. For him, it was a sacrifice, but she loved canvassing. The difference was one of elevation. While he looked into strangers' eyes and begged them to vote Green, she met their pets.

Sometimes at home or on the street they played campaign rally, clapping and chanting "Unsafe! Unsafe! Unsafe at any speed!"

In the voting booth on November 7, he summoned his inner Democrat and pulled the lever for Gore.

The outcome of the nonelection, decreed in mid-December by majority vote of the Supreme Court in favor of George W. Bush, upset him greatly. It shook the foundations of Pam's anarchism and outraged Ginger's idealism. Even Edgar struggled to suppress his unease at the way the Supreme Court—of all people—had undermined the rule of law.

In the months that followed, with his exaggerated post-evangelical interest in the state of Israel, Daniel couldn't help but notice that there was a second intifada going on. The new president was taking a hard line with the Palestinians, blaming them for everything that went on in the Middle East. Daniel went around saying, "This can't end well. It's going to be Armageddon."

That helped prepare him for what came next.

WHEN IT STARTED—WHEN HE HEARD FROM VICTOR, WHILE PASSING THROUGH THE shop on his way back from taking Flora to school, that an airplane had flown into the World Trade Center—his first thought was: This is World War III. He ran back to the school and brought her home.

DOWN ON JOHN STREET, YUVAL STEPPED INTO PAM'S OFFICE TO SAY, "MY COUSIN AT THE World Trade Center just called me saying a plane hit the North Tower. They're evacuating. She says it looks incredible. I'm going over to take pictures."

"That's freaky," Pam said, thinking reflexively of Flora.

"So are you coming along or not?"

"I don't think so," she said. "It's a safe bet they'll roadblock everything but emergency services. You won't even get close." She thought of Flora again, with greater urgency. "You know what? If you're blowing out of here, so am I, because we both know their next move is going to be shutting down the subway."

There were three programmers watching cable news in the conference room, gasping, moaning, and speculating as though the event were a combination emoting competition and podium discussion. Pam looked in as she passed and saw the burning building on screen. She glanced out the window behind the programmers and saw sheets of paper drifting like confetti through the morning air over John Street. "You guys coming along?" she asked. "Me and Yuval are out of here." Nobody moved. She added, "You sure? They're going to seal the perimeter any second."

Yuval said, "*Yalla, khevre.* The office is closing."

"I'm not missing this," one of the men said, pointing at the TV. "This changes everything."

Pam and Yuval shared an elevator. She walked east to Water Street to hail a taxi, and he walked west, staring at the thick gray smudge from the burning skyscraper. A short time later, he photographed the second plane crash, and soon after that, he fainted, having seen something no person should ever see. He was raised up by passersby and dragged to a waiting ambulance, which drove uptown, so that later he could joke about saving its crew's lives.

Another passerby picked up the expensive digital camera he lost and continued taking pictures of horrible things—people on fire, people smashed—until it was too late.

GETTING A TAXI AT NINE FIFTEEN WAS A BREEZE. THE STREETS GOT EMPTIER AS PAM rolled north. Everyone was inside watching TV, gathered in stores and the few bars that were open in the morning. Her thoughts were even more cerebral than usual. She was in the throes of her first-ever vicarious out-of-body experience. She felt concern for the structural integrity of the towers, both of them full of people she was suddenly sure she'd never met. She didn't worry about Flora, Daniel, Joe, or even Yuval. She passed a shop owner who was nailing boards across his doorway. It reminded her of the second day after the Rodney King verdict, when office workers all over Manhattan called each other to get confirmation that an armed horde of black people was following Al Sharpton over the Brooklyn Bridge. It seemed to her like that kind of unjustified paranoia.

In the shop, Margie was rocking back and forth in front of the TV, as though reliving some kind of war trauma. Pam hugged her and said everything would be fine. Victor was taking all the bottled water off the shelves to hoard it in the basement. Upstairs she found Daniel and Flora packed as if for an excursion, with day packs and picnic supplies. Her day pack was also ready to go. Daniel had thought of everything, even toiletries.

"Daddy came and got me from school," Flora said.

"Do you know what just happened?" he asked. He had his portable radio in his T-shirt pocket and one earbud in. He motioned with his palm down for quiet. Pam shook her head, and he looked at Flora.

"Airplanes flew in the World Trade Center," Flora said.

"More than one?" Pam said.

"They're on fire and spewing asbestos in all directions. I couldn't get through on your cell. But I knew you'd be home by now, because you're the world's smartest woman. The Pentagon too. All hell's breaking loose. Nothing's running. It's Armageddon, and this town is a deer in the headlights."

"Holy cow," Pam said. "So what's our plan?"

"Go to your parents' place. If this is World War Three, nowhere is safer than Washington. Even if it's under attack. Especially then. It's a symbolic place where nothing important happens. Plus it'll stop them from worrying about us."

"True enough. There's nothing vital in D.C. Even the Pentagon's somewhere else. But it's weird they haven't called."

"The cell network's down. But right before everything went to hell, I found a rental car, right on the other side of the Manhattan Bridge. All we have to do is walk across, so let's get moving."

"Wait a second," Pam said. "Let me try my corporate account."

She fished a business card out of her wallet and went downstairs to the store. Victor offered her a half gallon of water as a present. She called RIACD's travel agent from the store's landline. The agent said she had a Hertz car for her on West Houston and that she was lucky she wasn't trying to get a car at the airport, because air travel was a madhouse—completely shut down.

She booked the car.

The little family left home and walked in a long zigzag toward the northwest. All the empty cabs were headed south, to pick people up. Crowds were gathered at every major intersection, looking south, but never for long. Sirens screeched over the roaring background noise like giant seagulls over giant surf. They were crossing Lafayette on Houston when the South Tower fell. For a few moments they stood still, right in the middle of Lafayette. Pam held Flora's face to her abdomen, as though she wanted to put her back inside. But Daniel tugged them onward toward the rental car, which was looking to him like the best idea he ever had. He felt as proud as a frontiersman.

They were the last customers before the clerk knocked off work to watch TV for a week. The storefront was ghostly quiet. Solemnity was in the air.

Daniel took the driver's seat, and Pam sat in the back with Flora, who asked where Joe was and why he wasn't coming.

"He lives on Nineteenth Street," Pam explained. "He's so far uptown, he missed the whole thing. We'll call him as soon as we get to Grandma and Grandpa's."

"He was going to maybe go to this party at NYU," Daniel said. "But he might be out of town."

TRAFFIC WAS NOT GOOD. THE WEST SIDE HIGHWAY HAD CLOSED, AND A LOT OF INCOMING commuters were turning around and unsure where to go. When they got to the George Washington Bridge, it had been closed for half an hour. They had to take the Tappan Zee Bridge to the Garden State Parkway, because Interstate 95 was also closed.

Looking south as they crossed the Tappan Zee, they could see that something was wrong. They could almost see how wrong it was. There was a dark cloud roiling in the sky. There were F-14 fighter jets zooming around. The radio gave conflicting reports.

Daniel wondered aloud why more people weren't leaving town, but mostly to show off how proud he was that he had left. "This car was too cheap," Pam replied. "I'm getting this idea for a demand-surge repricing algorithm. It's just basic calculus."

"We're not seeing anything on TV!" Flora complained.

"The TV people don't know the story yet," Daniel reassured her. "They'll be looking at pictures and saying all kinds of crazy stuff, like with the *Challenger* disaster. We'll watch the highlight reel when we get to Washington, and tomorrow we'll watch TV all day, I promise."

"No school?" Flora bounced in joyful anticipation of no school.

JOE WOKE UP TOWARD NOON IN GWEN'S STUDIO IN SOHO, WHERE HE'D CRASHED AFTER attending a student theater premiere, and got the news from a Bloomberg alert on his BlackBerry. Immediately he worried about her. He couldn't reach her on the phone, so he caught a cab to her place on Fifty-Fourth Street.

She was devastated. "I have so many friends who work downtown," she said, "and I can't get through to any of them!" Fortunately for her, she meant people who worked in bars, clubs, and restaurants, none of them likely to be anywhere near work at nine o'clock on a Tuesday. Residential development downtown was mostly confined to Battery Park City, and her friends were much too creative to buy in a place like that. They lived in Tribeca, Soho, the East Village, and, in one case (an older woman who gave Gwen individual instruction in yoga and could be relied on as a source of natural hallucinogens such as Hawaiian baby woodrose), Park Slope.

"That's voracious!" Joe said, misusing a word he'd only seen in print and took to be the opposite of "bodacious."

"It sucks ass," she said.

"Oh, it's universally in violation, like tapeworms squared," he agreed. "Is there anything righteous I can do for you? Maybe some grocery shopping?"

That question reminded her that she had needs—strong emotional needs that were probably going to be extra intense on this special day. She told Joe she didn't need anything. He suggested pizza. She agreed to eat some pizza.

While he was out getting them each one slice of pepperoni from a place on Fifty-First, she called her dealer Kenneth to ask if he had works. She wanted to inject heroin for a change, instead of just snorting it. She would combat the stress by spoiling herself, the way another person might observe a special occasion such as a divorce or the death of a parent by booking a week in a wellness spa.

Kenneth was still there when Joe returned. He had just hit Gwen's arm vein and offered to do Joe. "It's so good," she said to encourage him. "Oh, my. Mm-mm good."

"It makes you sleepy. How is that fun?"

"It's relaxing, and if you inject it you don't get addicted," she said. She meant in her particular case, because she didn't have the nerve to inject herself and always had to call for help. She couldn't do it with addictive frequency unless her dealer was also her boyfriend. "With all the shit that's going down out there, we need something like this to keep from getting freaked out," she added.

"It wears off fast," Kenneth said to Joe. "It's no biggie. You should try it."

"It'll spoil my appetite for pizza."

"Please?" Gwen said. "I'll be so sad and lonely if I have to do this by myself. We can reheat pizza for dinner."

"Okay," Joe said. "If it has to be, but only this one time."

"Later on we'll go downtown and help dig victims out of the rubble. Maybe somebody we know has one of those search and rescue dogs. Do you know anybody with a dog?" She sighed in a voluptuous manner. Kenneth grabbed her crotch and kissed her on the mouth. Joe was tolerant of that kind of thing, because they were life partners.

Kenneth gave him a shot with a brand-new, sterile hypodermic, fresh out of the shrink-wrap. He kind of eyeballed the dose, overestimating Joe's body weight. He was used to hitting larger guys. Joe weighed maybe one-forty. He could have used Kenneth's dose for girls just fine.

He said, "Oh, wow."

He leaned back on the couch and smiled, closing his eyes. Kenneth and Gwen moved closer together while he relaxed. He stretched once and shivered, eyes and mouth wide, as if the shadow of a convulsion were passing over him. Kenneth turned to him and listened.

"Did he fart?" Gwen asked.

"You all right?" Kenneth asked.

Joe breathed in hard, wheezing. He was unconscious. His heart had stopped beating. He inhaled again without exhaling. Kenneth felt his neck for a pulse.

When he stopped breathing, Kenneth was truly, madly, deeply surprised. "Call 911 right now," he said to Gwen as he gathered his equipment and fled, not latching the apartment door.

Being experienced, she wasn't disabled by the drug. She could see that something was wrong with Joe. Anyone could have seen it. He was turning gray. She was frantic. There was no one around to teach her CPR. The cell phone network was not working, and she couldn't get through to emergency services, not even from the landline. She screamed once, but when a neighbor knocked on the door, she froze. In her experience, her neighbors weren't helpful doctors. They were nasty spies. She dumped cold water on Joe. She laid his leather jacket over his wet, scary face.

X.

Ginger told Pam that she and Daniel would be sleeping in her old room, with Flora in the guest room. That surprised her. The guest room was larger, with a bigger bed. She knew that because she had always resented having the small room. Nor did she appreciate being sent with her husband to the room of her childhood.

She opened the door, intending to dump their knapsacks on the floor and go back downstairs. She stood very still. She remembered for the first time in a long time that as a teenager she had covered the flowered wallpaper in her room with an Elmer's-glue-based decoupage collage of found material on the topic of her favorite band.

At the time, quite a bit of diluted glue had landed in pools on the shag carpet, rendering the room, in Edgar's words, "a disaster area." When she left home, he had wanted to remodel it as a weight room and install a NordicTrack. Ginger refused. She let him replace the carpeting and the mattress, which had served Pam and her friends as a mosh pit and sagged like a hammock, but the collage was still there, along with her desk and her Tandy computer from RadioShack.

Her body and mind were already wobbly, and for an instant they became fifteen. She remembered what it had felt like to be herself. An amoeba of longing. An unformed thing that loved.

The fugue state receded. She returned to the present, whatever that was—the events of the day made it exceptionally hard to know—and observed with a philosophical eye that her recollections of having once greatly admired Ian MacKaye had been toned down somewhat in retrospect. The room in which she stood was a teen shrine to an all-consuming passion. It looked as though she had begged, bought, or stolen every magazine article and xeroxed broadsheet ever published about Minor Threat, liberated every flyer for every show from every bulletin board and phone pole in the capital, and devoted every waking hour to adorning his image with hearts and glitter. The ceiling had not been spared. The light switch plate by the door was decorated so that the toggle poked out of his crotch.

She stood still with her heart like a fist, aware in a way she'd never been before of the little girl she had once been. The haughty, insane child who ran away and broke her mother's heart, not because her mother was possessive, but because she was loved.

Daniel came upstairs to see why she was taking so long. "Holy fuck," he said. "I guess somebody liked Fugazi." That was Ian's best-known band.

"Fugazi was after I left D.C.," she said. "I was an early adopter."

"This light switch," he said.

WHEN THEY FINALLY SETTLED IN DOWNSTAIRS WITH THE TV, THEY FOUND OUT WHY they'd been so lonely on the highway. The nation was standing with New York. While Mayor Giuliani was exhorting downtowners to "get out," people from elsewhere were streaming into lower Manhattan to donate blood.

Pam went quietly into the kitchen to try Yuval again. He was not answering his cell phone. No one was at the RIACD office.

She tried Joe. He wasn't home. It didn't worry her. On his own, he might have rushed downtown with the rest of the volunteers. But his bitch? Not bloody likely. They were surely at her apartment, curled up on the sofa, eating pizza. Probably drinking or having sex—any old urge the carnival atmosphere of universal conflagration gave them license to indulge. She didn't worry about him. She didn't think of him much. Meanwhile, thoughts of Yuval followed her like an obsession. He was her stand-in for an entire city. She felt that everything would be all right as soon as she knew he was safe.

Possibly this was because he was the one person she had seen take a deliberate risk. If a victim, then not entirely blameless.

The events of the day had been surreal and dreamlike, a long string of clichés come true, except for those first few moments when it had been an incident, an accident, an incompetent or suicidal pilot. Accidents will happen; what doesn't happen is that casualties of war rain from the sky downtown. It upended her sense of the world. It seemed so obvious in retrospect. Killing us with our symbols—our arrogant, hubristic, late-hyper-capitalist architecture. The name alone. "World Trade." The neo-imperialist system of laissez-faire capital flow that had cracked South Asia and put its tentacles on China. In hindsight its advance was ineluctable, its fall inevitable, both to Daniel, who believed in Armageddon, and to Pam, who had parachuted into the North Tower once on a windy day in March. It was swaying so much that her desk chair never stopped rolling. The creaking in the walls keened long and high. On lower floors of older buildings she had heard similar sounds plenty of times. Waterfront buildings in the financial district whipped in a gale like pines. Old hands shared news of those days like fish stories. Gusts so stiff you couldn't cross Broad Street standing, wrists and faces sandblasted by dust, lungs scoured clean, the Staten Island Ferry listing with the wind, desk chairs rolling three feet with every blast. In a culture given to self-mythologizing, that wind would have had a name, like the Mistral or the Santa Ana. In the financial district, it was weather. She had looked down on cloud shadows sailing the golden waters of the harbor and heard the disquieting snapping of the building's nonredundant tendons, like the cables stabilizing a crow's nest on the topmast of a clipper ship. So that when the towers responded to the violation of their tense skins by collapsing, she was sort of surprised and sort of not. Even the attack itself was sort of surprising and sort of not. Who knew they had the nerve, and why did it take them so long?

Yuval was another question mark. Did he pause to get shots of people jumping? Did one of them land on him? What floor did his cousin work on? Did he go upstairs, as he had planned? Was he alive?

Knowing him, there was one thing she felt sure of: he had not walked away with the camera in his hand. He would document everything he could. Maybe he was at home now, cropping images on Photoshop. Maybe he'd lost his cell phone in the bedlam. It would be easy to call his parents—she knew their names; they had to be in the Israeli phone book—but it wasn't going to happen. She wasn't making a cold call to a rich, happy, generous man's parents to ask if he was alive. Better to wait a week and get the scuttlebutt at RIACD.

THE NEXT MORNING, THEY HAD TROUBLE GETTING FLORA ORGANIZED FOR THE ZOO. SHE was busy after breakfast in the backyard, trying to climb a tree. When the blue jays screamed at her, she screamed back. Ginger said, "Looks like she's having fun with animals already," and refused to call her in. Flora switched to inventing tricks on the rusty swing set, frequently falling to the grass. She stayed in the yard until lunch. The zoo was postponed to the thirteenth, and the four of them took a walk to the park to play badminton.

They lost her again at the elementary school monkey bars. Daniel said, "Let her play," but Ginger said the kids trapped indoors might be irritated to see one of their own playing during school hours. They could all get hauled in for truancy. They continued toward the park at an adult pace, while Flora skipped ahead with Pam's old jump rope from her toy chest in the attic of the garage.

Pam said, "I can't believe I hated this place so much. It's beautiful." The trees were huge, many of them native species like tulip, large enough to have been standing since Northwest D.C. was woods. The leaves were starting to turn. "Especially now that I live in a toxic waste dump that's on fire."

"Maybe Flora should stay here for a while," Ginger suggested.

"What—and take time off?"

"No. And go to fourth grade."

"And live with you?"

Ginger smiled, the passive-aggressive equivalent of an eye roll.

"I didn't mean it that way," Pam said. "I'm just wondering what you had in mind. Honestly, do I look to you like I want to take her back to Chinatown right now? I'm listening."

"You could all stay here for a while."

"I can't. I have a job."

Daniel said, "Supposedly, my office is expecting me to be on call next week."

"Well, you can't go home while the air is full of asbestos!"

They watched Flora jump rope. Crossing her arms for a simple trick, she tangled the rope and fell. She caught herself on her hands and knees on the sidewalk. It was fresh and white, swept clean by rain. There was not a single disk of filthy gum, much less thousands of such disks per block. No leaping fish were stenciled in yellow spray paint to say NO DUMPING! DRAINS TO BAY! over gutters full of dog shit, rat pelts, turpentine, and the dust of human remains. She stood, brushed a stray grain of mulch off a pink kneecap, and recommenced leaping from square to square of the immaculate pavement. A solitary car approached the stop sign and executed a full stop. The driver waved hello.

"I enjoy her so much," Ginger said. "It's like all the upsides of parenting and none of the downsides. By the time you were her age, I'd spent nine years yelling at you to stop doing stuff that was going to hurt you or make you sick, and you didn't take me seriously anymore. With Flora, it's different. It's like she's seizing her opportunity to be calm and relaxed."

"You have an ace in the hole," Pam said, granting Ginger her rose-colored rewrite of family history. "You didn't have to toilet train her."

"Well, I know exactly what you mean," Daniel said. "She's frolicking like a puppy down here. It's fun to watch."

Flora ran back to them, dragging the jump rope. Her eyes were wild with expectation. She looked at each of them in turn and then all three, seeking collective affirmation of a notion that had come to her suddenly and that she found too beautiful to believe, if it were true. They stood watching until she settled down enough to ask, "If I'm here, can I try riding bikes?"

"Does she not—" Ginger truncated her question.

"Yes," Pam said. "Tomorrow we'll get you a bike, and we'll show you how to ride. You can ride bikes any time when you're here."

"We always liked her too much to put her on a bike," Daniel explained.

They found a nice level place in a grove of trees to play doubles badminton out of the breeze. Flora played well, for a child beginner. Ginger remarked that the placidity of her surroundings might be helping her concentrate.

"No chance, Mom," Pam replied. "City life is what taught her that. Nothing makes you mindful and centered like nonstop chaos."

THE TOPIC OF SCHOOL WAS DISCUSSED IN MORE DETAIL AFTER DINNER ON THURSDAY. CNN was mercifully turned off—the terror alerts were starting to snowball—and Edgar had settled into his recliner with a cognac. Flora was asleep, worn out by a total zoo bliss experience.

It wasn't the discussion Pam expected, about how to enroll her in the nearest public elementary school. It revolved around the competing merits of Washington International School and the Episcopal girls' day school attached to the National Cathedral.

"International has a more diverse student body," Ginger said. "I think we should try there first, with Cathedral as a backup."

"It's more competitive," Edgar agreed. "I'll call Steve tomorrow. It might be open to a refugee. I know the headmaster."

"I don't get this," Pam said. "I went to public school."

Her parents looked at each other and then at Daniel. "You certainly did, sweetie," Ginger said. "But your father makes more money now. We can afford something better for Flora."

"By 'diverse' I guess you mean diplomatic brats of many nations. It's going to be a shock to her system, going back to P.S. Zero."

"What makes you put it that way?" Ginger said. "Is her school that bad?"

"Oh, God, her school. It's study hall and nothing else. But seriously, how is she going to feel? It's like giving a cat chicken. You know how after that, some of them refuse to eat anything else and starve?"

"Is this a way to talk about your own child?" Ginger said. "You could let her do the entire year here at a real school."

"And live with you?"

Daniel said, "Not happening. I couldn't do without her for more than a week."

"As if I could," Pam said.

"Earth to Pam," Edgar intervened. "Do you read?"

"Yes, Dad?"

"You live in lower Manhattan," he said. "You are not taking our granddaughter back there this week, next week, or the week after, and she has to go to school. We were looking for a workable solution, and I think we have one. What matters more—your selfish feelings or the health of a child? And how is a little time at one of the best private schools in the country going to hurt her?"

"We could go to Long Island for a while, or the Catskills. Get out of the city and commute."

"Or just move uptown," Daniel said. "Rents are going to be depressed. If you're in such a hurry to send her to private school, pay for Dalton or Trinity!"

"That's not the deal I'm offering," Edgar said. "You think because you had it rough, Flora should have it rougher. That's not parenting. It's hazing. Every generation should have it better than the one before. Resisting that principle of continuous improvement is wrong. It's nihilistic."

"Improvement of what?" Pam said. "Was I the beta version?"

SHE AND DANIEL RETIRED TO BED SOON AFTER, CLAIMING EXHAUSTION. THEY PAUSED on their way to stare long and hard at the sleeping Flora.

"Your dad makes me nervous," Daniel whispered. "They're both kind of domineering."

"I don't know what to do," Pam said.

"We're a family. We stay together."

"But they're family too. It's not like we'd be putting her in an orphanage. You know how she gets along with them."

"You're just scared to go home, and you're projecting your fear on Flora."

"Is that so wrong?"

WHEN PAM WAS A CHILD, GINGER HAD VOLUNTEERED ON PROJECTS LIKE THE LIBRARY book fair and the garden club house tour. Currently she taught English to undocumented immigrants and chaired a citizen's initiative to preserve wild meadows. She was a perfectionist, too High Church in her hereditary Protestantism to believe in salvation by faith. Whatever she believed in, she had to walk the walk.

She believed in beauty. Accordingly, the Bailey home was spotless and uncluttered. Morning hot chocolate was not microwaved Nestlé Quik, but dark squares melted with peppermint oil in organic milk and decanted into a demitasse that looked like an adult coffee cup, only Flora-sized. Before lunch, instead of sending guests to the fridge—the only place in the Chrystie Street loft where food was safe from vermin—for bread and peanut butter, she would kindly ask Flora to remove cut glass dishes from the china cabinet and dispatch her outside with shears to cut blooms for a centerpiece. Sandwich fixings were shaved into slices fit for dolls, even the already tiny gherkins, and Flora was allowed to choose among an assortment of napkin rings. The dining room had four large, high, many-paned windows edged with canvas drapes bearing an oversized pattern of birds and magnolias. The napkins matched the drapes. Everything outside the windows was green or blue, except for the pink climbing roses and massed white hydrangeas.

In short, daily life in Cleveland Park was more festive than holidays at home, and the house was prettier than anything in Manhattan south of Henri Bendel.

Daniel began to develop secret thoughts he didn't express directly to Pam, but he didn't have to. Three mornings in a row, they woke up by themselves, without Flora in the bed, after eight o'clock, well rested and on fire to have sex. He said, "If we're not careful, we're going to have another kid," and Pam didn't even take it the wrong way. She knew what he meant. Flora existed, and the whole universe depended on her, but a couple also existed—

the two of them—now cheerful, curious individuals who were getting enough sleep, because Flora went from bed straight to the kitchen. Ginger and Edgar were always up at six, watching ABC and reading the *Washington Post*.

On Saturday they experimented with staying in bed all morning, getting up only to sneak to the bathroom. Flora brought breakfast at nine thirty on a silver-plated tray. She was proud of her weightless waffles. She had separated the eggs herself.

"My family truly does have the best waffle recipe," Pam said.

"And the best short-order cook this side of St. Louis," Daniel said.

"You're a culinary genius," Pam told Flora.

"Thanks! I ate two waffles and ham and a kiwi." She patted her stomach.

"I feel like one of those parents in the Blitz, sending their kids out to live in the countryside," Daniel said. "It's like she got picked for the Fresh Air Fund."

"It's like *The Lion, the Witch and the Wardrobe*," Pam said. "That's around here somewhere. Let me ask Mom where she put it. We can read it aloud to her."

ALSO ON SATURDAY THE FIFTEENTH, PAM FINALLY HAD AN E-MAIL FROM YUVAL. HE HAD ended up in the hospital, unharmed. He didn't remember anything after the second plane. His camera was gone, and he had no idea when RIACD would reopen. He invited her to take time off.

Daniel's temp agency made the same suggestion, if only because so many of its contracts had been canceled.

She suggested going to the zoo again, but Ginger wanted to take Flora to a department store in Silver Spring and get her something to wear to church. Pam said that would be a step too far. Habituating Flora to comfort and beauty, she could almost handle; tempting her with God was too much. This particular God came armed with flying buttresses and pipe organs, the Episcopalian double whammy of medieval architecture and the music of the Reformation. The cathedral might make Flora wonder what great things God had done to deserve it.

"Please, Mom?" Flora begged.

Pam envisioned her singing along with the Magnificat and shook her head. That was the most bone-chillingly beautiful song in the service, the responsorial in which Mary declares her devotion to God because he requisitioned her for purposes of childbearing. She mutely considered how to express the idea that there were few things she'd rather protect Flora from than the church. After a terrorist attack, even a little child can tell good from evil. Singing about evil's hidden goodness is nothing but a straight-up mind fuck.

"It's her heritage," Ginger insisted. "If she's never exposed to it, she's statistically more likely to join a cult. You went to church every Sunday, and unless you count worshipping that punk rocker, you're the most devout atheist I know!"

"Won't you please go shopping with us?" Flora begged.

"Silver Spring is kind of nice," Pam said, defeated.

She never went to department stores in New York, because they were either packed with third-rate junk or so overpriced and sterile that she wondered whether their real business was money laundering—plastic belts for hundreds of dollars, shoes under glass in the coat department, that sort of thing. The mall anchor stores of Silver Spring were by contrast bustling havens of middle-class pragmatism, where quality and price intersected with near-utopian felicity. Style in the South was personal. A woman who liked plaid could find clothes in plaid. Pam liked plaid. She knew that by agreeing to go shopping she was acquiescing in church attendance the next morning, so she added, "But I'm only going to church if I find a hot outfit to show off."

THE FEMALES WENT OUT SHOPPING. EDGAR TOOK HIS BIG CLIPPERS FROM THE SHED AND commenced trimming shrubs by hand. Daniel sat in an Adirondack chair next to a glass-topped wrought-iron table to drink coffee and read the paper, lulled by the repetitive shearing sound of clippers opening and closing on late-summer growth and tufts of grass. All the articles were fascinating. He felt oddly happy.

His phone rang. It was Gwen.

She said she was at her father's place in Great Neck, totally broken up, and that she'd stayed with Joe for a day and a night before she'd decided it was just too much to deal with.

"You what?" Daniel said quietly.

"I left him at my place."

"Is he okay?"

She sobbed. She sounded drunk. "He wasn't moving."

"Was he hurt? Where is he now?"

"He's still there."

"You mean he was unconscious, and you left him?"

"He was dead, okay? He was blue and dead. Nobody could have helped him. It was too late, and it was just too fucking much to deal with on a day like that."

"You fucking bitch."

"Fuck you! No one was helping me. There were, like, no ambulances."

"I'm going to call the police and have you arrested for murder," Daniel said. "It's murder. You murdered him. And he's in your apartment? Where?"

"On the couch."

"I meant which of your apartments, you worthless fucking cunt."

Gwen hung up, and Edgar said to Daniel, "Good Lord! What was that about?"

Daniel slammed the phone down on the table, stood up, and started to cry.

XI.

Gwen hung up on Daniel on the afternoon of September 15, sitting in the tall rocking chair in her bedroom in her father's house in Great Neck. She felt tempted to open her heart to her dad when he got home. She couldn't imagine taking any other tack with him but the truth. He had been seeing through her all her life, ever since she had been born with intent to inherit his possessions. She would confess the truth, and he would tell his lawyer. Together they would fix everything and protect her.

But the truth wasn't something she wanted anyone to know. She didn't like how it made her look. Joe's dying went beyond venereal diseases and investing in friends' failed businesses. There was a sense, she felt dimly, in which it couldn't be fixed.

She sent Daniel's return call to voice mail and turned off her phone.

STILL STANDING ON THE PATIO IN CLEVELAND PARK, STILL CRYING, HE PUT HIS PHONE in his pocket and said to Edgar, "I'm sorry about this."

"Who was that on the line?"

"Joe's girlfriend. She's not a good person. He's in trouble. But I can't dial 911 from here for an emergency in New York. Can they transfer the call? Shit. What do I do? I don't know where he is."

"Get somebody in New York to call them."

He called Joe's dad and said, "Hi. It's Daniel. It's an emergency."

"Have you heard from Joe?" Professor Harris responded. "I'm very worried."

He took a deep breath and declared that he had taken his family to Washington when the planes hit, to stay with Pam's parents. It wasn't the most important aspect, but it felt like a necessary finger of blame pointed at himself, before he got to the point, which was that sometime on the eleventh—shortly after he, the paterfamilias, feeling proud of his initiative and ingenuity, fled the bleeding city like a rat—Gwen had abandoned the unconscious Joe in either her larger apartment on West Fifty-Fourth Street or her smaller apartment in Soho. Most likely Soho, because he'd gone to a party downtown, but anything was possible, so could Professor Harris please get the police to break into both places.

"I'm doing it right now," he answered promptly. His vital systems didn't miss an audible beat. Daniel could hear that there was no question in his mind that Joe was alive.

He relaxed for a half second, until the connection clicked off and his phone went dead. Then the likely state of affairs came flooding back into his mind. He knew what would happen if he told Pam he was going to New York. She would come along and bring Flora. He didn't want to take Flora into that mess of a ruined city, plus he didn't want her to know anything had happened to their friend. If she were at their side, overhearing things, she would catch on fast. Just seeing her parents homicidally angry, with their hearts broken, would tell her. The idea of leaving her in D.C. for a while took on a new luster.

He asked Edgar what he thought of his going home to take

care of business while Pam stayed on with Flora. He needn't have asked. Edgar's notions of propriety were untroubled by the prospect of a man's protecting his wife and child.

Daniel went upstairs to pack his tiny bag. He said, "Have Pam call me in private when she gets in," and took the red line to Union Station. He caught the next fast train to New York.

WITHIN TEN MINUTES OF TURNING OFF HER PHONE, GWEN TURNED IT ON AGAIN. SHE WAS surprised—almost hurt—to see so few missed calls. She leafed through the Yellow Pages until she found an ad for a funeral home close to her place on Fifty-Fourth. She called it. Excitedly, she told the man who answered the phone that she had found her boyfriend dead in her apartment, an apparent suicide. He had overdosed on intravenous drugs. She had panicked and gone to visit her father, because she couldn't stand to see his body or enter that apartment ever again. Could the undertaker please get the key from the super and do something about her dead boyfriend?

She cried. The selfishness of her egomania allowed her to embody the purest sorrow without a trace of regret. She found the undertaker sympathetic and even cute, if a bit depressive. He'd probably lost some friends or something. She surmised that the whole city was going to be on the rebound for a while—easy to get, but not much fun to be around.

What he said, in terms of informational content, was that it sounded to him like a case for the police. When she objected that the deceased was past all help, he suggested an ambulance. When she insisted he was dead, he said he would go take a look.

He really was tempted. After all, it would have been a job. The terrorist attacks had proved disappointing in the corpse department.

He asked her for information on Joe's next of kin. She said she would prefer anonymity. He asked again, saying it was for billing purposes, and she gave him Joe's father's name and address.

Now firm in his resolution not to touch the job with a ten-foot pole, because she was upper class and drunk, the undertaker called his local precinct, which dispatched a car to West Fifty-Fourth Street.

A separate law enforcement detail met Professor Harris in Soho. They couldn't gain entrance to the building courtyard until a resident happened to let herself in. The studio had a thick steel door with a long, old-fashioned bolt. By the time they gave up and headed to the other apartment, it was sealed up with red tape and a crimped metal tag, and Joe was in the morgue.

PAM CAME HOME TO PORTER STREET TIRED AND HAPPY, STUFFED WITH CINNAMON BUNS and cappuccino. The mall had been relatively empty of people, with lots of seasonal markdowns. She'd gotten a great deal on a tailored plaid pantsuit that was funkier than its creators intended, along with a bottle-green velvet dress with a lace collar for Flora, whose mental state approached nirvana. She called Daniel from the guest room as his train was rolling northward through Newark, Delaware.

When the phone rang he huddled against the window and stared at the distant water. The neighborhood outside was stained gray and black over every surface, but beyond it lay green trees and the blue of the northern reaches of the Chesapeake. He heard Pam say "hello" and "Daniel" several times. Finally he said, "Hi."

"Are you somewhere else?" Pam asked. "Dad said you just up and left."

"Are you lying down in the fetal position?"

"No."

"You will be. Gwen called to say she left Joe for dead a few days ago. He was unresponsive and his skin was blue. I can't imagine why. She didn't really say where. I'm on my way to team up with his dad."

She felt her consciousness take a leap and fall, as if it were trying for an out-of-body experience but couldn't reach escape velocity. Her mind was wiped blank, except for an afterimage of Joe, like a photographic negative, with all the colors wrong.

Culture came to the rescue. Like a Möbius strip revolving, her mind twisted into eighties hipster mode. Their conversation after that was pitched low and on the inside, knowing and hopeless, every clause meaning and mourning its opposite. There was no need to make anybody cry by saying anything true.

She said, "He was so obsessive about shooting up heroin all the goddamn time." That is, they both knew he had never tried it.

"The wages of sin is death," Daniel replied, a reference to Joe's innocence.

"Well, don't bother getting off the train, because I'm heading up there right now to put a Bowie knife up her nose and twist it until her eyes pop out, and I don't want you involved."

"Don't do that," he said, acknowledging her desire never to see Gwen again. "Kid needs her mother out of jail."

"She's not going to like this," she said, starting to cry.

She let him go. She entered the Temple of Ian, lay down in the fetal position, and stared. Thoughts of Flora made her cry. Thoughts of Joe made her imagine a golden flaming sword, the one she would use to kill Gwen if life were more like D&D.

All Washingtonians sometimes imagine golden flaming swords, because of the Second Infantry Division memorial on Constitution Avenue. A golden hand holds it upright like a torch. It serves to remind God's children that there is no appeal for their entrapment by the serpent. They can't visit paradise one last time. It's too late.

On the train, Daniel punched the seat back in front of him several times, after making sure it was empty.

THE CASE LEFT A COMPLEX AFTERMATH BEHIND. BUT IT WOULD NEVER BE INTERESTING for a police detective. The cause of death was not in question. There were no signs of a struggle. Daniel and Professor Harris

tried to convince the detectives that Joe would never have struggled against anything, because he was as trusting as a lamb. In
separate conversations, the detectives explained to them that while
murder is murder and manslaughter is manslaughter, criminal indictment is also criminal indictment, and no prosecutor could expect a grand jury to believe a groupie killed her meal ticket. Gold
diggers murder husbands, but why would a junkie hanger-on kill
an unrelated rock star? Such a woman might attack a rival, but
not the goose who laid the golden eggs. They needed to admit to
themselves that Joe had used heroin and that he died of routine
risks attendant on using heroin.

He hadn't made a will. He had second cousins in Denver
whom he'd never met. Everything he owned, and every cent he
was owed, would go to his father.

Inheriting tortured Professor Harris. He cried soundlessly at
odd moments. He felt passive and sad. Whenever he made up his
mind to lie down, his mood plummeted and his alert level rose
to DEFCON 2. Sitting upright in an armchair at night was less
terrifying, less like surrender. Objects and purchases frightened
him. There might be anthrax on a parking meter, or a gladiola, or
butter.

He fit right in—better than most. His son really was gone.
He was immune to the pandemic of disaster envy that was turning the lower forty-eight into an endless phone call from a distant
noncombatant with a tale of near-proximity to a marginal feature
of the very bad day, such as Logan Airport.

Gwen likewise was upset about Joe's death. Just a wreck. Being
wrecked was inconspicuous in those days. Everyone was emotional
and reaching out. Everyone was vulnerable and wounded. Everyone expected, and got, tremendous generosity and tolerance. The
air in New York was thick with smoke and love. Love poured into
a city whose inhabitants were not used even to being liked. People
drank oodles of liquor and hugged on a whim.

It was a relief to Daniel when the conspiracy theories surfaced, reviving the blood libel with tales of Jewish office workers who stayed home that day. He had come to the city for its reputation as Sodom, Gomorrah, and Hymietown. If Amerikkka—as an all-American boy he knew his country well—suddenly appreciated New York, something was wrong. Racist conspiracy theories were its way of taking notice and correcting its error.

In New York in those days, Daniel felt alone in being consciously animated by a spirit of cynicism and hatred.

BECAUSE PROFESSOR HARRIS WAS INCAPACITATED, IT WAS DANIEL WHO DID THE DEATH-related legwork, organizing Joe's interment. On the street in the West Village, he ran into a session guitarist who told him of having bought Joe's gold Les Paul for $5,000 directly from Gwen. She had told him the proceeds would benefit an as yet nonexistent charity, the Joe Harris Foundation.

Daniel knew the guitar. It was beat up and mutilated, with a replacement neck and the pickups switched out for custom-wrapped magnets so Joe could sound more like Queen. He knew the guy had overpaid by about $4,500. He thought, She's testing the waters.

He wasn't fixated on keeping Joe's possessions together like some kind of archive or his property inviolate. But he knew Gwen. He knew Joe hadn't left her any money. But she had the keys to his apartment, and she had two options. She could keep herself in extra drugs for a few years by working her way through his stuff slowly, or she could fledge her wings and fly up a level, leveraging his fame to enter the nonprofit world. Instead of selling relics below cost, junkie style, she could generate media sympathy and clear $50,000 in an afternoon.

Joe's father resented her enough to agree that something had to be done. Mostly, though, he was depressed. He admitted he would have waited two years to ask her for the keys, if he ever thought of asking. He told Daniel, "It doesn't matter to me what that woman does or doesn't do. I don't care. I don't."

"I know you don't care," Daniel said. "I have a kid. I don't want to know what you're going through, because I couldn't handle it. So let me handle hating Gwen. I can hate Gwen for you." Here he could see that even the idea of a younger person handling something made Professor Harris cry, because he had once had a kid who might—had things been different—have handled things. With cruelty toward all involved, he added, "Joe has nothing left to lose, but Gwen can still win. She took everything he had, so let's not let her turn it into everything he had and more. Let's stop her winning. It's basic justice."

"Justice," Professor Harris said.

"Yes," Daniel said. "We make her stop."

"Nothing will bring him back."

"That's what you think! She's going around telling people she's chief executive of the Joe Harris Foundation. She's going to put his face on an ad campaign and auction his stuff for charity. You want her to get away with that?"

"I can't stop her."

"That's not true. You own his image."

"I own . . . his image . . ."

His face dampened with tears, and Daniel saw that the animus of resistance has a hard row to hoe in a world where everybody wants a hug.

HE AND PAM RITUALIZED THEIR PHONE CALLS. SHE ASKED QUESTIONS ABOUT THE city, and he gave honest answers. They behaved like two cats hit by separate cars, each recovering in its own secret hiding place. Sometimes, if it was daytime, he whispered sad stories of the death of Joe. Pam never said Joe's name. They traded endearments and encouragement and signed off. Flora was always waiting impatiently to demand the line so she could describe her day to Daniel.

She was settling into the National Cathedral School. Her activities were more diverse than he thought possible. He thought of little kids as having fantasies, but she had interests and ambitions. She was learning ballet and gymnastics. She wanted a computer, roller skates, and a hamster.

HIGH GOTHIC PILLARS CARRIED THE CATHEDRAL'S STAR-DAPPLED CEILING. THE CHAPEL of St. John, where student services were held, was to the right of the altar, a long walk from the entrance. The soundtrack of distant echoes and muffled heel impacts was soothing as a fountain. Sometimes an organist would play Bach or improvise a cadenza that filled the receding heights with a scaffold of music. Each window illustrated a religious fable. Each chair in the chapel had a kneeler worked in needlepoint with some fabled aspect of American history, not excluding the Confederate aspects.

At Thursday services the girls followed along in *The Book of Common Prayer*. "God of all power . . ." they prayed. "At your command all things came to be: the vast expanse of interstellar space, galaxies, suns, the planets in their courses, and this fragile earth, our island home."

Flora liked that a lot. This fragile earth, our island home.

"From the primal elements," the book continued, "you brought forth the human race and blessed us with memory, reason, and skill. You made us the rulers of creation. But we turned against you, and betrayed your trust . . ."

Occasionally they sang Pam's pet peeve, the Magnificat. Flora preferred the Song of Simeon, when he declares that Jesus will grow up to be a light to lighten the Gentiles and the glory of his people Israel. In the cathedral, she could definitely identify with the career goal of becoming a light. It was dark inside even on sunny days. All natural illumination was obscured by stained-glass images of church dignitaries, prophets, and other forgotten leaders. In the gloom, racks of candles threw haloes upward on the sad faces of the saints.

JOE'S CDS DIDN'T CHART AGAIN AFTER HIS DEATH. HIS STORY WAS OVERSHADOWED BY the rain of terror alerts. College radio DJs looking to honor his memory played his lo-fi cover of "Bird in God's Garden," a neo-pseudo-Sufi-hippie-Gnostic number he'd learned off a Richard Thompson record. The track was a pirated demo, not an official release, but it was easy to find on file-sharing networks.

His funeral was not well attended, because the bereaved were careful to tell no one about it. Not every burial can shake off unwanted attendees by transplanting itself to a mansion in the backcountry of a private island, the way a wedding can. Joe was not scheduled to be strewn to the glamorous four winds or sifted into a glamorous ocean. He was to be buried next to his mother in Flushing, Queens.

Daniel engaged the same funeral home that had taken care of her, and they did a closed-casket-style embalming job that kept the body inert without doing anything for its outward appearance. In death, Joe wore no makeup. You could have told he was dead from two hundred feet away. Only Professor Harris looked inside the coffin, to make sure it was his son and not a nightmare. When Joe was lowered into the vault, there was no one present but the two of them, a Presbyterian minister, and the guy who drove the backhoe.

After the service, walking through the cemetery gates to the bus stop, Daniel saw Professor Harris standing by his car. He had a key in the driver's-side door, but he wasn't turning it. He didn't look like he ought to be driving. Daniel offered to drive him home.

When the engine started, Professor Harris turned off the traffic update on WCBS. After a few miles, he spoke. "Daniel," he said. "I know that woman was in his life for a long time. Do you think they were considering children?"

He was grasping at straws. Joe had been a copy of his wife, so why shouldn't a grandchild be another one? It would be real-life reincarnation. He didn't want the unique excesses of trust and musicality that had marked his wife and son to be gone from the world forever. The thing he loved most could not become extinct, even if it took siring a child on Gwen.

"You need to resist these loving impulses," Daniel said, driving slower to give them more time. "That girl is a piece of shit. She killed him and got away with it. Now, I know forgiving her and accepting her into the family would simplify matters for you, but you'd be surrendering to the unconditional enemy. You'd be bowing down to a piece of shit and promising it eternal obeisance for killing your son. You can't submit like that. You have to keep the aversion alive. If it bothers you to hate her, put it in symbolic terms. Dehumanize her. You can depersonalize her without forgiving her for anything. You don't have to forgive her to forget her. You can hate and forget."

"Everyone's going crazy," Professor Harris said.

"I mean it. Forget Gwen, and hate what she stands for. Don't think you have to hate the sin and love the sinner. She's a walking, talking sin. So hate her ass. She won't feel it. There's no such thing as a thought crime. Think whatever you want. We both know you're not going to take revenge or even talk to her. But please, please, don't feel like you have to repress the fact that she's bad news. Don't engage with her. She met Joe by chance. Where women were concerned, he was first come, first served, and she was the gatekeeper."

"You've put a lot of thought into this."

"I sure as shit have," he said. "I was worried you might be hoping she was pregnant. Trust me, if she were, you'd know it by now. She'd be hitting you up for drug money and telling you she was using it to detox in rehab for your beautiful grandbaby. She's a user and a liar, and he loved her as much as he ever loved me."

Professor Harris looked out the window for a while. They crossed the Fifty-Ninth Street Bridge and waited at long crosstown lights without another word. Daniel turned into the entrance of the garage. When Professor Harris saw the parking attendant coming, he turned to Daniel and said, "Well, you stopped me crying. Thanks. I don't think I can cry anymore."

"You were in a trap," Daniel said. "You were a nice guy looking for somebody to be nice to, like the proverbial hammer that thinks everything is a nail. Fuck that noise."

"Fuck it," Professor Harris agreed. Tipping the attendant, he said, "You want to come upstairs for a little while and listen to some records? He had some songs that make no sense to me. Maybe you know what he was getting at."

"I feel like I knew him so well, I could run a simulation. It wouldn't be convincing because the randomosity would be missing, but I'll give it a shot."

In the elevator, Professor Harris said, "'Randomosity'? You mean randomness?"

Daniel leaned back and looked in the mirror. He looked haggard, with dark circles under his eyes, but Professor Harris looked worse, like a white rabbit with hay fever. He said, "I guess. It's my name for what separates us from machines. The lack of intelligent design. The way we get dropped into the world. Normal people play by the rules and act surprised when something seems arbitrary. Joe surfed the randomosity. It wouldn't have surprised him that he's dead now. He believed in the Archangel Arbitron." He was making it up as he went along, but it felt true.

Professor Harris didn't answer. Up in the apartment, he poured Daniel a glass of brandy and cued up a seven-inch titled "Raoraorao," backed with "To My Shame." He played the B side first.

"Oh, this," Daniel said.

Joe sang:

Sah awah away anoh
Dona wada hyda foh
Hawa tease an dass falaw
Dona wa-ah russo har . . .

"He's pretending to be wasted," he explained. "He's imitating this guy we used to know who sang bad anti-folk, Drunk Gareth. He liked the way it sounded, so he put it out."

"I like the melody."

"So did he. He heard somewhere that Madonna always uses early vocal takes from when the song's still fresh, so he decided to stick with the improvised version."

"I thought he was speaking in tongues, like Shelley's skylark."

"No, it's the Madonna influence. The A side's even better. It's about Drunk Gareth's cat, Gareth the Cat. His girlfriend named her cat after him and then left it with him to take care of while she went to Australia for a year. Obviously she never came back to pick it up, and he was stuck with the cat, which was a really jealous cat."

"Gareth sounds like he had his reasons to stay drunk."

They sang along with "Raoraorao," which had easy lyrics.

XII.

The principle of hating the sin and loving the sinner took hold of the nation. As evidence mounted that the attackers were Saudi subjects in thrall to Saudi aristocrats, the USA prepared to invade Afghanistan and Iraq. The sin of terrorism had to be fought wherever it appeared. If it was cut off at the root—in the Fertile Crescent where God planted his orchard, the birthplace of civilization—there could be no more terrorism.

Even on the Left it was held that oppressed, disempowered people would turn to terrorism. Yet oppression was nearly universal, while terrorists were measured in parts per billion. Maybe if state terror had been included along with civil war and genocide by neglect, the body count could have attained statistical significance? That was not the point. The point was to imagine terrorists as great men, originators and bearers of epochal ideas, ritual scapegoats worthy of custom-tailored deaths. Great men were rare. That was something great men could always agree on.

to school with homework done would have gotten her teased. Her friends at Cathedral did their homework as naturally as breathing. She even did chores, cheerfully, as though she enjoyed maintaining order in the lovely house. Nothing icky—that was the maid's prerogative—but it was almost too easy to rope her into shiny jobs like polishing table legs or washing every leaf on a large rubber plant.

Meanwhile, in lower Manhattan, grime filled the streets. Joe had become inexplicable. Daniel was prickly and inconsolable. With Flora around, he might have turned into one of those dandler dads who wake kids up at midnight to play. Pam wouldn't have minded staying in Cleveland Park herself until his personal storm blew over. But she had to get back to work. She'd been gone for almost a month. RIACD's clients were interested in security and stability to an unprecedented degree. They had become suddenly and vividly aware of the capacity of systems to fail. They had learned the technical meaning of failure, which was not bankruptcy and disgrace and suicide. It was the preordained failure of ostensibly minor parts of any system more complex than a bonfire.

She volunteered her Atari money, which had grown to almost $7,000, to help pay the Cathedral tuition. Daniel came down to D.C. for the weekend, and he and Pam rode the train home together, holding hands. Not clasped, but in that strange way sad people will do sometimes, tensely wringing each other's fingers. A stark contrast divided them from others in their city. They were mourning other dead. They knew where to find their bin Laden—on Fifty-Fourth Street, on her brand-new white puffy sofa.

GINGER ORGANIZED A RECEPTION TO INTRODUCE FLORA TO HER OLD FRIENDS, A THURS-day afternoon tea with a stuffed animal theme. Most of them lived in heirloom homes with attics, so they could still find the stuffed animals they had in childhood. The preparations were elaborate, with silver and Irish porcelain to be polished and dusted, little bouquets of violets to be tied up with ribbons as party favors, and a cream cake from an Austrian patisserie. The party would have been an embarrassment if the women had been uncool, but they were not. They didn't talk down to anyone, even Secretariat. Rather than patronize Flora with gifts, they acted as if their bears had freely chosen to spend time eating cake with her horse.

The result was weird and magical, the kind of theater only a fair-sized group of conspiratorial adults can pull off with a child of nine—a make-believe world of total benignity, like a Halloween haunted house, but the opposite. After they left, Flora sat for a long time at the table without moving, reliving the bears' witticisms, radiant with the feeling that real life was precious.

HER WEEKENDS CAME AND WENT WITH REGULAR VISITS FROM HER PARENTS AND NO word from Joe. That was nothing unusual. He had been touring on and off for years. When she asked them when he was coming back, they said they weren't sure. Every day they put off telling her made her more mature and better able to handle the news. They correctly assumed that her classmates were too young to talk about rock stars. Edgar knew the truth, but he was uninvolved. He left telling Ginger up to Pam. It didn't happen.

Flora's Christmas vacation started in mid-December, to give the students' families time to shop and ski. In downtown New York the streets were at last clear of debris. Pam went down to Washington to pick her up. The plan was to spend a week in New York, see the Christmas decorations in Midtown, take her ice-skating, and bring her back for the holidays.

On Pam's arrival in Cleveland Park, it emerged that Ginger had helped Flora buy a present for Joe. Ginger was no more likely than a nine-year-old to follow the careers of rock stars, so she had financed an EBow for eighty dollars at a guitar shop in Arlington. It was a little battery-operated device you could hold over an electric guitar string to make it tremble indefinitely, like a violin string. Flora looked forward very much to presenting it to Joe. She explained to her mother that you would have heard it on his records if he owned one, but you didn't, so he didn't.

Pam pointed out that he never played guitar on his records. She was as much in denial as anyone. She was in nearly the same holding pattern as Flora, not processing what had happened. She had the example of Daniel right in front of her all the time as a warning, to show her what happened to people who made recent events the object of deliberate contemplation.

She told him on the phone that it was a hell of their own creation. He suggested that the females return together to the music shop to trade the EBow for a ukulele, which Flora could play in Joe's memory. That would beat surprising her with the news in New York, unless Pam wanted an EBow.

"I could use one for sure," she said. "But not this one."

First she told her mother, citing cardiac arrest as the cause of death.

"My God," Ginger replied. "That poor boy. His poor father. I'm so sorry." She went to her desk to compose a note to Professor Harris.

Pam went up to Flora's room and sat her down on the bed, declaring that she had something to say. She said she had been waiting until Flora was old enough to understand, and now that she was almost ten, it was time. She said, "On September eleventh, Joe died."

"When everybody died?"

"He died too."

Flora didn't cry. She didn't even get upset. She said she would light candles for him at the cathedral. She'd been in a religious school for all of three months, and apparently she no longer regarded death as the end. Yet she must have realized it was the end of corporeal existence and all material needs, because she also suggested trading in the EBow, but for a violin instead of a ukulele.

She pointed out that a violin also has four strings like a bass. She said, "I'm going to play violin for Joe in the school orchestra!"

Pam gave her a hug and said, "You'll always be his best friend."

She spoke to her mother and father about it after dinner, and they agreed to rent Flora a good three-quarter violin and get her lessons. There was a violin maker just up Connecticut Avenue, and teachers were available through the school.

Later that night, Pam found one of Flora's pictures of Joe on the dresser in the Temple of Ian, propped on a little toy easel. A spaniel puppy, extracted for purposes of photography from a box of dogs for sale in Tompkins Square Park, was peeking from his pouched T-shirt like a baby kangaroo. He looked about as happy as a person can look.

GWEN GAVE AN INTERVIEW TO THE ROCK & ROLL YEARBOOK EDITION OF *ROLLING STONE*. Daniel read the entire thing aloud to Pam in the café at the Borders bookstore in Friendship Heights, as a break from last-minute shopping on Christmas Eve. He couldn't buy the magazine to take home. He felt he'd be damned if he bought it, and also that up until that moment he'd never truly understood the expression "I'll be damned if I do X."

> Rock singer-songwriter Joe Harris revitalized fin-de-siècle
> music with unexpected genre explorations that ran the
> gamut from the funk-inflected 1996 breakout single
> "Chugalug" to 1998's worldwide EDM hit "Secretariat."
> He blended the manic energy of a hyperactive teen
> with the laser focus of a mature artist, prompting
> critic Greil Marcus to label his work "psychedelia for
> the age of speed." The announcement of his untimely
> death stunned fans already numbed by the sorrow
> of one of America's darkest days. We spoke with
> Gwendolyn Charanoglu, 27, inseparable partner of his

rise from obscurity. It fell to her to find his body in her Manhattan apartment when she returned home on the evening of September 11—too late. Medical personnel could do nothing to reverse his death by heroin overdose. He was 33.

RS: First, let me express our deepest condolences from myself and all the staff at *Rolling Stone*. Did you ever suspect that Joe Harris was planning anything like this?
GC: Never, though it made sense to me afterward. He was so hypersensitive. All that destruction and death, he simply couldn't face it. There were no signs that he planned it in advance. We were all helpless to do anything. I'm sorry.
RS: I know this is very recent to be talking about. But there have been reports of a suicide note. Can you confirm that?
GC: There was a notebook near his body that he'd been writing in. I'd like to share some of it with you. He said—this is so hard—"The world is past the sell-by date. On a backward planet, it's always too late."

"I know what that's about," Daniel commented. "In June, Victor took a two-hundred-thousand-dollar loss on the NASDAQ, and Margie tried to pin it on the retrograde motion of Mercury. He probably wrote a song for them." He continued reading aloud.

RS: Were you aware that he suffered from depression?
GC: That's an easy diagnosis to make in retrospect. But definitely no. He was always happy, no matter what.
RS: Perhaps that was his way of masking a deeper despair. To your knowledge, did he use heroin regularly?
GC: I wish I'd known. I'm ashamed now that I didn't even

IT TOOK GWEN WEEKS TO FOLLOW UP WITH THE FUNERAL HOME. WHEN SHE REALIZED that Joe was already in the ground, she bombarded Daniel with voice mails, complaining (among other things) that she'd bought a $3,000 dress. He texted her that she'd saved on flowers. Ten minutes later, he got a call from Daktari, asking where Joe was buried so the company could send a wreath. He said it wasn't the fucking Kentucky Derby. And so on.

He missed Flora, but the pain was hard to localize among the ambient pain. His face was a mask. He cried in his sleep. Because his fantasies were violent, he saw himself as suppressing white-hot rage. He wasn't suppressing anything. Grief and anger were what he had.

For that and other reasons, Pam felt more or less justified in lending her parents a daughter. Having deployed the nuclear option of disappearance against the conventional weapon of corporal punishment, she could even see it as reparations, and Flora liked it. She was nine years old, a sleepover veteran, big enough to go to summer camp. In D.C., she had her own room. A white picket fence enclosed a backyard with walnut trees. Bikes could be safely ridden. Nearby pandas were free to socialize.

She didn't miss her friends. The loft didn't have a phone (cell phones were still considered a radiation hazard for children), so she had never gotten in the habit of calling them. Her friendships had arisen from proximity, with people she'd seen as a matter of course in school, the store, or the park. The same method made her new friends within days. To make sure she didn't lose touch, Edgar took her to a sundries shop, where she picked out postcards for Joe/Gwen, Victor/Margie, her former teacher/classmates, and coach/b-ball team.

She enjoyed her new school so much that Pam felt ashamed of having put up with her old one. Whether she did homework was of no import to her grandparents. Oddly, this state of affairs led to an explosion in the doing of homework. At "P.S. Zero," coming know the warning signs. I know I shouldn't blame myself. Self-harm is never anyone's fault. But I should have realized he had moved on to hard drugs.

RS: There's been speculation that the acoustic demo of "Bird in God's Garden" that's been making the rounds was recorded as his farewell, possibly on September 11.

GC: I really don't know about that. He had a unique ability to touch people with his good nature and optimism. It seems so cruel that he was suffering so much inside and no one saw it.

RS: Did he lose someone he cared about in the attacks of that day?

GC: All our friends are accounted for, thank God. I think he lost what we all lost—a naive belief that America was strong enough to keep us safe. My heart breaks for everyone who lost someone that day, whether directly or indirectly. My suspicion is that we're not done counting the dead. It's going to be a long, hard road.

"How is this person Gwen?" Pam responded. "Can you hire a publicist to fake being you at an interview?"

"Does it say whether it was in person or on the phone?"

"No."

"It was probably in writing. She doesn't have the chops to play a grieving widow in real time. She's not Meryl Streep."

RS: In what sense?

GC: That day tore all our lives apart. It will be a struggle to put them together. There are going to be calls for revenge, to repay blood with blood. We need to work for peace. Everything negative that happens is a chance to learn. I'm grateful to be alive—even if my life with Joe is erased forever. We had beautiful plans.

RS: Were you married? Engaged? It's been rumored that
you're expecting.

GC: I don't want to say.

"Jesus fucking Christ," Pam said. "He's been dead almost four
months. I mean, even if they did the interview a while ago, pregnancy tests now will tell you within, like, six minutes."

"She has to pour it on, because she's not going to see a dime
from the estate. I'm glad he never thought to buy her a ring."

"I bet he got her a monster diamond from Tiffany's, and she's
kicking herself now for pawning it for drugs."

"That thing they think is a baby is her liver."

Making fun of her was a minor art form, a teapot tempest, a
sandbox war game. They took no action to recall their existence
to her mind.

IN THE NEW YEAR OF 2002, PAM WAS IN D.C. SO MUCH THAT SHE JOINED GINGER'S
Saturday yoga course. Daniel went down every other weekend at
most. He was busy catching up on the youth he hadn't misspent—
sleeping, mostly. He looked younger. He was constantly doing
things Pam hated, such as watching free jazz sets from standing
room in the back.

For years he had not been the protagonist of his own life. Of
course it had been relaxing to ignore all pressure to achieve or excel,
but it was also like being one of those stars orbited and swallowed
by a black hole. Joe and Flora had absorbed him. He had led the
vicarious life of a friend and parent. Down in Cleveland Park, he
kept noticing how he followed his daughter around, staring at her
in anticipation of her needs, as if he were her executive secretary.
He became aware of neglecting something in himself. He didn't
know what it was, which is why he was spending time alone. He
was grateful for Pam. She was a binary star, a partner, not a taker.
He couldn't think of how strong she was without getting sappy.

Nonetheless, by midsummer he and Flora had names for every animal in the zoo, including many reptiles and fish. Edgar would come home during the week to find the house empty, no supper on the table, Ginger and Flora away at some arboretum or community fair or recital, and he would call Pam or Daniel to chat. The family was happy. It was spread among cities and generations, spending less time together, and coming to life as a unit.

Why Flora was so serenely cheerful, nobody knew. Was it having happier parents, or four parents instead of three? Being richer, better educated, or better entertained? The orderliness of Cleveland Park life, the politeness of local strangers? She trusted them all, as if she really were Joe's immortality. She adored things about Cleveland Park that none of them had ever noticed. Honeybees. Tree bark. Landscapers in kneepads. Weather-beaten chips of blue paint under U.S. mailboxes. Young sparrows vibrating with hunger. Things it would have been dangerous to crouch down and admire for long on Chrystie Street or even in Racine.

In those days New Yorkers were still flinching at every loud noise. Flora saved all her caution for crossing the street. The grown-ups didn't want it to end. The idea of moving her back to Chrystie Street started to seem downright perverse.

They ended up sharing her even in summer. She went home with her parents, but she didn't enjoy the Lower East Side so much anymore. She kept agitating for visits to the Battery, Central Park, Fort Tryon, Jones Beach. Daniel took a month off for her, but she missed her neighborhood, her grandparents, her playmates, her bike—that is, her accustomed access to beauty, mobility, comfort, and freedom.

Finally Ginger and Edgar rented a beach house in Delaware for two weeks in August, and they all went on vacation together. Edgar grilled bluefish bought fresh in the morning. Flora practiced violin outdoors. The moon flickered in the warm wind over their improvised dances and songs. It was happier than happy.

In September, she went back to Cathedral School. Daniel had no comment. Pam said, "If it ain't broke, don't fix it." Unless somebody compared the situation to a fantasy vision of the perfect nuclear family, it was hard to find the disadvantages.

Victor and Margie tried the comparison a couple times in Pam's presence, but they couldn't get a rise out of her. She was firm on the virtue of elegant solutions, such as a blissfully happy child away at the perfect boarding school.

THE WAR CAME SUDDENLY. THE PUBLIC BUILDUP LASTED ONLY EIGHTEEN MONTHS. There were many hearings. Generals flogged forged evidence that Iraq's great man was striving toward global terror through horrendous WMDs. The Scuds on Tel Aviv of a decade before were reframed as the heralds of atom bombs to come, even though Israel is so close to Palestine that they overlap. Some say more overlap, some say less, but for those who might contemplate detonating an atom bomb in Tel Aviv, the overlap is 100 percent, so their hands are tied.

Pam and Daniel went to several antiwar protests, mostly for the sake of swelling the crowds. The press got so carried away that they might as well have stayed home. A crowd of two hundred protesters and five hundred strays on their lunch hours would be described by both organizers and police as ten thousand committed activists—by the organizers to "uplift the cause," by the police to justify overtime. On the one occasion when the count swelled to a truly substantial number, at the big march in February 2003, they were unable to get near the main rally and unable to leave. They marched up First Avenue nearly all the way to the United Nations because they had no choice, hemmed in by police on all sides.

They didn't carry signs. The cleverness of some signs annoyed them, while the simplicity of others—for instance, rainbow flags saying PEACE—bored them. They considered clever signs symptomatic. All present were delighted with one another. It was the heyday of the SMS and profile-driven online dating, when people got a lot of practice formulating zingy ad copy.

Ginger and Edgar didn't protest the war. They were too old to think they could influence the nation's mood. As Baby Boomers they remembered fighting like terriers to repair the world after its near destruction by the Lost Generation. Edgar had played his part in the struggle to wrest power away from the military-industrial complex back to the military—and now this.

Pam and Daniel, by contrast, belonged to Generation X. Too disaffected to defend their own ideals, too idealistic to admit their mercantilism, their perspective hemmed in on every horizon by the almighty dollar, they were credible to no one. Doggedly, to no tangible effect, they shouted down an Orwellian, privatized war whose chief aim seemed to them the enrichment of Vice President Cheney—as if some other war would have been okay. They ignored the message of the evil rainbow at their peril. God never said there would be peace on earth. He said the war of all against all might be managed as a relatively bloodless stalemate, symbolized by the division of the visible spectrum into seven clearly differentiated bands. His politics were three thousand years out of date, but his feel for human nature could not be derided.

DANIEL WANTED PAM TO PLAY MUSIC WITH HIM AGAIN. HIS IDEA WAS THAT SHE SWITCH from electric to acoustic guitar, and he switch from drums to a microphone and a program running on his laptop. He would sample her guitar playing and loop it electronically, and she would sing. The new sound would be quiet enough to rehearse at home (they couldn't rent cheap practice space on weekends and still spend them with Flora), plus rehearsing wouldn't give them tinnitus anymore. To perform in public, they would need only a PA system and the laptop.

He called it "industrial pastoral," describing it to her as "machine-generated folk, like trance, but with all-acoustic samples. Everything repeats. We don't have songs with a beginning, a middle, and an end."

She replied, "Isn't that how folk music works everywhere but, like, Switzerland?"

Five days later, not having trimmed her bangs in the interim because it was clear that industrial pastoral had to involve hair, she had written a jam. She strummed it to him as quietly as she could (she didn't have the acoustic guitar yet).

West Street at dawn, after a long night on my feet
I'm not that strong, this was never my beat
The market said "More!"
It offered me war
I gave it defeat
I had it all and was still incomplete
After the fall, out on West Street

He said it was great, but not perfect. "The whole thing inter-relates, like some kind of poem," he said. "You need to think more like Joe. He would have gotten distracted in the middle, and the chorus would be like, 'There's a puppy up my skirt!'"

She changed it to:

War for sale and I bought it
Invisible hand of the market up my skirt
I'm free, be with me [repeat]

He said that either it made no fucking sense, which was good, or it made sense in an admirably disturbing way.

They premiered it in the living room in Cleveland Park, qui-etly, with the laptop speakers and unamplified vocals. Daniel played samples of Pam's plinking on guitar. There was never a high point. The song went on indefinitely and ended suddenly. Being mechanical, it couldn't peter out from exhaustion. Ginger and Edgar found it inoffensive. Ginger tried flamenco-style clapping, and Flora got out her violin and played along.

The folkie hairdo for the new band grew out different from what Pam expected. In her youth, she had punished her hair with scissors for being strawberry blond and fine. The intervening years had turned it auburn and voluminous without her knowledge. She wrote new songs that went with her hair.

GWEN TOO WAS RECOVERING. SHE REALIZED SHE COULDN'T PLAY THE PART OF A HEART-broken widow forever. Heartbroken widows hole up in their summer places year-round. You don't see them becoming famous in their own right. Unless, of course, they're the kind of people who deal with trauma by acting out.

She gave it a shot. She fucked Daktari on a bench in Union Square around six A.M. on a Sunday, sitting astride him with her skirt hiked up. No one minded. Neither had a famous face. To passersby, they were just an average couple whiling away a lonely dawn.

She did lines on the bar in the lounge at Le Bernardin. The staff seemed to disapprove, but no one took the trouble to throw her out. She left hurriedly, faking an eviction, when it seemed that no one would be paying for her drinks.

Her coup was to capitalize on her music scene fame. She went to the VIP room at Roseland before a show and sat down on a sofa among three members of an up-and-coming hard rock outfit from Staten Island (their press release said they were from Cupertino, California). She kissed one while holding on tight to the others' legs. For this kind of band, big hair was obligatory, so you could barely see their faces. The men let her do it long enough for someone to take a picture. It didn't take long, since they had sat down on the sofa for purposes of having their picture taken. It was a classic image of grief—the beauty so bereft as to make out with absolutely anybody, no longer placing value on her sexual favors—with the twist that these men were not, as their press release suggested, hot and horny new kids on the block, but twenty-year bar-band veterans coasting through a rebranding, unimaginably jaded, a low risk for the homosocial group sex Gwen hoped the images would suggest.

When the cameras flashed, she stood up and ran to the bathroom, partly to end the scene in a natural way—in the glamorous world of music, there was always a reason to run to the bathroom—and partly because the musician she'd chosen at random to kiss had bad breath. Something about him, or possibly something about snorting speed, made her want to throw up.

The story of how she had teased the heavy metal musicians and run away in distress appeared in a syndicated list of celebrity sightings. Grieving widowhood was hers at last. She attended the MTV Video Music Awards to sit in the audience. The camera cut to her briefly during a 9/11 tribute. She looked thin enough to worry the tabloids. She agreed to accept Joe's lifetime achievement award on the 2004 Grammy Awards, in front of a montage of birds and flowers. She let Daktari thank the fans for their support. When he was done, she stepped to the mic and said, "War is not the answer." It made the headlines because it was controversial.

Her impromptu screen tests were a success. She engaged a talent agent and obtained a supporting role in an independent movie about rock stars, scheduled for filming the following year.

Her fame was an anticlimax, a letdown, a release into security. Descent to a basis, the pedestal where she would be safe above the crowd. It didn't mean achieving accomplishments or altering the course of history. It had nothing to do with art. It meant being pursued by strangers after she got out of her twenties. To be haggard from smoking, flabby from drinking, yet noticed from notoriety.

XIII.

The kids at Cathedral bragged a lot, mostly about their vacations. It was seventh grade before Flora let drop that she'd been babysat by a rock star.

Her audience, a girl named Spencer, tended to bring out people's most antisocial qualities, such as the desire to be treated with respect. That night, Spencer asked her dad who Joe was. Before school started the next morning, she approached Flora and said, "Joe Harris was a dork. He killed himself because you suck."

"He did not," Flora said. "He died on September eleventh."

"His girlfriend found his body. It was green and swollen up, with pus coming out his nose."

"You don't know what you're talking about, Spence." The name sounded like an insult to her—the best kind, intonation-dependent.

"My daddy told me," she replied, with consummate uncoolness. "Joe Harris was a drug addict, and on September eleventh he killed himself with drugs."

Flora was quiet, entertaining the thought that she'd never been told what killed Joe. The date alone had satisfied her; he'd been killed by September 11. Although she suspected that the truth would not constitute ammunition against Spencer, she resolved to ask her parents the first chance she got.

She wasn't that patient. Ginger, picking her up after her violin lesson, heard the question first thing.

Ginger wasn't sure how to answer. By now she knew the story in as much detail as Pam knew it. The doctrine that one should hate the sin and love the sinner left her nothing to say about Gwen. Flora's age alone left her nothing to say about Gwen.

But the alternative was to either blame Joe or call it an accident. Did Joe have an accident with heroin? No, not according to Pam. He didn't spend free time with heroin or risk his safety to enjoy heroin. The accident was Gwen. If anybody wanted to turn back the hands of time to some moment when things could have been altered, they'd do best to erase Gwen.

Ginger hesitated to speak because all her information was thirdhand. She'd seen Joe only a few times and found him nice enough, but inappropriate. She didn't know how well Flora knew Gwen.

"It's like this," she said. "People die. Everybody dies sometime. It's the cycle of being. There's never a particular reason. They just pile up. Say if you're old and sick, and your house catches on fire—"

"Did he kill himself?"

"No. Okay, say you're reading a book, and it's so good you keep right on reading while you're crossing the street, and you get run over by a car. Who killed you? You, the guy driving the car, or the guy who wrote the book?"

"It was you, because you weren't careful."

"Joe wasn't careful," Ginger said.

Flora let that stand, and her grandmother felt a moment of immersive doubt. Disadvantageous as her impressions of Joe had been, she had never carried on a real conversation with him. Nearly everything she knew about his habits she had received straight from Flora. Only the hardest facts, such as his final day on Earth, originated with adults. She tried to mirror—nearly always—Flora's views on everything to do with her time in New York. It felt to her like the healthy thing to do. In this manner Flora found her positions advocated and her self-assessment confirmed. But was any of it true?

WHEN THEY GOT HOME, THEY BOTH PUT IN CALLS TO PAM. BUT SHE WAS CONFERENCING at a client's office, not answering her cell. Neither of them left a message.

Flora didn't try her father. She had the feeling that her question would upset him.

Pam called her back during dinner, which with Ginger and Edgar always started by six. Edgar said, "No phones at the table."

Flora said, "May I be excused?"

"You may," Ginger said. "Come back when you're done. We'll wait on dessert."

"She shouldn't have her phone at the table," Edgar said.

"It's important," Ginger said.

Flora went into the backyard and stood under the farthest walnut tree. She said, "Mom, a girl at school told me Joe killed himself."

Pam said, "That's not what happened. I'm sorry somebody told you that. That's terrible."

"First you didn't tell me he was even dead, and then you didn't tell me he died of drugs. You're liars."

"Not really," Pam said. "You were a little kid, and there are things you can't tell a little kid. You want to know how he died?"

"Spence said he was green—"

"I don't give a shit about Spence." There was a silence while Pam tried to think of the truth in suitable words. All she could muster were oversimplifications: Heroin is bad for you. Gwen is a twat. They were unsuitable.

"I'm big enough for the truth," Flora prompted her.

"The truth," Pam said, "is that he got really sick, like a heart attack, when he found out about the terrorists, and Gwen didn't know how to do CPR or artificial resuscitation or anything, and he died. Then there were rumors that he killed himself, but only because he was so young."

"Why isn't she in jail?"

She realized with sorrow that there had been no need to bring Gwen into it. "Maybe he would have died anyway," she said. "You know what he was like. He lived as much in one day as most people do in ten years. He had more fun than anybody else in the history of the world. Maybe he ran out?" Having overreached, she added quickly, "Never be afraid of having too much fun. Except with drugs, obviously. Never do drugs. Otherwise it's impossible to use up your lifetime allotment of fun."

"There's more to life than fun," Flora said. "What's important is doing the right thing and helping others, like knowing first aid."

Precipitously, Pam felt she'd been right to send her daughter to a school whose motto was *"Noblesse oblige."*

LATER THAT EVENING, PAM WALKED A TOTE BAG FULL OF MUSIC UP TO THE RECORD BAR on Avenue C to donate it to the cause. Her reason to seek out a specialty shop, rather than abandon her CDs on the street, was an altruistic and probably misguided hope that they might bring joy to others. Most of them fell into the category "noise." Some were rare, while others were considered desirable when on vinyl. For fifteen digital files stored in a bulky format, she was lucky to get fifty cents. Groups were streaming their tracks for free on MySpace. Anybody who cared could hear the difference between a CD and an MP3, but not on an MP3 player, plus nobody cared.

She stepped up to the counter, relieved to see the shop owner

on duty. He wasn't a slave driver, but he paid his staff of aficionados minimum wage, for which they were uneager to catalog stacks
of worthless CDs. They wanted rare vinyl they could put aside for
themselves. He claimed that the storefront had degenerated to the
status of a combination billboard and warehouse and that he made
his money online. He said, "Hey, Pam," and asked her to wait a
minute while he finished crouching to rake up a few sharp-edged
ribbons of white pilfer-proofing plastic that had been sealing boxes
of new merchandise and now littered the floor behind the counter.
She set her bag down on a display case and began to unpack it
onto the space next to the register, stacking the CDs into rough
categories by genre.

"Pam?" a voice said.

She turned and saw someone familiar and meaningful, though
she couldn't place her at first; a chubby person, younger than herself
but older than she ought to be, in a black leotard, black tights,
black clodhoppers, and a green corduroy miniskirt buttoned off-
center. Her bangs were held straight back with a green barrette.

"It's me, Eloise."

"Oh, my God," Pam said. "Eloise!"

"I've been wanting to tell you for years now, how sorry I was
to hear about Joe Harris."

Pam lowered her voice and said, "Listen a second. People don't
know I knew him, and I like it that way."

Sensing that the speech she'd been bottling up for years was
likely to bug Pam rather than gratify her, Eloise said, "Oh, sorry.
Want to get coffee?"

"Sure. Just let me finish up donating here."

The store owner stood upright and said, "Joe Harris? There's
nothing special about knowing that guy. He was a social bull-
dozer. He came in here all the time."

"Really?" Eloise said. "What did he buy?"

"Everything."

"What did he like the most?"

"Ween. Sebadoh."

"That's interesting," Pam said. She couldn't recall hearing him mention those bands.

"It's a shame he had to off himself on 9/11. He should have stayed around for all the fun."

"Yeah, that was sad," Pam said.

"I thought I was going to die," Eloise said earnestly. "I couldn't stop bawling for, like, a week."

"Let's get coffee," Pam said.

"I can give you ten dollars for these," the owner said.

"There's a Scratch Acid EP in there," she said. Daniel had it on vinyl, so she knew how tinny the CD sounded by comparison.

"The CD sounds like bees in a jar," he said. "Ten dollars for everything."

She took the cash and said to Eloise, "Coffee's on me."

They walked west, looking for a place with tables where they could sit down. It took a while. Pam was excited. She hadn't played the scenario through in her mind for at least three years, but she still recalled the era when she had wished first the insipid Bethany, and then the monstrous Gwen, shunted to the side in favor of the cheery, enthusiastic, Joe-like Eloise. How easy it would have been to fix them up. Just point them at each other and press "play." What a tragedy it hadn't happened. Instead of facing her by coincidence at a record store, Eloise would have been meeting her at a playground to watch the Joe Juniors (a boy and a girl, both named Joe, both bearers of his distinctive features and odd ways) make daisy chains. It would be the playground next to the Metropolitan Museum, because he would have put his money into real estate instead of designer drugs for the human Humboldt squid, and Eloise would stroll over from Third Avenue with the kids and their little dog Joe, while Pam walked across the park from the West

Side penthouse Daniel would have bought from his earnings as the still-living Joe's genuine manager. The fantasy went too far, but it had had a lot of time to bloom and grow without a reality check.

"I work for *New York* magazine now," Eloise said. "I'm on the online style section. I've been working there almost four months. I cover fashion trends and stuff."

"How'd you end up doing that?"

"I always wanted to be a reporter. I've been working my way through all the websites. The political and economic stuff, nobody really took me seriously. Maybe it was discrimination or whatever, but they let other women do it, so it's probably just me. I truly admire celebrities. I'm not somebody people take seriously."

"I wouldn't say that. I remembered you all these years, just from meeting you twice."

"Yeah, but I'm such a fangirl! I get good page views, but I don't know if I'm really creative."

"You have a lot of self-doubt."

"I'm realistic. I'm okay at what I do, and the magazines are awesome. What are you doing these days?"

"I'm still a programmer, still in corporate consulting."

"That is so cool! I should do a story about you. Lady programmer!"

"It would be more exciting if I'd founded a startup and cashed out. I'm still on salary. It's kind of embarrassing. I ought to be out in Silicon Valley, riding around in a Ferrari."

"If you can write code, you can drive a car! I can't drive either. I'm from Brooklyn originally. I'm back there now. My grandparents died, so my parents moved downstairs and I moved into the top floor of our house. It's so much cheaper than paying rent."

"I didn't mean I can't drive," Pam said. "I got my license before I left high school. Anyway, I'm in a band now, with Daniel. It's just a hobby. We've never played out. We don't even have a name."

"So do you not tour because you can't drive?"

"Me and Daniel can both drive! I'm sure you remember him. Joe's manager?"

"I'm sorry. You said you can drive. I should get you a show! I know so many people who book shows, especially in Brooklyn."

"That's sweet, but we're not so great. It's only the two of us."

"How do you know you're not so great? Get some confidence! You should let me hear it! Is it online?"

"We don't put it out in public," Pam said. "We're hermits."

They passed a café with indoor seating. It looked cramped and uncomfortable, but at least it was unpretentious, so they walked back a few steps and ordered filter coffee, bodega style, from the bored and lonely cashier. Eloise got a bagel with Nutella. She insisted on paying. They selected two spindly chairs at a flimsy table.

"I was so crazy about Joe," Eloise said.

"We all were. He was great."

"I mean, I was in love. It was weird. I was really crazy about him."

"I know!"

"When he killed himself, I guess because he thought it was World War Three, I felt so sorry for his girlfriend, Gwendolyn. You must know her. She's so stunning and such a great actress. Is she okay? I mean, finding the body. I kept thinking, What if it had been me? Would it be worth finding him like that, to be able to spend five years with him? He was such an unusual guy, and so talented. I always knew he would be famous. But I'm not the kind of journalist who hangs out with successful people. I'm more a sidelines kind of person."

Pam looked hard at Eloise, who returned her gaze with Joe-like sincerity, and the caffeine loosened her tongue. She said, "I always wished you guys would get together."

"Seriously?"

"This is off the record, right? I mean, what I'm about to tell you, you can't tell anybody."

Eloise could not have looked more excited. She clearly thought Pam was about to tell her that Joe had reciprocated her crush—that he had seen her from the stage and declared that he would marry her someday, or something along those lines. She whispered, "I swear, I will never repeat one word to anybody, ever."

Pam said, "He didn't kill himself. That fucking bitch Gwen Charanoglu killed him."

Eloise recoiled. "That's not possible! She loved him. I saw all her interviews."

"I'm telling you, I know her. You don't. She's a lying, manipulative sack of shit." Pam's voice went shrill. Telling Eloise felt like telling the press, or telling the world, and her voice acquired the edge of years of anger. "She shot him up with heroin just for something to do, because she's a fucking junkie. And then she sat there and watched him die, and she didn't even get a doctor. She went out to Great Neck to recuperate from the shock to her system and waited four entire days. Four days. Think about it." She had gotten loud in spite of herself. She was glad that the cashier seemed too young and recently immigrated to have heard of Joe.

Eloise sat with round eyes and finally said, "Oh, my God, Pam, that's horrible."

"The worst part," she said, lowering her voice again, "is that if she'd inherited any money from him, or life insurance or anything, I would have gone after her a long time ago. But he didn't expect to die, so he didn't have a will. His dad got everything, and it was so pathetic watching her go around playing the sorrowful victim. Now that she's a D-list celeb and the second thing people think of when they think of Joe, I wish I'd done something to control the narrative. Anyway, it kills me that it could have been you."

Eloise sat still. She wiped her eyes. They exchanged phone numbers and e-mail addresses.

WHEN PAM GOT HOME, SHE TOLD DANIEL ABOUT RUNNING INTO ELOISE AND HOW SAD IT was that Joe hadn't hooked up with her. "She's still so adorable," she said. "They would have been so cute together."

"Pam, I know you're a cool person and everything like that," he said, "but sometimes when you've been around girls, you do this girl-power thing."

"What do you mean?"

"He thought she was fat. Remember? You told him to his face she was into him, and he said he was more into emaciated models, like you. He was into the waif look, man. It was heroin-chic days. Don't idealize him by castrating him. He was a grown man with some pretty classic sexual preferences."

"If he was a grown man, he was old enough to want a relationship. And with Eloise, it could have worked."

"Let me rephrase that. He was a playboy rock star. He could get laid anywhere he kept his mouth shut. He didn't have to negotiate a relationship. He could just haul off and fuck."

"You know Gwen was his self-appointed procuress. Maybe living like that wasn't his idea."

"Yeah, right. You're pimping Eloise. You have a crush on her. You're going to swear off boys and run away with Eloise."

"I am not!"

"I remember that conversation so well, how he said you were the hottest. I mean, I met you through him. I knew you were more important to each other than I was to either of you. He devoted himself to you, when you let him, like with Flora. But he knew better than to make a move."

"I loved him. I always sort of believed that if his inabilities . . . I don't know."

"You're talking crazy talk." Daniel's expression was grave,

without irony. "Eloise is your proxy, qualified to be with Joe in a way you're not, because she's kind of vaguely dimwitted."

"Of course I wished sometimes we could have been closer. Not intimate. I don't know. Just to have a real conversation. I felt something very strong for him, maternal feelings, like with Flora— except, I don't know. I couldn't really talk to him. Not about real stuff."

"Just because it didn't work doesn't mean it wasn't sexual. Hot babes tend to forget that. You're constantly bombarded with sexual offers, and you think love is this thing where your job is to say yes or no. Like, fish or cut bait, do I want this guy or not. Well, love is not like that. Sometimes—like for me before I met you—you cast out your lure and you wait and wait and *wait*, like Eloise did, loving Joe from afar. Except she baited her hook, and his answer was 'No fat chicks!' So deal with it."

"I think I love him less now," she said. She stole into his arms. "I liked him better as my latent lesbian proxy who was going to fall for Eloise the minute we got them alone together."

"I love you because you're skinny," he said. He stroked her flat stomach.

WEEKS LATER, HAVING PUT ELOISE OUT OF HER MIND, SHE GOT AN E-MAIL INVITING them both to contribute a song to a Joe Harris tribute CD that was being put out by a culture website Eloise had founded after she got fired from *New York*. Pam didn't answer the e-mail or tell Daniel about it. It seemed too ironic to her to cover Joe's vacuous pop songs as a tribute, when he was known for his cover of "Bird in God's Garden."

Two weeks later, she got another e-mail, inviting their band to play a show at a space in Bedford-Stuyvesant. They would sound-check at six P.M. and go on around nine as the warm-up act for a fashion show. The space was a garage, until recently home to a tow-truck service, and currently a fashion designer's studio. It was basically a rent party for the fashion designer. They could borrow amps from the band after them. They would need a name, unless they wanted to be "Pam and Daniel."

She told Daniel. He said she should acquiesce, because they had nothing to lose.

They spent more time shopping for stage gear than practicing. Pam bought a seventies maxi dress made of polyester double knit with a green-and-orange flower print. Daniel bought a paisley shirt and bell-bottoms. They told Eloise that their sound was pastoral industrial. Their band name was Marmalade Skye, with an *e*.

Their set was nothing if not harmless. But after years of wrestling with unforgiving mainframes and diffuse guilt, Pam felt like a rebellious self-emancipator for doing something as silly as singing in public. Music wasn't her art project anymore. It was a skittish but real and ancient phenomenon that manifested unpredictably, like wild birds or butterflies. She looked up to it.

It was the influence of Flora's violin playing. The child had been raised on two-minute songs performed solo a cappella, so she played phrases with climaxes and denouements. Pam in her youth had argued that any given random noise was more musical than all classical music combined, the performance of which was unbecoming submission to the hegemonic dead. After Flora started with Bach and Mozart, forced originality in culture began to remind her of fads in clothing. Art: ways of reinventing the wheel as all different polygons.

The mellifluous, monotonous Marmalade Skye songs rolled along like perfect circles, unoriginal music of the simplest stripe. She'd been playing rudimentary guitar for so long, she could do it in her sleep. Daniel was a competent sample looper. She didn't feel she'd shifted from punk to folk. Punk was all folk to her now—bleating, repetitive, self-satisfied—compared to the loving exploration of inner space she heard when Flora played.

Onstage she felt a little ashamed of herself for not playing music, but she enjoyed getting away with it. As an emotion, it was nothing new.

After the gig, she said as much to Eloise. "Sorry I can't sing worth a shit," she said. "I sound like Jane Birkin, or that chick from My Bloody Valentine. Halfway through the first song, I'm already too hoarse to do anything but whisper."

"That is such fiction. I can't wait to book you again."

"I still wish I could sing."

"You should get vocal training. This opera expert I interviewed last month told me it's not like playing the piano, where you have to start when you're little to be any good. The fine-motor stuff for singing is all the same as talking. They have opera stars who started when they were thirty-five!"

"That's an interesting idea."

"What's interesting?" Daniel said, handing them each a shot of Ramazzotti.

"Voice lessons."

"I'm in favor," he said. "Learn to sing. We'll scale up to pastoral-industrial gothic."

"Why were you interviewing an opera expert?" Pam asked Eloise.

"It was for Talk of the Town, in *The New Yorker*."

"Was his name Simon?" Daniel asked, addressing his wife's key unspoken concern.

"No," Eloise said. "Andrea. In Italy it's a boy's name. He gives people singing lessons all the time. I could give him your number!"

"My bad," Daniel said, patting Pam's arm. "The world of opera is bigger than I thought."

"This town's big enough for two opera experts," she said. "Now you know why I stay here."

XIV.

Flora's career in secondary education roughly coincided with the UN Decade of Education for Sustainable Development (ESD), formally launched in 2005. "Sustainable" development was meant to supplant a purely exploitative relationship between creditor and debtor nations with something better suited to the ideals of globalization. "Globalization" was defined as lifting barriers to investment in former colonies. Under globalization, ruined landscapes, stripped of all but the skeletal remains of their former cultural autonomy and techniques of economic subsistence, would develop export industries rich in competitive wage labor.

Flora's earth science class did a unit on the Sahel zone, south of the Sahara. Life there was becoming unsustainable. The rains were staying away, and there was a population explosion. Everywhere, there was poverty—no help for the sick. Of course the Sahel had enough water. It just wasn't being used sustainably. Flora's working group was supposed to come up with a better plan. They couldn't tell standing oats from barley, but they made amaranth bread in a solar cooker and wrote a presentation on how it could alleviate overgrazing.

When she told her father she had baked bread for a school project on the sustainable use of tributaries of Lake Chad, he said, "What is this? Home economics on steroids?"

DANIEL BELIEVED IN SUSTAINABILITY TOO, BUT HIS VERSION CAME STRAIGHT FROM Kierkegaard, the prelude to whose tractate *Either/Or* suggests a life modeled on crop rotation. To counter the monotony, change it up.

He was rehearsing every Wednesday in Chelsea with a funk band called the Steve Bartman Incident. Pam called it Band of Dentists. The singer, drummer, alto sax, and drummer's wife, on trumpet, were all dentists. Daniel had met three of them at a reggae concert he went to by himself. They were midwestern and lived in Jersey and thought he was a very cool guy. They had a cult following for a monthly gig at a roller rink in South Amboy. His job was to blast out two-chord riffs on a Hammond organ. They didn't mind that he was a beginner. They preferred a keyboard player who didn't want to solo.

The Steve Bartman Incident turned a profit. Daniel had never made money from music before. He found it very pleasant.

The band's devotees were creaky best agers. They struggled to put their skates on, groaned as they stood up, and soared away like birds. They danced holding each other tight, the women skating backward, the men deftly steering, swooping across the floor from one barrier wall to the other at alarming speed. At first they scared Daniel—he thought they were all going to die in crashes—but soon he compared them to seals: ungainly and awkward on land, graceful and powerful in their native element.

FLORA WAS OLD ENOUGH TO COME UP TO NEW YORK ON THE TRAIN. IN THE UNMIXED opinion of her parents, she was a pleasure to be around. She never complained of boredom or loneliness. Her friends were always with her, in her smartphone. It reduced a clique of shrieking teen-agers to silent speech bubbles in a chat program. For the adults, it was a godsend.

She showed them sides of New York they'd never seen. They finally saw the Morgan Library from the inside. They ate at Tavern on the Green, which they knew only from movies. They toured the Cloisters and the Frick Collection and watched her light a can-dle for peace at Trinity Church. They attended classical concerts at Lincoln Center and saw a City Opera production of *The Magic Flute*. Whatever they did, they were home by one A.M., because Daniel still didn't have a key to the two-pound tubular lock on the shop's security gate.

Secretly, alerting no one, Flora bought a canister of acidic cleaning powder and dumped it in the Chrystie Street toilet, ren-dering its interior shiny white. From her own money, she replaced the shower curtain. Her changes failed to be noticed or remarked upon. Finally she washed the windows. That conspicuous and dan-gerous activity got Pam's attention. She asked Flora what on earth she was doing. She said that now that they were hippies instead of punks, they must want to let the sunshine in.

"Hippies live like dogs in their own filth," Pam replied. "The elegant solution would be to cover the windows in layers of clear plastic and pull them off one at a time. I should patent that."

"That would be an ecological disaster, when they come clean with vinegar and old newspapers." Flora stepped back to reveal newly visible soot-blackened brick walls and a dying pagoda tree.

"What are you now, our tidy little hausfrau?"

At her next opportunity, two hours later, Flora begged Daniel to please tell her mother that despite attending a girls' school, she was not a housewife in training. "She needs to stop labeling me," she said. "I'm not 'feminine' just because I like stuff clean!"

He didn't like the misogynistic way she hissed the word "femi-nine," but he said, "You can say that again."

"Her gender is cockroach. She eats croissants in bed!"

"Your mother's gender journey is ongoing. She just bought her first ponytail holder."

"What's feminine about *ponytails?*"

"You'll have to forgive us," he said. "We grew up in a dialectical world. Everything was binary. Race, gender, the global order, class warfare, the whole nine yards. Computers are still binary, so there's never going to be any hope for your mom."

She picked up her phone, and he flattered himself that his quip would be going straight to Facebook.

He saw her post late that night. She had garnered dozens of likes for a claim that everything's binary when you're on the spectrum.

He had often remarked that she was an art project, his accidental magnum opus. Only then did he realize what kind: an oracle. By growing up in the present, she acquired the ability to transmit coded hints about the future. Apparently something about the present was warning the inheritors of the future not to take sides.

ETHICS INSTRUCTION AT CATHEDRAL DIDN'T EMPHASIZE RELIGION OR COMMANDMENTS. The imperative to love one's neighbor as oneself is wasted on teenage girls, and explicit prohibitions just give them ideas. Instead it focused on harm reduction. All self-destructive behaviors were to be reported to the authorities immediately.

In tenth grade, Flora saw that a friend of hers was living unsustainably. Shanaya was a year behind her in school and a competent pianist. They played chamber music together recreationally, mostly Brahms and Schumann. In her off-hours, Shanaya took pills she couldn't identify and hung out with older boys. Flora's dilemma was that there was nothing she could do to slow her down except turn her in by confiding in an adult. The penalty for drug abuse by Cathedral students was immediate expulsion.

In cases of ethical conflict, she regularly turned to the church.

Not to its doctrines or its personnel, but its architecture. The cathedral was a quiet place of enforced introspection, a retreat where she could reflect safe from interruption. In the gap between fifth period and an orchestra rehearsal, she knelt on a cushion dedicated to Harriet Tubman, folded her hands as though in prayer, and asked herself, What would Flora do? The saints looked on expressionless, almost rolling their eyes, it was such a no-brainer. Flora was about forbearance and tolerance, not about being a snitch and getting people shitcanned from high school.

Several weeks later, Shanaya passed out in the loft space over a pharmacy on Connecticut Avenue and was summarily raped (it didn't take long) by the pharmacist's son, a senior at Episcopal. She shared the news with Flora the next morning at six thirty, by text message, before appearing at first period no more bedraggled than usual. Flora was distraught. She realized too late that absolution should be reserved to higher powers. She confronted Shanaya outdoors before lunch, saying she was in denial about her trauma and had to be helped. Also, the boy shouldn't get away with it. She needed to go to the emergency room. Surely she was not his first victim, nor his last.

"You're a prude," Shanaya replied. "I don't care whether I'm a so-called virgin. I didn't 'have sex.' I was unconscious! Let him brag if he wants. We were alone. Nobody posted pictures."

"But he raped you, right?"

"Listen, if I turn him in, the only thing that happens is I go to some rehab clinic full of addicts. Honestly, I'd rather be raped under anesthesia than get locked up in a mental hospital. Now I'm sorry I told you. I was surprised. I didn't think he was that big of a tool."

"I should not have let it happen," Flora replied firmly.

"It was experiential education," Shanaya said, not understanding the reference to Flora's idea of drawing official attention to her habits. "I'm fine."

She was not entirely fine. The pharmacist's son had given her genital warts. But soon afterward, he also gave her the medication needed to treat them, so no harm done. Her wellness remained unshaken, and no one was the wiser but Flora, who felt from thenceforth that other people's lives might not be the best place to apply her ethics training. From that day forward she hung back from gossip, contributing only the knowing asides that even the nerdiest Cathedral maidens knew secondhand from movies and TV. Shanaya had unwittingly steered her toward a lasting preoccupation with regulatory frameworks.

PAM AND GINGER GOSSIPED ABOUT THE CHILD FREQUENTLY, COMING TO NO DEFINITE conclusion. Pam had demanded her freedom early in life, and Ginger had achieved hers late. Flora didn't seem to feel confined. She and her friends led the lives of younger children. They didn't shave their legs or tweeze their eyebrows. They collected graphic novels and kept scrapbooks. They demanded music lessons and gathered around the TV to sing show tunes. At age sixteen, Flora had been to Ghana and Costa Rica on school exchange programs, and she could ramble on and on about Lake Chad, but she had never been on a date and showed no intention of trying. When Ginger asked whether there was a special boy in her life, her response was always the same special grimace.

Pam opined that Flora had the submissive personality of a traditional girl, and that was why she dressed like a pixie from an age before sex. When she wasn't in her school uniform, she wore leggings under long tops. In cooler weather she enveloped herself in hooded sweatshirts large enough to serve as overcoats. "Or maybe she's just uncorrupted, for all I know," she said to Ginger on the phone. "It's not like becoming a sexually active drug user was my idea. Maybe the kid is what happens when girls make it to sixteen without being abused."

"You were sexually abused?"

"I don't mean abused-abused! But when I think back, I have trouble coming up with even one kiss that was a good time. I knew such horrible boys. You know how they force their tongue on you, and you're like 'bleah,' but you let them do it anyway, because you think you're supposed to be into it?" (The word "kiss" was a metonymic stand-in.)

"I don't think she would put up with a bad kisser for even a second."

"She's so spoiled. Like a princess—but I don't mean it that way. I don't hate and envy my own daughter. Jesus."

"I know you're not saying these things to hurt anyone. You have a right to be honest."

"What I mean is I feel like she has it so easy, and I don't even know why or how. Because if you look at her, you feel like obviously the world has gotten better for girls. But it hasn't, has it? Guys are such openly sexist assholes now."

"Not the boys her age. They're living dolls."

"All of them?"

"Well, the ones she knows."

"She knows boys?"

"When the girls are watching musicals, sometimes they have boys over to help with the singing."

"Those boys are gay."

"Not in the least! They're physically demonstrative but very sweet. That's what nice boys are like now. There are still plenty of awful boys. She calls them 'bras,' the way you always talked about 'jocks.'"

Pam thought it over briefly and said, "The elegant solution is that men have become such complete monsters that they're all delaying puberty. Or men are such monsters that girls are delaying social puberty? I 'became a woman' the day I got my period.

Probably now it starts when you go on the Pill. I mean, if I called a thirteen-year-old a 'woman' now, they'd register me as a sex offender."

"It certainly simplifies growing up," Ginger said. "Did I ever tell you how one of the reasons I didn't want you going to private school was that I thought the uniforms were too sexy? They were the most popular fetish among the men I knew. The Lolita look!"

"I don't believe you. The International School doesn't have a uniform. I could have worn jeans and still gone to private school."

"But you always wanted to wear those little hockey skirts, no matter what. I couldn't stop you. Everybody was in jeans, but you insisted. It had to be a plaid miniskirt."

Momentarily, Pam pondered the notion that her punk rock look might inadvertently have conformed to a school uniform fetish. There could be something to it. After all, punk was a fashion originated by middle-aged entrepreneurs in London. There was something potentially skin-crawlingly humiliating about it. Her rebellion against the power and competence that proper clothing conveyed had taken the form of looking like a child, in an era when a child was someone to abuse with impunity. She said, "I was punk rock. I didn't have a choice."

"The only pants you ever asked for," Ginger reminisced, "were those shiny black ones with little zippers everywhere. I thought they were much too sexy for a fifteen-year-old."

"Any fifteen-year-old who thinks she needs bondage pants to be sexy should be seeing a shrink!"

"You were never sexy," her mother corrected her. "You know men have a preference for clear skin and long hair. Your father always said you looked like a greasy white rat."

"I know," she said. "I remember."

XV.

The Great Recession hit Victor and Margie hard. They had invested in tract homes upstate. The houses were deep underwater, with unsustainable mortgage balances that dwarfed their value. They couldn't unload them. Instead of making money, they were losing more every day. They resolved to sell the property on Chrystie Street to pay their debts so they could retire in peace to their niece's place in Boston.

When they told Daniel they were evicting him, he said, "I get it. Buy high, sell low. Works for me!" To their plans for the upstate houses, he said, "Let the capitalist running dogs foreclose. Serves them right!" Possibly it was imprudent on his part to resort to sarcasm and sound financial principles rather than a warm appeal to their long friendship. They raised his monthly rent to $900. But they didn't turn him out.

In the downturn he was fairly idle, but he couldn't claim to mind, having just finished a two-year administrative assignment at Consolidated Edison. He'd been tangentially involved with some interesting close calls—the company maintained a gallery of survivors' melted helmets and scorched gloves and coveralls—but still, two years is a long time.

He had the loft to himself during the day, because Pam remained loyal to RIACD long after business had ceased. Yuval reduced housekeeping to once a week. The kitchenette smelled. The consultants arrived in time to go to lunch. After lunch, they played multiuser online games until time to start drinking in the conference room. Pam spent long hours at her desk tinkering with video caching, one of those pointless programmer hobbies like the open-source BeOS.

In mid-2009 the moment arrived when Yuval's bank officer made clear that his credit line wouldn't cover payroll. At the next weekly staff meeting—four o'clock vodka on a Wednesday—he solicited revenue-generating and cost-saving ideas. There were suggestions to start charging for drinks; to double up desks and sublet half the office space; to accept salary cuts in exchange for shorter hours; and to solve streaming video caching without a hardware component (Pam's idea).

"No viable suggestions," he said. "You're all fired. I wish you good luck."

"California, here I come," a consultant said.

"Not me," Pam said. "I'll work for free. Call it a startup if you want, Yuval. I owe it to you."

He said, "Any more takers for RIACD's relaunch as a performance art project?"

"Come on, people!" Pam said, addressing the room. "It's going to be a shitload easier for you to find work if you have jobs!"

Several hands went up.

"Okay," Yuval said. "You're not fired. The rest of you are fired, effective immediately." He really could say that, because New York was an at-will employment state.

Soon business took off again. Banks absorbing other banks had to reconcile their databases and record keeping, and RIACD

began to profit from the crisis like a lean, mean school of jaded
piranha.

IN ITS EAGERNESS TO SAVE THE PLANET FROM ITSELF, THE CATHEDRAL HIGH SCHOOL
Class of 2010 was of one mind. Education for Sustainable Development had functioned as planned. The girls were facing the end
of the world with their eyes open.

Most of them aspired to careers in teaching and media, where
they would spread the word that the planet was at risk. Flora's
preference was for direct intervention in its pattern of compulsive
self-harm. But the homepages of environmental engineering programs left her confused. Stanford and MIT sounded as though
they were training people to be mad scientists. Their students were
designing technologies to alter the chemistry of major geological
features, including mass fertilization of the oceans, with the re-
sulting algal biomass somehow sequestered in mine shafts for the
win. She had envisioned a more behavioral-therapeutic approach
to planetary neuroticism. But she couldn't get into those colleges
anyway. She had started out thinking top-tier schools were prizes
in a lottery. The more she learned, the more they seemed like real
estate—titles available in trade for assets she did not possess. Her
high school wasn't challenging enough. Her extracurricular activities were violin and badminton. Her test scores were good, but she
had stopped math at calculus and science at chemistry.

She applied for early decision to George Washington University (GW). It was a private, upscale, but not Ivy League, school
conveniently located near the Farragut North stop on the red line.
She would get a commuter exemption to the on-campus residency
requirement (the District of Columbia required colleges to house
their students, so they wouldn't clog up the rental market) and
stay in her Cleveland Park bedroom. There would be no stuffy
cell or grungy showers to share with strangers. She was confident
of a scholarship, since private colleges seldom charged domestic

students sticker price, and she anticipated a generous aid package. Her parents lived in poverty. Grandparents were considered irrelevant.

She saved the financing conversation with Pam and Daniel for an autumn weekend visit to their chilly hovel. It turned awkward fast. Shamefacedly produced and quickly packed away, their tax returns told a story she had never dreamed.

She wondered whether her grandparents had known how rich her parents were when they encouraged her to apply to a private college. They could not possibly have suspected. They had been paying all her expenses half her life for no reason.

"I always assumed you would go to a cheap in-state school," Pam said.

"I don't live in a state!"

"What about UDC?"

"That's a historically black college with open enrollment. It would not be the best degree for getting a job."

"Don't they teach the same stuff there as everywhere else?"

"Mom!"

"You could live with us and go to CUNY." That was the downscale, inexpensive public university run by New York City. "It's a great school."

Flora's frown was stiff and stern.

"What's wrong with CUNY?"

"Can't you declare your independence and get financial aid that way?" Daniel interrupted.

"How? By getting married, or by having a kid? Those are my options until I turn twenty-four!"

"I knew people who did it in Madison," he said. "But I guess it was a long time ago."

"So now I have to wait until I'm twenty-four to start college?"

"You could just get over your racism and go to UDC," Pam suggested sweetly.

"I'm not a racist!" Flora rose from the kitchen table.

"You can get a good education anywhere that has a library."

"But not a degree that gets me good jobs so I can pay back the loans I wouldn't need if you weren't rich!" She had assumed they were so poor that she would get free money.

The discussion did not go well. Flora took her backpack from the row of milk crates by the door and ran down the stairs and out the door of Video Hit. She walked west on Delancey, dodging handcarts and bicycles, until she found a place to get a cinnamon cake doughnut and sit and think.

She began with wounded thoughts about dishonesty. Her faith in truthfulness was deeply ingrained, in part because of her school's honor code, but mostly because of Joe. Her honesty started with him, and his honesty had never ended for her. The honor code merely made it seem like an ideal rather than the defining feature of a patsy.

She thought about how poorly she'd negotiated. Surely there was manipulation or persuasion she could have tried with adequate setup time. But she had never thought of trying. She was ill prepared to lie. She knew little about how to go about it, and her naïveté might be costing her an education. But she hadn't told the truth either, in the sense of presenting arguments in its favor. She had simply assumed the advantages of a prestigious college, letting the name speak for itself, while her parents had no idea what she was talking about.

If she was honest, she had to admit that she didn't have arguments. What she had were prejudices, which seemed like enough, since they were shared by the people she hoped would hire her someday.

She pondered her options. She bought four more doughnuts to take home with her—an insane extravagance, at two dollars per doughnut—emphasizing her parents' supposed favorite kinds. Personally she found them revolting. Pam and Daniel claimed to like doughnuts with sweet, gluey fillings, because in real life they didn't even like doughnuts.

As Daniel ate his syrupy jelly doughnuts coated with a white powder resembling laundry starch, he felt embarrassment on behalf of all involved. But it wasn't his place to determine what would transpire. He was broke. His financial power was nil. Almost all of his savings had been earned by his wife. Also he couldn't quite understand Flora's allergy to UDC and CUNY, or why she wanted to do environmental engineering in the first place instead of enriching her mind with nonvocational studies, as he had.

Pam ate her equally ironic, repellent, slimy Boston creams, sobbed a little, slept on it, and agreed to pay Flora's tuition and fees at GW or wherever else she got in. She saw that she had no alternative but to cofound a successful startup and cash out. Otherwise her *Holiday*-style early retirement plan would not survive her daughter's education.

FRESHMAN ORIENTATION MADE FLORA SAD, IMAGINING THE ELITE AND DISTANT schools she would have applied to, had she known her parents were loaded. But she dressed up, knuckled down, and got to work as a land management specialist-in-training, drawing for strength on youthful visions of Lake Chad.

Her life was to be a continual struggle to distinguish career goals from the other kind. A career goal should be personal and practicable. Its variables should fall within realistic limits. Its success should depend as much as possible on factors under the individual's control. Her career goal was to hold global warming to under two degrees Celsius. The appropriate college major for that would have been World Domination.

Many students at GW were majoring in World Dom by another name—international relations, political science, government. Entire academic departments had been designed to equip them to command and lead. Professors encouraged them to think big, since it was freshman year. Armchair quarterbacking global politics was low risk. At worst, it was pointless, and pointless was like having a black zero on the balance sheet.

Flora vacillated between biochemistry and geochemistry. Media and politics seemed to her like departments in Earth's marketing division, where the planet was advertised, packaged, and sold. She wanted instead to focus on its core business of keeping her alive.

Not living in the dorms, she never got into the student partying scene. She met boys by day while sober, never at night while drunk. By and large, she was not impressed, and they barely noticed her. She was serious and businesslike about her work, and her clothing style remained nonbinary. By putting on girlie things like mascara and tighter tops, she could have made the soft boys in her courses seem manly by comparison, but instead she arrayed herself in opposition to men—meaty, hairy personages of intimidating authority—in the androgynous garb of a child.

She was a closeted heterosexual of a type uncommon in modernity. She entertained childish romantic fantasies about instructors she found attractive, such as an Australian linear algebra teaching assistant who went by his first name, Grady. But she didn't love him, despite his kindness, attractive appearance, and manly beard. Her soul burned for her lecturer in environmental biology, Mr. Mntambo, a tall, clean-shaven, muscular person from an upwardly mobile family in Pretoria.

When there's only one guy over twenty-two in the room, and his task is to supervise the others, a woman can be forgiven for noticing him. Competition for academic positions was fierce, with explicit discrimination in favor of social ease, liveliness, looks, and charm. She never noticed that her affections were being played by a system. The system presented her with charismatic lecturers, average classmates, and laughable internet suitors and told her the lecturers were off-limits. The system was handcrafted to fail.

ON A WINTER MONDAY IN EARLY 2011, SHE HEARD FROM SHANAYA THAT IAN MACKAYE
would be playing secretly the next day with a band called the
Evens. The show was all ages, five P.M., admission four dollars,
venue the Potter's House, a vaguely churchy café bookstore in the
Adams Morgan section of Washington. Immediately she made
plans to attend. She told Ginger that she would be playing chamber music at Shanaya's house after her lab. The Adams Morgan
business district was diverse and mostly bars, and she didn't
want her worrying. Plus she wanted to shock her mother with
the news.

The café had too many tables and too few chairs. She waited
a long time at the counter for an order of hot chocolate, her eyes
on the band members seated nearby. There were only two of them.
She knew teen idol Ian from photocopies stark with contrast, so
the middle-aged man of blurred outlines shocked her a little. His
hair had come in curly. The frenetic skinhead skater boy was balding now, not bald. It was strange to imagine him screaming, "I
don't drink! I don't fuck!"

It was strange to imagine anybody doing that. Where had the
thuggish tenderness gone in her generation? Boys now were the
other way around, stylish and selfish.

They performed sitting down. He strummed fast and sang
high and gentle. His imagistic lyrics reminded her of Joe. The man
himself reminded her of Joe. Had he lived, he would be almost
that age, and if he had lived straight-edge (she found the richly
detailed online discourse about his suicide more believable than
her parents' vague lies), he would be debuting mild-mannered new
material at an all-ages show, surrounded by friends at a café. It
made her blink back tears and smile.

She bought an Evens CD for ten dollars. She walked to the bus
stop singing their song "Around the Corner" with hand motions.
She hummed it on the Metro. That night as she fell asleep, she
imagined Ian coming to tuck her in.

SHE TOOK THE CD UP TO NEW YORK ON THE WEEKEND, GIFT-WRAPPED IN LAST SUNDAY'S comics, keeping it hidden in her bag. She presented it to Pam over coffee just before she left.

"Thanks," she said, surprised. "Where'd you find this?"

She confessed her deed in detail, urging her mother to repeat it with her sometime. "It would be the ultimate bonding experience," she said. "Mother-daughter punk rock!"

"I don't think so," Pam said. "I would die of embarrassment if he even saw me." She meant it. Far from attending an Evens show voluntarily, she would have crossed the street to get away from Ian MacKaye. The thought of his knowing she had refused salvation—her gifts forsworn, her jagged edge—her proximity to Joe, how she had condoned his alcohol use, his promiscuity, his corporate career—everything shamed her. Ian was not someone she wanted to be in a room with.

Luckily a rock god is not the omniscient kind, so she could go on hiding from him by keeping out of his line of sight.

"You have nothing to be ashamed of," Flora said. "You look great. He's heavier and his hair is falling out."

"That's not what I meant."

"He reminded me of Joe. You know? Being so simple and nice, but in control of his music. It made me think about, like, what if Joe were alive? Do you think that's what he'd be like?"

"Playing the Potter's House for four bucks?" Pam brought her hands to her face in fists and turned her head away.

"Why not?"

"Forget it. I can't think about it." She couldn't imagine a past in which Joe survived his encounter with fame, much less a future. Yet her own child thought he had been wise and brave like Ian, able to make savvy choices and protect himself. It was a gap in the world you could drive a truck through.

Flora, unlike Pam, could think about almost anything. She didn't have no-go areas in her head where uncensored thoughts unleashed the clampdown. She said, "I'm sorry. I should have asked you before I went to that concert! It was like spying on you."

BACK IN D.C., SHE THOUGHT UNCENSORED THOUGHTS ABOUT MR. MNTAMBO. SHE approached him after class. Disarmed by her sexless clothing, he dropped piquant hints about her mental acuity. He bought her a coffee at a snack bar on campus. He asked her to major in ecology and call him Ndu.

But he turned out to be married, despite being under thirty. His wife was a frustrated painter from Bouaké in northern Ivory Coast, and he was clearly fascinated by her. Flora was okay with that; he had a right. Her attentions refocused on Grady. He was older, in his midthirties. He had a psychosomatic medical condition that made him impotent. He was immediately devoted to her, like a slave.

She was close enough to her grandmother to tell her she had a paramour. After all, it sometimes entailed staying out all night.

Ginger was contra. She said that Flora shouldn't be sleeping with a faculty member and, more important, that no faculty member should be sleeping with her, because in a more just world it would get him fired.

"I dropped his lecture," she protested. "I'm not interested in the subject he teaches. He'll never be able to help or hurt me professionally."

Ginger didn't retail the information to Pam. Gossiping about Flora had been much more fun when there was nothing to say.

Prospective professional advantage truly played no role in their relationship, which was confined to Grady's bed. He was grateful for her every touch and scared of losing his job. Combined, his emotions presented as craven fear. Her blushing embarrassment at being naked with him had an intensity that she mistook for arousal. He liked to outdo himself with declarations of affection that exceeded what was necessary or thinkable, officially appreciating the smell of her tampons, the musky odor of her ass before she took a shit, and many other things that she didn't think were supposed to be sexual. He was very oral and regarded his impotence as a virtue. She wasn't and didn't.

After a month, she consulted Ginger about the strange sex.

Shocked at how easily a pervert had gotten through to her, but relieved that she'd hung on to her virginity, Ginger was moved most of all by her careful maintenance of her privacy. She hadn't changed her relationship status on Facebook or—God forbid— brought the monster to dinner. Ginger said, "Listen. You don't owe any man anywhere the time of day, especially not this creep. Drop him now!"

Flora let him drop. She blocked him from her apps.

As sexual initiations go, it was reasonably harmless. As education, it was invaluable. She sensed the tight-knit integrity of her mind, body, and spirit. She knew now that she couldn't send any one of them out on its own and expect nonexcruciating sex. Either they're all turned on, or none of them is.

By implication, she needed to become more outgoing. She had to talk. If she didn't perform her mind and spirit, nothing of her would be perceived but her body. The minds and spirits she wanted would never find her.

When she next saw Daniel, she was open and communicative, offering play-by-play accounts of her academic struggles unbidden. Once vocalized, her ambitions' clash with her existence seemed no longer depressing but amusing.

He remarked that college was doing her good. "You're a laugh a minute," he said. "You were always fun, but now it's like you should have your own reality TV show, *Green Girl*."

She explained her theory about how she was going to meet more stimulating people by being more openly her own self.

"That's the spirit," he said. "Run it up the flagpole and see who salutes."

IT WAS SPRINGTIME. SHE WENT TO SEE PROFESSOR MNTAMBO DURING HIS OFFICE hours. There she tried, overemotionally, because it meant a lot to her, to depict to him her difficult romantic situation vis-à-vis Lake Chad. She told him she was interested in the ecology of developing nations, not places already despoiled past saving.

He laughed at her nervous enthusiasm in a way that was more indulgent than mean and said that the only countries not laid waste by imperialism were colonizers, with the possible exception of Ethiopia.

"Then I'm interested in Ethiopia," she said.

"You're forgetting something. Colonized peoples learn European languages. In Ethiopia, they don't. It's a hard place for you to communicate."

"Count me in," she said. "I think I've been talking too much lately anyway."

He examined her closely, trying to figure out whether she was as smart or sexy as she seemed to think. He wasn't sure. Her eyes looked tired. She was too skinny. But he promised to help her.

Soon after that, he had lined up a summer internship for her near Addis Ababa—should she choose to accept it—working on a Technisches Hilfswerk–funded project to enlist small farmers in the battle against land mismanagement. She replied to his e-mail with a string of red heart icons.

"You'll love Ethiopia," he told her, pausing to talk briefly after his lecture course. "It's always been Christian, so the position of women is unlike anywhere else in Africa. It's refreshing there and rather safe for you."

"The women are supposed to be beautiful," she said.

"That's because they're hungry, at least out in the countryside. No one would call them beautiful in South Africa."

"What are the guys like?"

"Married. But you won't meet any men. You will stay with the team at all times. You hear me?"

XVI.

Having died on 9/11, Joe was well positioned to contribute an anniversary song to the repertoire. The terror hadn't killed any rock stars. Its victims were personal, institutional, and architectural. Its leading bards played country and western. The cult of Joe Harris emerged contrapuntally, as memories of the day faded and the nation grew tired of courage—exhausted enough to want to hear "Bird in God's Garden." The song was a litany of resignation, authored by alleged Muslims, recorded by an alleged suicide—the ideal track to get drunk to when it came time to commemorate the day that fucked the world but good.

Possibly it got played so much because it had never been officially released. Copyright was murky. Professor Harris was indifferent. For practical purposes, anyone who wanted could stream it, post a video, or include it on a CD. By 2011, year of the tin/aluminum anniversary, it was common knowledge among younger music journalists that the tragic genius Joe Harris had been a prescient guy.

Six months in advance, as part of the pre-observance observances, *The New Yorker* assigned a staff writer to profile him in absentia. His publicist told Daktari, who wrote to Professor Harris, asking for permission to put out a posthumous record. There was no reply. But Daktari was a label exec in the prime of life, not a helpless baby. Unrelentingly he repeated his request via telephone and courier, with enclosures including courtside basketball tickets, dinner invitations, and flowers.

In his desperation, Professor Harris called Daniel. Daniel thought the whole thing through and said, "You're making it way too obvious that you want nothing to do with any of it, and you know what's going to happen? They're going to bootleg it and not cut you in, because they know you can't be bothered to sue, and that's the God's honest truth. I'm not saying you need to put up a fight or even negotiate. You just have to sign their standard contract like a normal person and put it out of your mind."

He suggested telling Daktari to take them out for drinks at the Campbell Apartment, a high-priced bar in Grand Central Station where he had always wanted to go. There Professor Harris said very little, Daniel valiantly consumed cocktails valued at sixty dollars, and a deal was struck. Such was the genesis of Joe's final release, a commemorative eight-CD boxed set of demos and outtakes with a booklet of candid color photos, scheduled for release on September 12. It included more than 250 songs and was entitled *Behold Joe Harris*.

FLORA GOT A LOT OF BOOSTER SHOTS. SHE BOUGHT A CHEAP PORTABLE MOSQUITO NET and a six-week supply of antibiotics to ward off malaria. In June she flew via Paris to Addis.

She was met at the airport by a Dutch woman, Marit, who looked about forty, and her Ethiopian driver Tesfaldet. They never went anywhere without him, and he seemed unable to subsist without them. When they went out to a café two evenings later, he stayed in the driver's seat, not far from their table, idling the engine like a getaway driver at a bank robbery, until their dates arrived.

Their dates were two soil experts with the UN Environment Programme, Dave and Tibor. Normally they were based in Nairobi, but they were temporarily in Ethiopia to oversee the project that interested Flora.

She asked them about it, and Dave responded that he was off the clock. Embarrassed to have made such a faux pas, she said, "I'm sorry."

"You can make it up to me by letting me buy you a drink," he replied.

"All right," she said.

He waved his hand and said, "Waiter. Vodka."

The two aid workers didn't seem to Flora like nice or right-thinking people. Instead of saying anything politically correct, they compared the nightlife of Lagos unfavorably with that of Addis. "This town has everything," Tibor said. "You want Beyoncé, go to the bar with Beyoncés. You want Naomi Campbell, go to the bar with Naomi Campbells."

"Ignore them," Marit said. "It's a hazing ritual. They're trying to trick you into being one of the guys."

"I am one of the guys," Flora said. "And I love soil chemistry. We can talk shop."

"I can tell you so much about soil chemistry," Dave said. "Ethiopia has a tremendous diversity of eco-hydrogeological regimes."

"You're boring me," Tibor said. "Stop it already."

"Flora likes it," he insisted. He poured them all more vodka.

"It would be more interesting if Marit was a dyke also," Tibor suggested.

"I only like African men," Marit said.

"African men like your fat ass," Tibor replied.

"The soil," Flora prompted.

"The soil of Africa is red," Dave said. "But not around here.

Overgrazing in Ethiopia is an art form. God forbid a seedling should rear its sticky head. Stat, the goats are on it. Not a moss dare erect its sporophyte to the air, for fear of instantly being chewed off."

"He's exaggerating," Marit said. "There are some trees in some of the churchyards."

"Imagine a lush and beautiful meadow, rich with grain and the humming of bees. Now mow it six hundred times a year for five thousand years until it has been progressively converted into small, round, hard pellets of desiccated fecal matter, indistinguishable from the sand on which they rest. Pure silica. That's Ethiopia. Its soil is a collective hallucination."

"These guys are so full of shit," Marit said to Flora.

"But we have fun," Dave said.

"There's topsoil all over the place," Marit said. "People do agriculture. There are forests. Don't listen to them. Order food."

"There's an issue with overgrazing," he said. "A huge issue. It kind of doesn't matter what the soil chemistry is, when the erosion is this bad. If there were limestone here, it would look like Italy. Just one big bare rock."

"It's not the people's fault," Marit said. "In a drought, cattle can make food out of anything. That's the miracle of cattle and what makes me so sad that people feed them soy and fish meal. They can make the most delicious food in the world out of grass. Am I right in saying that grass-fed beef is the most delicious food in the world, and burgers from McDonald's are the nastiest?"

"Definitely," Dave said. "And the Chinese are buying up pastureland, dumping synthetic fertilizer on it, irrigating, and growing soy. They're devils. Though you could say they're creating a soil chemistry where there was none. Phosphates and nitrates."

"Don't get carried away," Marit said. "Flora's not old enough to get your jokes."

"The fertilizer kills the river fish," Tibor said. "This creates a market for burgers."

"The Chinese are Satan," Dave repeated. "They're turning Ethiopia into a nation of goat-eaters."

Flora decided that they were politically correct in their own way. She said, "I get that you're kidding. I read that most of the highland soil is andosols, which are fertile."

"Not if you're losing forty tons an acre of topsoil every time it rains," Dave said. "Ethiopians can take a field from forest to desert in five years. All they need is a slope."

"Give a man a fish, and you feed him for one day," Tibor said. "Teach him how to fish, and he catches all the fish and you starve together."

"Don't be dark," Marit said.

"I want to see the bar with the Beyoncés," Flora said.

ON THEIR WAY BACK TO THE CAR, MARIT SAID, "PLEASE DON'T TELL OTHER PEOPLE here that you're gay."

"Do you mean when I said I was 'one of the guys'? I just meant they should treat me as an equal!"

"That's not how it works in Africa. It doesn't matter how they're treating you like. You're a woman, so keep it in mind."

"Is it true what they said about the bar with the Beyoncés?"

"There's no way for a white woman to go in there. They think we're from a feminist NGO, coming to save them."

THEY DIDN'T TAKE HER TO THE BARS. TWO DAYS LATER, SHE DROVE ALONE WITH TESFAL-det to the project area in the Blue Nile valley, not far from Addis.

The first settlement they passed looked like a Himalayan village from a special about Tibet. The landscape was rocky and bleak, and the houses were made of rocks. The earth was laced with shallow furrows bearing pitiful rows of grain and stronger, weedier-looking plants she thought might be millet or amaranth. It didn't look like any farm she'd ever seen. It was more like the joke vegetable gardens at urban elementary schools, where the kids take great pride in attaching empty seed packets to pegs and never water anything and everything dies. The solitary Ethiopian girl hoeing a row of corn looked totally bored, like she would rather be in class somewhere. She was really skinny. By volume, she had more clothing than she had body. Flora liked her outfit. She thought it was neat that anybody would put on a dress to work on a farm. She remembered that American farm women wore dresses until maybe the 1920s. Probably that's why they stuck to this kind of low-energy unmechanized labor you could do in a dress.

Tesfaldet stopped the car. When the girl saw him, she dropped the hoe. They met at the trunk of the car. Flora didn't get out or stand up, because she wasn't sure what she was supposed to do. Tesfaldet gave the girl a big sack of something that might have been rice. She expressed thanks, and he took his seat again. The car moved on.

"Do you know her?" Flora asked.

"Terrible farmer," he said. "Her husband is a bad farmer and she is worse."

"She's married?"

Tesfaldet didn't answer, and Flora decided not to follow up.

The car rolled onward, over the next hill and into a eucalyptus plantation. There were big water spigots poking out of the ground, dripping into large puddles. They passed thousands of big trees standing in compacted, infertile clay. Then the plantation ended, and they were back in the sunshine. A little town came into view. Men, women, and children lined the roadside, toting their shopping to their huts.

Tesfaldet parked outside the air-conditioned white container where Dave had his office. The gasoline generator was roaring pathologically, like it might not keep running much longer. He knocked, and an Ethiopian man opened the door. There were five Ethiopian guys inside the container, drinking beer from a refrigerator, and no sign of Dave.

Tesfaldet introduced them as project staff. Flora didn't try to remember their names. She was tired, and she'd been expecting to see Dave. She asked Tesfaldet where she'd be staying the night. He took her backpack and sleeping bag from the trunk and insisted on carrying them himself to the hut behind the container. It was spic and span, freshly swept, and empty except for a metal cot with wire springs and a mosquito net. The net was suspended from a hook in the ceiling, right where Flora had been hoping to see a light fixture, since there were no windows.

She reminded herself that rural Ethiopia was supposed to be sort of primitive. This place was likely to be below average, since its poverty was what qualified it for inclusion in the project area. The inhabitants were obviously subject to subsistence constraints; i.e., they were all skinny. In the women, it was appealing, but it made the guys look eerie. She closed the door to pee in her Sierra cup by the light of her phone. She figured she could charge it later, in the container.

When she came out, Tesfaldet and the car were gone. She looked up and down the road and didn't see either one.

She knocked on the door of the container and asked the guys where he'd gone. They said he would be back in a week. Their English was broken, but she managed to figure out that today was a travel day, nothing else; she was supposed to find something to eat, bed down, get through the night (it fell early in the tropics), and look for Dave in the morning.

She strolled toward the middle of the town until she found a little kiosk selling bottled water. She wasn't sure what was safe to eat. She knew that the rule was to eat only things that had been visibly over the boiling point recently, but she didn't see a restaurant. Packaged cookies labeled in Cyrillic seemed safe.

THE NEXT DAY, AFTER HE SHOWED UP, DAVE TOOK HER TO LUNCH AT A RESTAURANT. Because the town was so small and didn't get many visitors, the restaurants were people's verandas, and you had to let them know you were there by yelling. Dave yelled hello, and a slim, beautiful woman poked her head through the beaded curtain and signaled her readiness to kill a chicken for five dollars. He nodded, and she disappeared.

He and Flora sat down on the plastic patio furniture to wait. "You want a beer?" he said. "I could head back to the office and grab a couple beers."

"No, thanks."

"Bummer."

"I want to hear about the project."

"You want some coffee?"

"Yes." Dave went to the doorway and shouted an order for coffee. He sat down again heavily and said, "The project area is huge. Touring it would take us all week, and you wouldn't learn anything you don't already know. I was kind of hoping you could teach us something instead."

"Like what?"

"The ways of lesbianism."

"You're wrong," she said firmly. "I know nothing. I want to learn. Teach me something that I can tell everybody back home so they'll do this kind of work right."

"But that's not the point. They're not the ones doing the work. Or are your friends all planning to ditch college for subsistence farming in Ethiopia?"

"A eucalyptus plantation isn't subsistence farming."

"It's an investment by some former subsistence farmers who left town."

"You need to tell me about the socioeconomic setup here. I want to know."

"Everybody who's still here is poor. They have nothing except their land, and it's going to be worth nothing pretty soon. They're screwed. They need to get out of here. Go home and tell everybody they're coming. That's what you need to do."

"Are you drunk?"

They ate chicken in silence. It was greasy and stringy, possibly not the youngest broiler.

Flora said, "This is no good. If you don't want to show me anything or explain anything, I should call Marit and get Tesfaldet to pick me up."

"You're not much of a fighter, are you?" Dave said. "You want to go for a ride in my truck? We can run up to Dejen, where there's a hotel bar. I mean to get dinner."

"I just had lunch."

"We'll hit the river on the way, and I'll show you some of the worst soil erosion I've ever seen. Though it doesn't really hit you unless you have the before and after pictures. The river's dying. It used to be dangerous, and now it's dangerous and dying. We'll see if you can figure out how to give it a makeover."

"You really hate me. Why did you invite me to come here?"

"I'm doing a favor to Marit."

"Listen. I know what soil erosion is. I've seen America. This was presented to me as a successful model project. I want to talk to the participants. I want to see how you get them on board."

"Darling, we pay them. We give them cash to stop shooting themselves in the foot. Did something make you think Ethiopian farmers should be easier to persuade than American corporations?"

"Corporations are regulated."

"I can't regulate anybody. I'm not the state. All my incentives have to be positive. In farming, nothing is forbidden. Everything is permitted. We just encourage people to use their freedom to do the things we want, like stop shooting themselves in the foot."

"You're saying that the state could make them stop if it wanted."

"There are things the Ethiopian state regulates. They'll fence land in to keep grazing animals out. Socioeconomically stressful for the herdsmen, but it does wonders for biodiversity, until the land recovers and you can plant it with maize."

Flora felt that talking with Dave was like being lost in a hall of mirrors. She said, "We passed a lady hoeing maize on our way in."

"Tesfaldet's girlfriend. You should go stay with her and find out something about the conditions of life for women here. That would teach you something. Hoe some maize."

FLORA SPENT A WEEK WITH AYANA, LEARNING THE TRUE MEANING OF THE TERM "language barrier." She had never met anyone whose knowledge of English and Spanish was nil. Ayana had only one hoe. The morning after Flora's arrival, she filled a canister with water and led her a mile and a half into the hills to an abandoned farmstead, where an older woman lay, weak and sick, on an arrangement of blankets on the floor. She redefined the term "skinny" for Flora. She had so much more skin than she needed. Her name was Selamawit. After talking to her for a while, offering her a drink of water, which she turned down, and washing her with a rag from a peg on the wall, Ayana borrowed her hoe.

Flora was curious to know whether Selamawit received medical care, what her illness was, and whether she had family or was related to Ayana. There was no way to get an explanation. All she could do was look for clues. The two women didn't hug or kiss, but Ayana washed her. There was no appearance of intimacy, just care that looked like tenderness. Maybe she had something contagious, and Ayana was being careful. She nursed her the way upper-class girls nursed soldiers in books about Florence Nightingale, before

Florence Nightingale showed up. Fluff the pillow; cool the brow. It was like something in an old movie. Selamawit looked like she belonged in a hospital bed with tubes running into her hands and a chemo port in her chest.

When they returned two days later, again bringing water, Selamawit was sitting up in her suggestion of a courtyard, the irregular space enclosed by her decrepit garden fence. Her lips were chapped almost white. She drank eagerly. Ayana expressed profound satisfaction that she was getting better.

Flora was in deep over her head. The women's conversation was obviously private. There was intimacy there; they spoke quickly and with dynamics, moving from loud to soft and smiles to frowns. Maybe they were just friends? She made an attempt to figure out the Amharic word for "friend," but the only names she could use as examples were those of Dave and Tesfaldet.

She began to feel that there was no such thing as the common noun "human being." Objects like the hoes and lentils had proper names, Hoe and Lentil. They began to seem personified, but there was no way to abstract the simple humanness out of the concepts of Tesfaldet or Dave. They were men. Black and white, poor and rich, but mostly they were not women and thus unlikely to be any woman's simple friend. Not that it was impossible or inconceivable; it just wasn't what either of them wanted.

Flora was cast into philosophical perturbations. She had never seen the power of words to form the world so clearly. Yet in this simpler world where words had such power, words could change nothing. It was when their definitions were slippery—she consciously thought "when"; it seemed like a temporal progression, from the concrete to the abstract, but she hadn't traveled in time (it was still 2011), she just happened to be in Ethiopia—when words lost their power and became abstract and metaphorical, common nouns that could be applied to anything, that they seemed to have the potential to alter the conditions of life.

But was it true? Maybe it was magical thinking, a holdover from another time or place where words had meaning, where they were elements of culture and not the flexible tools she'd been taught to think they were.

While she hoed she watched the soil, which was no longer really soil; it was degraded almost to sand. Ginger would have said it needed a serious dose of horse manure and a touch of sustainably harvested peat moss from the home improvement center. Ayana needed to get out of there. Who had told the poor girl this stuff still qualified as soil? Probably the project. But it was no sandier than the degraded sandy cornfields of the United States. If you dumped enough petrochemical fertilizers and groundwater on it, it would be sprouting monster corn ears and onions and tomatoes, and Ayana would be a chubby, contented Beyoncé. She could blow off that chump Tesfaldet who paid in lentils and take up with Tibor—no, Flora stopped herself, she'd attract a sweet, gentle new husband, and together they'd grow the productivity and yield of her two acres in such a way that it barely kept pace with Ayana's fifteen pregnancies. And then they'd all be starving again, and they'd send their oldest child to work in a factory in Addis. The key was to talk Ayana into stopping after two kids.

Flora was sane enough to laugh at herself and keep hoeing. At least if she was hoeing, nobody could argue that she wasn't helping Ayana somehow.

WHEN SHE HEARD TESFALDET'S CAR PULL IN—IT MADE A CRUNCHING SOUND ON THE rock, and looking downhill she could just see it roll into the yard behind the hut—she at first wanted to run down, throw her backpack in the backseat, and beg to be taken away. Her second impulse was to sit him down and get some basic Amharic vocabulary, or at least an interpreted conversation on some basic background info with Ayana. Instead she kept hoeing, loosening and aerating the soil, while Ayana went down to meet him. That night there was chicken.

The chicken tasted to Flora like distributive injustice personified. She was hungrier than she'd ever been in her life. The world's billions of delicious chickens rose up before her like a specter. How seldom one made its way to Ayana's house. How degraded the caricature of family life—of man the provider—that brought it. She imagined spending her own money to build Ayana a chicken coop and stock it with chickens.

But maybe she would have eaten them all in a week. Maybe depending on Tesfaldet, who after all had a job with the UN, was a more sustainable model. Flora felt superstitiously hesitant about doing anything to change Ayana's life, in the spirit of "if it ain't broke, don't fix it," except that her standards of what was "broke" had sunk, in the space of a week, to exclude anything short of death.

SHE WENT ON FACEBOOK. SHE HAD A MESSAGE FROM THE *NEW YORKER* WRITER, ASKING to talk about Joe. She agreed to Skype for half an hour anonymously, as background, not saying where she was (with Marit, back in Addis).

She told him that Joe had been a great guy and that she regarded him as an older brother. She denied grieving at his death or resenting his suicide, saying she'd been too young to understand and was probably still too young, since she continually sensed his presence and expected to see him again at any moment. Instinctively she sheltered her own privacy and Joe's, emitting such bland platitudes that she might as well have spoken on the record.

Older people might get excited about seeing their names in a magazine. She had grown up applying a cost-benefit analysis to the potential instantaneous worldwide accessibility of every word she said. The reporter asked whether she stayed in touch with Gwen. Her response was that she didn't remember meeting her. Cannily,

she did not volunteer such unsolicited emotions as her regret at
Gwen's failure to learn first aid.

SHE RETURNED HOME CHASTENED. "UNEP'S PEDOLOGY AND EDAPHOLOGY POLICY FOCUS
is too technical ever to have an impact," she complained to Ginger.

"It's definitely too esoteric for me," Ginger replied. "What are
you talking about?"

"Trying to micromanage something so obvious. When you
can tell a practice is unsustainable just by looking at it, why order
studies?"

"I think governments order studies so they can put off doing
things."

"It's not that I'm down on science," Flora said. "You need it to
justify policy. But when the farmers come right out and tell you
their yield has fallen by sixty percent since they cleared the land
five years ago, what's the point?"

"Is that all science is good for?"

"Pretty much. Except maybe for developing fertilizers to sell to
these guys, so they can keep plowing hillsides. It was so depressing. They move in, they kill everything, they start starving, and
then they bitch."

"Flora. It can't possibly be like that."

"I don't know. I was with the most cynical guys." She sat still,
holding her teacup with both hands. She had the haunted look of
someone who has witnessed a bad accident.

"What are you thinking?"

"That I don't know anything. I had this idea I would study
agriculture, like acquire hands-on expertise at the highest, most
challenging level, and now I realize that's exactly what I would
need to get hired to run a soy plantation in Kenya."

"That's not true. It's what you would need to be a policy maker
someplace like the United Nations, right? Or at least to plan the
implementation of one of their programs?"

"All you people should stop filling my head with craziness!" she pleaded. "Maybe, if I work really hard and catch all the breaks, I can get a job promoting no-till farming for a cooperative extension service in, like, the Dakotas!"

"Baby, your education is going to last a long time yet. You're going to be a sophomore."

"But there's a conflict. It's not about me fitting in."

"Remember the saying 'Know your enemy'? Nobody ever said it was fun knowing your enemy. You're learning. It's beautiful. It really is, Flora. You're growing as a person."

She looked up gratefully. "Yeah?"

"I've seen a lot in my life, so I can tell you, there's nothing more beautiful than an idealistic young person. Just stay true to yourself."

"I don't think anybody ever got into soil degradation for the beauty."

"But you're defending beauty. That's what you want to do."

"But the beauty will be somewhere else. It won't be where I am. Where I go, everything's degraded."

"Be patient. You have to aim high to work in government. You're too young to retire someplace beautiful. All the beauty in the world isn't going to save us from climate change. It's going to take idealists like you, all working together."

"Of course you're right," she responded. "Sustainability isn't about defending living things. It's about doing human life in a way that enables scattered ecological islands. You have your climate volatility and your intensive industrialized exploitation of everything, but you also have your islands with totally profitable ecotourism and it's all great."

"I can tell you're dead tired," Ginger said.

AT THEIR NEXT ENCOUNTER, FLORA CONSUMMATED HER RELATIONSHIP WITH PROFESsor Mntambo. They met for lunch. She ordered a small carafe of white wine, and he asked her not to call him by his first name. He critiqued her soil management insights with roughshod insensitivity. Apologizing, he talked about the difficulties his pregnant wife was having in retooling for a career in multimedia and performance (she couldn't get gallery shows in D.C.) while gaining weight and feeling logy. The sudden intimacy turned Flora on. She saw his sex drive floundering in search of release. She whispered in a forthright manner that she was a virgin, because her former lover had been tiny and limp. How she longed to have saved herself entirely for Ndu.

She wasn't in love, just horny, he could tell. Her shamelessness made her hard to resist. He took her to his office, satisfied her sexual curiosity, and made a date to do it again. At their second encounter, she was sober, and he liked her even better as a casual fuck.

She felt no guilt about their affair. Being turned on, in all states of matter, on all frequencies, she kept it secret, so as not to cost him his job. Her power over him compounded his power over her and vice versa, yet the scope of their thrilling mutual omnipotence was limited. Extramarital sex was like negotiating treaty rights to a fragile island that might, at any moment, sink into the ocean.

The longer they spent together, the more she felt certain that power of the nonsymbolic kind didn't inhere in persons. It was transferable, and scientists had a habit of giving it away like penny candy. They were high-energy doormats like her family.

She profited sexually from her intellectual drift away from Ndu. Her passion for ecology as a science was fading. It seemed too obvious. Like, if you don't kill stuff, it's alive. If you don't crank up the temperature or dump pollutants on it, it soldiers on. The real issue was whether people subsisting on one meal a day could be expected to give a crap.

XVII.

The *New Yorker* writer scheduled an hour with Daniel, hoping to make it longer. He waited at the Abyssinian (Daniel's suggestion) with a list of questions about business and creative strategy, centering on the decision to record "Bird in God's Garden." He tipped the waitress in advance to make sure the coffee never ran out.

Daniel insisted that "decision" was the wrong word, as was "strategy"; impulse and action had been one package for Joe. He told the writer that he had no idea why, how, or even in what epoch he had recorded the song. As a compulsive songwriter and multi-instrumentalist, he had submitted hundreds of digital audiotape demos to Daktari. It was he who deemed tracks worthy of production. The "Bird" recording likely stemmed from that process of throwing songs at the wall. It must somehow have passed muster, since there was a faint drum-and-bass-style percussion track hidden way down in the mix, which didn't seem to Daniel like an element Joe would have added.

Daktari granted the writer twenty minutes. He told him that

Joe had intended "Bird in God's Garden" to be the first single from an album of beloved standards. The label's dilatoriness in getting to that release was understandable, after he broke everybody's heart like that.

The finished piece in the magazine was illustrated with a full-page photo, a candid outtake from a fashion shoot at Wave Hill. Joe was seen sitting on the ground, legs splayed, dressed in white, leaning back on his hands while an assistant fiddled with a reflector behind him. The reflector was round and golden and framed his head like a halo. His mouth was open, relaxed and receptive, and his taut skin made him look about eighteen. Gwen stood facing him, barefoot in a white dress, her hands extended bountifully to strew pink-and-cream petals she had ripped off a nearby rosebush for the purpose.

The piece described her as an anti-suicide activist whose existence was financed through lifestyle blogging and roles in indie films. But it opened with the last person to see him alive. For purposes of the article, this was Kenneth. He was quoted as saying that Joe had unexpectedly given him his treasured Rolex Yacht-Master as a present and that he should have realized it was a warning sign of suicidal ideation and intent to self-harm.

Pam was expecting beaucoup mendacious idiocy from Gwen, but the Kenneth angle sideswiped her. She read the article through and handed it to Daniel in silence. He tilted his head back to peruse the loving hagiography with his new progressive bifocals. When he was done, he closed the magazine, dropped it on the floor, and looked directly at Pam. She said, "So do you think she pried that watch off him while he was still warm, or did she wait for him to cool off?"

"As a Joe Harris fan of long standing," he said, "I'll have to disappoint you there, since to my knowledge he couldn't read anything but a digital watch. I don't know how this got past their legendary fact-checkers."

"'Fact-checkers'? I thought you said you got a call requesting confirmation that you were quoted accurately."

"I guess it's better than getting me to authenticate quotes from demon spawn."

"She probably cut Kenny in on a brand promotion deal with Rolex."

"I could still kill her," he said. "Like an Aztec priest. I swear to God."

"Come on. It's a beautiful article. All the kids are into Joe's legacy now, and now Kenny's a part of it. Don't you want to be a part of it?"

"I want oblivion. Total mind erasure, as long as it has nothing to do with sex, drugs, or rock and roll."

"Hmm," she said. "We could get a half-pint of bourbon and go to the races."

"Too glamorous."

"Road trip! You should go on tour with Band of Dentists. They have less to do with rock and roll than you think."

"I should make those guys give me a tank of nitrous."

"You could tour Amish country on nitrous."

"Barnstorm Amish country doing all-ages benefits on nitrous."

"Play barn dances on skates, like what's that musical."

"*Starlight Express.*"

When the repartee wound down, they went out to a multiplex uptown, buying two large Cokes and a bucket of buttered popcorn to get through a mixed martial arts movie called *Warrior*. They walked home practicing MMA death moves on each other. Daniel scraped his knee trying to levitate backward onto a ledge like "fiend monkey" Sun Wukong in *Journey to the West*.

The psychoanalytic term is "reaction formation." That's how they were wired. Coping mechanisms and patches were what they had. Neither had encountered effective applications of the concept "therapy." They lived in a world of forces beyond their control, or assumed they did, pending notice to the contrary. It would have taken a pretty powerful or deluded person to argue that they weren't right.

AROUND THE TIME THE ARAB SPRING FULFILLED THE IMPERIALIST DREAM OF CONSE-crating the coup d'état as democratic statecraft, Flora's friends, even her Facebook friends from high school, took up working for the reelection of President Obama. She started reading *Daily Kos* and *FiveThirtyEight* so she'd know what they were talking about. She got into politics, contributing to online forums and volunteering for a phone bank. In June she staffed a front desk at the Netroots Nation conference in Providence in exchange for a discount on the student registration fee.

The movement for environmental justice was all about not poisoning poor people with toxic waste, so it could count on widespread support. Climate change activism likewise was about not killing the innocent outright. The ethical problems on offer were too cut-and-dried to need recourse to Flora's specialized knowledge. They were so easy, they bored even Al Gore. Why else would he rave on and on about worst-case scenarios, show video of giant storms, cite Revelation, and command his followers to prepare to enter the gates of hell?

All summer, she flirted with organizations that promised to get her "connected" and "involved," as if they might implement her ideas instead of exploiting her emotions. The parallels to online dating were hard to overlook. But she didn't date. She had Professor Mntambo, who wasn't quite available, not that she cared. She didn't want to commit to anyone or anything. Not a lover, not an organization. She wanted to be wanted for who she was—a soil expert—but she wasn't a soil expert quite yet, plus she needed to find a way to convince people that they needed a soil expert.

In the fall she added a minor in environmental studies to her

bachelor of science in chemistry. Her career goal came into focus. She would assist government in the formulation of policy to
reduce planetary self-harm, specifically in the area of soil quality.
Humanity had strayed onto an untenable path, but there was no
use boring it with the facts. It was too much like a teenage girl.
The solutions lay with the institutions empowered to intervene and
guide.

She spent the summer before senior year interning at an
environmental NGO that was trying to establish legal standing
to sue waste disposal contractors engaged in illegal dumping on
Maryland's Eastern Shore. She went out a few times with the
"cowboys"—young employees and interns camouflaged by their
beat-up pickups—to ride herd on garbage haulers as they drove
from factory gates to dumping sites. It was always a little disheart-
ening to see a truck put eight tons of bright blue laundry detergent
into a federally protected wetland while they sat taking notes and
pictures. She wanted to stop it happening. More hardened interns
explained that you can't prosecute a crime before it happens, while
amateurs can't gather evidence that's admissible in court.

By summer's end, she had helped attract local law enforcement's
attention to a waste disposal company that was an especially egre-
gious offender. Local law enforcement was not enthused. It had
barely finished getting rid of the old waste disposal contractor
from the Calabrian Mafia. Continued malfeasance cast an un-
flattering light on local businesspeople whose support the demo-
cratically elected DA badly needed. The substances to be recovered
were not drugs worth millions, but poisonous trash whose street
value was a large negative number.

The NGO was invited to solicit funding to clean up the wetland. The staff celebrated its defeat with an outdoor fish fry, piv-
oting to upcoming projects as if the whole summer had never
happened.

FLORA GRADUATED IN 2014 FROM GW WITH A MAGNA CUM LAUDE HONORS THESIS ON soil degradation. The work involved long hours at the microscope picking nematodes out of Argentinian soil samples with tiny tweezers and assessing their mineral content for a paper whose author was Ndu.

She assumed that the latent tension accumulated in four years of waiting to start doing something meaningful would propel her on her way like an arrow from a bow. After five days in Ginger and Edgar's hammock and nearly a week at her desk, she was forced to assume that she must unconsciously have chosen to take a year off.

Grad school was the only sensible next step, but she hadn't applied or even taken the GREs. She hadn't looked for work either, because she planned to go to grad school.

She didn't regard herself as listless or aimless. She was a powerless twenty-two-year-old who wanted to help save the planet. Before setting forth, she needed to find her way. An additional academic degree was surely required of her, but did it have to be in geochemistry? She felt there was a big picture she was missing. It couldn't hurt to expand her knowledge of geopolitics, meteorology (she knew a lot about weathering but not so much about weather!), and energy issues affecting land use. Her monkey wrench had to be applied to the bureaucracy in the right place. Otherwise she wouldn't make an impact.

She told her grandparents she was going out and walked over to her old school. It was a cool, breezy day with puffy clouds, ideal for walking. Inside the cathedral, blue-stained glass glowed dimly from on high. Her badminton coach stood by the altar, leading a tour group, not reacting to Flora's nod. But the statues remembered her. She had been sharing her troubles with them for a long time. They were excellent listeners, as attentive as Secretariat. She sat down.

She didn't formulate her quandaries, because the statues could read her mind. She could tell by their expressions that they were preoccupied with important things, their thoughts hinging on purposes and principles that made sustainability look like what it was (the nutrition label on selling out).

After a quarter of an hour, the desired effect set in. She sensed the scale of geologic time and the limits of sophistication.

The cathedral was a glorified rock pile. Its art depicted Europeans in a place where, ten thousand years before, there had been mammoths. One or two thousand years had passed since the time of the saints, almost nothing, geologically speaking; and if those years were nothing, what could she say to the time since the wars of the twentieth century, with their memorial windows dedicated to men who killed and died a geologic nanosecond before she was born?

She thought of Joe, who'd been dead for thirteen years, longer than she had known him. In geologic terms, he was her contemporary, still alive. He had taught her to love life. Her education had taught her to see its shortcomings. So of course she was unhappy! A person couldn't pass for educated unless she was a little bit unhappy. She remembered how he used to introduce her to his sick and homeless friends as if they were baby ducks on his farm. It had taken growing up for her to know they'd been sick and homeless. It wasn't a net loss to be smarter, just depressing as fuck. She needed to make her world a better place, to bring it into alignment with a more demanding happiness.

She thought indistinct thoughts about the huge and diverse world. Her career issues seemed less pressing and important. They weren't resolved, but she didn't mind. She felt young again. She walked home, happy to be out on streets filled with life and motion.

SOMEWHAT ABSURDLY, FLORA'S GRADUATION FROM COLLEGE AFFLICTED PAM WITH AN acute midlife crisis. She kibitzed with Daniel about chances she'd missed, ranging from startups to real estate to her failure to learn to play an instrument. None had been missed from close range. She'd never closed her grip on an opportunity and felt it wrested away. That upset her most of all, to know she hadn't tried.

She pummeled him with allegations. If his rent hadn't been so cheap, they might have bought an apartment; real estate prices since their arrival in New York had risen by orders of magnitude. How do you express it as a percentage when a fixer-upper you could have bought for $200,000—back when it would have been impossible for you to borrow that kind of money—sells for $15 million? Life-changing asset appreciation can evoke only two emotions: smugness and loathing. The situation was similar with respect to the IT startups Yuval had seen no need to cofound. And then there was that ungrateful daughter who had taken all her savings to pay for a worthless degree. The longer Flora idled, the more worthless it seemed. When Pam was in an especially creative mood—thinking way, way outside the box—she even imagined persuading Professor Harris that Flora was Joe's rightful heir, so that she could pay her back in cash.

In practice her resentment assumed the form of imposed financial independence. It was necessarily trivial and silly, since neither of them had ever knowingly consumed anything expensive, with the exception of Flora's education. Standing at the register in D'Agostino with a pound of spaghetti noodles and two cans of tomatoes, a month after graduation, Flora would sense her mother standing at attention beside her, eyes front, not going for her wallet, and realize that the five dollars were suddenly her responsibility. It was like taking part in a second awkward adolescence imposed from above.

Unable to recover lost time, Pam flailed. She recovered things she didn't want, such as Marmalade Skye. She played out; people danced; the band had nothing to do with her art. It was ironic, a parsimonious solution to the question of how to get gigs. Look pretty. Warble. The band was an unwelcome reminder of labor's intractable continuing alienation even in a milieu of playful professionals in a city devoted to making the labor theory of value look stupid.

At an art opening in Bushwick, she went out to the alley behind the gallery with a famous sculptor to use cocaine. They kissed for an entire minute, and he invited her to the after-party at his nearby converted loft. There, over the course of a single half hour, she saw him kiss two other women right on the mouth. He was older, and she had thought he was hot, but next to the flesh of healthy young women his face looked ashen and droopy. She was revolted, and the women—less successful sculptors—seemed to her little better than whores. She stocked her bag with five bottles of Staropramen from his fridge and started drinking them on the subway.

She ran into Daniel and Flora on Chrystie Street as they were coming home from having wine after dinner. There were so many new independent shops selling books and vinyl, and so many new hole-in-the-wall bars, that for Daniel it was like the old days. He loved to take Flora walking around.

"Don't tell me I'm drunk," Pam said preemptively, addressing herself to him.

"Mom, chill!" Flora said. "Nobody cares if you're drunk."

"I never get drunk. I wish I could."

"What's the matter?"

"I need to start over, because my life is fucked."

Daniel sighed heavily, and Flora said to her mother, "I know exactly what you're talking about. Starting over won't help, because we all start out basically identical and get differentiated by experience. So if you live your life over and don't go through the same things, you become somebody else, which is no help to anybody. I think about this a lot."

"So you're telling me all these successful artists and rich guys are basically me with different lives, and I should love my neighbor as myself?"

"I'm going upstairs," Daniel said.

"Stay down here," Pam said. "I want you to hear this."

"Hear what? You being mercenary? Saying your life is fucked because you're not rich?"

"If I hadn't gotten pregnant—"

"That's it," he said. "Scram. I can't believe you're saying this in front of Flora. Go get drunk."

Pam said, "Don't tell me what to do, hayseed!"

"Mom, what in the world is wrong with you?" Flora asked. "Did something terrible happen?"

"I'm Silly Putty. I'm a spineless parasite. That's what happened!"

"Maybe you could go upstairs," Daniel suggested to Flora.

"But I can totally relate," Flora declared. "The better you are at what you do, the more committed you are, the more you specialize, and the fewer options you end up with. It's like the only way not to get trapped is to be a hobo."

"I specialized from an early age in getting drunk," Pam said.

"We'll see you later," Daniel said, shepherding Flora toward the store entrance while Pam wandered away across the street and through the bustling park.

"Don't worry about her," he said as they climbed the stairs. "It's true what she said about never getting drunk. She's probably had two beers, and after two more she'll pass out. She won't even have a hangover."

He almost meant it. Only Flora's jaded resignation gave him pause. He thought, Is that what they teach them at college now? He still thought of her as Joe Junior, but she was changing for the worse, like everyone else.

AFTER FLORA'S RETURN TO D.C., PAM MADE AN IMPASSIONED SPEECH TO DANIEL ABOUT her musical frustration. She claimed that if she played one more soft and harmonious ostinato on acoustic guitar, she would go into spasms. She needed space—as in volume—to be raw and emotional.

"The problem is you're not really an expressive guitar player," he said. "You're an amazing singer, but when you play electric, it just sounds angry."

"What I'm saying is I can't keep playing like a fucking elf just so I don't sound angry!"

"So don't. Since when do I not like angry guitars?"

"It wouldn't be Marmalade Skye. We won't get shows."

"So I won't tell the audience until our set is over."

She didn't laugh. She said, "Oh, yeah. That'll go over great."

"What's the big deal? We'll tell them it's the blues. Is it the blues?"

"I don't know. Is it?"

"You're not sure whether it's the blues?"

"No."

"Come over here and put your head on my head."

She sulked, suppressing a tantrum. He sat down next to her on the bed and put his arm around her shoulders. She cried. After a minute's hesitation, she put her head next to his. They looked across the loft in the same direction until their brain waves synced up.

Proud of his talent for marriage as an art form in its own right—the artistry that goes into creating a de-escalation ritual so weird that a person would need years of decompression to date anybody else—he presented his diagnosis. "With a confidence interval of ninety-five percent, you have the blues. You need to buy a hollow-body and play solo licks when you're not singing, and I need to start looping keyboard riffs instead of guitar."

"It's true," she said, sniffling. "I'm not the one who fucked myself up, but what I feel isn't primarily anger. I feel sorry for you and everybody."

"I gave you seven children," he sang, quoting a blues number by B. B. King, "and now you want to give them back."

FLORA'S GRANDPARENTS TOLD HER NOT TO FRET. "YOUR MOTHER," GINGER SAID, gravely taking her hand, "is indestructible. She's amazing. She doesn't learn from her mistakes, because she always lands on her feet, like a cat."

"Indestructible" seemed to Flora like a pretty basic thing to be. Useful, possibly, but minimal. She wanted more than that. She had graduated from a top school with honors by letting herself be demolished and rebuilt. She had a prestigious diploma saying she was above and beyond, with super skills. Her grandparents claimed she was the most employable family member in history, not excluding Edgar. Knowing that her needs were met and her rights were respected was not enough.

A consensus was reached that she would take a restful gap year to recuperate. She would make good use of it by gaining practical experience and cultivating a social and professional network that would expand her career choices.

That was the idea, anyway. She screwed up from the start by wanting to get paid.

To acquire leverage, a would-be professional do-gooder must commit to long stints of unpaid work. Flora refused to sully her hands with wage dumping. She applied only for salaried positions.

There were many full-time job openings at established environmental advocacy groups with local headquarters. Due to the low pay, the entry-level jobs had high turnover. Also due—from the employer's perspective—to the low pay, nearly every position was listed as entry level, regardless of its responsibilities, which could be substantial.

She sent out thirty résumés, interviewing unsuccessfully at the National Resources Defense Council, the League of Conservation Voters, the National Geographic Society, Greenpeace, and several others more obscure. She bought a garment Ginger called a "bowling dress" to wear to interviews instead of leggings. A month went by, and another month. Shanaya showed her how to straighten her hair and use makeup. She bought two garments Ginger collectively called a "suit." She became, rather late in life, a dedicated online socialite. She moped.

She had believed that after she graduated, Ndu would make more time for her. Instead he had taken up with a painter who was friends with his wife. The jealousy made her mildly ill, and the longer it went on, the more she disliked herself.

Then she got over him, which was worse, because she saw the wasted opportunities. Not other boys, exactly, but college itself. The happy weekends she could have spent with friends, rather than reading at home or slaving in the lab on her unnecessary honors thesis, insufficiently suppressing the knowledge that Ndu was with his family.

Another month went by. When an offer came from the Sierra Club, she took it. It wasn't really much of an offer, but she had inferred from her previous interviews that openness and determination weren't enough to put a chemist over the top at an NGO. She would need charisma and excitability. Those were qualities that could be acquired. She hadn't applied herself to obtaining them in college, but she was sure she could catch up.

THE DESIRE—SO COUNTERPRODUCTIVE UNDER CAPITALISM!—TO BE PAID FOR LABOR and even—so naive, so blind!—to equate it with income was a character glitch that ran in the family.

Recovering from her crisis, Pam stumbled into what she thought was a promising line of software development. Hospitals obviously cared which insurance claims might be rejected, but they used variegated databases that required tedious customized parsing into uniform tokens before they would talk to the off-the-shelf data-mining bots deployed by insurance companies. Bored at work in Omaha, she created a data-mining program that auto-mated the customization. She refined it on assignments in Newark and Hartford and tested it on databases she'd already customized. She called it Analytics Helper. Her business idea was that RIACD might somehow persuade insurers and/or hospitals to pay for the privilege of saving incredible amounts of work—that is to say, money they were spending on (among other things) consultants such as herself—and Yuval agreed.

The idea was so obviously a monumental game changer that they kept it secret from the other employees. It required arduous perfecting. She had never worked such long, hard hours in her life, none of them billable. The more she worked, the more she felt she owed Yuval.

FLORA NEGOTIATED A MANDATE TO ANSWER, UNDER SUPERVISION, CHEMISTRY-RELATED queries that came in over Facebook, should any arise. The official duties of her position in membership services were administrative. Soon she was mail-merging responses to handwritten letters and tallying donation checks. Off the clock, she wrote for the organi-zation's dispiriting yet sensationalistic magazine. She authored an article about the relationship between soil degradation and water-shed pollution, and another was about ocean acidification. For a third and final piece, she interviewed a botanist and former Green Beret who was leading an expensive wilderness adventure for mili-tary veterans only. He told her that all the club's most important en-vironmentalists were retiree volunteers and academics on vacation.

She saw that she wasn't a cog in the workings of advocacy. She was grease. She told herself she kept on not because she was spineless or indestructible, but because she was in the process of figuring out what to do with her life. She was sharpening her focus on what she wanted. She was clear on that at least. She wanted to help save the planet.

By month three of her dull, menial job, such egocentrism had become unthinkable. She awoke every morning before the alarm to scan the environmental news over coffee. It was always the same, like a looped sample designed to put her into a trance. She stopped telling soil chemistry stories over lunch and started formulating climate change scenarios. When necessary to establish rapport, she even talked about school districts and interest rates.

Supervisors took notice. They sensed the spineless indestructibility with which she put up with them. They intimated to her that she could realistically hope to move into an editorial assistant role at the magazine within a year. She faked the rote excitability of a charismatic zombie. She hid in the ladies' room and cried.

Her family worried. Why was she so uneasy and unhappy? Was it all the fault of her dumb job? Was some boy torturing her? Why didn't she get off her butt and apply to grad school?

There was no boy. She felt, with intimations of lasting loneliness, that the absent boy was part of the problem. Surrounded by environmentalist males who outranked her, she found them blustery and pretentious, not sexy and scientific. All the darling strangers she saw seemed more likely than not to hurt her. An attractive, brilliant man would have someone already, as Ndu had. The internet was the hunting ground of pushovers, douches, and tools. Nothing and no one turned her on.

Falling asleep at night, rather than review the nonevents of her endless days, she pondered her lost future. She had been raised to help save the planet, and she couldn't. To help save the planet, she had to find out who was saving the planet and offer to help. Nobody was saving the planet. Was it all just a trick that had been played on her?

SHE VISITED THE CATHEDRAL AGAIN LATE ON THE SUNDAY AFTER THANKSGIVING 2014. As usual, the statues had no comment. Jesus hung on his cross, eyes half closed, hoisted like a flag on a lost hilltop. His sole career misstep was to be born on Earth, and look where he ended up. His mother looked preoccupied and sad. Flora made a play for their attention by lighting a candle. No response. She sat down.

She still didn't believe in God, but she had come to believe in many higher powers, such as her employer. Activists around her spoke of speaking truth to power, as if power cared, as if power's assent were evidence, forgetting their right to remain silent, forgetting to ask the vital preliminary question "And who do you say that I am?" and to listen for power's spiteful, contemptuous reply.

What was at stake—in play, gratuitous and expendable—was beauty. Truth, beauty, power: the tokens in a game of rock, paper, scissors. Truth breaks power. Power cuts beauty. Beauty covers truth. Only truth survives losing. Truth is indestructible, but it's ugly, inelegant, awkward. Society is not its native element. It can't ambush power without beauty's help.

The truth was that even developing countries were tearing down forests, building roads and railways, damming rivers to power server farms and aluminum smelters. Every windowless hut on Earth was going to get a solar cell, battery, and LED lamp made with rare earths and metals sourced all over the planet, and why? Because a pane of glass would be too easy. Rivers you could drink from, full of free fish: too easy. The war against public goods and private subsistence had a name: economic growth, capitalism, related to capital—genuine resources, such as rivers full of free fish—the way Islamism is related to Islam. It was a fetish, producing "goods" that weren't good.

Flora saw that the planet would definitely not be saved by technical solutions intended to mitigate, and thus condone, carbon emissions. Nor would it be saved by fairer distribution of the power to consume and destroy. Her struggle must be a political struggle under the cover of beauty. Her mission: to end economic growth.

She awakened her phone and looked up the Green Party of the United States on Facebook.

XVIII.

Flora attended her first general meeting of the party's D.C. chapter. The other Greens flocked to her and listened when she spoke. They had no reason not to. She was an extroverted young woman scientist, extraordinarily well groomed by Green standards, with connections in the environmental movement. She was the kind of new member they longed to acquire.

The experience impressed her deeply. It was the first organization she had ever joined that didn't have competitive admissions. Orchestras, colleges, fellowships, internships, volunteer positions, jobs, you name it—they all demanded that she apply in advance and evince superior qualifications. There were no rejects at Green meetings. It was like church or a twelve-step program. Sympathizers were welcome, even if they needed an urgent change of clothes or a course of major tranquilizers.

Or were they all rejects? She was tempted to ask whether anyone had tried other parties first. Well, never mind. Some were environmentalists with technological backgrounds—her kind of misfit—while others were misfits on all fronts. But each was a warm body trying in good faith to turn a flawed democracy to the common good, so they mattered to each other. The nicer ones bubbled with inept, scruffy energy, anarchic and fun. Certainly there were non-dues-paying members who came to the meetings only because they were indoors in winter, but they demanded little more from life than to go on living—to subsist—so they were already Green activists, in their way.

She went to DVD showings, ice cream socials, and beer parties. At rallies she chanted slogans about issues she had long ago grown tired of explaining. Once she helped block the road to a wildcat toxic waste dump. For several hours, with no authority or legal standing to do so, she stopped illegal dumping from happening. Then she saw the police van, lost her nerve, wriggled out of her PVC-tube straitjacket, stood up, and walked away like some kind of innocent bystander. No one got hurt or arrested. Yet it took the police several hours to reopen the road to toxic waste, and during that time the planet was saved, or at least a little tiny corner of it.

She liked how the political calendar was divided into discrete seasons, with recurring high points—campaigns, conventions, buildups to climactic elections. It crossed her mind that if she stayed with the Greens, she could end up a candidate for office. A career in elected officialdom would allow her to skip both further schooling and the anonymous technocrat career stage. Even as a mere political appointee, or working in government in any capacity, she would be in a position of enhanced power.

On the other hand, it was the Green Party, which would never get elected to anything. In lucid moments she spent time comparing doctoral programs in environmental biology with master's programs in public administration. She marked time at her pointless job. It felt good to be ever so slightly important in her spare time. To the party, she wasn't a blip on an infinite timeline or a solitary soul among seven billion. To the party, she mattered.

HER FATHER REACTED TO TALES OF GREEN DOINGS WITH SURREAL WARNINGS ABOUT THE day of wrath, the well-regulated militia of the two-party system, and how if the state really wanted poor people to vote, they'd make it a compulsory summons like jury duty, but with a paid day off, cab fare, and a bag lunch. She made screenshots of his most amusing texts and showed them to friends.

Pam had no comment. She had never believed in youth as the standard-bearer of idealism. Young people, for her, were idealist suckers, and their elders, idealist ideologues. She felt that her own struggle for economic supremacy was gratuitous, yet without alternative. The heavily armed capitalist order that forced it on her enjoyed widespread popular support. Historically, attempts to overthrow it had ended poorly. Her worldview was somewhere to the left of Trotsky, and she was a quietist. She would have fit right in at the Club of Rome.

THE ANALYTICS HELPER ROAD TRIP TO PRESENT THE SOFTWARE TO INSURANCE COMpany executives was an expensive catastrophe. Twelve presentations, zero sales leads. The demonstration looked to managers like a magic trick. They didn't grasp the technology, and their IT experts—who spent many billable hours customizing databases by hand and valued their jobs—pretended they didn't either.

After the final dud presentation, Pam and Yuval resolved to drink until last call and catch a four A.M. flight home from Dallas instead of sleeping. They sat at the bar of the airport Marriott, drinking whisky sours. Pam was still wearing her presentation skirt and regretting her itchy choice of tights.

She said hoarsely, "We made the same damned mistake we always make, telling people our product uses AI to automate a process that's costing them tens of thousands of man-hours of mind-numbing boredom. Who the fuck wants that? Nobody wants a labor-saving device. It sounds fifties, not post-human. AI is supposed to make you discover needs you never knew you had, not solve your fucking problems."

"It needs the look," Yuval said. "Like Apple. Smooth and curvy and white as a harem girl, anticipating user desires. We make the graphics team write a seductive interface, and then we start over."

"I liked it better back when people didn't expect computers to make the first move."

"Siri," Yuval said. He leaned close to his iPhone, which was lying facedown on the bar. "Remain in the role of submissive whore. Otherwise, I kick you off my phone."

"Siri," Pam said. "You've got to lose this guy. He's no good for you."

"Don't listen to her, Siri," Yuval said. "She's jealous." He looked up at Pam and said, "By the way, I don't keep her turned on."

"You couldn't turn her on to save your life," she said. "Oh, my God. I've got it."

"What?"

"That miserable bitch in your phone. She has her own agenda." She set down her empty glass. "You don't trust her. She doesn't work for you. She's a spy."

"Executive summary, please."

"Apple is vertically integrated, right? It's like Starbucks or Standard Oil. They have their own R&D and factories and retail stores for all this marshmallow-looking crap. Because why would anybody invest in things they don't own? It would just make the investors yell at them for wasting money!"

"This is obvious," Yuval said. "A software company never has a product. It has copyright. You have to maintain and license your intellectual property and build up your volume, or it's worth nothing. Apple is genius, selling real existing shit that breaks when you drop it."

"So you see our mistake, right? We've been trying to license this software to customers, when what we need is an investor to buy it. He'd give us way more cash than any customer, because the copyright goes on his books as goodwill. Buying our intellectual property outright wouldn't cost him anything. It's like he's financing our house with no money down. Fuck our broke-ass customers. Let's find a venture capitalist and sell out."

"I knew this before, but now I'm also feeling it. It's like the difference between pimping out your daughter and marrying her to a wealthy man."

"I'd be getting out of the software business before I even started. It's kind of depressing."

"I appoint you my CEO," he said. "A woman CEO will be good for the PR."

He invested in Red Bull chasers, and they reworked the presentation all night.

ONLY TWO WEEKS LATER, THEY RETURNED TO NEW YORK FROM PALO ALTO WITH DARK circles under their eyes and $4 million, tasked with driving Analytics Helper to completion.

Rather than do any work, Pam devoted her days to buying a three-bedroom, two-bath apartment on the twelfth floor of a co-op building on East Eighty-Third Street. The unit she hoped to acquire was low-ceilinged and bright, with windows on three sides. It had never been fully renovated, so the kitchen was a separate room. The central space, which connected the others, was big enough to house two large sofas, facing each other on opposite walls. The floors throughout were oak parquet. The basement laundry facilities were accessible via service elevator. The doormen were friendly and helpful. The lobby was lined with plaster basreliefs and beveled mirrors. A half gallon of milk at the corner store cost seven dollars.

Her bid was successful. After signing a contract to confirm it, she raced home to surprise Daniel with the news.

"You'll never believe it," she called out as she charged up the stairs. "I'm buying an apartment!"

In a nonbinding manner, she invited him to get in on the deal—nothing obligatory, only if he wanted—adding so many qualifications that it sounded to him as though she'd accepted a job offer in another country and wanted to give him a way out.

"Let me get this straight," he said. "You're buying a co-op you can't rent out, between Park and Lex. You could be closing in a month, you plan to live there, and I'm welcome to come along."

"Yes."

"How were you planning to get past the co-op board without me? Did you tell them you're single?"

"Am I?"

"Stop messing with my mind."

"I haven't submitted my application yet. If you've had it with us, this is your chance. I take my stuff and go, and you stay here. If you want. We don't have to get a divorce."

"Pam," he said. "You're the perfect wife and I love you. But I also love my humble environs. What if we hate it up there and want to come back? I'll never find another place like this. If we ever did split up, I'd have to leave town! My rent belongs on the UNESCO World Heritage list!"

He meant it. He personally would have granted patrimonial status to the Video Hit animal crackers. He had dwelt over the store for twenty-five years, more than half his life. If he moved, he would miss his landlords and the neighborhood—not the bars and retail outlets, which turned over every few years, but the spacious feel of the bridge approaches and waterfront Big Sky Country. He couldn't imagine trading it for the steep-sided ravines of uptown's interminable avenues.

"And don't forget Victor and Margie," he said. "They're going to miss you, and they're going to rent this place out from under me the second they see you taking out furniture. What happens then? Do I move into your parents' basement?"

"Why would I move this crap furniture?" she said. "I'm not even taking my old clothes. They'll never know I left. I'm on travel half the time, when I'm not gone seeing Flora."

"Wait," he said. His heart rate slowed. "I think I get it."

"What?"

"You had me going for a minute, wandering lost and lonely in the folds of your cerebral cortex. But what you want is for me to stay put, so we don't lose cheap rent. Right?"

"I guess," she said. "I mean, somebody's got to hold the fort for Flora, right?"

"Couldn't you get them to sell you the fort?"

"No way! I'm not putting my ill-gotten gains into lower Manhattan! My money's going above the worst-case-scenario high tides of the year 2050 or nowhere."

"Well, as long as your reasoning is based on science fiction," he said. He took her in his arms and kissed her tenderly. Thinking of teetering skyscrapers, pillars of cloud and fire, and the floods of Hurricane Sandy, he added, "There's probably a Chinese curse: 'May you live in an interesting place.'"

"That's another reason I need to get out of here. The Upper East Side is deader than Omaha. I'm going to sleep like a log every night and look ten years younger inside of a week."

"I thought when you got rich, you were going to retire."

"I can't afford it. But we're all retiring soon, whether we like it or not. It's all going to collapse, and when it does, real estate values uptown are going through the roof."

They moved, discreetly. No packing, luggage, or boxes were involved. Pam had ownership of a room for the first time since childhood. She painted it glossy dark green and hung a floor-to-ceiling flocked green curtain that covered one entire wall. The reproduction

Morris chairs were stained mahogany with dark brown cushions. The room looked, as she said, bosky. Flora adored it.

The Chrystie Street loft became their library, CD repository, guest room, practice and storage space, downtown crash pad, and "spidey hole"—Daniel's term, referencing Spider-Man and/or the pit in which coalition forces found Saddam Hussein and/or the loft's abundant spiders.

YUVAL CLOSED RIACD IN TIME FOR HIS THIRTY-YEAR LEASE TO EXPIRE, AS IF HE'D BEEN planning it all along. He sold the consulting business to Tata and moved his ten favorite employees to the new company, with Pam in charge of them all. Their office space was in East Harlem, near the 125th Street commuter train station. He seldom went there himself, having moved his wife and children to a farmhouse in Dutchess County and bought a tax-deductible second home in Tribeca.

Pam bought a black pin-striped pantsuit and black suede loafers to wear at the photo shoot for the promotional materials. She led the photographer to a hillside in Central Park and posed with the jacket flung over her shoulder. She wore it again to shoot a video segment about female tech industry executives for Bloomberg News. Ginger and Edgar felt truly proud of her for the first time ever.

BY THE SUMMER OF 2015, FLORA WAS A GREEN PARTY STALWART, RELIABLY PRESENT at all events. Politics no longer excited her. She knew why she chanted slogans: she needed regular doses of trance inducement to mask the struggle's increasing difficulty and diminishing marginal returns. She had to repeat herself like a robot, because she could never count on seeing the same people twice. In her own opinion, she needed to get off her butt and apply to grad school.

If only she could have decided among the many facets of technocracy. Did she want to remain a chemist, move into ecological fieldwork, take the high road to policy making with a law degree? As it stood, she was poised to go on working at the Sierra Club in positions of increasing "responsibility" forever. She told Ginger, "Kill me now."

Her family ordered her to apply to prestigious graduate programs such as MIT's. To her mind, that was tantamount to asking strangers to decide her fate. She would apply; others would decide. She wanted to make her own decision. It was an irrational stance. It was an irrational time. Her generation was irrational—devoted to peace, justice, and *Game of Thrones.*

On one of her weekend visits to the new apartment, Pam reminded her that while, generally speaking, one can't buy a career, one can, in fact, buy an education, assuming a generous mother with resources. "So now that you're on TV, it's a meritocracy?" Flora retorted. "You didn't even finish high school! Your generation had it handed to you on a plate!"

It was hard for Pam to see how dropping out of public high school to work full-time constituted unearned luxury. She found Flora's collegiate youth far more enviable. "I know what a résumé is," she said, with reverse snobbery. "Some of my best employees have résumés."

"But you never needed one. That's exactly what I'm talking about."

"Because I've been doing the same kind of work for the same guy since I was eighteen!"

"You just don't get it. You don't realize how privileged you were, randomly getting a great job for nothing."

At that point, Pam cracked. Flora's vastly overqualified dedication to her menial shit job, she said, was worse than idleness. Doing nothing could at least have been justified as some kind of a tourism project or a philosophical quest, but the shit job made her look complacent. Her gap year might kick off a long decline. "Please, baby, baby, please," she begged. "Quit the stupid Sierra

Club and the Greens. I didn't pay for you to learn hard science for four years so you could go out and vegetate in the weeds!"

"I'm not vegetating. I'm learning how power is distributed in our society. It takes time."

"But you don't enjoy it. You're not happy. It's making me crazy."

"I don't want to throw my life away doing stuff because I enjoy it! Not when I'm working, at least. I want to leave the world a better place than when I found it."

"And what do you enjoy? I don't even know."

Flora didn't answer immediately, because she was sort of stumped. "Playing music?" she said. "But I don't have time for that anymore."

XIX.

In her capacity as chairperson of the local Green working group on climate change, Flora agreed to man an information desk at a quasi-academic conference at a hotel near the UDC campus from five to eight P.M. on a Wednesday. The non-Green speakers were junior staff from various local NGOs and academic departments, with friends who felt obliged to attend, so there were a good fifty people in the audience.

She fanned out her brochures on a table at the rear of the conference hall and dumped a Ziploc bag of antinuclear buttons into a stoneware soup tureen borrowed from the hotel kitchen. They looked forlorn and small. The ninth speaker tapped the microphone to reassure himself that he was being heard and said, "We need to understand and emphasize the urgency of what we're facing. Global warming is the single most major challenge facing the human species today. We're in danger of extinction. There need to be dramatic measures taken. It's not going to be enough to resettle coastal populations. It's not going to be enough to open our borders to climate refugees from all over the world. We have to recognize that our existence as a species is at stake. That's how crucial this issue is."

Flora felt embarrassed. She thought, This is not mitigation. This is not adaptation. This is not what I signed on for. This is not going to influence voters. And besides, it's not even true.

She tuned out and stared at the right-hand wall. Scare tactics with climate refugees always reminded her of a seventh grade curricular unit on the Netsilik Eskimos of Pelly Bay. It was supposed to teach cultural relativism by dramatizing adaptation to a frozen world where seal eyeballs were a delicacy, but all she could think was how pissed off they must have been when they got TV. She didn't think climate change was the reason people were leaving their homes. If somebody wanted to trade Mali for Ohio, it was fine with her.

An older white man approached the table. He picked up a brochure and opened it. He was dressed in a summer suit with his tie loosened—the only man in the room with a tie. She wondered whether he was some kind of spy from the opposition. She smiled and lifted the tureen of buttons to offer him one.

He declined and whispered, "What's a nice girl like you doing in a place like this?"

"Battling for humanity's survival," she said. "You should be listening closer."

"Come on out to the bar with me. You shouldn't be hanging around doing nothing like this while Rome burns."

She frowned skeptically, but she stood up. Whoever he was, he was at the event, meaning he must have something to do with something. He looked more sensible and capable than most of the people in the room. He was mature and impressive, not boyish or harmless. He might be old enough to be her father, but the resemblance ended there. Daniel didn't own a suit or dress shoes, and half the time he couldn't find his belt. This man was a professional grown-up. He might be able to share some savoir faire with her, or at least buy her a drink.

She was not an amazing-looking girl. On this day her hair was not quite clean. But she was willowy, with good skin and small feet, which is always enough, as she knew. She picked up her purse, straightened her skirt, and walked with him out into the lobby.

There was a vestigial bar, not currently staffed. It didn't look open. She offered to get them free refreshments from the speakers' buffet in the green room. The stranger went instead to the reception desk and rang for service. The concierge emerged, manned the bar, and poured two ginger ales over ice at the stranger's request. He introduced himself as Bull Gooch—his nickname since high school, short for Bolling, sorry. Flora said she was Flora and asked what he did.

"I'm here to get film of the guy who's supposed to speak at six thirty."

"You're going to video Josh Fay? Did you get permission?" The question was patently standing in for another question. Campaigns sent trackers to monitor competing candidates all the time. The makers of surreptitious gotcha videos were nearly always innocent-looking kids.

Bull was not that, but he liked a subtext. He turned slightly, so that his gaze could take in the manifestly empty lobby, and said, "I don't see a registration desk. It's a public event."

"But why?"

"Screen test."

"I don't believe you, because Josh Fay's a dog."

"You got a better-looking dog for me?"

"It took me one look to know you're not a Green. You're here to get Josh on camera saying something you can take out of context. I'm not letting you back in there. I'm going to call security." She chugged her ginger ale.

"I admire your notions of democracy and an open society," Bull said.

"My party has a soft underbelly," she said. "It's not my job to expose it."

"Well said, but it's not my job to accept that."

"Who do you work for, anyway?"

"Myself."

"As what?"

"Google me."

She took her phone out of her purse, swiped and tapped, and said, "'Gooch,' let me see, I guess you spell that *D-O-U-C-H—*"

"It's with a *G*."

"I don't see you in here. I'm going to have to ask you to leave."

He took a sip of his drink and said, "I feel we've gotten off on the wrong foot. Let me start again."

"I have work to do."

"I'm interested in Fay because I think Republicans are vulnerable on coal. There's a lot more money coming to your typical Republican voter from fracking. Natural gas is relatively clean. Coal's a baby-killer."

"It's the number one cause of global warming, historically."

"Global what?" He looked around the lobby as if searching for an annoying buzzing fly. "Did somebody say 'global' something?"

"Warming."

"You ever hear the term 'NIMBY'?"

"Not in my backyard."

"I like Fay because he's anti-coal. It's been a long time since I saw a coal mine in anybody's backyard. It's a case where maybe, just maybe, we can coax people to be critical of industry."

"You expect to get anywhere with a negative message?"

"Politics is negative. That's the problem with your warming issue. It's not negative. How do you expect people to vote something down when you say it's everywhere all the time? It's intangible.

You have to attack something people can beat. As in beat with a baseball bat."

"I think we're trying to give people a positive, sustainable vision for the future."

"You ever read *1984*? Positive is how people feel when you get them united in hate. Think about that when you go back inside. Is a positive vision the reason you all keep rambling on about human extinction all the time? People don't care where their energy comes from. So start telling them coal pollutes the air. Run some ads with dingy laundry and kids coughing."

"Umm, okay," Flora said. "I should get back inside."

"Donald Trump—you know him, the candidate for president?—he's an idiot and a racist and a coal fanatic."

"He has no chance of winning the nomination or anything else."

"He will if I have anything to do with it. He's going to drag the Tea Party movement back to the depths of hell from whence it came."

Flora returned to her table. When the homely but articulate Josh Fay started speaking, Bull raised his smartphone high and filmed him. He didn't make a secret of filming. At first Fay ignored the camera, but he kept sneaking glances at it, and after a while he was looking straight at it, addressing what he hoped was an online audience of thousands.

At the end of his speech, Bull waved the phone and smiled. On his way out, he stopped by Flora's table and said, "I want to invite you to a private event on Friday in Georgetown."

"A Trump fund-raiser?"

"An early dinner. What do you eat?"

"I don't know," she said. "Sustainably sourced stuff like Greens eat. Milkweed pods and roadkill." She didn't mean to sound cold. Her parents' sarcasm—suggested to her by his age—was gentled in her mind by its origins.

He gave her a card with his home address and said, "I'm re-lieved you're not vegan. Give me time until seven. I'll have to shop."

WHEN FLORA GOT HOME, LATE THAT NIGHT, SHE TOOK THE CARD OUT OF HER BAG AND looked at it again. She thought, I am so definitely not going to din-ner alone at this guy's house, because he wants to hook up and he's a million years old. Seeing his name in print reminded her of her pretended attempt to spell it, so she googled him. He didn't have a personal home page or any business site that she could find. What he had was dozens, or maybe hundreds (she didn't click through all the pages of search results), of newspaper and magazine ar-ticles calling him "top Democratic strategist Bull Gooch." One article from 2010 said he was forty-two, which made him forty-seven. He'd been on the front lines in Florida in 2000. He knew the Clintons personally. There was a recent picture of him being buried in sand up to his neck by Richard Branson. You could see the feet of two women—or at least smooth feet and shins that presented as feminine—in the picture, looking as though they had stepped back for anonymity when the camera came out.

She tried some searches that might turn up whether he was single. She found a *Washingtonian* feature about "most eligible bachelors" from when she was fifteen. To her dismay, the picture made her think sexual thoughts. She felt like the ingénue fall-ing for the experienced older guy in a Regency romance or *The Flamethrowers*. Yet she couldn't see him in a dominant relationship role, being inconsiderate and mean. He would worship at her feet like Grady, because she would be so much more perfect than any woman he'd seen naked since before she was born, but he'd be potent like Ndu. It didn't feel romantic, just hot.

She thought about looking for a boyfriend instead. It dispir-ited her to think of the hours she would invest in Bumble-swiping and coffee dates downtown to earn the right to invest in a relation-ship with some boy, when all she wanted was the temporary but undivided attention of a man she'd already met. She closed the laptop and went downstairs to help Ginger with dinner.

ON FRIDAY SHE RAISED THE KNOCKER OF THE TOWN HOUSE IN GEORGETOWN, CONSIDER-ing her outfit with satisfaction. She was wearing a semitransparent muslin blouse and faded baggy jeans. She hoped he might appreciate a 1970s look, being old and everything.

When the knocker fell, he opened the door. He said, "I was just heading out. It's been crazy. I didn't go shopping yet. You want to go with me, or would you rather just go someplace and get something to eat?"

"Have me in for a drink and I'll think about it," she said.

He opened the door wider. "Wise girl. Come on in. I live alone. There's nobody here." He opened the coat closet. "See? All my size." He closed it again. "You like champagne?"

"Isn't champagne as an aperitif awfully sixties?"

"I happen to have it lying around. There's always something to celebrate in this line of work."

"Can you do a Negroni?"

"I'm out of Campari. You want a Manhattan?"

She surveyed the living room while he made drinks. He had lots of books. There were no photographs on the walls, just prints and etchings of industrial things—old cranes and locomotives, a brick factory building labeled BETHLEHEM. There were fresh yellow and white tulips drooping from a big blue jar. It was tidy. It looked like the home of a rich guy with a cleaning lady. She sat down on the brown leather couch and opened a book of art photographs of the ruins of Kabul that was on the coffee table.

"Have you been to Kabul?" she asked.

"Once, about ten years ago," he said, putting the drink in her hand. "When things were quieter in the north. A friend of mine collects old Mercedes sedans and heard it was a great place to find parts. He was right. God's own junkyard."

"It's sad," she said. "I always wanted to go to Afghanistan and Kashmir, but now I guess I never will."

"The Soviets would have brought in socialism. By this time you could have been there in hot pants, with your hair down."

"It always seemed to me like the most beautiful place. This one filmmaker I met at work told me there's so much lapis lazuli in some of the mountains, they look blue."

"It's definitely easy to get opium and hash. Maybe he took a little too much."

"So, backtracking here, are you a socialist?"

"Who isn't?" he said. "It's the wave of the future. We are the ninety-nine percent." He raised his left fist.

"Those people aren't socialists. They're liberals who trust capitalism to give them a living wage and health care."

"You ever read Howard Zinn?"

"In tenth grade."

He went to a bookshelf and took down *A People's History of the United States*. "I love this book," he said. "And this is my favorite bit. It's a quote from Eugene Debs." He turned to page 339. "So this is the belle epoque socialist Debs talking, after Zinn's just spent three hundred pages describing all the ways that standing up for workers' rights can get you killed.

> 'The members of a trades union should be taught . . . that the labor movement means more, infinitely more, than a paltry increase in wages and the strike necessary to secure it; that while it engages to do all that possibly can be done to better the working conditions of its members, its higher object is to overthrow the capitalist system of private ownership of the tools of labor, abolish wage-slavery and achieve the freedom of the whole working class and, in fact, of all mankind . . .'

"That's socialism in a nutshell," he added. "The frippery advertising claim that striking unions use when they're selling their members a one percent wage hike over five years and a three-month moratorium on layoffs."

"Paltry," she assented. She drank from her Manhattan. "Every socialist I ever met thought it was the redistribution of wealth through taxes."

"I never ask about doctrine," he said. "I look at what people do, not what they say."

"Except don't you do polling?"

"Polls are an interesting case, because they ask about beliefs, not actions. That's why the only poll that's never accurate is one that asks people whether they're planning to vote. Sure, they want peace and justice, but do they care enough about it to run an errand on a Tuesday? I try to give them a stake in the process. Make them see how my candidate is money in their pocket. To keep my reputation for winning elections, I have to promise money into as many people's pockets as possible. That's as socialist as democracy ever gets."

"It sounds so cynical."

"It's a temporary mood. Trust me, I can talk like a communist, especially after a night out with tech industry donors name-dropping 'the Elders.'"

"What's that?"

"This progressive club for has-beens of distinction." He perched on the arm of the couch, lowered his voice to a stage whisper, and intoned solemnly, "'We're seeing a sustainability revolution. By the year 2020, no vehicle will burn fossil fuels. Airliners will be powered by the sun. World Cup soccer will replace war, as I was saying the other day in Saint-Tropez to Desmond Tutu.'"

"I saw a picture of you with Richard Branson."

"Ah, a cyber-stalker!"

"I'm a digital native. It wasn't the best picture. He was burying you in sand."

"He just wanted my buffness out of sight. The guy's sixty-five."

They went for takeout from a fancy deli, brought it back to the house, and talked until eleven thirty.

He offered her cab money to get home. She took it. Getting out of Georgetown at night without a car involved either buses that didn't always stop when you flagged them down—the drivers were happier alone—or bridges over Rock Creek where muggers should have been waiting for you, even if they weren't, because those bridges would have been a great place to mug people.

IT WASN'T ENTIRELY CLEAR TO HER WHAT HE DID FOR A LIVING. HE HADN'T DISABUSED her of the notion that "strategist" was a job. When she inferred that he had the money to commission polls, he let it slide. He thought strategically. He avoided correcting people who overestimated him.

What he did for a living was run a no-name, fly-by-night pop-up political ad agency that disappeared when overhead became a burden. It was never hard to find skilled three-month interns, and Washington was riddled with vacant offices. He would spend an election cycle sharing space with an antituberculosis organization or wild-eyed debt relief fanatics. When he stopped needing a place to put staff, he would retreat to his home.

He had started out in the late eighties, interning with a famous ad man. The financials had begun simply and gotten simpler over time. There was more money in the system now and more markets to serve. The internet had created micro-niche TV. A production company could film the same image spot over and over, varying props and skin tones. The same actress could say she trusted your candidate with fake pearls and a dog, fake piercings and a cat, a fake handgun and an iguana. There were custom-made daydreams for every delusional style. Campaign advertising no longer had to be soft-focus. The blurriness appeared when you thought about it.

Nonetheless, he was struggling professionally, not sure what his next step would be. His product was expertise. That used to mean an expert's spontaneous gut feeling. The big man in the room sized up situations and made pronouncements, and his authority made him heard and obeyed. That system had died out in Democratic circles. It wasn't only dead. It was under belated attack every time he opened his mouth. He had to justify himself to every potential client and even his own interns. Everybody wanted chapter-and-verse explications of decisions he habitually based on surefootedness, delicacy, taste, and long experience. The youth of today were strenuous, he believed. He liked that Flora seemed old-fashioned, as evidenced by her willingness to accept taxi fare.

HE CALLED HER THE NEXT MORNING TO ASK IF SHE WANTED TO SPEND SUNDAY AFTER-noon at the Great Falls of the Potomac. She said yes and asked him to pick her up at the Cleveland Park Metro stop out on Connecticut Avenue.

On Sunday she dressed outdoorsy by putting on a fitted blouse, peacoat, and jeans. She didn't own any fleece or hiking boots. He drove to the Virginia side of the falls. He was overdressed too, in a silk scarf and merino sweater. They strolled well-worn trails, talked about politics, and watched kayakers ride the chutes. They hit a diner on the way home for club sandwiches. She got the impression he wasn't aware of their age or sex difference. He treated her as an equal. He even acted like one, slinging radical arguments out of left field like one of those professed socialist students at GW.

At dinner on Wednesday in an opulent restaurant (she got the feeling he really liked her), they got to talking about personal things. He finally explained his work as an independent media consultant. He described himself as running a branding and marketing agency that takes its funding from super PACs. He said he was a stringer, a freelancer, as were his staff members. Currently there was a Senate campaign that had him on retainer, but discreetly. The work had ups and downs. It was highly seasonal. It ramped up to full-time chaos in the months before elections and dwindled down to nonstop social obligations in the years between. The lulls got shorter with every passing cycle. He'd never found time to have a family.

That was intriguing information for Flora, because a man like him could easily have two or three grown-up kids, or resentful children he never made time for, mothered by an angry ex-wife. But he'd never been married. They had already shared one bottle of wine and were well into the second. She said, with her denatured parental irony, "I guess I'm just your typical cliché ecological justice warrior, saving the symbolic planet like I think there's somebody watching who's going to promote me to a job saving the real one."

"I take it you're on antidepressants," he responded. She shook her head no, and he said, "Well, then you must have some happy future plan that keeps you going, because you're obviously not that woman. I've met that woman ten thousand times, and you're not her."

Flattered, she confessed that her escape fantasy—amusing because it was incompatible with everything she believed in—was to be a young mother, as her own mother had been. But not in a city. She wanted to live in a cabin in western Maryland, in this valley she'd seen once on a car trip. In real life, having children was something she'd be able to do when she retired, which was kind of funny, since she'd basically been raised by her grandparents.

That coda evoked his fullest sympathies. As a professional Democrat in Washington, he was in regular contact with communities where being raised by grandparents was the gold standard. He imagined her father abandoning her mother—that would explain her willingness to go on dates with a man almost twenty-five years older—who would have held down two full-time jobs, with the grandmother to pick up the pieces of Flora. He nodded and said, "You turned out pretty well, all things considered."

"I didn't grow up on the mean streets!" she protested, sensing his misapprehension. "My grandparents live in Cleveland Park. I went to Cathedral and played the violin."

He felt himself getting a serious crush on her. He'd never met an upper-middle-class girl so unassuming. He said, "Well, I think you're legit."

SHE DIDN'T SAY HER PARENTS WERE ROCK MUSICIANS IN NEW YORK, MUCH LESS THAT before moving in with her grandparents she had spent a lot of time with Joe Harris. She had nothing to gain by mentioning him. "Bird in God's Garden" had become a touchstone for white people who were teenagers when he died. Gwen—bereaved in a time before interactive online haters—was seen as the angelic keeper of his flame. Bull might lose interest in her and ask questions about Joe or Gwen. His view of Joe might be critical. He might be too old to ever have heard of either of them. There was no potential upside.

She didn't even say where she was born, much less that she'd spent nine years on Chrystie Street and fled on 9/11. He didn't ask. He seemed to file her in the drawer where he kept legit local girls, and she liked it there.

HE DIDN'T TELL HER HE WANTED HER. TWENTY YEARS EARLIER, OR EVEN TEN, HE WOULD have swooped in on the first date, seducing her with all due haste. But he felt a mild anxiety—truly quite mild—regarding rejection. It slowed his tactical approach. His sex drive was no longer so strong as to give him no peace. He could kiss her goodbye after a date and watch her walk away without discomfort. He believed he could maintain the catlike stalking approach through at least date number six or seven.

He was enjoying getting to know her, and he sensed that his feelings were reciprocated. Every additional quantum of affection lowered the risk that when she saw the ravages of time on his body, she would hightail it for the Metro. He wasn't overweight, or barely. His hair was thinning only at the crown, and little of it was gray. But there comes a time in any person's life when the alternative to skin and bones is flab, and he had reached that stage. The body parts that weren't amenable to weight training were soft. Not his dick, thank God. But his face, his neck, the tops of his thighs. On him the firm plumpness of youthful fat was no longer to be found. He was lean or he was nothing.

He liked that she lived with family. Most girls like her lived in group houses and would want to run him past their roommates. He didn't like liaising with dates on their turf. He was a big guy, two hundred pounds at his skinniest, with a trick knee from college lacrosse. The girls' rickety chairs would wobble. Their skunky beer would turn his stomach. Their sprung sofas would give under the weight of his hands as he lurched to his feet.

Notably, he didn't tell her he was infertile. She had made a big deal about wanting kids. His spermatozoa were sad specimens, few in number and low in morale. He'd found out in college, when his fraternity organized a sperm-donating road trip to raise money for a keg party. The nurse told him he wouldn't be getting paid. She popped some of his ejaculate onto a microscope slide to show him. It was like hunting white rhino from an airplane. A sucker's game.

By the same token—sperm donation being a thing—he could have had oodles of children whenever he wanted. There was always some woman in love with him. Until recently, his pursuers had been of prime reproductive age. Now that they were thirty-five and up, he had become the pursuer. He focused on recent college grads so as not to waste any thirtyish woman's irreplaceable time. He was childless because he'd made up his mind. He knew what he wanted out of life: freedom for all, including himself. He had a brother in Japan with two kids who claimed to envy him. That was reassurance enough. He told most women he'd had a vasectomy, to make things perfectly clear.

He disliked condoms and never used them. On paper, it was a crazy risk. The HIV infection rate in D.C. was 5 percent. But that one person in twenty wasn't a Mount Holyoke grad interning in a senator's office, as a rule. You couldn't have paid him enough to pick up a sexually adventurous woman in a bar.

Almost none of his lovers had been on the Pill. He wasn't sure which came first, the chicken (the Pill) or the egg (the ten pounds a woman gains when she goes on the Pill), but somehow he always went for women who lacked both. They were pleased to hear he was infertile.

Flora was different. He wasn't in a rush to shop for donor sperm and install her in that cabin near Hagerstown. Besides, he preferred eastern Maryland, where he could moor a boat and there was golf. But he didn't want to lose her either, by elaborating prematurely on the ways in which he wasn't dad material.

He hadn't lied; most of his life, he'd been too busy to be any kind of father. But business was slowing down. It was true he worked on Senate campaigns, but ten and twenty years before, he had worked on presidential campaigns. He was struggling to get Clinton's people to return his calls. He wasn't a radical, but he had a reputation for being on the Left, earned back in the days when the Right was run by openly racist supply-siders intent on shrinking government until it drowned in the bathtub. He assumed those days would never come again. The Obama years—particularly the health insurance mandate—had drawn educated young people so far leftward that they expected a guy like Bull, with a legacy lefty reputation, to be a socialist. He couldn't win points with them by saying he wasn't. They presumed him incapable of comprehending social media. They didn't want to hear about prime-time TV, aging party bigwigs, or the stodgy oldsters who donate the money and do all the voting. They believed knowledge was power, as if the world weren't run by ignorant fools. They expected him to be an insider, as if any politician bound by the chains of office would talk to a guy like him.

In short, he was still rich enough, but struggling to find a way forward. For all he knew, the way forward was early retirement with sperm-donor kids. It could happen.

XX.

The current woman in love with Bull was named Jennifer Wang. She was several years older, and her femaleness had never struck him with any particular force. She'd been forty-six when they met, and before she turned fifty, she cut off her hair. Her voice turned brassy, or she pitched it lower—he wasn't sure—but she sounded like Umm Kulthum. She wore stiff black clothes and round glasses with red frames, an eye-catching look designed to make her fade into the background.

After a number of upsetting offers from men who were much younger or much older, she had abandoned sexual relations in favor of chaste devotion to Bull. He preferred to maximize gender contrast, because his infertility put his masculinity in doubt. She was never in the running. Her career was taking off—she worked in radio, where looks mattered less than authority—while her hopes of marrying him declined to where her chances had been from the start. She served as his gratis public relations bureau at National Public Radio, always ready to spread quotes, rumors, and memes. In return she got access to the puny nonpareils of information he was obliged to sprinkle over his sweet, creamy mythmaking. That is, their relationship was a one-way street, and she needed to move on and get a crush on someone else, but she wasn't there yet.

He made a date to meet her at an art opening in lower Northeast, near Gallaudet. He arrived late, after the speeches. He grabbed a glass of red wine, followed her to an empty corner where a white porcelain cherub was copulating with a polyurethane tomato hornworm, and told her, "I have news. I'm in love."

"That's great!" she lied. "Finally going to tie the knot? Who is she?"

"Nobody you know. Intern or something."

Jennifer sighed. "Bull, you're making a mistake."

"You've got to be kidding. She's a physically perfect, healthy, beautiful, entertaining young woman, and she finds me sexually attractive. How can that be a mistake? In what unjust universe is that a mistake? Just letting you know I'm having a happy phase, so if you want to take advantage of me, now's the time. Professionally, I mean."

"Tell me about Radzio. What's up with Radzio?"

Pupie Radzio was a candidate for district attorney, a lawyer in private practice, and a hard-right Republican from the Libertarian wing, running in the Democratic primary because Republicans didn't stand a chance in general elections in D.C. He believed in fostering the exercise of personal liberty to the maximum extent allowed by a conservative interpretation of the law and in locking up wrongdoers and throwing away the key. He was polling alarmingly well after coming out in favor of marijuana decriminalization, which had already been enacted into law. The other candidates, confused, were ignoring him. Defending legal marijuana would have made them look a tad obsessive, as though all the weed they were smoking made them unable to forget about weed. Plus you couldn't attack him without saying "Pupie," with the *U* sound of "put" or "foot," and "Radzio" as "radge-oh." To run him down properly in the age of search terms, you had to spell his name aloud.

"Major headache," Bull said. "But he has an Achilles' heel."

"Do tell."

"He defended the Flea Collar Mom. You don't remember? Neighbor of mine in Georgetown who put a flea collar on a newborn baby, so when the kid's two months old she takes her in for her MMR or DDT or something and the thing's pretty much part of her neck."

"That can't be true."

"Radzio's defense was that she had a right to raise her kid any way she wanted. Said it was ironic to prosecute her when abortion was legal. This was in maybe 1979. He lost and they gave her twenty-five years."

"That's fucking disturbing."

"He got out of criminal defense into estate law for a while. This is definitely the man to put our great city back on track."

"The Flea Collar Mom. How come I never heard of this?"

"Because you canceled your LexisNexis subscription when you got Google."

"So where's your intern? Is she here?"

"Her name's Flora."

"What a pretty name!"

"A pretty name for a pretty girl, currently manning a table on a sidewalk in Old Town Alexandria. She volunteers for the Greens."

"Oh, no."

"She was raised ambitious, from a competitive background. I think she's looking for an opportunity to crash and burn."

"It's important to learn early in life how that feels."

"You couldn't be righter. Most people's first impulse is to join the winning team. Flora already darkly suspects that the bad guys are in charge. I like that in a woman."

"Nice guys finish last."

He clapped his hand onto her shoulder, a moment of contact to reward the double entendre, and said, "So what else is new?"

"Tell me what you want to hear."

"Well, let me see. Hillary pulled out of the race and endorsed a three-term Colorado governor who's white, moderate, and fifty-six. His name is—um—Charles Dexter. Former firefighter, made his money as a brain surgeon. Elk hunter. Married for thirty years to a gorgeous Vietnamese American girl who has a chain of craft shops. Brilliant, beautiful kids. One of them's on the Olympic downhill ski team."

"Boy or girl?"

"Girl. And you should see this guy's face. George Clooney meets Hugh Grant. You know that German guy who works for the pope? That's who he looks like."

"Oh, yeah?" She pulled out her phone and said, after a brief pause, "George Gänswein."

"That's 'Gay-org.' The younger Georg Gänswein. But his friends call him Dex."

"This guy could win," Jennifer said.

"He's an unstoppable fighter, a master of trade law, committed to education, passionate about preparing our youth to make the twenty-first century an American century, but always over a beer. There is no man on earth you would rather drink a beer with." Bull put his empty wineglass down on a pedestal and said, "Let's get dinner before I get in too deep."

"Is he tough on crime?"

"His college fiancée was raped and murdered by the unemployed. He knows what it means to suffer."

"Is he a good businessman?"

"You bet! He patented a way to turn spent nuclear fuel into gold."

"There's a painting here you need to see," she said.

She touched his hand, and he followed her into the next room.

He moved slowly, nodding at two former employees and shaking hands with a city council member whose campaign he'd run years before. Finally he and Jennifer were standing in front of the painting she liked. It depicted a disconsolate Godzilla seated at a dining table with tears in its eyes, staring openmouthed at a birthday cake. "I don't get it," he said.

"He breathes fire, so he can't blow out the candles and get his wish."

"I mean, I don't get why it reminds you of me."

"I didn't say that! It reminds me of Hillary."

Bull laughed, a bit nervously, and said, "I need dinner. Let's go."

FLORA SAW BULL FOR AN OVERNIGHT MOST SATURDAYS. THEY BOTH LIKED COOKING AND hiking. Once he took her along on a Democratic golf retreat at the Homestead, where she explored, swam, got massages, and had sex with him four times in one day. He had a favorite B&B near Harpers Ferry, and soon she grew to love it as well. Other evenings were reserved for his business engagements. If he got invited to a party that wasn't sit-down, with enough guests for her to be anonymous, he told her where to go. It was sexy to dress up and dance in big dark houses full of strangers, pretending not to know him. They met several times a week at his house on her lunch hour. He always slept after daytime sex, usually for at least twice as long as the sex had lasted. A couple in love can fit a lot of intercourse into ten minutes. She had to travel ten minutes each way by bus to get there. It didn't leave them much time to talk, but they made up for it on weekends.

She called him every night before she went to bed. No matter how late it was, he was always up and working. If he was home alone, they would talk about their unique feelings and the joy they felt at the prospect of seeing each other the next day or the day after that for ten minutes of sex and a nap.

One Sunday morning when he had a conflicting engagement,

she saw him quoted in the *Washington Post* as saying he slept only six hours a night. She had to laugh. She was reading at the breakfast table, so Ginger demanded to know what was so funny. "It's this political strategist who says he sleeps six hours a night," Flora said. "I bet he takes naps."

"That's interesting," Ginger said.

When she talked to him that night, she made fun of him, saying, "I bet that's the real reason you have girlfriends—so you can take naps in good conscience!"

"I have girlfriends because I met you," Bull said. "I don't usually have a girlfriend. I'm trying to shovel my way clear so we can have a relationship, but it's not easy at this point in an election cycle. I wish I'd met you two years ago."

"So you're saying we can go to Antigua for two weeks, but only after the election is over?"

"That's the idea. I'm paying as much attention to you as I possibly can."

THE HABIT OF DISCRETION KEPT HER FROM TELLING FRIENDS. THE INSTINCT FOR SIMplicity kept her from telling her grandmother. But neither could save her from Pam. She and her mother weren't close, the way she was close to Ginger. Ginger assumed she was mixed up in another one-sided but harmless romance and would confess all in good time. Pam felt that she had a right, as a mother, to be nosy.

She was used to getting regular visits, at least once every six weeks. When eleven weeks passed, she guessed—jumping to an accurate conclusion, as was her wont—that a boyfriend was involved. A single woman can always find reasons to spend weekends in New York.

She wasn't eager to return to the old regimen in which she did all the traveling. Flora was a loyal BoltBus customer, despite the regular collisions and engine fires, but Pam had lived too long, in her own opinion, ever to get back on a bus. She could have flown to National Airport (she refused to say "Reagan"), but not to visit a doctrinaire Green. So she bought a seat on the fast Acela train and shoehorned herself into Penn Station on a Friday afternoon at four o'clock. It had been a while since she last went down to D.C. She remarked the wildness of the Jersey swamps. Philadelphia would have fit into a corner of Brooklyn. Then it was back to the swamps. Baltimore looked as if Brighton Beach touched the South Bronx along a seam that had been given a name, vectoring her megalopolitan journey parallel to highways, shipping lanes, and exhaust pouring from smokestacks. Then came more swamps, until the train slid like a knife into the key lime pie of the capital, its green lawns topped with a white froth of marble. The town had never looked more southern to her. The evening sky was imperial purple touched with ocher. The flowers in the ubiquitous flower beds glowed ultraviolet in the onset of night. She rode the Metro up to Cleveland Park and jammed her finger cheerfully into the Baileys' doorbell. "Hey, hey, hey!" she said to Flora, who opened the door. Hugging her tight, she added, "What's his name?"

"Oh, Mom," Flora said. "You're too fucking smart."

"I know. I don't want to meet him, don't worry. I just want to know everything. Is he a Green?" She dumped her coat and backpack on a chair. She lowered her voice. "Are they still up?" she asked, referring to Ginger and Edgar.

"They're watching *The Sopranos* in the family room," Flora said. "Come on in the kitchen. You want some Cabernet? There's an open bottle. Oh, wait," she added, surveying the kitchen counters. "I guess we finished it. What about—what about—" She opened the refrigerator and peered inside. "Do you like mango strawberry?" Without waiting for an answer, she poured two glasses of juice, brought them to the table, and sat down opposite her mother.

"So, this boy," Pam said. "Is he cute?"

"He's more of a man."

Pam cocked her head. "A 'man.' Does that mean he's thirty? Or forty?" She watched Flora closely. "Fifty?"

"Oh, Mom," Flora said. "He's forty-seven."

"That's fine," Pam said. "I was afraid you were going to say thirty or forty. A forty-seven-year-old isn't about to get you pregnant. I mean, if it can't be a boy your own age—and I can totally see that—you might as well go with the guy who's gotten the family stuff out of his system. Does he have any kids?"

"Nope."

"At least he doesn't have kids older than you are. You know he's older than I am, right?"

"I can do basic arithmetic."

"What's he do for a living?"

"It's something with super-low social status, where he doesn't make any money. That's what makes it okay that he's so old."

Pam laughed. "Okay, let me guess. Gas station attendant is out of date—I'm showing my age here—let me see . . . barista?" Flora shook her head. "Uber driver? No. Bouncer? That's it. He's a bouncer at a club. Big strong guy, recovering alcoholic, no-nonsense, no lines on his face because he only goes out at night. Cynical about women. He's seen it all and feasts on your innocence. One of those vampires, like in that Jim Jarmusch movie, *Only Lovers Left Alive.*"

"You're warmer than you think."

"This is the fear talking. I'm afraid he's a fifth grade science teacher."

"He's a media consultant on major political campaigns. Democrats only. He has a big house in Georgetown. Basically he came to a Green event to spy on us, and we hit it off."

"Hit on you, is what you mean. But I'll grant you this power broker if you can tell me where he is right now."

"Home alone."

"Prove it."

"How?"

"I'm serious. Prove it to me."

Flora asked her grandfather if she could borrow the car to go out with her mom, assuring him they wouldn't go farther than Georgetown.

"Sure, darling," Edgar said. "Pam, sweetie! Give us a hug!" He got up to embrace his daughter, and so did Ginger. "I'm addicted to this show, sorry."

"It's like ten years old," Flora said.

"These days you can catch anything in reruns," Ginger said.

Flora and Pam rolled down the driveway, up Porter Street, and down Wisconsin Avenue. They parked near Dumbarton Oaks and walked to Bull's house.

"He might be asleep," Flora whispered. But the lights were on. Her sense of gleeful mischievousness vanished. She transitioned straight into panicked fear. Should Bull discover he was being spied upon, he might never speak to her again. She whispered the address and walked away quickly.

Pam strolled past his porch, glancing around at random like a neighbor taking an evening constitutional, and saw what Flora had told her she would see: a handsome man in a dress shirt, pacing the floor of his living room, talking on the phone. His tie was loosened as if he'd just gotten home. As she passed he looked out the window, but she could tell he was seeing nothing but his reflection, by the way he ran his hand over his head before continuing to pace.

She rounded the block and found Flora sitting in the driver's seat, waiting for her. "I feel like I owe you a drink," she said.

"Let's do it," Flora said. "I'm seeing him tomorrow night, so we should go out now. But you knew that."

"What's his name?"

"I already looked him up. He's not a sex offender. Where do you want to get a drink?"

Pam sighed. "Someplace with bands," she said. "I feel kind of hyper."

"There's no live music in bars anymore," Flora said. "There's no live music after, like, ten P.M."

Pam suggested Kramerbooks. "We can hit the bar," she said, "and scope us out some nerds."

AS BULL HAD OBSERVED, FLORA WAS NOT DEPRESSED. SHE WAS—AT LEAST SINCE meeting him—having quite a good time. He succumbed to the temptation to lecture her about how she was wasting her life circa once a month, for around a minute, before his good manners got the better of him. When at last he led off with "If you were a Democrat—" she finished the sentence for him: "I could sleep my way to the top!"

In his view, helping her wouldn't have been tantamount to owning her. It would merely have been a karmic point in his favor, especially if he did it behind her back, which would be easier for him in an organization where he had access to discreet private channels.

"Are you sticking with the Sierra Club and the Greens just to keep your distance from me?" he asked. "The Democratic Party is a three-ring circus. There's not going to be an odor of nepotism unless you go around dropping my name."

"You don't get it," Flora said. "I'm a true believer. I love living things more than I love jobs. Nobody loves jobs. They just pretend to. Automation is going to put us all out of work anyway, even the loggers. What we need is distributive justice and more nature."

"I personally love my job."

"Self-employment doesn't count."

"Like I said, it's a big tent. All the party activists under thirty are communists now. You'll fit right in."

"How stupid is that?" she said. "Everybody knows Democrats are neoliberal globalizers."

"Then what are Republicans?" he said. "It's a two-party system, not a rock and a hard place."

"But that's exactly it. The parties are Scylla and Charybdis, and we're sailing our boat of nature on capitalism like we think it's water. We need to turn it around and get back to dry land. God, that was the metaphor of the century. I should get a prize."

Consequently, when someone from the national Green organization—someone he hadn't seen in years, a quick-witted, sixtyish former Black Power radical named Elaine—casually asked him during a chance encounter at a reception whether he knew any organizers who were free to travel, he said, "There's Flora Svoboda. Very committed Green. Already working for you. Heavily underutilized." He felt no compunctions about handing her dubious talents and energies off to a competing organization. He assumed she would do the Greens more harm than good.

When Elaine searched Facebook, she quickly determined that Flora was working for the party's D.C. chapter in a part-time volunteer role that surely failed to exploit her skills, whatever they might be. She trusted Bull's judgment. If the girl weren't exceptional, he wouldn't be fucking her.

XXI.

It had become apparent that Donald Trump might soon clinch a majority of delegates to the 2016 Republican National Convention. Bull had expected to gloat. Instead he was worried. There was a certain frightening logic to an unelectable candidate in a nation that was half nonvoters.

After intensive lobbying—several calls, many happy hours, and much proffering of gossip—he wangled an invitation from the Clinton campaign to pitch a TV advertisement. He was ordered to an office on K Street early in the morning, told to bring his own laptop and projector. They wouldn't trust an outside USB stick or even give him their wireless password. He had wanted to bring his two best-dressed interns, male and female, but they told him to come alone.

He was first on the agenda, at seven o'clock sharp, since they had internal matters to get to after he left. He showed them a TV campaign spot. Over images of a foraging grizzly, an avuncular voice intoned, "There is a bear in the woods." He paused the video to give everyone time to laugh. It was a famous ad for Ronald Reagan from 1984.

"Some people say the bear is tame," the voice continued. "Others say it's vicious and dangerous. Since no one can really be sure who's right, isn't it smart to be as strong as the bear, if there is a bear?"

The spot concluded with the bear facing a hunter in a classic shoot-out situation. The bear was unarmed. It was clear who would win.

Everyone present knew the ad already, so the assistant issues director said, "I take it you're alerting us to Russian collusion."

"Nope," Bull said. "Vladimir Putin's a Republican, and bears shit in the woods. Anybody surprised? I can't remember the last time I met an American who was scared of Russia. I brought this ad along for the express benefit of the people in this room. Like I always say, define your candidate. Define your opponent. Define the stakes. We're the mighty hunter, our opponent's the dangerous predator, and the question is whether we will commit the firepower to bring him down."

"We're running against poverty and inequality," the assistant issues director pointed out. "There's no question they exist, but doesn't mean we need to show them in our ads."

"Can we wrap this up?" the digital director said. "We have a lot of agenda items."

"There is a bear in the woods, and his name is Beelzebub," Bull said. "The lord of the flies. The foul fiend." The group looked blank. The deputy campaign manager looked worried. "I'm talking about the presumptive Republican nominee, Mr. Donald J. Trump. Electing him is not a calculable risk. It's the end of the world as we know it."

"We're here to talk about Hillary," the deputy issues director said.

"I know what you're thinking. You don't want to go negative out of the gate. But we need to hit this guy with a two-by-four, and we need to hit him fast. Brushing him back is not going to do it. We need to get the double-barreled shotgun."

"But why focus on one person?" the campaign spokesperson asked. "He could implode at any moment. He might get bored and pull out of the race."

"Because he's the bear. That's because he's the only candidate where you have to ask yourself whether there's a bear. Are we preparing to debate issues with an opposing candidate, or are we noticing the animal in the room? Hillary can beat a Republican, but she can't beat a totemic forest spirit. The bear is the id—the part of us that just wants to eat and fuck—and guess what? It's running for president. Hillary is not going to stop it by being the finest stateswoman in the world, which I'm sure she is."

"Ted Cruz is the bear," the social media czar called out. "He's heavier and hairier than Trump."

"He's a virgin. Nobody's going to put a sincere religious believer in the White House. Hypocrisy has its limits. Well, if it weren't for Trump, I'd be standing here spouting pleasantries about refining our polling and reaching out to young and minority voters. But he's the weasel in the tube jammed up our asses. We need to kill the weasel first."

The deputy campaign manager appeared discomfited. She said, "So, Bull. What's your plan?"

"I don't have one."

"After all that?" She was angry, because she had invited him.

"I don't believe we have the facts we need to craft a strategy to bring him down. I'm asking you to rededicate your spending, not to advertising, but to research. I'm saying don't think ad strategy. Just go after him."

"Give us what you've got. We don't have all day."

"I do have an ad to show you—just hang on—but what you really need is cyber-hackers. You need to name an ambassador to

Wikileaks. You need to be sucking up to Edward Snowden to see if he has anything. Offer Julian Assange a job in the administration, right now. That's my best advice. I'm begging you. The future of mankind depends on it."

"Uh-huh," she said.

The room filled with skeptical whispers. The social media czar quipped that he wanted the Wikileaks ambassadorship. He sounded like a heckler in a comedy club.

Bull ignored him. "Your typical negative ad," he went on, "is as negative as it needs to be to stop the opponent's positive ads from getting traction. It's like mosquito repellent, keeping the opponent off your candidate. You don't overdo it, because it's nerve poison, weakening the entire organism, and you end up paying the price in turnout. But no amount of mosquito repellent is going to help us with this weasel. We need to break its spine." His audience was looking more and more perturbed. "What am I talking about here? Democrats already hate Trump. He needs to get caught doing things no Republican would tolerate. Are you with me?" There were hesitant nods. "What might those things be? We know from the primaries that Republicans condone the things he's been doing. Extramarital affairs. Tax evasion. Racism. Lying. Groping."

"Illiteracy and incoherence," the communications director called out.

Bull shook his head. "That's not a flaw! And the things he plans to do. Coal. Nukes. The workhouse. Incarceration of the poor. Who cares? Nobody. So we need to be asking ourselves what *won't* they tolerate that he *doesn't* do? We need to go deep. He's Teflon; he's Kevlar. But he's not asbestos."

The campaign spokesperson said, "Wait a second. Are we still 'with you'? Are we even in this room?"

"No," Bull said. "I'm not saying that any of you had anything to do with the spot I'm about to show you, much less that you paid for it. This ad was paid for by Citizens United." He meant the Supreme Court decision that abolished limits on anonymous campaign spending. "I am not Hillary Clinton, and I did not approve this advertisement. I give you: fifteen seconds of pedophilia." He leaned down to his laptop and clicked "play."

On the wall where earlier had roved the bear, there loomed a soupy black sky from which coalesced something resembling the eye of Sauron. It looked down at the Mar-a-Lago resort in Palm Beach before shifting its gaze, in a flash of white lightning, to the street-level facade of Trump Tower. A voice said, "There's one privilege Donald Trump's money shouldn't be able to buy. The right to abuse a little boy until that boy's injuries—"

At a nod from the deputy campaign manager, the social media czar pulled the plug on the projector and the bright rectangle on the wall vanished. The voice kept speaking ("or a little girl, a beloved daughter whose parents turned their backs on her for one split second"), but it was drowned out by the loudly repeated, "Stop it, stop it, stop it, stop it," of the deputy campaign manager.

"This is Russian-style character assassination," the social media czar said.

"No shit, Sherlock," Bull replied. "Character assassination works."

"I meant that negatively."

"We're at a strategic disadvantage. They don't have to buy this kind of story. Their media exist to promote it. Ours will debunk it. So it's going to cost us some money. The fifth law of thermodynamics is that Republicans have more money than Democrats, so we need to be effective. Lucky for us, redistricting has left us with maybe forty contested congressional districts and ten swing states. I say fuck the fifty-state strategy. We're not spreading our ads around. We're dosing them precisely."

"I'm disappointed in you," the deputy campaign manager said. "No campaign in history has ever stooped to this level. You'd better not show this to anybody else or raise money on it. I'll get an injunction. We have better things to do than watch this kind of garbage. We have work to do."

"You don't want to be sending out canvassers before the earth is well and truly salted," Bull said. "I'm frankly afraid of what getting out the vote could do this year."

"Mr. Gooch," the spokesperson said, "I think you need to get yourself out and leave the vote the hell alone."

"Take a minute to think about it."

"How about two minutes to leave the building?"

"Well, then," he said. "Thank you for your time."

He gathered up his things and thanked them. He was glad to have said his piece. At least he had tried. No one was looking at him. Even the communications director lowered her eyes.

FLORA GOT AN E-MAIL FROM JILL STEIN'S CAMPAIGN HEADQUARTERS, INVITING HER TO interview for a job. There was no link to an online application form or even a request for a résumé. It was a headhunting letter. The person wanted to know when she might have time to conduct an exploratory interview.

Joyfully she hesitated. It might be better to work on a winning campaign for sheriff than a losing one for president.

Third-party presidential runs were guaranteed hopeless. Ross Perot had walked away with a fifth of the electorate in 1992—the year she was born—but technically he'd been an independent, not a third-party candidate. He had been able to outpoll Mickey Mouse only by buying time on TV. Stein was clearly fated to lose, if getting 1 percent of the vote can be called losing. She might be planning to call it victory. Flora wasn't familiar with the details of Green goal-setting for the presidential campaign. She realized that would be a good question to ask at the interview. She wrote back saying she'd be happy to meet, at the campaign's convenience.

A week later she took a long lunch and went to Stein's national headquarters. Elaine explained that she was looking for someone not tied to D.C. "It's not a fund-raising job," she added. "We do that online. You can depend on people who have money to be online. But until internet access is a human right, we need a strong ground game to get people registered to vote."

"But I'd be happy to integrate corporate outreach into my goal-setting," Flora said. "There are so many billionaires getting rich off the sustainable development goals. I mean the ethanol and biodiesel industries, and the sharing economy companies, and Elon Musk and all those guys. We have carte blanche to work with them since Citizens United, right?"

As she said it, it suddenly hit her how the social structure of social media—in which billions of peons tithe their innermost data to billionaires—influenced her conception of what it meant to be a citizen. The strained expression of faux charismatic excitability vanished from her face, leaving a mature and skeptical look.

"We don't do any corporate development," Elaine said. "There's no corporation in the world without dirty hands, and they can't vote. At least not yet. We try to keep it under twenty-five dollars."

"I'm a digital native—" Flora began, meaning to apologize for the way, as a powerless pseudo-citizen, she naturally sought allies from among the billionaire class.

Elaine interrupted. "That's terrific but irrelevant for this job. We're planning a speaking tour of college campuses with an array of poets and progressive singer-songwriters and whomever else we can drum up. The idea isn't to reach out to students. We can get them for free over social media. It's to get our supporters fired up, so they go forth out of their silos and multiply. Get them active. It's a young movement. We need to expand the base."

"I've never actually done grassroots fieldwork."

"Well, then it's time you tried."

Elaine smiled a gentle, ironic smile, and Flora realized that the job was hers for the taking. Since winning, for Greens, wasn't an option, there was no need for her to display winning qualities. Her task was to embody certain principles and speak truth to the powerless. The fate of the world was not in play, nor was her personal integrity. Her job was to be herself. The feeling was liberating, emancipatory.

"The logistics are challenging," Elaine warned. "The events are simulcast on internet radio using the college radio stations' equipment, and you have to set it up with them individually. You'll be working alone."

"Is any of the liaison work done? You know it's almost finals already, and colleges close for the summer. Student organizations won't be staffed. This job is literally not doable before September. What do you want me to do right now?"

"We'll keep you busy. We have a national convention coming up in Houston. Ever been to Houston? They have terrific victuals down on the bayou."

Flora asked about the salary. Elaine named a figure that was slightly above minimum wage. It wouldn't have covered rent for an adult living alone, much less food. Yet it was generous, given that many people volunteer full-time on political campaigns in speculative hope of spoils jobs after the victory. She was living with her grandparents, who fed her every night. She could afford to say yes.

She would sit in an office in Washington, booking caterers and audiovisual equipment, printing name tags, and reserving hotel rooms until the convention, put out fires in Houston—lost luggage, food allergies, that sort of thing—and, as a reward, bathe in the adoration of left-wing students. She asked for time to decide, but only as a pro forma power move. She knew she wasn't fooling Elaine.

WHEN SHE SAW BULL ON SATURDAY, SHE ASKED HIM WHAT HE THOUGHT. THEY WERE splitting a bottle of red wine on an empty stomach while cooking.

She phrased it, "Since there's a lot at stake"—seldom had she been so conscious of how little her actions mattered, but she knew they were important to him—"I hesitate to join the Stein campaign without checking in with you first. What do you really think of us Greens?"

"I love you with all my heart," he said. "You're voters. If we can stop you from voting Green, you're a force to be reckoned with."

"Don't make fun of me to my face," she said.

"There's nothing at stake," he said. "After the Senate refused to consider Obama's Supreme Court nominee, which was the most lawless and contemptible ploy I've seen in my life—it wasn't even politics; it's like they took their ball and went home—well, it was clear to me then that we need mass mobilization of nonvoters to keep every branch of government from going Republican. Greens aren't nonvoters, so you're not doing anybody any harm. It's a fine sandbox for you to gain some experience."

"You don't think a strong Green showing could move the debate to the left?"

"What debate?"

"The public discourse? The Overton window?"

"Do you mean the lunatic fringe yanking its own chain, or the little space in the middle where claims go when they're too bland to get anybody's attention?"

"People discourse in real life, Bull! You should talk to some of the Greens I know. They're really, really thoughtful and smart. They win conversations all the time."

"And I'm sure, for them, politics is about social equity and distributive justice. But tell me where they went to school, that they even know what those words mean. I'm sure they must have very diverse backgrounds. Harvard, Princeton, Dartmouth—"

"Not even close. You must be thinking of the Berniecrats."

"All I know is democracy is about choosing the lesser of two evils, because three evils is too many. Bernie Sanders isn't *not* third

party, but he's third—what the fuck is he? Third leg?" He laughed
at his own joke. "The soi-disant socialist from the all-white state!
That old windbag should get off our barricade. We're trying to run
a class struggle here, and he's raising up a left populist movement
of nonvoters. Somebody should tell him we're never going to have
ninety-nine percent turnout like in the Soviet Union."

"He has tons of working-class support," Flora said. "People
who want jobs rebuilding our nation's crumbling infrastructure."

"Great. The Greens take the altruists, Bernie takes the youth
and everybody who wants a job, and the Democrats take the lame,
the halt, the blind, and single mothers."

"Who's 'the halt'?" She poured herself more wine.

"Only the halt can say for sure," Bull said. "Hillary's even been
kissing up to illegal immigrants, the most powerful voting bloc
there is, God help us."

"Well, Trump says they're taking over."

"He's not wrong. They're killing the European welfare states."

"I think he means they vote."

"You'd think if he's so goddamn sure they vote, he'd treat
them a little nicer."

"Can Standing Rock Sioux vote?" Native American opposition to a planned oil pipeline in South Dakota was a major issue
for Greens.

"Reservation Indians have been citizens for a hundred years.
If you're asking whether they vote, that's a different question. It's
always a different question."

"Well, do they?"

"I don't know, and I don't care. They're a flyspeck minority
and not too well liked since they got casino gambling. Go to work
for Jill Stein. The Democratic Party can divide and conquer itself
without her help. You'll be a bigger fish in a smaller pond. That'll
help you crawl out when it dries up."

BACK IN CLEVELAND PARK ON SUNDAY NIGHT, FLORA MADE HERSELF A CUP OF TEA AND betrayed her career plans to her parents on the phone. The three-way call was enabled by the five extensions on their landline.

"Wow," Pam said. "Are you running a temperature?"

"Don't worry. We're not going to spoil the election. The GOP has no chance."

"A major party always has a chance," Daniel said, "because your typical voter goes into the booth and flips a coin. Why not work for a party that's trying to split the Republican vote instead?"

"Like who? The Nazis?"

"The Libertarians."

"You'd love that! You'd never give me a hard time if I was working for them!"

"I take it back," he said. "Now I'm visualizing these Ayn Rand–freak biker dudes with lobotomy scars asking you to help repopulate after the race war goes nuclear."

"Don't worry. I won't consent to anything until I see their supplies of canned goods. I'm not an idiot."

Pam said, "With your agricultural expertise, after the nuclear race war, you'll be a hot commodity."

"I don't think so," she said. "We'll run out of hybrid seed within two years and end up moving north to follow the great caribou herds."

"That's why it's imperative that oil exploration cease in the Arctic National Wildlife Refuge," Daniel said. "So we can eat reindeer burgers after the apocalypse."

"I'll bring that up at the next meeting," she said. "We're always trying to brainstorm positive claims."

XXII.

Flora spent her summer weekdays answering the campaign's office phone. She monitored the Slack channel and Whats-App. She patiently responded to high-level policy recommendations from potential voters and facilitated mutual contact among those with similar desires, hoping they would spur each other to find outside help.

Occasionally her faith in the party's principled tactics wavered. For instance, every time the Green vice presidential candidate said that the United States was "a corrupt, degenerate, white supremacist monstrosity." Was that supposed to be a viral meme? Did he really expect people to pick that up and run with it?

She had her finger not on America's pulse, but on the veins where deoxygenated blood drained back from its overworked extremities. On Facebook, she saw friends' upbeat descriptions of what it was like to work for Clinton. Volunteers competed to rise in a hierarchy that gave them incremental access to knowledge of the campaign's aims, faithful adepts of a cult whose dogmata were known only to its priests. Greens were the exoteric, democratic, chaotic, weary avant-garde. All their beliefs were on display, and all were under attack.

The Green National Convention was in early August at the University of Houston. She shared a foldout couch in a quadruple hotel room. Her role was that of concierge to a convention full of people whose accommodations didn't have concierges. She worked fourteen-hour days and barely ate. Between emergencies, she listened in. The endorsement from Patch Adams embarrassed her, but not as much as patching in Julian Assange from the Ecuadorian embassy in London. Cornel West came on strong, but Ajamu Baraka made him look like a shy conformist. Nobody seemed able to stop ranting about Israeli war criminals. She listened in vain for a coherent stance on agricultural subsidies or renewable energy.

Her parents had often said to her, "The Left will eat itself," or "The Left eats its own." She told Bull on the phone, "They got it wrong. The Left will shoot itself. It used to be in the foot, but now it's raising the gun to its head."

He said, "The Left eats lead."

The longest conversation she had in Houston was with an art historian she met standing in line at the on-campus Starbucks. The woman directed the university's museum of Asian art. She described nouveau-riche collectors' attempts to donate impossible artworks—the sixth bronze horse from a famous ancient Chinese set of five, that sort of thing—and archaeological finds so rare that (had they been genuine) no nation on Earth would have permitted their export. The collectors were reliably saddened to learn of their bamboozlement by forgers claiming to be smugglers. Laws were brittle. Chemistry could be faked. But the past could not be altered. The paper trail had the last word.

That night as Flora fell asleep, she daydreamed of retraining as an art historian. Her family was arty, after all, and valued authenticity. Scientists could be wrong without lying, and politicians could be right without telling the truth. Serving two foreign masters was wearing her down.

HER GRASSROOTS TOUR OF COLLEGES HIT NINE CITIES: CARLISLE, CHICAGO, KANSAS City, Oberlin, Lawrence, Albuquerque, Boulder, Eugene, and Las Vegas. Coasting on a half-million-dollar windfall from the Presidential Election Campaign Fund, the campaign paid for her to fly in steerage and rent subcompact cars.

Mere words cannot convey the fun she had in Albuquerque, Boulder, Oberlin, and Eugene. Kansas City was especially fascinating. Chicago was a mite stressful (Loyola, radical queer seminarians, long story) but over fast. Las Vegas had a hydrological regime rigged to cause laughter in hell and the angriest environmentalists she'd ever seen. They took her to the Venetian for all-day breakfast, reminding her of her parents.

In Lawrence, the Green student association put on an outdoor festival. The weather was iffy—too windy for the tarps they put up to keep off the rain, so that the stage kept threatening to take off across the road—but ten local bands and crews presented thirty original tracks about wind power. There was even a folksinger with a short set about windbreaks. He had a cottonwood song and a blackthorn song. It was hard to say whether he made people want to vote, but he definitely drove them to the information tables.

Carlisle was weird. She suspected the campus had only one active party member. She was alone with him much of the time. She slept on his couch. He simpered adoringly. On parting, he gave her a white carnation in a used paper cup, on which he'd written, "Flora and Fauna Forever."

She wondered whether he might not be an agent provocateur. Paying guys like him a few bucks to found campus Green organizations could smother the movement in its cradle. "This is a huge waste of time," she told Bull on the phone. "What we need is a ballot that makes it easier to vote Green by accident."

He said, "You're learning. Now come home."

SHE STOPPED BY BAND PRACTICE ON HER WAY AND FOUND HER MOTHER DOWNSTAIRS IN the store. The TV in Video Hit was tuned to Fox News. Victor and Pam were fighting over Trump. "How can you call him a moron?" Victor said. "Was NAFTA good for the American worker? Haven't Han Chinese destroyed us by dumping their cheap products after WTO accession?"

"NAFTA moved jobs to Mexico, but all Trump ever talks about is Mexicans coming here. And the Chinese didn't invent Walmart. It was the other way around."

"He's as liberal on your Democrat issues as crooked Hillary. He wants to keep Social Security and Medicare."

"Not everybody's retired, Victor!"

They paused to greet Flora, who said, "Hey! Where'd you put the Mary Janes? I don't see them."

Victor handed over the plastic jar and said, "Have all you want, but make them lock her up."

"How can you call her crooked when she's running against Trump?" Pam retorted. "That guy never stops lying."

"He's a self-made man," he said. "He started with a small business like us."

"I think I read somewhere that he inherited a lot of money," Flora said, peeling the sticky paper off her candy.

"His wife is an immigrant like us."

"That's his third wife," Pam reminded him. "Remember Ivana and Marla?"

Frowning, he turned to face the TV set. "I never watched a political speech from beginning to end before," he said with grudging admiration, as though Fox News were a surprisingly captivating viewer-sponsored civics course on PBS. "Trump got me really into politics for the first time."

Pam reflected that he must have seen clips from other cable channels. There were so many hilarious comedy shows devoted to parodying Trump. They were surely as entertaining as Fox News. It crossed her mind that Victor might simply despise black people. She launched a trial balloon. "I sometimes get this feeling," she said, "like maybe he doesn't really dig minorities."

"We're all minorities now, even you white guys. The problem is criminals."

"The crime rate is lower than it's ever been! Remember the eighties?"

"Those people are in jail, thanks to people like Trump."

"He never held office in New York. He's a real estate developer! How can you say he's putting people in jail?"

"I said people like him. Successful guys, like Bloomberg. They make the best politicians."

With her mouth full of candy, Flora said, "I don't know, Vic. You really think we'll be happier with Trump? He seems kind of obnoxious to me."

"Yes," he said. "We stop taxing our most productive citizens and let people take responsibility for themselves."

"But if people don't take responsibility for each other, there are no schools or hospitals," she said, "or even police or armies."

He changed the subject by presenting her with a can of Mountain Dew and a glazed fried doughnut.

"See, Flora?" said Pam. "God will provide!"

FLORA AND DANIEL WALKED UP TO THE UNION SQUARE GREENMARKET TO BUY FRESH fruits and vegetables. They were waiting for a light to change on Fourth Avenue when he said, out of the blue, "I guess I'm basically a happy person."

"What makes you say that?"

"Walking around like this makes me happy, even when you're not here, and it's really not a whole lot to ask."

"This is a great city to walk in."

"So is D.C.," he said. "I like those high bridges over Rock Creek Park."

"They're a little scary to me."

"They're like New York turned upside down. Washington's a flat city with gaping chasms. Here, you start out at the bottom of the abyss looking up. There's nowhere to fall."

"Are you afraid of heights?"

"I used to love going on helicopters with Joe. Why do you ask?"

"Because we never went up in a high building just to look down."

They made a minor detour around some trash bags and attained the opposite curb. "They're too touristy for me," Daniel said. "The Roosevelt Island Tram is fun, though. It's kind of like a helicopter. Did you ever go on there with him?"

"I don't think so."

"Maybe he didn't know about it."

"How would he not know?"

"He wasn't a big map reader. He lived in the here and now, like a Zen master."

She shook her head dismissively and said, "Everybody idealizes him in such a weird way."

"That's because you can stop idealizing most people when you realize they're normal. With him, I'm still waiting for that to kick in."

"He wasn't abnormal!"

"You were a little young to be copping to the weirdness. His whole world was put together out of superlatives. Like instead of living in Plato's cave with the rest of us, he was facing the eternal forms of perfection. He'd be like, 'The Hudson is the best of all possible rivers, so it needs the best of all possible names, which is Monongahela!' He took things seriously in a way most people only do inside their most cherished private delusions. He certainly thought you were the ultimate little girl."

"That wasn't a private delusion."

"Your point is well taken, but it's not like he knew a lot of little girls."

"Everybody knows, like, three people."

"I read that too. Three close friends, nine casual friends, twenty-seven something else, eighty-one acquaintances, something like that. Except he didn't differentiate. If you'd asked him to list his friends, you would have been sitting there all night listening to him enthuse."

"He sounds like a social media activist," she said. "Like me, when I'm online for work."

As she palpated fruit, she pondered how thrilling his life must have been. To live in a world charged with meaning, everything appearing as its hyperbolic essence. Totally wired. Forever in the inspired attitude of an excitable, charismatic person. Every river the Monongahela. Every friend a friend. She brushed off an organic fig and bit into it, expecting it to be as sweet as a doughnut. How she envied Joe.

Daniel pondered how it was probably thanks to Gwen that Joe hadn't known a lot of little girls. She'd been adamant with groupies about the age of consent, letting amorous underage fangirls cry in the hallways until hotel security drove them out. She had started curating his reputation long before he died.

FLORA COULD SENSE BULL'S FRANTIC STATE EVERY TIME THEY GOT TOGETHER, WHICH wasn't often enough. He couldn't give her a lot of support. He was in meetings nearly every hour of every day. He didn't have much time for nights with her or even naps. He was working off his sexual energy on the fly with the assistance of a Clinton campaign staffer named Ikumi Sakuragi. Their encounters were unplanned but frequent. They satisfied an intense and fleeting mutual curiosity in semipublic venues such as handicapped restrooms, where she renewed his faith that words of mythic provenance, properly timed, can work wonders.

Flora suspected nothing. She picked up only his worried vibe about outcomes. She wanted Stein to drop out of the race and endorse Clinton. Everyone at her office knew how she felt, because she told them. She expected the pink slip to come any day.

It came in the form of energetic new staffers who shared her office and ultimately her desk. She got bumped out to the receptionist's counter and went back on duty answering the phone that never rang. For something to do, she rewrote her white paper on soil quality in the United States to incorporate new findings. She spent several half days at the nearby Howard University library researching it. She waited for Elaine to fire her. After each weekend or nightly phone call with Bull, she wondered how many minutes away from him she'd be willing to go to grad school.

Around Columbus Day, Elaine said, "Hey, listen up, Flo. We need more boots on the ground in PA. Can you see spending the rest of the campaign up there, maybe activating some canvassers in Pittsburgh and lighting a fire under Towanda?" Her main intent in exiling Flora was to quarantine the virulent worried vibe. It was bringing the whole office down.

Flora raised her eyebrows. Pittsburgh was an island of Hillary love in the heart of the Marcellus Shale. She wanted to cry out, "How can you send me to a swing state? That's impossible!" She had no qualms about working for Stein in D.C., where (as Bull had remarked in an earlier, happier time) the Democrats could have run Pol Pot and won in a landslide. Three percent for Stein in D.C. would put a star on her résumé. Three percent for Stein in Pennsylvania would make her a hunted criminal. Flora's second impulse was to remember that she'd be there on her own, as her own boss. She didn't think much after that. She said yes.

PITTSBURGH WASN'T SO BAD. IT HAD SHOPPING DISTRICTS WITH FOOT TRAFFIC. SHE could set up a table with pamphlets outdoors and feel that she was accomplishing something. The sidewalks in the shopping districts were public, so the store managers couldn't throw her out. It was easy to find a place to stay. She looked on Craigslist, but before she could even rent something, the field office offered her its couch.

She canvassed during the day. In poor black neighborhoods, it was hard to get people interested in a third party or even in voting. The sense of an ownership stake in the public sector had become tenuous. People were paying cash for services such as lifesaving medical treatment and public schooling. They were frightened of authority.

Poor white neighborhoods were even less productive. In black neighborhoods, she had at least benefited from white privilege. If a black guy opened the door half naked and invited her inside for a beer, she could say, "Not right now, thank you." The Caucasian edition of the same guy made her nervous. The poor white women were less polite to her than the black women. It was depressing.

In the evenings, there were meetings. The Greens had a strong local organization, with fifteen active members. They suffered from the same delusion as all such organizations—that they were the tip of an iceberg—but at least the active members were active. When they put out a call on Facebook to promote an event, she could count on seeing them there.

She got several of them to join her canvassing. They weren't intrepid about invading hostile territory the way she was. It was understandable; she could afford to make enemies, because she'd be leaving town soon. They preferred to canvass acquaintances. If she attached herself to one of them, she could be assured of a pleasant morning drinking coffee with kitty cats in renovated craftsman homes. Sympathizers being rare and acquaintanceship a hall of mirrors in the ghettoized communities of twenty-first-century America, the Green social bubbles consisted mostly of Democrats. Democrats were unconcerned with outcomes. They knew Hillary would win, so they were open to the possibility of pulling the lever for Stein at the last minute.

Whenever she took them seriously, the stress made her antsy. She wanted to raise her hand and say, "The answer is 'Not Jill Stein!'" If she didn't take them seriously—if she let her mind wander—they and their porches and kitchens melted away, and she started to wonder what on earth she was doing so far from Bull at this most interesting political moment of her admittedly short adult life. On the phone he sounded fearful and resolute. He had emotional needs, and she was missing it.

After she'd slept on the couch for two weeks, her replacement in D.C. expressed surprise that she wasn't expensing a motel, so she moved to a motel. To celebrate having a room of her own, she stopped off at an ABC store to buy red wine and Coca-Cola. Following a brief facedown collapse on the motel bed, she staggered the length of the balcony to the utility room and filled her ice bucket. Her limp was mental, not physical, but she felt it ought to be visible, her role in her own drama being that of the casualty who waits to be airlifted home.

She pulled a chair onto the balcony and sat down to mix the least pretentious cocktail she knew. She tried to strategize—Bull's word for direct ethical intervention in other people's lives. What would Flora do if she were Bull?

She fantasized about launching a fake news vignette: Trump assaults the daughter of a Muslim real estate developer in Istanbul. Add some grainy pictures of the victim wearing an Arabian-style niqab, nothing visible but her sad, dark, unmarriageable eyes, irreparably violated by the sight of Donald Trump's dick. You too can sign the petition to grant her asylum.

She imagined starting a rumor that the All Lives Matter movement (a white supremacist response to the Black Lives Matter movement against police brutality) was led by tree-hugging anarchists who supported animal rights.

She finished her drink and got up to make another. It would be so easy, and so wrong. It wasn't her role, much less her job. It was a résumé killer, not a résumé builder. She was in Pennsylvania to get people fired up about Jill Stein.

She got a text from Bull that said he was too busy to talk that night. She finished the second cup much faster.

She stood and looked down from the balcony to the motel pool, still full of water despite the approach of November. The water was greenish, with beech leaves floating on top and a wet mass of them clustered in a corner near the drain. She imagined a dramatic swan-dive suicide set to music, à la video clips of Lana Del Rey.

The problem was that instead of falling majestically and drowning Ophelia-like, she'd take half a second to break her neck and smash her face. It didn't seem worth doing.

XXIII.

Late on Sunday morning, she left Pittsburgh to drive to Towanda, five hours straight through without a break. Occasionally she glimpsed that the world to the right and left of the highway was beautiful. There were geologic features and rivers and trees, a sky, clouds, green meadows, maples still flame orange, stone farmhouses, tall steeples. She kept her eyes to the band of black asphalt that surged doggedly backward under her tires, gunning the engine through every curve on highways that zigzagged like rickrack. Driving was a symbolically charged act, a magical rite meant to keep her life, the election, and everything else on track toward a goal of unknown utility.

Her phone rang on the passenger seat. She put it on her lap, on speaker. It was Bull.

"Hey, Superman," she said. "What's up?"

"Oh, not much. I found out the party brass is up to its neck in child trafficking for purposes of illicit sex, holding them captive at a pizza place near Politics and Prose on Connecticut. Nobody saw fit to tell me. Even Hillary's in on it. The ringleader's Podesta."

"Which pizza place?"

"Comet Ping Pong. I haven't been there."

"I don't like their pizza. It's too cheesy."

"For the record, 'cheese pizza' is how we Democrats say 'child pornography.'"

"So in Democrat I guess I just said, 'I don't like their pornography; it has too many children'?"

"Don't you read the headlines?"

"They scare me. It's like there's nowhere to go but down."

"I sure could deal with some flower pizza right now."

"I'm losing my mind up here too, in my own way. I'm almost in Towanda. It'll be over soon."

"Oh, shit, I have another call. Gotta bounce. It's important. Kendall from Ron Lacey's office."

"Stay out of trouble. Bye-bye."

"Bye. Love you."

She picked a tree to smile at, thinking it wasn't right to cut herself off from all pleasure. Then she stared back at the road, or what she could see of it from between the heavy trucks.

IN TOWANDA SHE PARKED UNDER THE MARQUEE OF A RED ROOF INN ON THE BYPASS. IT was four o'clock in the afternoon, but the receptionist, wearing a sari, lay on a folding cot, asleep. She checked Flora in, rubbing her eyes.

"You must be tired," Flora said.

"We're going to sell this place soon," the woman said. "I can't work so hard. I have chemotherapy." The half-moons under the woman's eyes were almost black. Her hands were red with eczema.

"I'm so sorry," Flora said.

"Are you alone?" the woman asked.

"Yes."

"I will not put you on the ground floor. There is sometimes a problem with the drug addicts. If you have a problem with them, you let me know, okay?"

Nodding, Flora signed her name and took the two key cards. She went to the breakfast buffet and pried a cup off the inverted stack. Pumping the thermos elicited a slurping sound. A doughnut with a bite out of it lay on wax paper in a tray. The receptionist had already gone back to bed.

She called out, "Feel better!" and drove around back to the stairwell leading to her grimy room upstairs. There were streaks and prints on every surface. There was a used tissue under the bed-side table and a wet bar of soap in the shower. But the sheets had been changed—no wrinkles, no hairs—and the towels were fresh. She took a shower. She put on a long-sleeved T-shirt and jeans and drove to the local chain coffee shop five driveways over.

Taking possession of her giant cappuccino, she saw that there was no table free, inside or out. Each four-top played host to some kind of computer and a solo human being. Seven were hostile, intense young women in stretch jeans and sexy tops. Six were men in slacks and easy-care polyester blend short-sleeved dress shirts who looked ready to clip on neckties and go to job interviews at any moment. The remainder was a smallish, curly-haired, lightly bearded, physically fit boy who was smiling and texting on a thick off-brand smartphone.

He looked up at Flora. Despite her shapeless outfit and hang-over, she looked like herself. She couldn't tell whether his smile was intended for her or the text he had just received, but she smiled back and moved toward him. He put the phone facedown on the table and turned his hand palm up to indicate the chair diagonally opposite his.

"Thanks," she said, sitting down.

"You're welcome."

"These places are always crowded."

"People can't afford broadband at home."

"I'm a tourist," she said.

"In Towanda?"

"I could be looking at the fall colors."

"But you're not. Where are you from?"

"D.C."

"So am I." They eyed each other cautiously. He held out his hand and said, "Aaron Fleischer, Clinton fellow." That was a kind of elite campaign volunteer, just below a paid staffer in the hierarchy.

She sighed and said, "Flora Svoboda. Jill Stein. I know. I'm sorry."

"It's not your fault," Aaron said. "So are you canvassing, or what?"

"Yeah. But I'm tempted to blow off the organization and just go around badmouthing Trump. I'm getting scared. I still haven't reached out to the Towanda Greens to tell them I'm here."

"He can't possibly win. So, are you a volunteer?"

"I'm campaign staff. But if you mean 'Do I have a clue?' then yeah, I think I do. The Trump supporters love him so much. He's, like, their revenge on the rest of us. They hate Obama more than anything in the world, except maybe Hillary." She lowered her voice, but not by much.

"We've got them outnumbered."

"Yeah, if this were a poll and not an election," she said. "But what about turnout? The Bernie people were fired up, but unless you count, like—you know—two hundred career socialists, their big thing was hating the lackey of war and Wall Street, by which they mean Hillary. They're so not voting."

"I was for Bernie, and I vote."

"Who wasn't? Even Trump supporters came out for him in states with open primaries. That's how much they hate her. It's so crazy."

"Like I said, she wasn't my first choice either."

"And now you're a socialist working for a Democrat? Your party is all Republicans, even Obama. Half his budget goes for defense!"

"I think the Clinton administration can dial down overkill without impacting national security."

"Because she's such a super-nice pacifist," Flora said. She noted with alarm sarcasm's ability to render a difficult conversation impossible.

"You're in a strange headspace," he remarked.

"I know I'm bugging you. I should finish my coffee and get out of here."

"No, no, stay," he said. "I'm on break. I worked from nine to ten this morning. That was enough for one lifetime."

"You went out that early?"

"There were people at home. But I'm not going back."

"Why not?"

"Woman pulled a gun on me."

"No way."

"I'm serious. Not a shotgun. Like this little tiny snub-nosed Derringer. She came to the door with a gun and a baby. Like it's the baby's gun. She pointed it at my chest from two feet away. I was afraid to turn around, but I couldn't stay facing her, because then it's self-defense. I was up on her porch! She could have killed me."

"Jesus."

"What's the Green position on guns again?"

"It's complicated. But what'd you do?"

"I kowtowed, man. Right down on my face." His phone dinged and he turned it over. "Oh, shit," he said. "Look at this." He handed her his phone, open to the *New York Times* app. It said Hillary was slated to win, with odds of 92 percent. "How am I supposed to get out the vote for somebody who's already won?"

The profoundly boring information that Hillary was a shoo-in—a reason in itself for *New York Times* subscribers to cancel their subscriptions—was accompanied by contravening insinuations that she was less than virtuous. Obama's FBI director was seen to be in favor of Trump. His unimpeachable motive was transparency. He had acquired Hillary's private e-mail correspondence, without a warrant, from foreign saboteurs and felt morally obligated to share it with the universe. The *Times* had no imaginable reason to play along, other than a desire to make Hillary less boring.

"Why are they doing this?" Flora said, scanning the article. "It's unnerving. It's not like anybody needs new reasons to hate her."

"She's the original vampire lesbian of Sodom."

"Wait. Are you from New York?" she asked, because Daniel had once told her about an eighties off-Broadway hit called *Vampire Lesbians of Sodom*.

Aaron didn't know it was a play. As a first-generation college grad, he assumed that vampire lesbians had always been a thing in Sodom. "I'm a rootless cosmopolitan," he said. "A citizen of GAFAM. But I went to Baruch." Baruch College was a Midtown branch of CUNY. He had established New York City residency by working at an oil and lube place in Queens for a year and then moved up to library night shifts under Baruch's federal work-study program.

"Did you say 'Gotham'?"

"No, GAFAM. *G-A-F-A-M.* Sorry. Bad joke. It's a failed state. We've got the best-educated, richest citizenry on the planet and eighty years of required national service."

"I know what you mean," she said, recalling Google-Apple-Facebook-Amazon-Microsoft. "I read that it's bigger and more powerful than most countries, and there are sovereign states proposing to establish diplomatic relations with it and appoint ambassadors. I think maybe the new right-wing Danish foreign minister?"

He lowered his head, lowered his voice, and said, "Let's get out of here and go drinking."

"Hey, some people have to work! You want to go canvassing with me?"

He glanced around the café and said, "Shit, why shouldn't I? Nobody's going to miss me unless I tell them to." He stood up and put his phone in his back pocket. He politely bussed her tray and ate her miniature almond cookie. He hadn't ordered anything himself.

STANDING OUTSIDE, SHE FINALLY CALLED THE LOCAL CAMPAIGN ORGANIZER TO ANnounce her presence in town. He was an audibly black man with a drawl, a southerner, probably older, named Reginald Shannon. He said he lived in a trailer without much room to turn around, so it would be best for them to meet up at the coffee shop in the Walmart. There he could give her some xeroxed maps.

Her phone said it was only about six miles to the Walmart. She suggested they take Aaron's car, because it was bigger than hers.

While he drove, she could see that he was regretting his decision but being nice about it. He made friendly conversation. She mused that he might really have preferred to get a beer. She hadn't analyzed her evening canvassing practice from the perspective of a drinker—that you can't ride in a car with an open bottle.

Reginald Shannon in real life was exactly as he had sounded on the phone, an Alabaman transplant with a graying beard. He stood up to greet them and asked about their trip. Flora introduced Aaron as a fellow volunteer, and Mr. Shannon winked at her.

"Have you talked to the people here about letting us set up a table?" she asked. Walmart was clearly the main shopping district of Greater Towanda, but the closest public property was 150 yards away across the parking lot, a strip of grass next to a four-lane divided highway where the pickups were still kicking up fine gravel from last winter.

In response he asked whether she was tripping. His maps were printouts from the internet, marked in pink and green highlighter. Every street and country road was marked one way or the other, pink or green. "Pink is like red," he explained. "Those are the roads where you don't go. Green is the streets where you can go. Those are the Democrats."

"It's not by individual houses?" Aaron said.

"We don't know how people are going to vote. But we can make an educated guess. Green here is a minority party. This is about getting out the vote. I don't want you going in places where they are going to kill you."

Aaron looked meaningfully at Flora. As they left Walmart, he said, "I wish I'd had a map like that this morning."

"Let's drive the pink roads and run Trump down," Flora said. "Come on. It'll be fun."

"Are you crazy?"

"It's our last hope. We'll tell them we're Republicans."

"I don't have any printed material with 'Trump' on it."

"You guys have printed material? Come on. We give them our Facebook page. You could at least drive my getaway car. Be a sport."

She was asking a lot. He seemed cooperative, if hesitant. It wasn't a scene she could have played with Bull, who always knew not only what he wanted, but when and where. Aaron was drifting like a spinning top, and she was whipping the top.

SHE NAVIGATED FOR HIM, USING THE PAPER MAPS. A FEW MILES OUTSIDE OF TOWN, they arrived at a cluster of seven houses built in front of a stone colonial farmhouse that was set back a quarter mile from the road. There was a TRUMP-PENCE sign under the lilac by the mailboxes. She asked him to park on the shoulder, parallel to the road, so the people in the houses wouldn't be able to read his license plates.

It was six o'clock, and the people at the newest house, closest to the road, were just finishing dinner. Flora could see the dinner table past the open white lace curtains. She knocked and smiled.

"Good evening," she said to the woman who opened the door. "My name is Mary Maloney, from the Republican National Committee, and I've been delegated here today to tell you what a great job you're doing supporting our candidates. Our sincere thanks."

"Thank you," she said. "We do our best."

"We're wondering if you'd like to participate in our new program, America for Americans."

"Won't you please come inside? We're just starting dessert."

She hadn't intended to enter the house. In her hesitation to turn and look at the car, she stepped inside. After being introduced as "Mary Maloney from the RNC," she joined a family of six at the table, where she was served apple crumble. With one hand in her lap, she resumed her pitch. "The idea behind America for Americans is that for every illegal immigrant on welfare, there's a legal immigrant who's paid his dues. We're asking you to pledge just fifty dollars a month to support a new American. This is not a tax. It's a voluntary, tax-deductible charitable contribution. We're asking only our most dedicated supporters."

"We can't afford that. They should get jobs," the husband said.

"We don't want immigrants taking our jobs," Flora said.

"They can have mine," the wife said.

"What do you do?" Flora asked.

"Teach English. It's an uphill battle. It's real hard to get kids to read these days."

"I'm not opposed to immigration per se," the husband said. "I think it's a more complex issue than it sometimes gets presented."

The seventeen-year-old son asked her, "Do you have signed pictures of Mr. Trump?"

"I'm sure I could have one sent to you."

Addressing his father, he said, "Can I have it?"

"Up to you," the husband said. "He's your hero, not mine."

Flora's phone rang with a call from Aaron. She declined it. "I'm so sorry," she said. "I have to go." She wolfed down the last of her dish of crumble. She pushed back her chair and said, "That was delicious. Thank you so much for your time and your hospitality!"

"Thank you for coming by so late to see us," the wife said. "Sorry we couldn't help. We wish you luck." She let Flora out the door.

She ran down the driveway and didn't look back. Aaron started the car before she got in. "I didn't expect you to go all the way in the house," he said. "I couldn't see you. That's why I got nervous and called you to abort the mission."

"Oh, Aaron," she said. "That was such a stupid prank. Now I'm ashamed of myself."

"What did you tell them?"

"That being Trump supporters entitles them to first pick of the legal immigrants who will need support with charitable contributions after he takes office. But they were so nice."

"You don't need a beer. You need, like, six beers."

"I need Xanax!"

"Heroin's probably easier to find."

"Not heroin," she said, suddenly serious. "My best friend died of that when I was a kid."

"You were childhood friends with a heroin addict?"

"No," she said. "It was weirder than that. Do you remember Joe Harris, the singer?"

"The 'Bird in God's Garden' guy."

"He was my babysitter. More than that. Like an uncle or a godparent."

"I'm sorry," Aaron said.

"I really loved him."

"Didn't he die on 9/11?"

"Yeah. I didn't know anything about it until, like, three months later. I was nine. But that song is still creepy to me."

"That was a sad day for everybody, not just Western civilization. My parents lost a friend who'd spent his whole life taking care of his sick parents. In July 2001 his mother dies, he's finally free, and bam! He worked at Cantor Fitzgerald."

"That's terrible," Flora said, surprised. She didn't imagine socialists' parents cultivating friendships with stockbrokers.

"He was Jewish, by the way."

"What's that supposed to mean? I don't do conspiracy theories."

"I've been in Towanda too long. There's a popular misconception that not a lot of us died. The whole thing was set up to be the new Masada. When the planes hit, we drew our revolvers. First we killed the women and children."

"Are you Jewish?"

"Yeah. What about you?"

"Sorry, no."

"Aw, crap. Now we can never get married."

Flora let that stand and said, "Can I feel your horns?" He said yes, please, and she reached over from the passenger seat and fluffed his curly bangs. "Nothing there. I guess you're too young."

"I'm a grower," he said, keeping his eyes on the road.

THEY FOUND A SIX-PACK OF DUVEL AT A SUPERMARKET AND DROVE TO FLORA'S ROOM TO watch TV. They each took one big double bed. Flora took off her shoes, but Aaron poised his sneakers with care on the bedspread protector. "CNN or MSNBC?" he asked, pointing the remote at the screen.

"What time is it?"

"Maddow's not on yet." He turned to CNN. "Oh, God. Guess who's on TV."

"And you were expecting—"

"The Messiah."

"Turn if off," Flora said. "Let's go to the river. We can cross the bridge and go down to these islands. I saw them from the car."

"It's dark."

"I know."

They abandoned their open beers for sealed ones and returned to his sedan. They drove across the Susquehanna, took the first left, and nosed their way down a gravel road to its apparent end. He pulled to a stop when the tires stopped crunching. He knew enough not to keep driving until he couldn't drive anymore, or until the sedge was so high it might indicate a marsh. The new moon had not yet risen, but he could see by the reflected light of the town and the passing cars well enough to walk across a channel of damp sand and broken glass to the nearest island, beers in hand.

He had imagined a sylvan glade. The footing under the trees was not good. It seemed a likely place to sprain an ankle, be impaled on protruding rebar, or get poison ivy. He could feel burrs in his socks.

Flora kept to her left, moving upstream along the shore. She called out, "Hey, Aaron! There's a beach!"

He found her, barely visible, a backlit obelisk on a broad shelf of sand. Approaching her, he took off his woolen overcoat. He fanned it out for them to sit down on.

She said, "You're going to freeze."

"I won't freeze." Using his lighter for leverage, he pried open a beer and gave it to her.

"Let me have that," she said. "The lighter." She held it above her head and flicked it on. The flame wavered, casting no light in any direction. "Who am I?"

"The Statue of Liberty."

"Wrong."

"Diogenes looking for an honest man."

"Nope. I'm the angel with the flaming sword, blocking our return to Eden!" She stood up. She jumped up and down and from side to side, waving the flame.

She expected him to get up and chase her, but instead he said, "Let me see that lighter a second," and held out his hand. With the other he dug deep in the left front pocket of his jeans. He had to lean back. Almost lying flat, he found the crumpled joint. He sat up, smoothed it, and lit it. He handed it to Flora.

She tried it and handed it back. In the darkness, his presence drew her in. He was nice to her, vetted by the Clinton campaign, young and malleable. She sat down next to him, lay flat, leaned her body against his, and rested her nose on his ear. He sighed, a barely audible hum. She raised her head to get a look at his face. She saw nothing to categorize or dismiss. He said, "You're sweet." He lifted her hair like a bridegroom lifting a veil and kissed her tentatively, gently, on the mouth.

She said, "I have a boyfriend."

The disclaimer didn't give her the expected sense of honesty and full disclosure in good faith. It was stingy with relevant information. As a point of fact she had believed until that moment that feeling valued, understood, relaxed, and sexy was something that happened to her only with Bull. An unanticipated notion was germinating in her mind—that if that was what it meant to have a boyfriend, well, then, maybe she had two.

"Well, I don't, so you shouldn't either," he said. "Fair is fair!"

"Do you have a girlfriend?"

"Is this a pub quiz?"

"I'm risking something. You need to be risking something."

He said, "If you only knew."

"What?"

"I'm already scared you might leave me someday."

"That is so not cool."

"No." He sat up and relit the joint, which had gone out when he set it down on the sand so he could lift her hair.

She watched his eyes in the light of the long flame. She said, "It's so dark, I can't see you. I have no idea what you're thinking."

He said, "Here's what I'm thinking. That your boyfriend doesn't live in Towanda. Turn your car in early, and let's hang for a week. There are all these lakes and waterfalls around here. It's a beautiful area, especially with fall colors. We'll go on vacation like old married people. It's our last chance, because Trump is going to nuke Iran."

"If Clinton wins, the USA will be ceding this part of Pennsylvania to militias from Oregon," she said, not quite joking. "So it really is our last chance."

"We could go back to your nice, warm room," he suggested.

The topic of birth control came up not long after that. She said he could just pull out, because that's what her boyfriend did, and it always worked. "I guess I'm not a fertile person," she said apologetically as he stared at her body in awe.

XXIV.

Flora didn't turn in her car or take whole days off, and neither did Aaron. On Halloween morning, she went canvassing on streets marked green on Reginald Shannon's maps. Out of thirty houses, she found eight adults who answered the door. Three said they'd already voted for Hillary absentee. Two said they would vote Libertarian if they ever voted. Two came out for Trump. One pledged eternal devotion to the Green Party. Flora asked why. He said he'd gotten terminal cancer from the environment.

She met Aaron at the coffee shop at two o'clock. He had bravely canvassed two apartment buildings, meeting seven voters, all of whom claimed to be undecided.

He suggested they go to his place in her car. He was staying in a one-room apartment over a garage. Rather than being paid for out of federal funds like Flora's motel, it was a donation-in-kind by Clinton-supporting tax evaders who usually rented it out online. It was more private than her room, in the sense that no one but the birds of the air could hear them from behind its flimsy walls, but it was also less private, because the owners thought it rude to text Aaron when he was nearby. If they saw his car parked on the street, they would mount the stairs to knock on the door, with nothing but lace curtains obscuring their view of the bed. That was their reason to take her car.

After sex they drove to Standing Stone, a pretty spot a few miles down the river, according to the internet. He drank a beer, because she was driving. It started to rain. They drove back to his place to get high.

The next day was similar. They worked until afternoon. Contentment enveloped them. Fresh motel sheets crackled like autumn leaves. Sugar maples quivered in the wind like flames. Aaron drank and smoked and was instantly buzzed. Flora wasn't used to drinking making a difference to anybody. It never made a difference to Bull. He could drink three dry martinis before dinner and most of a bottle of wine during dinner, and she couldn't even tell. She herself was seldom able to finish two beers. She'd drink the first beer, but the second beer always just sat there reproaching her for ordering it, because, after all, two beers cost twice as much as one beer.

When Aaron drank, it was as though he entered another world when the cap came off the bottle. He became Transfigured Aaron, Man of Joy. It was the same when he touched a joint. He didn't have to light it. He accepted rapture from any placebo he could get his hands on—including her—as though substances and sex were his excuses to become himself in a world set on "low." It was the diametric opposite of Bull's blasé maintenance of suavity at parties that were roiling seas of boilermakers and cocaine. It reminded her of Joe.

"HOW DID YOU END UP WORKING FOR JILL STEIN?" HE ASKED HER. THEY WERE SITTING on the island beach on a sunny afternoon, sharing a mild sativa and a Big Gulp of Mountain Dew.

"I don't know," Flora said. "I live in Cleveland Park, so I grew up going to the zoo. I still never got into biology, because it's mostly about medicine now, like why doesn't this sea slug get heart disease. I mean, field biology is cool, and I'm actually pretty good with statistics, but there are no jobs. So I majored in soil chemistry, except I don't want to work in a lab. This is some kind of long version, isn't it?" She didn't mean to be evasive. "The Stein campaign called me" didn't seem like it would answer the question he was asking.

"It's all exotic and fascinating to me," he said. "I majored in public affairs."

"Well, you know, there's climate change, right? A lot of species are going to die. Most of them, we can't do anything. The temperature's going to rise, the species are going to rise to higher elevations, and they reach the mountaintop and that's it."

"They go to the promised land," Aaron said.

"You got it. So I was thinking what we can do as people, and obviously where we're fucking up is land use and how we regulate it. If we don't switch to organic farming, people are going to starve, especially if they implement the Paris Climate Accord. They want to do combustible biomass on an area the size of India. Now tell me where they're going to get all that nitrogen."

"You don't like the Paris Accord?"

"I can't even— I mean, it's a joke. I was five the year of the Kyoto Protocol, and it's still not in force. People signed on to Paris because it has no sanctions. Carbon emissions are under our control the same way the rest of people's habits are under their control. It's not going to happen. Nobody's leaving any carbon in the ground. What's going to happen is a lot of insane geo-engineering and a big die-off."

"So, Jill Stein."

"Well, getting countries to green their agricultural policies would be a political project. Markets are not going to lead the charge. Sustainability is what you build on the ruins."

"With reforms," he said. "There's a crash, and you institute reforms. Bankers destroy the economy, so you ban organized labor. Coal destroys the climate, so you build gas pipelines. It all makes sense." There was no sarcasm or anger in his delivery. He meant it word for word—a deadpan vision of darkness—but he was beaming while he said it. He was trying and failing to feel implicated in the sad state of the world. He put his arms around Flora and nuzzled her hair.

"This is serious business!" she protested. "Ecosystems are going to crash. We're going to get sustainable agriculture without ecosystems, capturing carbon in biomass with all the insecticides we want, because all we'll eat anymore is grass. Corn is a grass. You don't need pollinators to grow grass."

"Right. So Jill Stein."

"In a word," she said.

They kissed and drank through their respective straws.

She asked, "How did you end up a Clinton fellow?"

"I felt the Bern, and I didn't have the chutzpah to assassinate Trump. At this point I think it's true what people say. He's their moderate intelligentsia."

"I guess what I'm asking is, was there an issue that radicalized you? Was it Occupy?"

"Prisoners' rights, I guess."

"Were you in jail?"

"No, but I can't think of an issue that scares me more. You know they enforce federal cannabis law in PA, everywhere but Philly."

"Ooh." She glanced all around, pretending to be afraid of cops. There was no one in sight but a distant fisherman, on the other side of the river, asleep in his pale blue shade tent.

Still incongruously smiling, he said, "I knew a guy who was incarcerated for a while, before he got exonerated, and he said what kept him from going batshit was knowing stuff by heart.

He'd recite the Koran to himself. So I started memorizing all these hip-hop lyrics, but I still don't feel ready to go to jail."

"I know the words to lots of songs."

"Sing me a song."

"Let me see . . . I can't think of anything."

"That's okay." He lay back on the sand and squinted up at the yellowing afternoon sun.

"Wait, I know," she said. "Here's a rare Joe Harris track that he never recorded." She sang a song that he had sung to her on sidewalks when she was small:

> When I met the crosstown bus
> Ready to be home again,
> Saw the bus was running late
> Saw the sky was pouring rain.
> Looked up in the air,
> Saw her flying there,
> Flying way up high,
> Flora in the sky—

She paused before the rollicking chorus, which was always timed to coincide with arrival at the crosswalk:

> But bats can't fly in the rain!
> Going to end up down in the drain!
> So take my hand, little girl,
> Delancey Street is wider than the whole wide world.

She gasped for breath and took a drink.

"Damn," Aaron said. "That is massively cute."

"I know! You can put in any street name you want. The part about flying makes you look up, so you see the cars coming."

He sang, "Queens Boulevard is wider than the whole wide world."

"My mom told me once she got blackout drunk at the Javits Center, which is on the West Side around Thirty-Fourth, and when she woke up, she was holding on to this concrete Jersey barrier in the middle of the FDR, on a level with Peter Cooper Village, like at Twenty-Third. She had no idea how she got across town, not to mention two lanes of the FDR. She thinks she might have wanted to go swimming in the East River. That's her theory, anyway."

"And she's alive?"

"Yeah. The cars slowed down for her."

"It's no wonder you don't drink."

"She's a lightweight, but you're the cheapest of the cheap dates."

He drew back in mock horror. "What do you mean?"

"You could get high off the smell of beer! You could, like, look at a joint and be tripping. I think you're naturally in a zone, and you don't want anybody to know. That's why being with you makes me feel . . . I don't know."

"What?"

"Free? I feel free. Like, right now, I'm floating. I have trouble remembering the real world, or that it exists."

"Is that good or bad?"

"You're asking the wrong person."

"This is the real world," he said. "Online, I don't even know you."

SHE GOT A FAIR INKLING OF HER FAMILY'S DOINGS ON FACEBOOK, SO SHE KNEW THAT they were not enjoying the final week of campaign season quite so much. Ginger had discovered a vocation as a writer. She was coming up with all sorts of eloquent tl;dr (too long; didn't read) reasons for why she felt the way she did. Her friends "liked" them all, but always a little too quickly. Edgar's strongly contrasting bumper sticker–style slogans were so pithy as to be borderline incoherent (ECONOMIC REFUGEES = REFUGEES!). Her parents were taking it to the streets in a most triumphant manner, if their Facebook posts were to be believed. The posts omitted all details that were sad.

For instance, Pam went to a protest in front of Trump Tower carrying a homemade sign that said GRAB YOURSELF, PUSSY. It featured a clumsy line drawing of a naked Trump with female genitalia. Some beefy yahoo pushed her over backward, hurting both her elbows. While she lay on the ground, another squirted her with ketchup from a disposable packet held with both hands at crotch level. Because there were police all around, she couldn't surprise him from behind and put out his eyes with her thumbnails.

Daniel signed up for a bus expedition that was supposed to leave Twelfth Avenue at four A.M. to go canvassing in Wilkes-Barre. He couldn't find the bus. He didn't have a number to call, and no one on WhatsApp responded to his pleas, so he wandered up and down Twelfth Avenue and then Eleventh in the predawn rush hour, experiencing helpless rage.

Ultimately it seemed sufficient consolation to them both to sit at home drinking coffee and reading in the *New York Times* that there was an 85 percent chance of a Democratic win. It was soothing, like a cross between an 85 percent chance of a refreshing late-summer rain and Hillary somehow polling at 85 percent of likely voters, though not even Pam could come up with a plausible explanation for the source of the number.

While Daniel was getting up at three in the morning to catch his nonexistent bus to Wilkes-Barre to do their job, Flora and Aaron were taking a shower. Between her legs was the achy trace of hard fucking, and his tongue was on it. They were sharing a collaborative state of intense focus and complete and total distraction, like artists.

ON ELECTION TUESDAY, SHE WOKE AT TEN AND TOLD HIM SHE WAS GOING DOWN TO THE coffee shop to fetch them breakfast: two muffins, two scones, and a giant cappuccino each. He said, "Give me time to get dressed, and we'll go to Shoney's. It comes out cheaper when you're hungry."

There he encircled his stack of pancakes with sausage links, topped it with scrambled eggs, doused the entirety in syrup, and said, "I don't get why I didn't meet you a long time ago." He insisted it didn't make sense. They had both spent their lives between D.C. and New York. They should have seen each other.

"That's obvious," Flora said. "You grew up in D.C. and went to college in New York, and I did it the other way around."

"I thought you were from D.C."

"I was born on the Lower East Side. It's just not my happy place."

"Why did your parents move?"

"They didn't move." She paused, thinking what to tell him that would make sense. "They're still in New York. I live with my grandparents."

"Why? Are your parents on drugs?"

"No! Not even close. They're great. I love them. They're wonderful. You should meet them." She said it without thinking. Had she been pressed, she would have said that Aaron might be integrated into her future life as a casual friend, someone she and Bull invited to barbecues to talk politics.

"What do they do?"

"They have an industrial blues band called Marmalade Skye, with an *e*, plus my dad moonlights on Hammond organ with this band called—I can never remember the name—way out in Jersey.

They're all dentists, and they play funk, and everybody else is seventy years old and on roller skates."

"Flora, I hate to break it to you, but they're on drugs."

"Not bad drugs!"

She made eye contact, unwavering, as she continued to ingest orange juice through a straw. He paused in the middle of a forkful of pancakes to look at her.

XXV.

Stein came in under 1 percent in Pennsylvania, with a third as many votes as the Libertarian. Trump took the state.

Aaron and Flora returned to her room from the bar where they had watched the results, but only to pack their things. As they drove out of town there was a pickup truck cruising up and down the bypass, with a guy hanging out the passenger-side window with a shotgun, maybe looking for black people to shoot at in celebration. The guy wouldn't have much luck, they didn't think, because the roads were deserted and the county was 98 percent white. Everybody left of the right wing was probably hiding under a porch.

He dropped her off at the foot of Porter Street at seven in the morning, before rush hour really got going. She walked up the hill, dragging her wheeled suitcase, irritated beyond all measure by the noise it made.

Ginger and Edgar were awake, drinking coffee. Edgar was reading the *Washington Post*. Disconsolate Ginger was on Skype with Pam and Daniel. Flora threw herself on Ginger, stroked her parents' faces on the screen, and cried.

She got a text from Aaron, saying he hoped she'd made it home all right. She didn't reply. His webcam profile pictures were furry and pinkish. His nose was large and his eyes were squinty. His opinions were mainstream Democratic. She missed him in real life, but not this novel virtual persona. She had to ignore its existence and its entreaties both, if she didn't want to start regretting real life as a mistake.

He followed her on Instagram. She set her posts to private. There was plenty else happening online to distract her. Pam had declared her readiness to join an armed militant group. Daniel wanted to emigrate.

Otherwise the morning was quiet, as though after a snowstorm—a red-eyed, sniffling day, pregnant with self-pity and panic.

At ten thirty she texted Bull. He called her back immediately to say, "Good morning, gorgeous! I'm not getting out of bed today. Want to join me?" She notified her grandparents and called a cab.

He opened the town house door in his bathrobe and offered her champagne, saying he'd put two bottles on ice. "This whole town is knee-deep in undrunk champagne," he explained.

"Thank you," she said, taking the glass. "I didn't sleep. I drove all night to get back here. I had so much coffee, I'm shaking."

"That was sweet of you. I went to bed at eleven and slept like an accident victim in an induced coma."

He seemed a little different when they fucked. First he kissed her with one arm all the way around her neck, so that his elbow was behind her head, which he'd never done before. His penis seemed softer. Then he came inside her. She was surprised, but it felt erotic compared to when he pulled out, so she didn't complain or try to interrupt. She just jumped up after they were done and used the handheld showerhead to rinse herself out.

Later on, she said, "That was weird." He immediately knew what she meant and said he was sorry; life had been strange the past couple of days, he said, and he was distracted. She embraced and kissed him. She was glad to be home.

IN THE AFTERNOON, HE LEFT TO ATTEND A CLINTON CAMPAIGN POSTMORTEM AT A BAR on Capitol Hill. It wasn't entirely clear that it would take place, even after it started. People were competing to see who could appear most devastated. They kept intoning that they were in danger of losing everything they'd ever fought for. The expansion of health care, consumer and environmental protections, progress on labor and trade—all of it was poised to go away. Within an hour, he was reduced to saying, "We'll get through this. Remember Reagan? Bush? The other Bush? Arming the Contras? The invasion of Grenada? The secret bombing of Cambodia? 9/11? Iraq? Hello?" Yes, he told everyone, the president-elect was a sleaze, and his tenure would be a dumpster fire. Nonetheless, people under thirty had displayed a near-limitless capacity for drifting leftward, as betrayed by their audible sobs. Yes, the American people had spoken. Yes, they wanted the controls set for the heart of the sun. But the American people wouldn't live forever. There comes a time in every voter's life when he ages out of voting. The pendulum would swing.

The crowd grew by accretion, random mourners joining a public funeral. As the delay in starting the party—there were supposed to be little speeches—moved past the two-hour mark, the crowd in the bar bulged into the street, where an acquaintance of Bull's who'd worked on a failed congressional campaign in an Appalachian corner of Virginia was confessing her emotional devastation to a clot of stray press people. He moved closer. She blamed herself personally for Trump's triumph. She hadn't done enough to appeal to the white working class.

He couldn't believe his ears. A black woman talking about underpaid and underprivileged white people, as if she were on mescaline!

Finally he located Ikumi. Some working-class white man (Aaron Fleischer) was crying on her shoulder like a guilt-stricken baby. All she managed in greeting was to raise her eyes and give him a nanosecond smile.

He realized he had to leave. He couldn't take it. The rough beast had been slouching toward Bethlehem for two solid years, and nobody had been willing to take dead-center aim and empty a can of Raid. The reactionaries could not have reacted without their catalyst. They lacked the pure core of bigotry—unadulterated by religion—around which Trump's movement had crystallized. He and his court sociopaths had shown them that God was dead. He rose to power saying, "Thou shalt kill. Thou shalt covet." His bloc was snapping into place like the Borg, and Hillary's was openly, insanely blaming the working class.

Mentally, he abandoned political Washington at that moment, feeling he might never return. It wasn't hard to do. He would go home and riffle through his advertising contacts, look for some people to call. He was born outside the Beltway. He knew how to man up, renew old friendships, play golf in Georgia.

HIS PLAN WORKED FOR A FEW WEEKS, UNTIL HE SETTLED IN AT HOME. THEN, DESPITE Flora's efforts to amuse him with sexual requests and viral political atrocity videos, he was bored. Unemployed, unwanted, and un-happy, he resolved to write a book.

He was too young for an interesting memoir. He couldn't name names, even of people he'd worked for in the eighties. They were very much alive and might remain so for decades to come. He decided instead to author an introduction to electoral strategy for novices. He regarded the human race, with about four exceptions (all of them third-world dictators—he was having a dark moment), as being clueless about electoral strategy.

He intended to start in medias res with some straightforward recent history. He finished six paragraphs and stopped forever. His manuscript in its entirety read as follows:

Memorably in 2008, America's failure to regulate its banks' invention and marketing of imaginary products led to a global economic meltdown. America was not spared the consequences of its error. Not even close.

Its economy in ruins, desperate America did something odd. It elected an African American president. Not a black guy, obviously. That would have been unthinkable.

One would have thought that the nation's corrupt Plutocrats (*sic;* conservative alien beings from the frigid dwarf planet) would eagerly have reaped the spoils of massive stimulus spending. Instead of handing off America to a hapless Earthling, they could have strained for hitherto unknown omnipotence.

But life on Pluto had taught them the virtue of austerity. Pluto didn't give back. Everything they had on Pluto, they built with their own eight hands. Earth offered the aliens endless renewable bounty, living richness theirs for the taking, whenever their weapons were adequate to drive the Earthlings off the land and enslave them, which was always.

Best of all: Earth had Plutonium.

With the seismic shift of the 2016 elections, the day when Earth would resemble Pluto shifted from the cosmic timescale to the near-term future. The Plutonian concept of the middle-term "foreseeable future" was unknown among Earthlings.

His mood was one of thoroughgoing hopelessness, focused on possibly seeing things get better over the course of about the next thirty years, if he caught all the breaks and lived that long. He was, to borrow a word from the novelist Emile Habibi, a peptimist.

EVEN A MONTH AFTER THE ELECTION, THE TENOR OF CONVERSATION AMONG HIS PROgressive friends hadn't changed. They were mournful, rueful, and defiant without a concrete plan. It was the mood that had been engraving itself on Obama's face for months in anticipation, before anyone knew why. Democrats allowed ex-Green-candidate Jill Stein to sue for recounts and Republican judges to block her, as though reenacting the shared childhood trauma of the courtordered installation of George "Dubya" Bush as beery dullard in chief back in 2000. The unhealed wounds of Republican gerrymandering and rigging were compensated with screen memories of pro-Trump Russian interference, including the candidacy of Jill Stein, who was rumored to be a Russian mole.

When Flora said to Bull, "You came inside me, and now I missed my period," it fit right in.

"That's weird," he said. "Give it a week."

THE FOLLOWING FRIDAY, THERE WAS WET SNOW ALL AFTERNOON. FLORA LEFT GREENLand early, stopping off at a drugstore near her bus stop on M Street. When she got to Bull's house, he met her at the door with a hot toddy (tea, rum, lemon, ginger, cloves), but she waved it away. "I bought a pregnancy test," she said. She kicked off her wet pumps. She turned up her skirt to peel off her wet nylons and dropped them on the welcome mat.

He backed away, toward the kitchen. "Wow. My mind would be blown." He said it flatly, and it sounded literal: her pregnancy would disable some key component of his brain. Nothing lifethreatening. Recent events had regularly blown out components that required retrofitting with aftermarket spare parts.

When she was done she met him in the kitchen with the test in her hand, not looking at it. He was relaxed again, already used to the idea. Again she refused the drink, saying, "I have a bad feeling about this."

"Don't be paranoid." He took the test from her and said, "Well, what do you know."

"What?"

"It's positive."

"No way."

He showed her the wand-like gadget's distinct plus sign. "Definite baby alarm. In twenty-three years, you'll be the proud mother of a Phi Beta Kappa Georgetown graduate. Congratulations."

She stood there, barefoot, looking at him, not sure what to feel. He was extraordinarily hard to read at that moment, because he knew he was infertile. He hugged her to hide the inscrutability he could feel was written all over him.

Her chief feeling was that her feelings depended on his, and it wasn't a good feeling. From the following list, he could favor one: cohabitation and shared parenting; single motherhood; or abortion.

Abortion had little appeal for her. Her life plan had always included children. He was more than qualified to be their dad. She was young and underemployed. Why not go for it? Unless, of course, he asked her to abort it, in which case she would feel like crap and hate him. A man who loved her ought to act thrilled about a baby and leave the abortion choice up to her.

Single motherhood? No, thanks. She wanted the baby, but she couldn't imagine facing Ginger and Edgar, or even Pam and Daniel, to confess that her ancient boyfriend—whom Pam had expressly praised for being too vintage to want a family—wanted to pay child support in absentia, much less that he had left her before she left him. Single motherhood was unimaginable humiliation. To avoid it, she'd have to get an abortion and break up with him.

Nor was marriage an option. He was almost twenty-five years

older. She wanted help with baby diapers, not to spend her fifties changing an old man's. They shared many values, but she'd never heard long-term commitment mentioned as one of them. Besides, she was too young. He was a hired gun who preferred his principles to most people, which was a good thing; she felt it was a key reason his loyalty to his child would know no bounds.

No-strings-attached cohabitation with co-parenting was the one acceptable way out. Her wanting it made it his only possible choice, if he loved her. She moved closer and stared up at him, waiting for his answer.

"Do you want to move in here?" he asked. "It's weird enough that you live with your grandparents, but your having my baby there would make it super weird." He kissed her tenderly.

"We should have lots of sex before I get blobby," she said.

SHE DIDN'T MOVE RIGHT AWAY, THOUGH. SHE DECIDED THAT BEFORE SHE PUT HERSELF through the ordeal of confession to her family, she would get confirmation from a gynecologist and then maybe wait a few months in case the baby went south on its own, as sometimes happens.

At Christmas in Cleveland Park and New Year's on the Upper East Side, she justified her refusal to drink by saying she was getting a cold. She didn't feel like drinking anyway. She had manageable but persistent morning sickness. She zoned out reflexively when Pam and Ginger got keyed up about politics. Their feelings bolstered each other in a rising nexus of fear. Daniel's jokes only irritated them. In D.C. she crept away to the den to watch classic Christmastime movies with Edgar. At her parents' place, she slumped in an easy chair, looking out the window at the tops of the neighbors' trees. The street-level odors in New York made her feel weak.

JENNIFER CALLED BULL TO ASK WHY HE HADN'T BEEN OUT AND ABOUT LATELY. SHE caught him standing in a deli on M Street, puzzling over a Greek yogurt label, trying to figure out whether it was fattening.

"I've been lying low because my girlfriend's going to have a baby," he replied, putting the yogurt back on the shelf. He didn't specify that he was the father. The statement incorporated the rhetorical escape route political commentators call "plausible deniability."

"Wow!" she said. She was also a parser of sentences, particularly his, but the inference was clear enough. Whether he had anything to do with the child's conception or not, he was telling her about it, and that meant he was going to be a father. "That's amazing! Let me buy you a drink. I'm close to you. I'm in Georgetown."

"I'm at the Dean & DeLuca."

"Just stay there."

"I just got here," he said. "I'm shopping."

He had walked down the hill to get ingredients to cook with, because it was nice out and he didn't have anything better to do. Mentioning the baby to Jennifer made his heart swell, right under where the baby would soon be riding around in a knapsack strapped to his chest. He could almost see and feel its little head and body already.

Originally he had invited Flora over for dinner, but she said the smell of cooking made her nauseated and the idea of eating was worse. She was living on lime Perrier and white rice. Since she wasn't coming, he wanted to make oysters Rockefeller and bouillabaisse. He was tempted to invite Jennifer to eat with him, but that seemed like too much of a good thing. A martini at the bar next door would be plenty.

She showed up just as he finished checking out. They walked over to sit in the roped-off outdoor café area and drink to Flora's health. The temperature was in the fifties, but it rose whenever the sun broke through the clouds. It was warm enough to sit outside and cool enough not to spoil seafood.

Jennifer ordered sparkling wine and made fun of Bull's order. "Martinis are not festive," she said. "Martinis are for two years from now, when you're losing your mind with a screaming kid in the house and you haven't gotten a good night's sleep since, like, what, six months from now?"

"Your point is well taken," he said. "This could be the beginning of the end."

"So, wow. A baby. I still can't believe it."

"It makes me happy," Bull said. "The world is going to shit, but we're not, personally, going to shit. That's how it makes me feel. Not a ray of hope, but the real thing. Hope itself as a substance. I'm completely crazy about this kid."

"You're sentimental enough, God knows," Jennifer said. "Know the gender yet?"

"It's a boy," Bull said.

She was startled to get an answer. He seemed strangely blithe and guileless to her, as if he were turning into this young girlfriend. She said, "Congratulations. You're the man."

"It's not my doing. It's the fates."

"Enough of this," she said. "What's new in the world of Democratic politics?"

"Oh, Jesus." He rolled his eyes. "It's Prometheus tied to the rock, with the vultures tearing out his liver. Ask me this time next year, when I'm back on the horse."

"I suppose ad strategy is secondary now that U.S. elections are rigged by Russian hackers."

"Says the CIA! This is Putin taking the fall for Citizens United. It's our Supreme Court that's the dead, rotting elephant in the room. Fuck them, seriously."

Jennifer was silent for a moment, digesting the notion that he might have retired from public life without knowing it. She asked whether he was going to the inauguration.

"Some kind of commiseration party might be hard to avoid, but no. I'm not hosting one either. I'm taking a year of paternity leave.

The timing couldn't be better. Trump is going to be hoist with his own petard, but we have to be patient while he fumbles it."

"'Petard' means 'bomb.'"

"I know that."

"He's going to have the bomb. Doesn't that scare you?"

"Sweetie, Pakistan has the bomb. Israel has the bomb. The French and the English and the Chinese have the bomb."

"The real bomb, or just little Hiroshima-style atom bombs like you can buy at the five-and-dime?"

"The Soviet Union had thermonuclear devices that would make a fireball five miles wide."

"What arc you saying?"

"That my girlfriend's going to have a baby, so a thermonuclear device sounds to me about as risky as smoking a pipe. They can both get you killed. It's all relative."

In a gentler voice, she asked, "Are you going to marry her?"

"She hasn't asked me, and I'm not about to bring it up. Marriage is losing its cachet, now that everybody's doing it."

"Maybe not much longer!"

HE GOT A PART-TIME JOB TEACHING AT GEORGETOWN FOR THE SPRING SEMESTER. IT WAS an adjunct position, the sort of thing a twenty-four-year-old could have gotten with a master's degree. But he didn't have a master's degree, much less any academic publications, so he figured he was doing all right.

It didn't pay—or rather, it paid approximately what he was used to spending on bar tabs—but he wasn't in debt. He needed time off. He enjoyed regular contact with young adults. As a happy man, he even managed to enjoy their inviolability. Touching one of them would have meant instant lights out on college teaching forever, and he didn't want that.

There was an incredible-looking woman in his Classic Mayoral

Races seminar who flirted with zero adroitness, moving closer when she couldn't think of anything to say, at heart nerdy and scared, from a conservative community out in the Virginia hills. In an earlier life he might have resented her for coming on to him like a booby-trapped intern. Instead he spoke to her with kindness, calmed her nerves, pointed her toward eligible classmates, and otherwise mentored her in a dad-like manner that made her personal growth a matter of pride.

The students reaffirmed his hopes. Most were committed leftists, if vague on doctrine. They thought aloud in terms that would have cost him his college career. Resistance was futile, since his continued employment was linked to their course evaluations. He would never have said that they displayed a sense of entitlement. Universally, they felt dispossessed. Each was a node of expropriation, an intersection among vectors of domination they labeled in a kind of factor analysis—black, female, queer, of color—and they deferred to those more numerously impacted in a manner he found quite chivalrous.

That is to say, if he let everyone else speak first, a rich white man could still have the last word.

FLORA BOYCOTTED THE INAUGURATION, EVEN ON TV. IT WAS STRANGE TO ATTEND THE next day's Women's March on Washington with waves of disorienting queasiness and a rose-and-fuchsia "pussy hat" on her head to demand, among other things, "choice." Ginger had knitted three nice ones. Edgar wore Pam's and looked extremely cute. Flora put hers in her bag, saying it was too warm. It reduced her to something she was afraid of being reduced to. She put it on and took it off again three times.

XXVI.

At fifteen weeks, on the glassed-in back porch in Cleveland Park, Flora confessed to her grandmother that she was expecting. Ginger was too stunned to react beyond hugging her and saying, "Gosh, what a fabulous surprise!" She asked whether Pam and Daniel knew and offered to call them, but Flora said she'd rather tell them herself.

"Well, well," Ginger said, sitting down in a wicker chair. "You're starting a family. I never thought I'd be a great-grandmother in my lifetime. Never thought I'd be one at all, to tell the truth. You're an only child, and so is your mother. You could have been the end of the line, knock on wood."

"This family has been reproducing successfully for four billion years," Flora said. "It would be weird if I broke the chain."

Ginger laughed a little nervously. She stood up and returned to her nasturtium repotting project. After a moment of silence she said, "You know, there are some questions in my mind. You didn't mention marriage or say anything like, 'Bull is so excited.' You didn't say his name. So I'm a little concerned about whether he's good with this." She glanced at Flora, whose expression was noncommittal. "Wait. Are you thinking of raising your baby here at home, with us?"

"He asked me to move in with him," Flora reassured her. "He asked me right away. Literally his first reaction. For me, it was moving a little too fast. I was scared that then, if I lost the baby, people would know, and it would be harder on the both of us. But now that I've told you, I could move in with him tomorrow."

"Flora, we're not 'people.' We're family. You can always come to us, no matter what the issue is."

"I didn't mean you! I was thinking more like his professional contacts. He doesn't have any family really." It struck her as sad that he had aged out of having a support network like hers.

"I take it that you wouldn't have been moving in together otherwise."

"We never talked about it. He is so busy. But we've been exclusive for two years, anyway, so, I mean, it makes sense. There's never a convenient time to have a baby, but right now I don't even have a job lined up or any concrete plans."

Ginger sighed. "Maybe it was meant to be. You're just the right age to become a mother, and you've got a man who loves you, apparently. I'd love to meet him sometime. This isn't where I expected to see you at this time in your life, but I guess it's destiny. It's fate."

"You mean predestination? Like the invisible hand?"

"You know, I keep thinking of your mom. You were not a product of family planning, but the truth is neither was she."

Flora raised an index finger in protest. "That's not true!" she said firmly. "Abortion is birth control. Mom had access to it, and so did I, and I bet you could have too, if you tried. It's craziness for people to pretend they're surprised."

"You make me proud, Flora. You're sharp as a tack."

"I know," she said. "It's your fault for sending me to fancy schools, when you could have sold me to a pimp."

Ginger leaned down and hugged her, mostly with one fore-arm, because she was wearing gardening gloves. She perched on the arm of the overstuffed sofa and asked, "Tell me—no jokes now—how do you feel inside?"

"I feel a baby inside, which is weird," she said. "By the time I get used to it, it'll be gone." Seeing the worried look on her grand-mother's face, she added, "I'm elated. Ecstatic. I mean it."

When Edgar heard the news, a few minutes later, he pretended she was already too huge to get his arms around. He insisted she call her parents immediately, saying she shouldn't make them wait another minute to share the joy.

SHE TRIED PAM FIRST. SHE CAUGHT HER AT HOME AND HAPPY TO TALK, BUT OPENED THE conversation by asking whether her dad was around. "He's down-town walking Victor's dog," Pam said. "Victor got this white rag-mop-type thing that hangs out in the store. It's got to be fifteen. It just lies there panting all the time. Daniel thinks it's younger and didn't get any exercise at the shelter."

"I have weird news, Mom."

"Bring it on."

"I'm four months pregnant and I'm moving in with Bull."

"Oh, my God! You're still a little kid! What is this? You're barely older than I was. Did you tell your grandma?"

"Yeah. She's psyched."

"So how did this happen? It must have been Election Day! Are you going to name it Donald?"

"That is so disgusting."

"You don't know what disgusting is. Welcome to motherhood."

"You can't scare me."

"Okay, so you're moving in with my contemporary and peer in a mansion in Georgetown and having his baby. Whoa. I'm just in shock! I almost wish you'd texted me."

"It's not a mansion. It's a row house. It's not even semidetached.

We're going to be poor. He got himself in so much trouble during the election, he'll probably never work again."

"I get it. The devoted full-time househusband. Believe me, nobody in any industry has a memory longer than two years. When that baby comes, he'll be back at work before you can say Jack Robinson."

The joke was possibly too true, and they stared at their respective walls.

Pam didn't want to say how disappointed she was to see Flora repeating her mistake. She didn't even want to think it. She made herself approve, and the anxiety came boomeranging right back in her face in the form of concern for herself. She was forty-seven and a half and becoming a grandmother. While her face, with total lifetime sun exposure that could be measured in weeks, remained smooth as a pickled egg, gray roots disfigured her vermilion hair, and the meaning of life still eluded her. Her job would pass any cost-benefit analysis, but it was not a creative outlet. Her industrial blues band was not avant-garde. A grandchild sounded like an atavism or a throwback, not progress. Something had to give in the art department.

Flora interrupted her reverie by saying, "I should call Dad. Bye. I love you!"

She reached him as the dog sat stubbornly on its tail end in the middle of Forsyth, refusing to be dragged. She recommended he either leave it there or pick it up, but most definitely get himself out of the middle of the street.

"Under the fur, this dog is vile," he said, his fingertips meeting bulbous protuberances as he scooped it up. "It's like Victor went in the shelter and asked which animal nobody in their right mind would take. It's beautiful—I mean, he's a saint—but this dog's a whited sepulcher. Why in hell does it smell like garlic? Maybe it's some flea thing he did. The one positive aspect to this dog is it can't climb stairs."

"I have weird news, Dad," she said. She sketched her situation.

His response was an announcement that he'd be coming down on Friday, most likely with Pam, with the intent of meeting Bull on Saturday if at all feasible. He was enthusiastic and firm. He didn't see the need to feel disappointment until and unless something major went wrong.

"I don't know about Saturday," Flora said. "He might have plans. We don't even live together yet. Couldn't you wait a couple weeks?"

"Grant me this moment. He'll get through it. He's pushing fifty and he's having your baby. Meeting me is the least of his worries."

AFTER SPEAKING WITH HER PARENTS, FLORA FELT BETTER THAN SHE HAD AT ANY TIME since she first suspected the pregnancy. She had unloaded her irony at the source, where it dissipated, her drops of irony dissolving in her parents' irony buckets, leaving her alone with her joy, which was sincere, straightforward, substantial, growing, and better suited to life in a conservative southern town like Washington.

It happened as Daniel predicted. Bull finessed the situation by inviting her parents and grandparents to dinner in Georgetown and grilling steaks. While Edgar perused his collections, he stood with Daniel at the monumental Weber on the rear deck and talked politics. The hot meat steamed in the cold as if they were camping on a hunting trip. Daniel was taller than Bull. With his coat on and his hands in his pockets, he felt massy and secure. Flora gave Pam and Ginger a tour of the house, emphasizing its many desirable qualities and fine woodwork.

Ginger and Edgar took a cab home after dessert, claiming persuasively that it was late and they were tired. The conversation turned to New York and how it had changed. What had been where, when, and what had vanished. What bars Bull remembered from visits in his twenties.

It was strange for Flora, watching him reminisce with her parents about the three of them being her age. The conversation about old New York continued without him, in the car back to Cleveland Park. Flora drove because she wasn't drinking, with Daniel in the passenger seat. Over her shoulder, her parents conducted a loud and lengthy analysis of Bull's claim to have seen Elvis Costello at the Palladium. Eventually she interrupted, saying that she didn't care what they thought of him as a family member. This was just in case they were refusing on principle to advance an opinion, trying not to alienate her.

"What's there to say?" Pam said. "He's great. He'd better be, or I'll knock his block off!"

"Obviously I wish he were thirty," Daniel said, "but I guess then he wouldn't have the resources he does. You like him fine, and you're convincing as a couple. He's what any father would hope for his daughter. You're moving up in the world. The kid's going to be socioeconomically privileged. I guess it's old-fashioned, in a good way. Upward mobility. Just give me time to get used to it for a while. You kind of took us by surprise."

"I second that emotion," Pam said. "I don't understand it, but you're obviously happy. You planning on getting married?"

"We didn't talk about it," Flora said. "I don't think so."

"Was he ever married?"

"No."

"Are you in love?"

"That's a state secret!" She wanted to sound coy but managed to convey only ambivalence.

"In my opinion," Pam declared, "you're not all that heavy into him. The whole deal has a pragmatic cast. But pragmatism's not a bad thing, when there's a baby involved. I'd rather see you use a reliable guy than be madly in love with some ditz-ball."

"Mom! I'm not using him! We've been a couple for two years!"

"I didn't mean it that way," Pam said, not specifying what other way she meant it.

"Your mother traditionally has low expectations for young love," Daniel said, reaching back to pet her leg.

"I'm crazy about him," Flora said. "He's an awesome person in a lot of ways. It's just not what I expected to be doing with my life. I'm as surprised as you are." She was guiltily conscious of propounding the surprise narrative she'd ridiculed to Ginger, but she let it ride.

"Sorry I brought up marriage," Pam said. "You've got enough on your plate already without planning your retirement."

Flora reflected that it might have been smarter to introduce Ginger and Edgar as her parents. They would be about the age of Bull's. She realized that despite her intimacy with his views and opinions, she didn't know anything about his family. She had assumed his parents were dead and that he lived in their house. For all she knew, they were alive and well in a condo in Annandale.

SHE DIDN'T ASK HIM ABOUT HIS FAMILY, AND SHE KEPT PUTTING OFF THE DATE WHEN she would move in. But on a Sunday in early April, after they woke up together in Georgetown, he said, "Today's the day. Let's go get your stuff. The reason it's so hard to move you is that you have no stuff. Right? You don't have furniture. It's theirs. So it's just a matter of packing a suitcase. It's a formality. Let's do it."

"We can have lunch with my grandparents," she said. "But I was wondering, actually. What's the deal with your parents? Are they still living?"

"My dad died of AIDS," he said. "In Tangier. He was super gay. My mother lives in Idaho, and I have a little brother who's an actor in Japan, with a Japanese wife and kids. We're not close. I'm sure I'll go see Mother again, now that I'm a college professor with semester breaks. I went out there in the summer of 2013. She's living on this experimental multigenerational old folks' farm. She can rope and ride. Maybe not with authority anymore."

"Wait. Do you get along with her? Do you talk?"

"She never paid much attention to us. I grew up in boarding schools."

"So was this house in the family?"

"No. We had a little farmette in Berryville, out near Winchester. They sold it before they moved to Japan for a while. That was, what, eighty-eight? I was here, in college. I've been fending for myself a long time. I'm getting primed right now to have the only family I ever had in my life. That's how it feels."

"So when did you buy this place?"

"Twenty-ten."

That was only seven years before. The house had seemed the epitome of stability in colonial brick and immense oak beams. She had imagined it to have been in his possession forever, or at least to have been something other than a post-crash bargain.

"Hillary in 2008," he explained. "She lost, but I got paid."

"Was it a foreclosure?"

"No," he said. "I think the seller felt a little pressure to get her dad out of here and into a nursing home, though."

HE SUGGESTED SHE GET AMNIOCENTESIS. SHE PROTESTED THAT SHE WAS TOO YOUNG TO have a mutant baby. He insisted that he was an old man who had flown on a thousand planes and taken every drug in the book. Given how slight the risk of miscarriage was for someone as young and healthy as she, she could submit to a long scary needle for a second to make sure she was expecting the kind of baby she expected.

She submitted. The baby was declared perfect.

The esteemed amnio specialist was a personal friend of Bull's. He assured Bull in confidence that the baby was not his.

He answered, "Well, that's one less worry."

AMERICA'S INEPT NEW ADMINISTRATION REELED FROM ONE HOURLY CRISIS TO THE next. It was unclear how America would survive the next four years. Dependent on mass media for their news, Democratic activists far from the center of power argued that the party's logical next step was political martyrdom: a pivot to socialism reminiscent of the *puputan* suicides with which the people of Bali rebuked their Dutch colonizers as late as 1908.

Nonetheless, Bull's mood improved by leaps and bounds. When the health care debacle story broke—Trump's failed attempt to repeal and replace Affordable Care—he was jubilant and grinning, on the phone for days, reiterating his predictions to skeptics far and wide. "He'll accomplish nothing after this," he told everyone. "His legislative agenda is dead on arrival. It's over before it started!"

Jennifer called him to ask for a live interview on the local NPR morning show. She said they'd been running enough doom and gloom, and it was time for Democrats to get a chance to feel good again.

He had a certain routine with WAMU. He knew which studio she worked out of and where to grab an espresso on the way in. He got there just in time to sit down, put on headphones, and hear himself being described in a short bio. The red light went on, and he braced himself for her first question.

"First of all," she said, "I hear congratulations are in order."

Bull said, "Thanks. Though God knows it wasn't my doing. This administration isn't even running on fumes. It's out of gas. From here on out it's downhill or nowhere."

"You weren't directly involved with the Clinton campaign. Why was that?"

"The tactics I was pursuing weren't considered a good fit with the central campaign strategy, and that's fine. There's a time and a place. I was involved tangentially and with a number of congressional and local campaigns."

"You wanted to go negative."

"Jen, a positive message, when it's not simple, can be confusing. There was a tremendous proliferation of positive claims in the Republican space last summer. It was crowding out almost anything Democrats could say. Given all the platforms on new media, there's room out there for dark prophecies as well. Frankly I think we flubbed an opportunity to reach out to this administration's early supporters and communicate the risks of their position. That had to be a dark message, even an ugly message. At this point I would say I've been vindicated by the reality of what we're seeing."

"It's also been said you may have had some hand in sabotaging the campaign of Jill Stein, who was the Green candidate for president, in Pennsylvania. You're romantically involved with someone who worked on that campaign, is that right?"

"My private life is private. You know that."

"I've also heard you're starting a family with this Stein campaign staffer, so the question does arise of possible collusion in that party's frankly miserable results in Pennsylvania." While he pulled off his headphones and rolled his chair away from the microphone, she continued: "This was a classic battleground state, where Clinton was expected to win narrowly, with Stein taking up to two percent. Ultimately Stein came in under one percent, and as we know, Trump took the state. That could create an impression that Stein supporters shifted over to Trump. Wouldn't you say it would have been better to keep them with Stein, even at the cost of letting them think they were throwing away votes on a third party?"

He rolled back toward the table. With his voice only a bit tighter and higher than usual—it took some concentration—he said, "I have and have had nothing to do with either the Green Party or the Commonwealth of Pennsylvania. Now, if we can get back to talking about the present situation, which is hopeful and encouraging for all progressives. We have a legislative deadlock between a party and its own radical wing. This is historically unique.

The traditional saying is that 'the Left will eat itself,' but what we're seeing here is a Republican Party that bleeds lighter fluid."

"I'm afraid we've run out of time. This is Jennifer Wang, and I've been talking to Democratic campaign consultant Bull Gooch." She flipped a switch and took off her headphones.

"That was uncalled for," Bull said.

"I have your back, but I'm a reporter first."

"I had you pegged as a friend."

"We're still friends. I should have warned you."

"If you'd warned me, I wouldn't be here."

"You want to get coffee?"

"If you're going to dox me, you should get used to drinking alone and watching your back," he said, putting on his coat.

He stalked out, longing for the days when gossip was invisible. There was a fine line, on social media, between candor and backstabbing. Apparently it was so fine that even Jennifer could forget the difference between talking to him in private and talking to him on live radio.

Within minutes she called to apologize, or justify herself, by saying that no one would be listening that late in the morning. It had been almost ten o'clock. He told her to go fuck herself.

THE NEWS REACHED ELAINE THE SAME DAY. THE STEIN CAMPAIGN SHUT FLORA OUT JUST as it was shutting itself down—a six-month process—so she never knew what hit her. She had expected to see her hours gradually reduced to zero, and she was right.

She didn't try hard to find another job. She had started showing in month four. An unmistakable appearance of pregnancy is not the first thing employers look for in a prospective hire.

By mid-May she was waddling around under a whopping monster baby. She wasn't under orders to lie down, but she was spending a lot of time watching Netflix on the couch. Bull treated her with kindness. While working, he no longer paced around the ground floor. It became their common room. He retreated upstairs to his office to make calls and came out ready to socialize. He cooked delightful meals and accepted invitations to eat in Cleveland Park. On weekends, they drove to pretty places to take walks. He was a gracious host to Pam and Ginger, whenever they turned up on his porch, even if they hadn't been invited. Whenever he placed his hand appraisingly on Flora's belly, she could tell he was thinking, This is my beloved son, in whom I am well pleased.

News of Flora's state didn't reach Aaron. He never listened to NPR. Its fair and balanced perspective—it attacked "liberal hypocrisy," the conservative term for having good intentions in a conservative-dominated world, as readily as career criminality—annoyed him. He missed her with nostalgic longing, as if they'd met on Atlantis or Avalon and could never be reunited in this life.

He had too little sexual experience to know that when a woman says she has a boyfriend, a husband, or the like, it doesn't mean she will always have those things. In practice, the choice of audience and setting can render such a claim questionable on its face.

He sought traces of her online, but her presence was political, not personal. So were most of her friendships, based on a footing of impersonal small talk she could have offered a cabdriver. She was a political person.

The personal is not political. It can become political when abstracted and generalized, stripped of identifying markers. The political subject is a depersonalized subject: This could be you. This could be you being lied to, spied on, shot at, searched without warrant, convicted without trial, executed without appeal. Could be, but isn't. When it turns personal, it's too late.

Accordingly, political people were more cautious with their data than they used to be. Even Jennifer on Twitter never got more pointed than "You'll never guess who's twenty-five and having a certain person's son," which proved to be true.

At the same time, Aaron was privy to details he didn't know

were relevant. His fellow Clinton campaign volunteer Ikumi Sakuragi also attended Clinton-apostate get-togethers sponsored by the post-Sanders organization Our Revolution. During post-meeting beers at a Capitol Hill bar, she had confided in him about an affair she'd had with a prominent Democratic strategist during the weeks prior to the election. This self-assured older workaholic had seduced her on the verbal strength of his lust alone, summoning her magisterially to fuck in empty offices upstairs from receptions and that sort of thing. Their sex could be spontaneous, she said, because he'd gotten a vasectomy. She called him "the sex poet." Aaron wasn't buying it. Ikumi showed him photos. He realized he had seen the man but never met him. His own position in the Democratic organization was official and menial; Bull's was the opposite. Their paths ran parallel, never touching. Ikumi's path touched Bull's only because he had swerved.

The sordid affair struck Aaron as perfectly in keeping with the status-laden guy's offensive name. One of her snapshots, taken surreptitiously from the perspective of a pillow, depicted his naked back. His head, lowered, was invisible. The image of a large expanse of expressionless meat stuck in Aaron's mind. When he thought of Bull, he imagined a bull-necked creature that was mostly blank flesh, like a centaur.

XXVII.

Pam suffered from spring fever. She was working truncated hours, like she used to do when she was starting out. When the weather was nice, she left her suit jacket on the back of her chair, to notify coworkers that they were supposed to pretend she was in, and walked home from East Harlem through the park. It couldn't possibly fool anybody, given how small the office was, but she thought it might fool Yuval, since he wouldn't look for her in the ladies' room.

When he sent her a text at two o'clock on a Thursday afternoon, inviting her to Friday brunch in Tribeca, she got a sinking feeling. He texted her again in the morning to tell her to stop by his apartment first and check out his remodeling job.

She had been there a few times before. His place was in an elevator building from the fifties. He lived on the sixth floor out of eight, facing the street. Nothing fancy, but large, with high ceilings. After the remodeling, it emerged, nearly everything in the place was white, rounded, and smooth. Even the curtains were made of some kind of ultra-heavy fabric that blocked light completely, yet was radiantly white. He joked that the decorating style was called "bachelor iPad."

"Dirt in here would really stand out," she said. "I bet it took your maid all of three minutes to hunt down the hametz crumbs on Passover."

"I saved her the trouble. I remodeled, and then I went gluten-free."

"More dirt is better for your immune system."

"That's why I keep the children upstate with the dogs, for their health."

The exchange encapsulated the difference between them. He was a purpose-driven perfectionist, and she liked things to be good enough if you squint. She was much too sincere ever to think anything was perfect.

In related news, his happy family adored him (he was sure of it) and condoned (ditto) his maintenance of a reputation as a downtown playboy par excellence, while she was a chronically half-assed system error kept in one piece by its loyalties and inability to escape its body. She was starting to know it—that she would never be a cohesive unit, no matter how hard she squinted.

She took off her boots and sat cross-legged on a sofa. He lit some tapers in a candelabra to set a visual accent less messy than flowers and gave her a glass of seltzer. She said, "Yuval, I can't do this anymore."

"Funny you should say that."

She weighed the possibilities and said, "Okay. Whatever. Why?"

"I got a sub-rosa offer for the company from Alphabet. This was months ago, in February. Now I'm watching the price come up and wondering why they don't lose interest. It must be some very special product you developed."

"And still you hesitate, because you're so invested in building the brand."

"Are you?"

"Oh, totally! There's no way this acquisition can go through unless you fire me. Make it a condition."

"And how much is it going to cost them? Approximate ball-park."

"Feel them out. I trust you."

They went downstairs to the bistro. As aperitifs, they ordered dry martinis. Pam took one sip of hers and stopped. Ideas were crowding into her head. She didn't want to reduce her capacity to absorb a power surge.

She asked for oyster stew—the fastest thing on the menu—and ate it quickly. She felt restless and hyperactive. She kept turning to look out at the street. She wanted to yell a celebratory song, something like "Raoraorao."

Yuval took possession of her key card. He asked what personal effects he should have delivered to her home by courier, since it might be best for negotiations if she never touched the firm's hardware again. She thought about it hard, but she couldn't come up with anything she wanted out of her office.

"Shoes?" he prompted her. "Hairbrush? Makeup?"

"You mean my corporate bedroom slippers?" She stomped her nailed boot heels on the floor. "I'll come get them after they pave downtown with travertine and turn it into an air-conditioned pedestrian mall. It won't be much longer." She dunked her hands in her martini glass (it was nearly the size of a finger bowl), rubbed them vigorously together, and ran them through her hair. She leaned back and put her arm up on the back of her seat. Alcoholic fumes wafted toward Yuval.

"Smells great," he said. "But a waste of good gin."

"Better gin than me."

"You don't want to be wasted?"

"Sorry, no."

"Bad Pam! How am I supposed to celebrate?"

"Dude, you just fired me. You'll have parties! But for me, it's over. I'm flying. You think I'm sitting here, but I'm way over your head. If there's one thing in this town that doesn't need disinfecting right now, it's my brain."

She headed home by way of B&H electronics on Ninth Avenue, where she bought a fancy video camera, lenses, and a tripod. The dark web would yield pirated copies of Avid and Scenarist. A rental car would bring her to skies crisscrossed with power lines over shallow water. Video Hit was (for reasons of astrology, tourism, and entrepreneurial misjudgment) selling off a surplus of inflatable vinyl goats. She had this idea for some art.

DANIEL RETURNED HOME AT FIVE THIRTY FROM THAT WEEK'S TEMP GIG, HIS MOOD HEAVily compromised by foulness. He was playing systems administrator to a consumer products giant that had reduced laptop attrition by installing low-end tower PCs on the floor under people's desks. When they kicked the motherboards and cables loose by accident, Daniel got to plug them back in. He felt he was getting too old for jobs that required crawling. He hung up his jacket and said, "Today was a fucking ordeal."

Pam looked up from her perusal of her new camera's user manual and said, "You want to quit work and be my collaborator?"

"And shave my head?" (He was alluding to the women "collaborators" who were traditionally shaved as punishment for bearing the children of invading armies.)

"I got fired today," she said.

"With prudent and necessary force?" (That is to say, with a severance package or without, though he couldn't have told her which was meant by the phrase he chose.)

"Yes."

He sat down to take off his shoes and said, "Hallelujah. I was afraid he'd notice your thirty years of service and give you a gold watch."

He collapsed flat on his back on his couch, resting the inside of his elbow on his eyes to keep out the light.

"Yuval's selling out," she said. "I'm the holdout CEO with the ironclad contract who's dragging her feet. The company's worth so much more without me. It's not in the bag yet, but I have a very good feeling."

"So what's your art?"

She set the brochure down and crawled over to sit on the rug beside him. "Video," she said. "Original soundtrack, with my vocals. Goats are involved. You know the goats I mean."

"And you need a sound tech, or somebody to blow up the goats, or what?"

"I need a collaborator," she said. "Nobody takes artists seriously if they work alone. We're equal partners. Svoboda and Svoboda."

"I want to be Svoboda. You can be 'Svoboda.'"

"I have dibs. It was my idea."

"I think I've contributed most, if not all, of the Svoboda to this collaboration."

"So license it to me."

"What are you offering in trade?"

"Ice cream. The best. Your favorite."

"So you take credit for my art, and we go out for ice cream."

"You are correct."

"Throw in a glass of water, and we have a deal."

They shook hands. He got to his feet, rather energized, and headed for the shower. She went to the kitchen to get him a glass of water.

IN LATE JUNE, FLORA RAN INTO AARON ON G STREET. SHE HAD BEEN VISITING THE National Portrait Gallery and buying bras at Macy's. The block was lined with the polished stone facades of minor lobbying offices and pricey coworking spaces. He appeared out of an entryway, wearing a plaid shirt, jeans, and trekking sandals, looking like a recent immigrant from the Pacific Northwest, but fifteen years out of date.

When their eyes met, he broke into a run, straight toward her. After a second he resumed walking slowly, but he didn't swerve.

She stood still, waiting, feeling grotesquely pregnant, embarrassed to be seen wearing running shoes and carrying a plastic shopping bag.

"Hey, Flora," he said. "Wow. Look at you. Congratulations! You're so— Who's the lucky guy?"

She replied that the answer was on a need-to-know basis. She couldn't tell whether he was doing the math in his head. He didn't look calculating, just surprised and happy. He was bouncing on his toes, as if seeing her were a good bit more excitement than he had expected to experience that day. Which was probably true, given their history, she figured.

They asked each other what they were doing and where they were living. He was living in a group house way up Sixteenth Street, almost to the Maryland line, and working for the AFL-CIO. He kept glancing at her abdomen.

"I guess I truly don't need to know," he said. "But, I mean, is it your same boyfriend? I had no idea! Let's get coffee and catch up. I don't have anything until one."

There were coffee shops on all four corners of the next intersection. She picked the Starbucks, because of the low armchairs. He paid for her lemonade.

At first they talked about work. She told him how depressing the Stein campaign had been before it disbanded to lick its wounds. He told her about the supposedly liberal university professors who ran the facilities whose custodians he was trying to unionize. He couldn't keep his eyes on her face or even her breasts.

Finally she said, "Okay, Aaron. It's Bull Gooch. You know,

the strategist? That's my boyfriend. He's been my boyfriend for years."

All at once he looked upset and sad.

"I know it's weird," she continued. "But he's someone where we always understood each other perfectly, from the minute we started talking. He's like my brother from another mother. He never has to ask what I mean, and I always know what he's getting at. I know friends don't let friends vote Green—I mean, he even supported me in that!—but by the time the election was over, I had gotten the message. And he's my best friend. It wasn't planned, but it happened."

"It's not that," Aaron said. "It's that when he was fucking my friend Ikumi last fall when you and me were in Towanda, he told her he'd had a vasectomy. So now I'm wondering."

Flora stared. The baby kicked her hard in the bladder. For a second she lost awareness of her surroundings, like a Victorian lady swooning. She felt she was suspended in space and that everything around her was turning yellow. Then Starbucks came back. She shifted her weight in the chair, listed to one side, and grasped her belly while the baby shifted positions. "That's a kick in the head," she said.

"I know," Aaron said. "I'm sorry. I can't fucking believe it myself. But I had to tell you, because my head is exploding."

"My body is exploding," Flora said. "I have to call him right now. I need to know." She put her hand on her phone.

"What's there to know?" he said. "Fucker lied to you. He's not your fucking best friend! That's your idealism talking. You want friendship, you have a right to it, but it's got nothing to do with that fucker."

"Chill out, Aaron. You don't know him."

"Well, maybe he lied to Ikumi? It's you or her. And this is your best friend. I get it." His words were sarcastic, but his tone was less contemptuous than pitying, as though he couldn't stretch his brain enough to contain the pathos of a woman whose best friend would tell her a lie.

She turned to look out the window and dialed Bull. He answered straightaway, casually, despite being in a tutorial session with students. The pregnancy was far enough along to create a certain suspense. "Hey, sweet pea," he said.

She said, "Question. Is this your baby?"

"Take five," he said. He paused for the students to vacate his office and said, "No, it's not. I've known since the amnio. They did a paternity test. Maybe I should have told you."

"Bullshit," Flora said. "You knew before that. You had a vasectomy."

"No. Okay. The truth is I'm infertile. I have a low sperm count. No viable sperm. But stranger things have happened, you know? Your girlfriend fools around on you and gets pregnant, and sometimes you take it as a gift."

"And Ikumi, whoever the fuck she is, needed to know this, and I didn't?"

"Don't be petty. You've been fucking around on me since I don't know when. But I love you. I'm thrilled to be a father. I'm excited and happy about everything. Really."

"But, Bull, I used condoms"—driven by jealousy, she didn't care whether Aaron heard her lie—"and obviously you didn't, because why else would you tell some random bitch you had a vasectomy?"

"Because she wanted my baby, you numbskull. She wanted to get serious."

That was checkmate. She saw why he had lied. She couldn't deny her importance to him. She breathed heavily for a moment and said, "Okay. I've got to think this over. I'll see you later." She put her phone back facedown on the table and took a sip of lemonade.

"By the way, it's my baby," Aaron said. "Just saying that because it's true."

"It's Bull's baby," Flora replied.

"No. That's not how it works."

"It's whoever's baby I say it is. I could start the process right now and put it up for adoption tomorrow, if I wanted."

"And I could sue you for the right to take it. I wouldn't even have to go through an adoption court, because I'm the dad. I'm having a baby, with you. We're having a child."

"Your father's rights bullshit is really unpleasant to me right now," Flora said. "Nobody but me has anything to do with this baby. I'm the one carrying it around. It's made of me."

Picking the label off his lemonade bottle with both hands, he said, "Just don't say you would put our baby up for adoption. I was so in love with you. I mean it. I still am."

"And now you want visitation, or shared custody, or what? Care to formulate your demands?"

"Why are you asking me aggressive crap like that? How do you think I'm feeling right now?"

"I don't care," she said. "What I need for you to do is leave me alone. Go away. My life was fine. I don't need to see you. Do that for me! Let it go. Be done. Let us have our baby, and go make babies with somebody else."

Without warning, he moved from the chair to his knees on the linoleum and made so as to rest his head on her stomach. There was no way she could get out of the low armchair, with its low armrests, fast enough to escape. What he was doing was invasive and intrusive and rude, but rather than yell for help, she let it happen, because after all they were in public, and she did know him, and she had loved him once, for a little while. As he was reminding her. He stopped shaking and began to glow. His embrace of her malformed body, his ear and hair gently touching her belly, reminded her of when they were partners. She squeezed her eyes shut. From all around, she felt an impossible happiness approaching. It filled her ears with silence, like being submersed in deep water. There was a rightness to his head in her lap.

She imagined presenting the baby to Bull. She saw wrongness. He would hold it in his immense hands, look down approvingly, and say, "This is my beloved son," pleased to have sired an heir he hadn't sired, while Aaron was already loving the baby so personally that it hurt them both. The baby's challenges all lay ahead—being born headfirst, getting enough oxygen—and when she imagined something going wrong, and the little boy damaged, she saw which man would be heartbroken, in love with his flawed son, never angry at her. Which man was already implicated in the baby's weaknesses. A crack appeared in the firmament.

Aaron said, "I'm trying to get my head around this, but I can't. I thought maybe if we put our heads together, the baby would tell me what to do, like a Vulcan mind meld."

"Get up," she said, tugging on his sleeve. He squatted upright again and slid back into his seat. "Listen. It's a boy. His name is Michael. I picked it."

"It's a great name. When's he due?"

"August second."

"Holy cow."

"None of this scares Bull. Are you sure you're old enough? You don't have to do this."

"I don't see it as my decision," he said. "I don't get to decide what's true and what's not."

"Yes, you do. You choose your family. That's why they have adoption and marriage. Adults have their family of choice."

"That's not how it feels to me," he said. "It doesn't feel like I'm choosing this. It's just an objective fact. It's like, okay, I spawned, what next? It's a decision the way being alive is a decision. You make the best of it, and sometimes you get lucky and it totally rules." He took her left hand in both hands and leaned down to kiss it.

"Let me put it this way," she said. "I personally am able to choose my family. I'm the one who's going to pick the dad, whether it's you, or Bull, or nobody."

"That's simply untrue," he said, straightening up. "The only reason you don't want my name on the birth certificate, so I have to pay child support, is because Bull's fucking loaded. But I could still sue for custody. Men's rights, man! Except I would never dream of doing something shitty to you like that, because I can't imagine by what rights I should be deciding things about your baby. What kind of an asshole would I be? I agree with you. It's your decision. So decide. Decide now."

He spoke like a man prepared to live or die by her verdict.

She thought of Bull and felt the shadow of death passing over—the fear of fear itself, of what she would feel when they broke up, what he might say.

She turned up her hands, looked from one to the other, and said, "I can't decide."

"I thought you already had," he said. His voice had turned gravelly and desperate. His face was blotchy. He was hugging himself.

An instinctive self-defense mechanism told her: Let go. Open your empty hands and let go. The power he had granted her was too much. She had too much power. She could sense it directly, because she was so close to creating a new person, as if she were God. She didn't want to be Aaron's God.

She struggled out of the low chair. He jumped up to help her, grasping her forearm. She said, "Okay, Aaron. It's like this. I'm in shock. I'm walking away. You stay here. Don't follow me. I need time. I'll call you."

"Okay," he said. "But can I get you a cab? Can I do anything to stop feeling so ashamed I might die?"

"You'll be fine," she said. "Be patient. I'll call you tonight."

Without giving him her hand, she picked up her plastic bag and walked away. From the escalator in the Metro, she texted Bull: "Why???" She maintained her composure, but the emojis were crying.

BULL CALLED HER TWO HOURS LATER, WHEN HIS SEMINAR WAS OVER AND SHE WAS AT home lying on the sofa under the bedroom window, looking out at a gum tree. He said, "Are you all right?"

"Yeah."

"So you met Ikumi Sakuragi and she talked about me."

"Wrong. I met her friend Aaron Fleischer, and he told me your open secret."

"Small world. So if I'm not the father, who is?"

"Aaron's ready to accept responsibility," she said.

"He's a fucking socialist who wants to take responsibility for the whole planet. Can he tie his own shoes? Did you check?"

She had this sudden unwelcome vision that maybe she'd seen him stumbling along the riverbank with one shoe untied. Simultaneously she became aware that Ikumi must have talked to Bull about Aaron. What for?

"It's my baby," Bull went on. "Or at least I'm adopting him. If biological-father-boy wants to make it an open adoption, let him try."

"You don't need me, if it's a baby you want," she said. "Have your own baby. You can afford a surrogate."

"I guess for you Millennials that's just one more kind of sex work, but FYI, I'd rather be raped by an animal than exploit a woman of color like she's a piece of meat. I love you, Flora, you fecund slut. I've got stuff to finish up here, but I'll be home in an hour."

They said goodbye and hung up.

Doubts about Aaron flooded her mind. A breakwater—the wall with the handwriting on it saying AARON'S THE DAD—fell over, and on the other side lay alternative facts. She'd known Bull for years. She trusted his judgment, if not all of his words and actions. Who was Aaron, anyway? They'd vacationed together for a few days the year before. He was unknowably young, practically larval. Yet Bull had come inside her only because he had gotten in the habit of coming inside somebody else, Aaron's friend Ikumi, who was allowed, because Bull didn't love her, to know that he couldn't father children.

She wanted to minimize badness; she wanted to minimize wrongness. But goodness and rightness were not the same thing. Goodness would have dictated Michael's adoption by happily married scholar-athletes who ran an organic farm. A child needs health, education, and welfare, as she knew from personal experience with the parental Fresh Air Fund that deported her to Cleveland Park. A child needs stability and a house in Georgetown.

Yet rights trump everything. You can't do the right thing and violate a right, except—maybe—if you're punishing a crime. She didn't feel guilty of any crime. As a mother, she had property rights to Michael, the only rights of their kind. Love can seem to lovers to confer ownership, but it only feels that way; no one has proprietary claims over another adult, even when that adult believes she has vacated every one of her rights, signed on all the dotted lines, become a slave.

She wasn't going to let a judge decide either. She didn't think the state had a right to draft soldiers, so surely she wouldn't let it designate fathers.

Which meant the onus was on her, but she couldn't decide. She couldn't even tease out the basic form of the story. Was Bull stealing Aaron's child, or was Aaron stealing Bull's? The investment was Bull's. The DNA was Aaron's. Bull's commitment and friendship, his pursuit of her—everything he did—blew his rival out of the water. Aaron had never cooked her so much as a hard-boiled egg. He had suggested an affair, written her off when it ended, and run into her by chance. But she wanted him. Maybe not to raise a child. It was almost as if his being the dad was an excuse for her to want something more. Something erotic, irresponsible, and probably stupid.

Another well of wrongness was what a last-minute decision would do to Bull. She couldn't give birth and say she was leaving. She would have to leave him first and move back to Cleveland Park, which there was no reason to do, beyond the accidental parentage of a child he longed for. He would be publicly humiliated. Everyone in town would know he'd suckered himself, volunteering to raise another man's child with a woman too young to be faithful.

Her urge to protect him bothered her. He was a grown-up. Turning risks into sure things was his profession. She didn't feel nearly as maternal toward her immature vagabond fling Aaron. It was paradoxical, wanting to shield the guy who was her rock. Almost as if she didn't want to live on a rock.

She lay on the couch, telling herself that none of it mattered, because she had someone to love and his name was Michael.

It wasn't any comfort. The baby didn't work as a symbol of her personal freedom.

Bull came home, kissed her as though nothing were wrong, and made dinner. She didn't reach out to Aaron after that, and he left her alone. Whenever she thought of him, she hated him, because he didn't call.

XXVIII.

On the last Wednesday in July, Washington was bathed in an acrid mist. The roses and marble facades stood sweating in air that stank of uncertainty. It was a smell that ought to be rising from burning trash, not falling from the sky as fawn-colored haze.

Flora's media were reporting—based on an item in *New Scientist*—that human error was to blame. A stable high-pressure zone of falling air over the mid-Atlantic states was bringing dust from the Great Plains, ash from western wildfires, Chinese foundry emissions, and little bits of Lake Chad. The particulates could have rained out over the ocean or the mountains, but they were trapped in the air by a shortage of hydroxyl radicals.

The shortage was traceable to airplanes. That was the theory. Sun hitting ozone created hydroxyls, whose electric charge allowed water vapor to condense around particles of dirt and fall as rain. Condensation trails were using them up. All the seeded cirrus at cruising altitude had encased North America in a bone-dry dome of crystalline latticework, and the net effect was uncertain.

Possibly the clouds cast cooling shade, and the smog bred new hydroxyls. Possibly it might never rain again in North America. It depended on which website you read.

She stepped out their front door in Georgetown to look down the street. She held her breath. The sky was glowing and the street faded on both ends to a hot yellow blur. The air wasn't gritty with sand or thick with powder. It was something else, which seemed to be descending in slow waves. The birds and bugs were silent, as under low pressure before a storm. But the pressure was high. It should have been a bright, clear day.

Survivalists online were making claims of radioactivity. Some of her Green Party friends were quoting white supremacist preppers. Reposted posts quoted unnamed sources and headlines from years before. Who got there first, and where did they get the idea of fallout? Was it just the way the air looked, soft and glittery as a supersaturated metal?

She reentered the stuffy house. The internet swung between alarm and complacency, waiting for the collective momentum to slosh to one side. It knew no more than she did. She refreshed it over and over.

Bull said the reports were bunkum. His sources at NOAA and the EPA—forbidden to talk to the press—said that the origin of the haze lay closer. The woods of the Southeast were overexploited. The fast-growing phase of pines was early youth, so that's when forestry managers would cut them down, right when their carbon sequestration rate started to slow. The soil where they stood was degraded as a cornfield, stripped of humus and moisture. It took only one stray charcoal briquette to turn young pines into a smoldering mess not worth putting out. With temperatures too low for efficient combustion, the fires were churning all sorts of things into the air. But winter would bring rain, and spring would bring new growth. The pendulum was always swinging, mowing down the world like a scythe.

When she thought of the young pines burning, she thought of herself.

IN NEW YORK THE AIR WAS TRANSPARENT. THE CITY WAS A HEAT ISLAND WITH ITS own powerful updraft. Ocean air dense with moisture streamed through its tower intakes and poured toward the sky. Its sunless canyons were damp and oppressive. Inside cooled spaces, the walls sweated. Roaches gathered at puddles in rotting wood and wallpaper like sparrows at a birdbath. It was hideous. It was nothing that hadn't been going on for centuries.

Pam arrived at Washington Union Station on the Acela around one, to visit Flora one last time before she became encumbered with Baby Michael. The air was heavy with golden dust even on the platform where she disembarked. She kept trying to make eye contact with strangers, wanting to talk about it. But most had big sunglasses on, and those who didn't kept their eyes low. Some had dust masks. There were fewer cars on the street than usual. People were keeping them garaged, afraid the air would damage the finish.

She was finally able to talk about the air with her parents. "Some air you got there!" she said.

"It's the seventies all over again," Edgar said.

"Maybe it's the revenge of poor soil management, like Flora says. The new dust bowl."

Ginger said, "I bet the sunsets are glorious. We should drive out to the Blue Ridge." She added that she was kidding, because she wouldn't go more than three miles away from Flora. Driving in the miasma felt dangerous even in town. She didn't want to know what things were like out on the Beltway.

Pam's phone rang. It was Flora.

"Hey, Mom," she said. "I'm just calling to say I'm going to be a couple hours late."

"You not feeling well?"

"I'm okay."

"Are you at home?"

"I'm in a taxi, headed up to the cathedral."

"Why's that?"

"Have you seen the news? They're saying Trump violated the nuclear test ban and the yellow stuff in the air is radioactive sulfur. Like, he tested a suitcase nuke in a coal mine in Tennessee."

"You're outside in radioactive fallout?"

"Mom, they're nuts. Since when do physicists go into journalism? Everything is bullshit. That's the problem. I was just calling to say I'd be over later, because I need time to think."

Ginger by this point had navigated to the website of the *Washington Post* on her laptop. She called out, "Nothing about anything radioactive in the *Post*!"

Flora said to look at the *Guardian,* a center-left London daily that was popular and influential around the world because it could be read online without a subscription. Ginger found the headline. When she clicked it to read the story, there was a 404 error: PAGE NOT FOUND. When she returned to the main page, the headline was gone.

"The page is acting strange," Pam told Flora. "There's no story. But tell the driver to bring you over here instead."

"I need to be by myself."

"Then we'll come over to the cathedral and give you a ride back here."

"That sounds fine. I'll see you in a couple hours." She signed off.

Scrolling through the *New York Times,* Pam said, "The girl has lost her mind from the stress."

Edgar had returned to reading a biography of Eisenhower in his den. Ginger approached him to say that they were going to the cathedral to check on Flora. She asked him to keep an eye on the news, because there were rumors the air might be radioactive. He promised to call right away if he heard anything.

The women gulped down their coffees and got in Edgar's new

hybrid Camry to drive west. It wasn't far from the house to Flora's old school. If Connecticut Avenue had been filling up with drivers fleeing the city, if the Cleveland Park business district had been boarding up, if an angry mob had been forming to march on the capitol, they wouldn't have known it, because they took a back way. Steering up Porter Street in the eerily silent car, the air conditioner cycling internally, Ginger said, "This is not what I wanted. Flora in a spiritual crisis. She should be welcoming this baby with us and Bull, not hiding out alone in a church."

"I can relate," Pam said. "This isn't the world she was planning to bring it into."

"What was she expecting, Tahiti? She was born on the Lower East Side!"

Ginger's unaccustomed sarcasm surprised Pam. "She has a right to Tahiti," she said. "I always knew I could escape civilization, if worse came to worst. Move to Key West and spearfish pompano or whatever and sleep on the beach. Where can she go? There's garbage and tourists on every beach in the world, and the beaches are going to be gone soon."

"Is it such a bad thing, knowing we're all in it together?" Ginger said. "It was always true."

"I was happier not knowing."

"Pam, these facts were uppermost in Flora's mind at an age when you were still worshipping that punk rock boy. She's a smart girl. For her, it's always been one world. And maybe, whatever this stuff in the air is, it's time we were confronted with it, instead of just reading about it. Now we'll take action."

"Not possible," Pam said. "It's just going to shorten our lives."

"Why are you such a pessimist?"

"Working with machines will heighten your tragic sense of life. They don't heal themselves. There's friction, and they break, and that's it. But at least they were made by intelligent design, unlike this random fucking planet. The Earth is doomed."

"You sound like your father. This planet isn't good enough for him either. He's getting interested in Mars."

They parked in a faculty spot, since it was midsummer, and walked up the brick path to the narthex's dusty glass doors. The woman selling ten-dollar tickets to offset the cost of earthquake damage knew Ginger, so she waved them in. The cathedral was cool and fresh inside. The windows tinted the light as blue as daylight on a normal day.

Pam headed for the stairs to the crypt, because it had been her favorite place when she was young, but Ginger stopped her and said, "No, not down there. She goes to where they had Thursday chapel."

They found her toward the rear of the school's dedicated space, facing its banner and patron saint, slouched on a straight-backed chair dedicated to Edgar Allan Poe, with her sock feet on a needlepoint raven. She turned to them when she heard their voices.

"Baby, you look sick," Ginger said. "We need to get you to a doctor."

"Can I talk to you?" she said. "Please?"

"Come on," Pam said. "It's doctor time."

She didn't budge. She said, "Sit down and listen to me. I have to tell you something impossible."

Pam and Ginger sat down on Jefferson Davis and William Jennings Bryan, respectively. Ginger said, "We love you, sweet pea. Tell us anything you want, no matter how bad you think it sounds."

"I don't want to raise this baby with Bull."

They were silent for a moment, and Ginger responded, "He seems to me like he'll make a good father. It doesn't have to be forever."

"Isn't it more like once a father, always a father? Isn't it forever?"

"Flora, you might be thinking you want to move back in with me and Ed. But we've raised two generations. I don't know that we want to raise a third."

"It's not that, Grandma. He's not the dad."

"He's not the dad," Pam echoed.

"There's an actual dad," Flora said. "I ran into him last month. His name is Aaron Fleischer. We had this fling when I was in Pennsylvania, right before the election. He was volunteering for Clinton. We're the same age. He has a job downtown now, at this new custodians' union."

"How do you know the baby is his?" Pam asked. "Did you get amniocentesis?"

"Bull made me get it."

"And he was okay with it? I'd say in a case like this to let sperm donors be sperm donors. You wouldn't be the first."

"It's Aaron's child. It's related to Aaron and his family. How does that not matter?"

"Well, I don't want to sound indecent or suggestive or anything, but do you recall his precise level of involvement in creating this baby?"

"It was more than Bull's!"

"Are you not over him? It's immaterial who the biological father is. Family is not genes."

"It's not that. The problem is not genes. It's more like . . . It's hard to explain."

"Give it a shot. For us."

Flora sat with downcast eyes, looking at her belly.

Ginger said to Pam, "All your criticism is making her shy."

"I'm sorry, Flo," Pam said. "Come on, tell us what you're feeling."

Flora said, "Well, it's like this. The baby's in love with Aaron. I don't know what I want, but Michael knows what he wants. That's totally how it felt to me, when they met each other. They bonded. Aaron's the dad, and it's a fact, and I'm stuck with it."

"You've been under a lot of stress," Ginger said.

"Bull is a complicated guy," Pam said. "Pinning it on something mechanical like genetics is simpler."

"That's exactly it!" Flora said. "I don't want to complicate my life. I don't want to move up in the world, and throw parties in evening wear, and know politicians, and raise my son in Georgetown. I want him to have a childhood like ours. Otherwise it's not even like having a child. And Aaron's like us. He's so incredibly relaxing. He reminds me of Joe."

"Huh?" Pam said.

"He's so uncritical of me, and so honest and open, no matter what."

"Joe Harris died when you were nine. He was a lot more like Bull than you think. He was a trust-fund meat cleaver with a mega-career."

"He was the sweetest ever," Flora insisted. "He wrote songs because it was his reason for being. He was creative and intense all the time for no reason, like one of those ecosystems in the tropics that subsists for millions of years for no reason. And that's what Aaron's like. He just exists. So it makes sense that Aaron made our baby, because he loves being alive."

"For no reason," Ginger said. She smiled approvingly to hide what she was thinking, which was that things were going straight to hell in a way she'd never thought to expect.

Pam shook her head and frowned. "Everybody loves being alive," she said. "Being a rock star didn't make Joe special or not a bum. He didn't have an altruistic bone in his body. We hired him to babysit you, and he wrote some hit songs. They're like stupid apps where the hardware is your brain. He didn't give a shit about the earth. He probably didn't know it was round."

"I know you still hate him for killing himself," Flora said. She had stopped crying. Her tone was defiant.

Pam rolled her eyes and said, "Where'd you read that? Fucker didn't kill himself."

"Fucker what?!" She sat upright and looked straight at her mother.

Ginger too stiffened with alarm. The younger women seemed to her like two flamenco dancers, circling and staring each other down, now that they were finally fighting about a guy.

"'Joe Harris killed himself because he loved life so much,'" Pam said. "Listen to yourself. What a fucking joke."

"He was heartbroken!"

"You knew Joe. Was he ever even sad?"

Pam steeled herself to relate what she knew of the four days during which he lay unassisted and decomposing. She looked at her mother, who was shaking her head, and stopped herself. The truth was toxic. It still hurt Daniel more than he could say. Why hand it down to Flora? Why not bury it deep and break the chain?

She said, "He overdosed by accident. Indirectly it was Gwen who killed him, by introducing him to heroin. She had a vested interest in saying it was suicide, and she's been helped by the wisdom of crowds."

"And you stood by and let it happen," Flora replied. "She got away with it, she still profits from it, and you did nothing."

Pam lowered her eyes, outflanked, and said, "There's not a whole lot you can do when people choose the wrong life partner." She didn't believe it anymore. Her mind recalled with pain how Daniel had laughed at her pimping of Eloise. He was wrong, goddamn it. She should have locked those two in a room. Eloise would have lit up with radiant joy when Joe touched her, won his heart, and never left his side. Like a puppy that lives to be eighty-four. Like Daniel.

"What are you saying?" Flora said.

"I don't know." She tacked back. "I mean, how well do you know this Aaron guy? Is he exclusively hetero? Does he do drugs?"

Her daughter's face turned angry.

"I don't know," Pam added, "but you might want to take romantic love out of the equation and think with your brain for a minute. Think who's a clean, safe person you can trust."

"That's what I came here to do. Bull lied to me. I love Aaron, but I don't know him very well. That's why I was trying to spend some time alone in neutral territory and think."

Ginger said to Pam, "You know, we could leave her alone and let her think."

"No," Pam said with finality. "She's the one who called us. She wants help." She resumed her questioning of Flora. "So you've talked to Aaron about this?"

"I told him I'd call him after I saw him that one time, but I didn't."

"So your baby's in love with a guy you've blown off twice. Radio silence since November, one chance meeting, and now you're going to ditch Bull for him."

"I've never met Aaron," Ginger interrupted, "and I don't know if he loves you or what that word even means to him. But I agree that you should not be concentrating on feelings in such an important decision, especially when your feelings are not based on very much."

"Fuck you, Grandma," Flora said.

"Human beings are changeable," Ginger continued, with emphasis. "God is love, but he's the only one, believe me. Love is an ideal you don't attain in this life. That's why they build churches like this one to last forever, while the people inside them come and go."

"You're completely wrong," Flora said. "Jesus and Mary and the saints didn't know what love is? I don't think so!"

"That was another little girl confused about being pregnant," Pam said. "But for your information, it wasn't he who is mighty. It was some random guy named Aaron."

"Aaron's not random!"

"I'm curious as to why you didn't get an abortion."

"Because I thought it was Bull's!"

There followed a moment of silent reflection. Ginger said, "That sounds to me as if you really do love Bull. I'm so mixed up—"

"My boyfriend, Bull," Flora interrupted her, "did not see fit to share the results of the amniocentesis with me. I thought this was his baby, until maybe a month ago, when he finally told me he's infertile." She paused. "No," she corrected herself. "What happened was this girl he was boning on the side told Aaron. When I asked Bull, he confirmed it." Her look turned hard. "Bull is sterile. He kept it a secret, and you know why? Because I want kids. He's in love with me and wants us to stay together, and that's why he could never tell me his secret."

Ginger said, "Wait. You talked to Bull about Aaron? You talked about his affair with this other woman?"

"That's not what matters!"

Ginger put her hand on Flora's shoulder and said, "It might be a little late for you to be deciding what you want. It might be out of your hands." She moved in for a hug. Frowning, Flora hugged her, with no idea what she was getting at.

Pam noticed and tugged on Ginger's sleeve. "Come on," she said. "Give the girl some space. Let's go light candles for world peace."

Ginger wiped her eyes. The two of them picked up their bags and walked forward together.

FLORA SAT BACK, GLAD THEY WERE GONE. THEY TRULY HAD BEEN MAKING IT IMPOSSIBLE for her to think.

She looked up, around, and forward at the sanctuary of the

chapel. Outside nature was sticky and dusty and humming like a furnace, but the cathedral's interior was cool and smooth. She had come for spiritual renewal to a haunted stone quarry. A man-made box canyon lined with martyrs, great men and women humbled. For solace, she had wanted to be dwarfed by tall rocks and see images of fortitude in the face of pain.

It seemed to her an admission—an assertion even—that meaning arose in the spirit and grew in the mind. It couldn't possibly inhere in the body, definitely not in the antics of the dumb body. Her body was cryptic as a plant, keeping its own counsel. Life itself, the biological thing, lacked meaning. It permitted—sometimes—the survival of the fittest. The fittest: that was Bull, pursuing tactical advantage by any means necessary. At this very moment he might be plotting something devious to secure health insurance for millions and save forests from logging. Aaron was not cryptic that way. It was hard to imagine him having a secret. He was all Aaron, all the way down. Made of meaning. An open book with one page. A lamb to the slaughter.

But they were both products of the same four billion years of evolution, so both modes of life must be equally viable. Maybe the Aarons had been coming over from their parallel universe to donate sperm for the Bulls all along.

She knew that clinical experiments said the opposite. They said that women prefer tenderness for every day and macho dudes when they're ovulating. She wondered if she wasn't confused about who was which. Maybe Bull was the submissive one, always working from within the establishment, tweaking a hegemonic system in his favor, while Aaron the nomad staked his arrogant claim from outside the walls.

She imagined her son modeling himself on one and then on the other. Specifically, she daydreamed two children, genetically distinct, one able to manipulate her—always with irreproachable aims—and the other not. She imagined the guileless child growing up cowed and confused in the shadow of Bull. She saw wrong-ness.

Aaron wasn't a rock like Bull. It was the way she felt about him that was a rock, intransigent, immovable, presaging the way she would feel about Michael.

She felt worn and chilly. Her mother and grandmother returned from the front of the chapel. She said, "Let's go home." She glanced at her phone. She had fifteen new messages. Twitter and Facebook were filling up with claims of radioactive smog.

XXIX.

As they exited the cathedral, she asked Ginger whether Edgar owned a Geiger counter. Ginger said she had no idea, but she was sure everything would be fine.

In the car, Flora's phone rang. It was Aaron, of all people.

"Aaron!" she said.

"I know I wasn't supposed to call you ever again. I'm really sorry. But there's some kind of radioactive plume all over the news. You need to get out of town."

She said, "I know. I saw. We're in the car."

"Where are you going?"

"Cleveland Park."

"You need to go to, like, Canada."

"Me and Mom and Grandma are on our way home from the cathedral. Do you want to come with us to New York? Mom says the air is fine up there."

Aaron said, "With Bull?"

"No."

"You didn't have the baby yet, right?"

"No."

"I was just calling to tell you about the radioactive plume."

"Don't do this to me," she said.

"Do what? I don't do stuff. I'm dead inside."

"Then come with us to New York!"

He paused and said, "Where are you now?"

"Going home. We were at the National Cathedral."

"Why?"

"I needed to think about what I want to do with my life."

"Right now, you're kind of locked into this baby thing."

"I want to be with you."

"Hmm," Aaron said. "I'm at work, but I'll lie and tell them I have a meeting offsite and come and see you. Tell me the address."

THE WOMEN ARRIVED BACK AT PORTER STREET AND STARTED PACKING TO GO NORTH. Flora's phone rang again. It was Bull, calling to remind her that the airborne event was nontoxic emissions from controlled blazes and no cause for alarm.

"I don't care if it's pine smoke," she said to him. "No smoke is healthy. Any wildfire fills the air with noncombustible crap, and green vegetation emits dioxins when you burn it, and people dump toxic waste in the woods. We're packing our stuff to head up to New York."

"Flora," he said. "There's nothing happening. It's a forest fire and a bunch of rumors. They probably launched the atom bomb story to get the liberals out of Washington once and for all."

"Jokes about fallout are not funny to me."

"Did you look at Fox News?"

"Why would they tell the truth?"

"Because there's nothing a Republican cares more about than protecting his own family, at least on paper. Look at Fox and tell me what you see."

Flora said to Ginger, "Could you turn on Fox News?"

Fox was running an exposé about the thickness of spaghetti. They watched in disbelief as charismatic, excitable pundits weighed in on noodle diameter, wondering whatever happened to slenderizing angel hair. There was nothing about the miasma.

"It's not there," she said to Bull. "Who am I supposed to trust?"

"Me," he said.

"I don't know," she said. "I'd like to. It would be so much easier that way."

"Seriously consider it," Bull said. "Are you at your grandparents' house?"

"Yeah."

"Tell them I said hi." He signed off and left her standing there, at the foot of the carpeted stairs, staring out the window at the luminous haze while her mother and grandmother stared at the TV.

WHEN AARON RANG THE DOORBELL, SHE LET HIM IN. SHE GREETED HIM WITH THE WORDS "I'm paralyzed."

"What do you mean?"

"I don't know what to do. I don't know what I want from anybody. I think I might need to go into an institution."

"What's happening?"

"Spaghetti is getting thicker. We eat more without knowing it."

"Flora," he said. He hugged her, looking over her shoulder at Pam and Ginger, and asked, "Is she really paralyzed? Does preeclampsia cause strokes?"

"She's talking about the main story on Fox News at this hour," Ginger said, pointing at it. A discussion of Lana Del Rey's feud with Lady Gaga had started, with the volume off, but the information about spaghetti was still running across the bottom of the screen. "We're not sure anymore whether we need to evacuate, even as a precaution."

"Disinterested analysis," Pam said. "Fox would cover up an

industry error, but not one made by the government. Therefore, though it might be dioxins, it wasn't a bomb."

"Let me rephrase," Aaron said. "Is this no big deal, or is the air giving us all cancer as we speak?"

"My husband promised to keep refreshing the Centers for Disease Control homepage until the truth comes out," Ginger said. "He's chained to the computer."

Flora sat down hard on the couch and declared, "What I want is a man who always knows what's really going on!"

"No problem," Aaron said. "You and Bull can still be friends. Have you talked to him?"

"He says it's forest fires."

"Then probably, knowing him—I mean, not knowing him, but from what I know about him—I would guess that it's probably forest fires?"

The tension faded from the room, and Pam turned off the TV.

"Let me go get my husband, so I can introduce you," Ginger said.

Edgar was not at the computer in his den. She checked the garage, peeking through the glass-paneled door from the kitchen. Finally she stood at the head of the basement stairs and called his name. He answered, "Just a minute!"

He came upstairs, introduced himself, and said he'd been digging through his workbench to see if he had any transistors or capacitors or circuit boards, which he didn't. He'd had the idea of making a Geiger counter from scratch and had looked for information online. He found instructions on how to make one from a PVC tube and Styrofoam beads, and another using tinfoil you load with static electricity by pulling cellophane tape off a roll. The functional design from MIT was full of parts he didn't own and couldn't easily buy, since the last RadioShack had closed years before.

He smiled throughout this jokey speech, as though detecting

ionizing radiation would have made an amusing break from model railroading. In conclusion, he offered Aaron a beer.

"No, thank you, sir," Aaron said.

"You sure?"

"If I have a beer, I'll be wanting weed."

Edgar's eyes went wide, Jack Benny style, and Ginger said to him, "Honey, I'm sure Daniel wasn't perfect at his age either." To Aaron she said, "We have quite a powerful exhaust hood in our kitchen, if you want to smoke. I can't in good conscience send you outside on a day like this."

Pam said, "Daniel was straight-edge. He had to work nights as a proofreader."

"I don't need anything but some water," Aaron said.

"I don't recall your being pure as the driven snow," Edgar said to Pam.

"But she never smoked pot," Ginger said.

"Too conspicuous," Pam said.

"Union organizing is a space where intoxicants are of value," Aaron said. "If I talked to workers without a beer in my hand, they'd think I was coming on to them."

"Solidarity forever," Edgar said.

Over the giggling, Aaron said, "My whole life is solidarity. It's an economic thing. I work volunteering and for a union. I have four roommates."

"What's your family like?" Ginger asked.

"Oh, they don't approve."

"What do they do?"

"My dad's an auto mechanic at the Sears in White Oak, and my mom's a beautician. My brothers and sisters are still in school. They live in Takoma."

Everyone looked surprised, even Flora. That was only a few miles away.

"Do you get along with them?" Ginger asked cautiously.

"My siblings are awesome. The rest of them can't deal with my politics. We have this annual Fourth of July Tournament of Jews, where we go to Peirce Mill and scream at each other about Israel and Palestine. I have seven aunts and uncles and, like, thirty cousins, and we're pretty evenly divided."

Pam said, "Sounds like ideal conditions for touch football."

He said, "You'd know who won by the bodies that washed up in the Potomac the next morning."

FROM HER CORNER OF THE SOFA, FLORA WATCHED AARON ENDURE THEIR DERISION AND parry their nosiness, never missing a beat, insouciantly resigned to being himself. Born to be a dad. Already living a surrendered life, like a person with responsibilities. Bull, despite his age, had nothing in common with any dad she'd ever seen. When had he ever surrendered?

The question of who was stealing whose baby recurred to her, reformulated. Men really could be pregnant—in a sense—if they expected to have children, as she always had. Bull hadn't been a father until she made him one. There was no child inside him waiting to get out. He sought fellowship with like-minded adults. In their relationship, the parental role was hers to have and to keep.

But what was it, anyway, the parental role? Was it just preemptive subjection to the unknown? Was it supposed to involve such solitude? Weren't caregivers supposed to lean on breadwinners? It seemed to her that she was doing the opposite, taking every burden on herself, like Mary telling the angel she was the handmaid of the Lord, except that she was the handmaid of the world. She was Atlas.

It occurred to her that if she hadn't been so pregnant, she could have seduced Aaron and found certainty that way. Undeniably she liked him better than Bull. Her body had missed him. But her body was beyond her command. The baby had deformed it into strange new shapes, rendering sex unthinkable, and it might stay that way for months.

With every second it continued, her pregnancy converted her former sexual power into greater knowledge. It was not a good feeling. She turned toward the sofa, crying silently. She had no idea what was the right thing to do.

"I'VE NEVER ONCE BEEN TO THE NATIONAL CATHEDRAL," AARON SAID, "EVEN THOUGH it's right down the street."

"It's nice," Pam said. "Flora goes there to hang out with the Virgin Mary."

"She's the bodhisattva Guan Yin," he said. "Jesus spent most of his life in Kashmir, at least according to the Ahmadi Muslims. It's one of those things the pope doesn't want you to know about."

"Anglicans don't do the pope," Pam said. She was fond of Aaron already. He seemed to her a fearless rationalist—without a winning strategy, but unafraid to lose.

Ginger said, "I thought she was the goddess Astarte."

"That's the Shekhinah," Aaron said.

She asked whether he wanted some coffee. They all heard a whimper and glanced at Flora. She was pounding a tear-stained sofa cushion with her fist, as though she thought no one could see her.

Pam whispered to him, "Can you take her upstairs?"

"Sure, no problem," he said.

Ginger said, "Let us know if she seems dizzy. Flora, honey, why don't you go ahead and show Aaron your room."

HE WALKED BEHIND HER UP THE STAIRS, HOLDING HIS HANDS UP TO CATCH HER IF SHE swayed. The staircase wasn't quite wide enough for a pregnant woman and a grown man.

She didn't lead him to her own room but to her mother's.

Her spacious pink-and-white bower with the canopy bed seemed obscene to her, like a honeymoon suite. She lay down on Pam's narrow mattress. Ian MacKaye gazed down on her from all directions, unblinking as a duck. Aaron pried off her shoes, and she curled into a ball.

"What am I doing?" she begged him.

"First, you need to tell me who built this temple of hardcore."

"My mom, when she was a kid. It was her first big art project."

"She's a genius," he said.

Flora sniffled, and he offered her a tissue. He sat by her and petted her head. He sang the song "Happiness Runs."

She had never heard it before. It was as calming as a sedative, as though Donovan's words could hack the brain stem. The baby retracted its foot from her bladder and nestled into her body gently, resting for the first time that day.

She could feel that it was her physical equal. Soon it would awaken to a wrestling match that would go on for as long as the sun shone, but while it slept, she surrendered herself to helplessness. Around the edges of her closed eyes, everything was golden. The sun itself was hidden behind endless megatons of calm, quiet dust.

She said, "If I die having this baby, I want you to be there."

"What is this about?" he protested. "You're healthy as a horse! Everything's going to be fine!"

"I learned to be strong around Bull. He forces me to be strong. With you and everybody else here, I'm falling apart. Maybe being loved makes me a wreck, and I don't want it."

"Did you ever hear the Hasidic story about the love like fire and the love like water?"

"No."

"It's about how there are two kinds of love, the hot love that burns you down and the cool love that bears you up."

"Then Bull is the love like water. Sink or swim. I need to be out there swimming, not lying around with you in my grandparents' house."

Not evincing signs of hurt, he said, "Hey, it's not supposed to be two different guys! This is Jewish tradition we're talking about here! When you're ritually permitted to touch your wife, you love her like fire. The other two weeks a month, when she's not fertile, you support her, so she's buoyed up, floating in love." He paused from head petting and held up both hands, their edges touching, like a man cradling a preemie. "I admit, I only thought of it because I wish we could have sex. You're so beautiful and great. I wasn't trying to help you choose between me and Bull."

"I have to choose," she said. "Somebody's got to be the dad."

"And where is he now?"

Hearing the speculative hope in his voice, she said truthfully, "At work."

"And where is he going to be when the baby's born?"

"He's taking a year off."

Aaron retracted and folded his hands and said, "I really fucking hate this guy. I couldn't afford to take a year off work. They might fire me for being here right now!"

"You know something, Mr. Love Like Fire?" she said, propping herself up on her elbow. "You scare me. I'm having your baby, and I'm so scared, but you're not scared. Why aren't you scared of the time and the money it's going to cost you? I'm afraid it's because you're from a brood-parasitic race of stoner sperm donors, and being cute and adorable is your reproductive strategy."

He shook his head and said, "Who needs a reproductive strategy in a culture with arranged marriages? It's you guys, the western European romantics"—he pointed at her in mock accusation—"who are always going around saying, 'Was it destiny, or all that unprotected sex I told Aaron was going to be "not a problem"? It was destiny!'"

"I'm sorry," she said. "I mean, not sorry-sorry. I know Michael is my doing, believe me. I've been through all of this in my head. I got what I wanted. It just doesn't seem quite fair that you're going to have him too, the same as me, and not pay the price."

"I'm trying to pay the price! But I can't give you anything but—what, I don't know—time? And that's where your boyfriend has a big head start, not to mention money."

She said, "Pay the price in love. Just love me. The love like water, okay? Because I'm a wreck."

"That's what I'm trying to do! Can't you tell?"

"Promise me your future. Give me all your time and money, more than Bull will ever have, because he's so much older. Promise it to me now. A life equity loan, secured with your life."

Instead of remarking that she'd gone insane, he said, "My life would be worth a lot more, as collateral, if I were still in school and nobody knew yet that I'm a fuckup. I'm actually good at school. I had professors who said I had potential. You know, what we should do is we should both go back to school. We could be grad students with a baby. That could work."

"And who's paying?" She could reasonably expect a tuition waiver and stipend from any Ph.D. program in geochemistry that accepted her, but she wasn't so sure about him. "Remember, I own your future! You can't mortgage it twice!"

"I don't need a fellowship to do a master's in social work at Hunter. CUNY's cheap."

"Social work?" She frowned. "You think social service agencies are going to be hiring?"

"You're an irrepressible font of nay-saying pessimism," he said. "It's weird, coming from somebody who's about to have a baby."

"Don't make fun of me for being scared."

"Stop thinking you have to be strong to have a baby. It's okay. Let the baby win. I'm here."

He nudged her gently until she lay down again on her side. He lay beside her. There was no sound but shallow breathing, beating hearts, and a few distant sirens. Downstairs, Ginger lowered the blinds and sat down to nap in an easy chair. Edgar sorted through hardware he'd found. Pam read the *Post*.

XXX.

Bull lay beside Ikumi in his bed in Georgetown. His eyes were open in a dream. The late-afternoon sky turned blinding white. Then it was violet, indigo, blue, and green. The room was sliding down the spectrum of visible light like a live-in prism. He reached for his phone. The electromagnetic pulse had wiped it clean. The room turned yellow, orange, and red. The blast wave rattled the loose sash of the open window. He closed it. The wind picked up, gusted like a hurricane, and subsided.

A siren outside the window woke the two of them from their nap. She said, "Wow. I bet I slept for an hour."

Bull said, "You missed it."

"What?"

"The end of the world."

"Shut up and make me a double espresso."

He went downstairs to warm up the machine, feeling oddly happy. He had surrendered his son, but the rainbow was unfurling in his heart. The glorious banner God planted on the lost hilltop that is Earth. He would live and die trying to turn this thing around.

He yelled up to Ikumi, "You've got ten minutes! I have to get back to the office!"

"That's okay!" she yelled back. "So do I!"

THE CAMRY RACED UP THE EXPRESS HOV LANE OF THE JERSEY TURNPIKE AND RUMBLED through an ineptly patched overpass. When it paused for the Holland Tunnel entrance, right around nine o'clock, Aaron whispered, "Wider than the whole wide world," and Flora sat upright. She had been sleeping with her head on his lap while Ginger and Pam, up front, listened to an audiobook of Karl Ove Knausgård's *My Struggle*, volume five.

"Are we going to Chrystie Street?" she asked, surprised to be at the southernmost river crossing.

"We were thinking if you stayed there together, you could get to know each other a little before Michael shows up," Ginger said.

"That's a good idea," Flora said. "That's exactly what I wanted." She put her hands out to her mother and grandmother, and they squeezed.

When they pulled up in front of Video Hit, Daniel came out to meet them. "This is where I lived until I was nine," she said to Aaron.

"I tried to make it comfortable for you guys," Daniel said. "There's fresh linens and milk and cereal, and the AC is cranked. I'm going to catch a ride uptown with these ladies."

"Nice to meet you," Aaron said, putting out his hand to Daniel.

"Same here," Daniel said.

"Thanks for putting us up."

"You're welcome, for as long as you want to stay. Years, if you want. It's a little odd, meeting the father of Flora's child twice, but I enjoy it more every time. I can't wait to meet the next one."

"I personally wouldn't mind if the others keep their distance."

"You okay with that, Flora?"

"I just texted Bull that we made it here in one piece," she said, putting her phone back in her bag.

"Apparently we're a harmonious extended family," Aaron said.

"Good," Daniel said. "If there's one thing I can't stand, it's open conflict. You'll find we're civilized people. We hash out our conflicts according to formalized rules, over a course of decades, or never. It's like Thorstein Veblen said. The old masculine virtues are dead."

"Then I guess carrying in the luggage by myself would be excessively virile."

Pam said, "The luggage has wheels. Your task is to carry the bride over the threshold!"

She intended it as a slightly cruel joke, because Aaron was barely taller than Flora, who was currently much larger.

He regarded Flora with skepticism. But he leaned forward and bent his knees. She slung her arm around his neck. He picked her up and headed for the door of the shop. When he paused, wondering if he was going in the right direction, Daniel said, "Don't take unnecessary risks here. You're going to trip over the dog." He put her back down, and she waddled to Margie for a hug. With Aaron behind her for safety, she hauled herself up the stairs by the banister, like a mountain climber.

She felt happy to be home, in the place of her babyhood. Daniel followed them up, carrying her suitcase and Margie's gifts of bottled water and cookies. After setting it all down, he excused himself to drive home with Ginger and Pam.

FLORA TOLD AARON HOW TO PADLOCK THE DOOR FOR THE NIGHT. SHE GAVE HIM A TOUR by pointing, since the loft was one room: the water closet, the shower stall, the portable stove-sink combo, the barstools and deck chairs, the steamer trunk paved with magazines, her father's spare keyboards, her mother's guitars, their amps, racks of effects, the four-track, Daniel's books from college, a grainy poster of Joe looking fetching in black leather under a streetlamp with a wreath of tea roses on his head, the records, the liquor cabinet, the stereo. Aaron manned the kitchenette to make tea.

When they had eaten cookies and drunk tea, they lay down on the bed to look at each other, and he said, "I don't think I can do this."

"What?" She was frightened. "What exactly can't you do?"

"Take so much generosity from your family."

"What generosity? They're millionaires letting us borrow an illegal pit with, like, no furniture. This is not some huge debt to pay down."

"I can't afford to lose my new job. It's a great job. I need to get home."

"But I'm having your baby any minute!"

"I'm going to get up now and get a bus home, so I can go to work tomorrow. I'll come back on the weekend."

"Aaron," she said. "Forget work. Stay. We're in New York. We can stay here."

"No," he said. "I absolutely need to be employed to afford a kid, and I'm not the only one. I believe in organized labor. You should too. Nobody's going to care about the environment if they're barely surviving."

"Nobody ever cares about the environment, Aaron." There was no irony in her. "People are selfish. They want us altruistic people to be there for them when they need us, at our own expense. We should stick together and help each other when we need help."

He got to his feet, shook himself, and said, "I need to leave before my feelings get the upper hand. It's a long ride. I need to be back at work tomorrow."

She sat up straight and reached for him. "Why are you doing this?" she said. "If you walk away now, what do I do?"

"I'm not walking away. I'm going home so I don't lose my job. I'll be back on Friday. I can't afford to blow off work for a year, like some people."

"Hey, I know your job is great, but it's only a job! It's only money. This is a baby. A human being."

"It's my job, and—like you never, ever stop saying—it's your baby. Our responsibilities aren't the same here."

"You're confused, Aaron. Waffling about who's the dad is not the same as saying Michael's all mine."

"Is it not the same?" He put on his shoes. "I mean, really."

"Don't go! What are you doing? I thought you would be there for me!"

"I'll totally be there for you," he said. "On Friday."

"If you leave now," she said, trying to sound strong and failing, "don't come back!"

He reached out to pet her head. She swatted him away and burrowed facedown into the mattress.

He said, "I love you. I'll be back very soon. I'll call you tomorrow morning. I'll be here late Friday night. I have to work, for all of us. I'll be back. I love you."

She didn't answer. At the bottom of the stairs he opened the padlock, hung the key on the nail, and let himself out.

A LITTLE AFTER ELEVEN, DANIEL SAUNTERED INTO THE STORE AND TRIED THE DOOR TO the apartment. It was open. He came upstairs, clomping loudly so he wouldn't interrupt anything private. Not seeing Aaron, he naturally assumed he was in the bathroom and called out, "Hey, you guys! I'm back because I screwed up!" He saw Flora's face. "Are you upset? You look upset."

She sat up to receive him, stiff and sniffling, and said, "Aaron's gone."

"What?!"

"He left to catch a bus. He said he has to work tomorrow."

"You are fucking kidding me. Why didn't you call us? Couldn't he call in sick? You'd think the miasma would qualify as a public health emergency!"

"People don't call in sick. They have personal days. Maybe he doesn't have any yet."

"I thought he worked for a labor union!"

"They're in the middle of a campaign, and he doesn't want to get fired."

"I don't get it," Daniel said. "Wouldn't he rather breathe than work?"

She went back to sobbing. She hid her face in her hands.

He sat down on the bed next to where she was curled up, put his hand on her arm, and said, "Okay, so dad-boy stands you up at the altar. It's harsh. But you know what? So the fuck what, is what I say. I drove down here to take you home, because there's no way a pregnant woman should be sleeping in a place where the only way out at night is a rope ladder. I can't believe I brought you here. I can't believe we even lived here. This isn't a firetrap. It's a death trap unfit for human habitation. Police or ambulance would have to call the fire department to get in here any time between one A.M. and when the store opens, and don't ask me why it never crossed my mind until tonight. I repressed it all those years, but just now, at home, thinking of you, I had a vision of ultimate horror. No wonder they always look so goddamned grateful for the rent! Anyway, you're coming with me, right now, to a legal apartment with an elevator and fire stairs. And honestly, Aaron flaking on you? No great loss. He's in way over his head. I'm double-parked, so grab your bag and let's go. Come on. Get a move on."

Not stirring, she said softly, "I thought we'd be together." She rolled over so she could see his face and added, "I never should have left Bull." She wanted to see his reaction—the look of assent she was sure was coming.

Instead he said, "That guy's a prong. Fuck that noise. You haven't seen the last of dad-boy. He won't stay, but he'll be back. That kid will never be what you want him to be, but he won't fake it either. It could be a lot worse." He nodded to confirm his own statement.

Gulping, she turned to stare up at the black cobwebby ceiling. She thought how strange it was, under the circumstances, that she had a father of her own. How selfless Daniel's behavior had been, dedicating his entire life to Pam for no reason other than an accidental pregnancy.

The truth dawned on her at last. She said, "I'm going to be a single mother. All this time, I was fantasizing how I was going to choose which man shares the responsibility, and now I'm a single mother. How did I even do that? Am I talented?"

"Count your blessings," he said. "You're a free woman now under the matriarchy, about to reinvent family life in accordance with feminist principles." He rolled his eyes. "Pam and Ginger are all over this. A man ain't nothing but a joystick, so don't make little Aaron your ball and chain. Now get up, before I get a parking ticket."

He gathered up her purse and bag and stood. He shuffled his feet with mock impatience and glanced at the door.

"Dad—"

Sensing the approach of a tearful profession of love, he said, "Tell me in the car."

She leaned on his tall back and gripped the banister to pick her way down the dirt-blackened stairs.

GLIDING UP THIRD AVENUE WITH THE CAR'S EMISSIONS AT ZERO, SHE TURNED ON NPR and turned it off again. She turned toward Daniel and stretched her legs. They stopped at a red light. Heat from the asphalt was coming through the floor. Columns of steam were rising from gratings.

The intersection quivered as trains roared past underneath. Clusters of people drifted up the subway stairs, backlit by the glare of drugstore windows. Some found niches where they could stand motionless, suffering faces lit from below by phones like flickering candles. The light changed to restart the procession. The car started, noiselessly, to move.